HER VAMPIRE OBSESSION

HER TASTE IS ADDICTIVE AND I WILL NOT SHARE HER. NO ONE GETS HER BUT ME.

Dexter

I've lived a long time. Some might say too long. I honestly don't know what drew me to Lucius' club in Tucson, of all hellish destinations, but dark and self-destructive thoughts have increasingly beckoned to me, as of late.

Then I meet her.

She challenges me from the very start and awakens something I'd thought long dead and cold inside my soul. Even her name should burn my lips, yet I can't let her go.

But when pieces of the past catch up with us, will I be able to keep her safe?

Eilidh

I've spent most of my life running, but that bastard had my number from almost the second our eyes meet. He's the first of his kind to break through my defenses when I thought I was safe here, of all places.

He's done worse than steal my heart--he's given me hope.

Now what the hell do I do?

Especially when it looks like my past is catching up with us.

This time, I might have run out of options.

Note: Lesli Richardson also writes as USA Today Bestselling author Tymber Dalton

HER VAMPIRE OBSESSION

LESLI RICHARDSON

MIDNIGHT ROMANCE

ACKNOWLEDGMENTS

HUGE thanks to Lee and Renee for asking me to be part of this fantastic series with a bunch of other talented authors! I really enjoyed the Bad Boy Alphas series, and love vampires, so I might have had a massive fangirl *squee* when they approached me!

To my growlie cuddly pet Viking, who knows exactly why.

AUTHOR'S NOTE

Before you even ask, it's pronounced "AY-lee." Hey, the characters name themselves.

And you can find out more about the Data-X labs, Garrett Green, and the other Tucson shifters in the Bad Boy Alphas series by Lee Savino and Renee Rose.

A few characters in this book are begging me to write their stories, so that will happen. As well as some others who spoke up during the process. Also, I plan on writing a new series inspired by some of the characters in this book, but I don't want to give away too much, so stay tuned...

1

D^{*exter*}

"I MUST SAY, I was quite intrigued to receive your call, Dexter."

Lucius Frangelico, the self-proclaimed "vampire king," studies me with a very practiced tip of his head and a smile that, combined, are supposed to elicit a certain reaction from most people.

I am not most people.

And he's not *my* king. I damn sure didn't vote for him.

Not that I have any desire to challenge him for his throne, either.

Yes, he apparently has one of those, too. If he thinks he'll make me take a knee for him, he's mistaken.

"Why is that, Lucius?" I'm well aware I'm probably one of very few people walking the face of this planet who know what he is, who can get away with not using honorifics with him.

"I've extended *how* many invitations to you over the years, all met with silence? And now..." He lets his words drift into silence between us.

I settle back in my chair and swirl the glass of bourbon in my hand as the silence descends. I won't try to bullshit him—that'd be useless and stupid. Just because we're both eternal doesn't mean I should waste our time.

"Between us?" I finally ask.

He tips his head again.

"On paper, I'm scouting for expansion opportunities. Tucson is an ideal location for a new casino, and I've nearly aged myself out of Atlantic City." I sip my drink and savor the sharp bite of the liquor. He doesn't press or interrupt me.

Like me, he's a patient man.

It's a skill we've honed over the many centuries spanned by our existence.

I take another sip of the bourbon and savor it. I would miss bourbon. It's the closest thing I've had to experiencing the sun in over a thousand years, once I lost—

I clip that thought short.

The sun isn't the only thing my soul deeply mourns.

Rolling the liquor around on my tongue for a moment before I swallow, I finally let the words coalesce and fall from my lips.

"Between us, I'm wondering what a Tucson sunrise might look like."

Beside Lucius, Selene lets out a soft gasp. She's his queen, always by his side.

Not just because she's a wolf shifter he turned, either. Although that is a very good reason.

She's far more deadly than Lucius and me combined, and she's his mate, his wife...

And his bodyguard.

Even Lucius' well-paid and highly trained security team cowers before her, vampires and humans alike. I saw the way his men tip their heads to her and averted their eyes when she entered the room. It had nothing to do with her being Lucius' love and everything to do with their abject terror of her abilities.

While I had waffled a little over my plans, seeing how happy Lucius is with his mate reminds me how empty and cold my own life is and has been for...

Well, forever, it feels like.

Maybe I will look for my first sunrise in close to two thousand years. Greet it with open arms instead of running from it. What started as an idle thought several months ago has become an increasingly strong instinct as of late. But first, one last business victory.

Lucius *tsks*. "It would be a shame for you to do that." Hell, he even sounds sincere.

I smirk at him over the rim of my glass. "Why, *uncle*. I didn't know you cared." My sire has been dead for ages—not by my hand, thank you very much—and he and Lucius were sired by the same vampire. My sire was several hundred years older than Lucius.

So, yeah. Technically, he is my uncle. I'm also not stupid enough to think Lucius truly gives a damn about my existence one way or another, as long as I'm not causing him trouble either way.

"I always did like you," Lucius quietly says. "You have a backbone and integrity."

"Plus, I've never tried to kill you."

He returns my smile. "I will not deny that colors my

opinion of you in a favorable direction." He sounds like he just walked off a BBC soundstage, while I dropped my Scottish accent once I relocated to the States. I tend to sound like someone from the Midwest now. "You are one of the few I have known this long who have not tried to overthrow me." A scowl flickers across his features. "Come to think of it, you are the *only* one I've known this long who has not tried to overthrow me."

"How many others have you known as long as we've known each other, Lucius? There are few as old as we are." I sometimes envy younger vampires' ability to recite their exact date of birth...and rebirth.

Lucius and I come from a time well before calendars were rewritten around the birth and crucifixion of a Nazarene carpenter. In fact, I believe Lucius predates those events by a bit.

He smirks. "Well, there is *that*. Still, the sentiment remains."

"I have no interest in politics, and you know it. I never have."

His lips curl in another smile. "Yet another reason I like you."

"Politics is an unwinnable game. I prefer capitalism." I sip my drink. "It's far bloodier. And more profitable. It also neutralizes politics. With enough money, you can buy what and who you want."

He actually snorts. I wasn't even sure he was capable of humor like that.

Selene's quiet voice draws my focus. "You're not *really* going to do that, are you? Meet the sun?" She was turned so recently she hasn't yet lost her humanity, her empathy. Some vampires manage to hold on to a modicum of that—such as myself.

Others come to see humans as nothing more than food and prey, instead of living, breathing beings with lives and dreams.

Once again, I focus on the liquid in my glass, gently swirling it, so I can breathe in its scent. "I haven't decided yet, quite honestly. It's not exactly a new idea for me, but the notion hasn't passed the way it usually does."

"What you *need* is a distraction," Lucius insists. "You *must* come to the club tomorrow night. Seems I remember you know how to wield a riding crop." He smiles. "Paris, wasn't it?"

"Milan." I don't need sex. Not to sound like an asshole, but I can get that whenever I want it. I have no desire to take it without consent, either. I outgrew that nonsense about the same time I was turned.

Without consent.

It was one of my younger "brothers" who killed our sire. My brother had also been turned without his consent, but his turning and weaning had been even more cruel than mine. It rendered him practically feral and barely coherent. Once he was strong enough, he killed our sire. Then he greeted the sun the next day because he'd been driven mad by both what he'd done to our sire, as well as by the effects of being turned.

Yes, I'm guilty of having stood by and watched it happen. Allowed it, even.

Fate in action.

Obviously, I'm far stronger than a human. Outwitting one, wooing one—those are pleasures I will never take without working for them. I won't allow myself to violate consent for the average innocent.

"Why did you open a club, of all things?" I ask. "And why *here*, of all places? A vampire, in a desert?" In the short time it's been open, Club Toxic has developed a rep among multiple species, but especially vampires.

Lucius smiles. "The cover makes sense, when you look at the larger picture. Besides, I like the area, and the situation in LA was no longer...tenable. On multiple fronts."

"You're surrounded by shifters." I hold up a hand to Selene. "No offense intended. I have no issues with shifters."

She smirks. "None taken, but only because you look like Ianto, and I love *Torchwood*."

Honestly? I couldn't tell you what I look like. It's been over two thousand years since I've seen my own reflection, and I'm not narcissistic enough to have my portrait painted.

Before I can ask what Selene means, Lucius speaks. "Nonsense. We're not surrounded—it's a target-rich environment." He smiles. "We have an agreement, and we have been mutually beneficial to each other. We don't hunt them, and they don't hunt us. When a human accidentally discovers their secret, they have one of our kind wipe it from the human's mind, meaning they don't have to kill the human.

"There is also strength in numbers, even as diverse as we are. Working together has shown everyone that setting aside petty, past differences is a boon for both. Especially against common enemies. Tucson has a large enough population that it allows for ample, safe feeding for us. I keep my nest tightly in check and remind them it behooves them to keep the shifters happy, and we help the shifters keep their secrets. Likewise, they help us keep ours."

"Are the shifters happy to have 'leeches' living in their midst?"

He smiles and shrugs. "The arrangement holds." His smile fades. "When traitors in my midst threatened that arrangement, I took care of them and made an example out of them to prove to the shifters that I can be trusted. And again, when a rogue nest tried to usurp me, we were allies against them. *That* is all that matters."

"It certainly seems like a unique arrangement compared to elsewhere." Usually, shifters and vampires avoid each other. If forced together in close quarters for too long, there is inevitably bloodshed. In a fair fight, vampires can usually beat shifters.

But shifters have a highly refined sense of smell and the ability to hunt in the daytime, meaning vampires are vulnerable.

"The shifters and I agree in more ways than we disagree," he says. "It was simply a matter of allowing them to see I am a man of my word. I helped eradicate a blood slavery ring in the area, for starters. Shifters being sold as sweetbloods. I help protect us all against the government. The local werewolf pack Alpha has seen I don't hesitate to eliminate those who would move against me or against the shifters we have allied ourselves with. Any vampires who don't wish to abide by my rules can happily fuck off and move elsewhere, outside my territory, or die. I allow the shifters to take care of their own, as long as they don't interfere with my...business, and they do the same."

I risk a smile. "And do you have the shifters over for tea and biscuits?"

His jaw tightens, but he doesn't rise to the bait. "Not exactly."

Selene giggles. I amuse her, which is one reason I'm now sitting in Lucius' living room. Other than sunlight and stakes to the heart, Lucius has only one weakness—Selene.

I envy him that comfort.

Even if she is easily the scariest creature on the face of the planet.

"How do you get around their squeamishness about us hunting?" I ask.

"It's amazing how many humans will volunteer to be cows when you throw in orgasms." He smiles again. "And money. There are also the...less desirable populations. Criminals. Did you know you can find registered sex offenders' information right online? It's publicly available for anyone to see. No one complains if one of them dies. We're careful to do it in stages, and to wipe their minds after every blooding."

"It's a twofer," Selene says, flashing canines as she smiles. "In a couple of years, Tucson will be one of the safest cities in the country."

"And more people will want to move here," I note. Ingenious.

"Exactly," Lucius says. "And it stays safe. There are also plenty of criminals out on parole who have trouble finding honest work. We are willing to pay them cash, and all they have to do is stay drug-free and not reoffend. Again, it helps keep the area safer. Also, I've forbade my sired from siring any new vampires of their own without my permission. It's a death sentence, if they do. They also know if they leave a trail of corpses, I will allow the shifters to take care of them for being rogues, if I don't stake them first myself."

I'm actually the only resident vampire in Atlantic City, that I'm aware of. I made it clear it was my territory, and that I would welcome visitors who cleared their visits with me and agreed to abide by my rules—no bodies, no sired, and no setting up a permanent residence. That I would provide them an ample list of volunteers happy to "play" with them and let them feed, or they could buy ethically acquired blood through me.

It's worked for me for over fifty years.

Which is another reason why I'm here tonight discussing this with Lucius.

"To be clear," I say, "I'm looking to set up a human-centric resort, not a vampire one. I run the company, but no one other than six trusted employees who've been with me for decades know I'm a vampire. I'm not looking to challenge you for control of the area, which is why I'm here discussing this with you in the first place." He knows exactly what I'm *not* saying—I'm not going to pay him tribute.

"What do I get in return?"

"Cover, increased transient populations of tourists to feed from, and, as long as your people don't kill, I'll allow them greater access through paid staff positions, as well as send guests to your club through recommendations. Meaning more jobs for vampires who wish to settle in this region, with your permission, of course. I will also contribute very generously to local politicians' campaigns and pet projects, in conjunction with you. I'll back whatever political issues you wish to forward for your own interests, as long as innocents aren't harmed, and I'll stand behind you in full support if anyone tries to move against you."

He slowly nods. "That *is* tempting."

"No killing or siring on my property," I add. "Not looking to increase the population. And any feeding done on my property must be with consent. For any vampires from out of town who wish to stay with me, I will source purchased blood exclusively from you." That will mollify him.

"I thought you said it'll be a human-centric resort?"

"It will, but I would be remiss not to include a section dedicated to catering to a specialty clientele. North-facing rooms with completely sealable shutters, and extra security features for the rooms. Specially trained staff, some of whom will be happy to consensually...satiate guests' hungers, if desired." I've already perfected the formula at my current hotel.

"I have heard favorable reports about your operations in Atlantic City." Well, of course people have reported back to him. I would have been shocked if he hadn't sent spies, vampire or human.

"There's a reason I'm as old as I am without a nest of my own," I remind him. "I do not piss people off, and I can back up my words with actions."

"And shifters? Will you be talking with them as well?"

"I feel I must. I know they run a fight club in town. I'm sure they would love access to whales willing to get the full experience of betting on live fights. I can buy a lot of law enforcement and local officials with the kind of money I'll be bringing with me. Convince them to look the other way. I'm certain I can talk the shifters into agreeing to a mutually beneficial deal. Another reason I wanted to talk with you first, since you and the Alpha are on reasonable terms with each other and have a stable treaty in place. I am showing you respect by coming to you first for your permission and blessing."

I see him struggling to not openly preen. Yes, I know how to appeal to him. "Does this mean you will come to my club tomorrow and postpone your ridiculous idea about meeting the sun?"

Tipping my glass so I can drain the last of the liquor, I nod. "I suppose I should hang around a little longer. See if my mood permanently changes."

He looks to Selene. "Please bring us a decanter of the special vintage, my dear. *Un*diluted. Three glasses."

She arches an eyebrow at him but rises and leaves the room.

"Special vintage?" I ask as I lean forward and set my glass on the coaster on the coffee table separating us.

"I do not wish to say anything else until you taste it. But it is...*exquisite*." His eyes actually light up.

"Why, Lucius. Should Selene be jealous?"

He grins, showing full fang, very amused. "Not in the slightest. First, you taste. Then we will discuss. I actually think you might be the answer for each other's mutual...situations."

The old bastard has my interest, and he knows it. Selene glides back into the room and carries a tray holding three crystal wine glasses and a matching crystal decanter, the latter of which is filled with a dark red liquid I know isn't wine. She pours three generous servings, not spilling a drop, and serves Lucius, then me, and takes the final glass for herself before settling on the sofa at his side once more.

Being a polite guest, I wait to waft it under my nose until she's settled, but when I do...

Holy fates!

My eyes fall closed. A buzz fills my head, and my mouth *waters*.

Lucius laughs. "Ahh, I knew you'd like it."

I haven't even tasted it yet, and I already want to meet and mate the creature, regardless of gender, whose veins could produce such a heady bouquet. "Shifter?" I manage, forcing my eyes open.

He's still smiling and sipping. "To be honest? I don't know *what* they are. Which is exactly why they are currently under my protection. Taste it, Dexter."

I do. Brilliant colors of flavor explode in my mouth like ripe berries and sweet honey.

My god!

It's enough to make me want to believe in happy endings of the non-pornographic kind.

I must be wearing a "look" because Lucius smirks. "Once again, I'll ask if I can persuade you to postpone your silly notion of greeting the sunrise."

If my heart still beat, it'd be racing in my chest. Even my cock stirs, eager to learn more. "Only if you promise to introduce me to them." I know he's being cagey for a reason. He's trying to hook me and reel me in. "How much money will this cost me?"

He exchanges a glance with Selene. "I wish I could quote you a price, but I cannot. They are their own person, and it is a...unique situation. They've been with me since I opened the club. I also wish I could say they are an experienced sweetblood, but they are not."

"They're not? This *isn't* sweetblood?"

"They have never been blooded, only...donations. In addition to working for me, I 'ethically source' their blood from them for more than fair compensation. Usually, I dilute it by mixing it with other batches. I can charge more for it that way and make it last far longer."

"And they're not a shifter?"

He shrugs. "Come out tomorrow, meet them, and tell me what you think."

I swirl the glass under my nose again, deeply inhaling. I feel like I've never seen colors before this moment, never had the ability to smell anything, until now.

For the first time in too long, I eagerly *want* to see another day.

So to speak.

I'm torn between wanting to guzzle the remainder of the contents in two or three swallows, and slowly sipping it for hours. When I finish, Selene automatically moves to refill my glass, pouring me what's left in the decanter. I know she didn't spike it with something because she poured all three servings from the same decanter.

"What did I do to earn such good graces from you, Lucius?"

Honestly? I'm starting to feel a little drunk. Or, maybe that's his goal.

He shrugs. "You are family, in a manner of speaking." His smile fades. "I have lost too many. And, as you said, you have no desire to overthrow me. You have no nest of your own."

"And?"

He smirks. "And my sweet pet is very territorial. Were I not already madly in love with Selene, yes, I would be tempted to explore something more permanent with... them." He tips his head, indicating my glass. "Trust me, I felt the same way you did when I first sampled this. There are extenuating circumstances as to why I never claimed them, but I cannot and will not explain in more detail until after you meet them in person." The love in his eyes as he looks at Selene nearly breaks my heart. "We were not meant to share a third for anything than the occasional sip, and this person deserves someone to love and protect them."

By the time I finish the second glass, I truly feel *very* drunk. As the driver returns me to my hotel, I'm lost in thought.

Absolutely, I want to meet the human who made me feel this way.

What I'll want to do with them after that... I guess I'll have to hope for a miracle.

After returning to the hotel, I retreat to my room, where the head of my security has already ensured that the bedroom windows are more than adequately covered. I take a shower, still lost in thought about the exquisite taste rolling through my system.

While I'm in there, I take my cock in hand and slowly start stroking. Lucius knows about Robert, and that I've had lovers across the spectrum. I can't help wondering why he's withholding even that much info from me.

As I close in on my first truly joyful orgasm in too damn long, I also realize I neither care about the person's gender, nor Lucius' reasons for withholding that info. All I care about is how I feel...*alive*. Pre-cum leaks from me as my hand strokes my cock. I wish it was a willing mouth or pussy —or ass—I was stroking into, but I'll settle for this because of how light my soul feels.

A sensation I'd been certain a mere twenty-four hours ago that I would never experience again.

I want to hold them, tease them, feel their willing flesh squirm against me as I do all sorts of delightfully evil things to them, all while giving them as many orgasms as I can wring from them.

If that blood wasn't from a sweetblood...

Fates, what will they taste like once I've coaxed them into the depths of subspace? Spanking their ass with my hand until they're red and squirming—

That's the thought that sends me over the edge. The first truly good orgasm I've had in a disturbingly long time makes me pump cum all over my hand and the shower wall and leaves me a little weak in the knees.

How much better will it feel when I spend inside them? Because make no mistake about it, I'm already determined to win them over.

I *must*.

Even an hour after dawn, I still lie wide awake in bed

and stare at the ceiling. What *is* that feeling coursing through me?

Excitement. Anticipation.

Need.

I think the last one terrifies me, at least a little.

And it's *exactly* why I will go to Club Toxic tomorrow night.

Because who doesn't need a little terror in life to break up the monotony of a never-ending existence?

2

E *ilidh*

HMM. Blue, today?

I tuck a strand of hair behind my ear. It's a cobalt blue wig, sort of a jaw-length pageboy with blunt bangs that hang just over my eyebrows. I haven't worn it in several weeks because I was kind of stuck in a mood. Before that, I wore it pretty much every other day for about a month, until I got tired of it. It's one of my favorites, though.

I always wear a wig. Sometimes they look "normal." More often, they're a color. The ones I wear to work at Club Toxic are nearly always a *loud* color.

Pink, green, purple, rainbow, silver, gold.

Yes, I think the blue today.

After fluffing my wig in the mirror, I remove it and secure my hair. The wig has to stay firmly on my head all night long during my shift. I won't have time to screw with it.

No one at work gets to see my real hair.

Ever.

In fact, few people ever see my real hair.

Mostly because it's fickle and temperamental. Today, it's a dark, golden blonde, honey with amber and russet tones. But I could wake up tomorrow, and it might be jet black with a stripe of solid white.

Or auburn brown. Or so deeply reddish orange that it looks like a wig.

There is no rhyme or reason to it. Sometimes, it'll stay one color for weeks or even months at a time. Then... *poof.*

The only thing I can control about it is the styling and length, but I rarely get it cut at a salon. I keep it trimmed long enough I can pull it into a ponytail, not much longer than shoulder-length.

It's done this all of my life. I think sometimes it has to do with my mood, but it only changes while I'm asleep.

Yes, I've tried filming it, and the camera or phone or whatever I use always fails. I finally gave up trying because it's too frustrating when that happens.

My mom always nervously laughed it off as fickle genes, likely from my father's side. He apparently gave me my violet eyes, too.

Except I can't ask him about them because he's dead. I have literally zero information about him or his family, other than his real first name and the last name of Smith. I was only eight when he died.

But that mystery will remain hidden in the past, the way the rest of my history is forever buried, since both of them are dead now. There's no one I can talk to about them, no one who knew them except a close family friend of Dad's, whose full name I don't even know and who I haven't seen since Dad died.

Once I have my wig firmly anchored in place and I brush it, I apply a light dusting of makeup and do a quick twirl in front of my bathroom mirror. I always wear bike shorts under the short black skirts I frequently wear to work a shift at Club Toxic, like I am tonight. I'll wear jeans, too, but it's May in Tucson right now and already hotter than balls out, even though the temps will drop after dark. The shorts help keep my full thighs from chafing and give me an extra layer of protection if any of the customers get a little too handsy when I have my hands full of drinks and can't defend myself.

Not that they get handsy with me—or any of the other servers—more than once.

I pull on thick, wool socks, lace up my black Doc Martens, and give myself another look in the mirror. The comfortable sports bra I'm wearing helps push my girls up under the black Club Toxic T-shirt. The shirt's neon pink logo lays right across the girls and will glow in the black lights. Lucius allows me latitude with my uniform that no other employee gets, and for good reason.

I make him a fuckton of money, with relatively little outlay on his part. It's a win-win situation for both of us.

Plus, I'm close friends with his mate, Selene.

My shift doesn't start until six thirty, and the club doesn't open until seven, but I have keys and an alarm code. I make sure I'm at the club by five thirty this time of year.

Well before twilight sets in.

Ironic, I know. I'm afraid of the dark, and yet I work in a club full of vampires.

I mean, it's not the vampires I'm afraid of, obvs. Or of the other races who live in and around Tucson. It's not even the dark I'm afraid of, per se.

It's what's sometimes *in* the dark that I don't want to face. Because if I'm not careful, I'm afraid that, one day, those things will find me again.

And that the next time they do, I might not be able to escape.

TECHNICALLY, I'm the assistant manager at the club, even though I told Lucius and Selene I didn't want a title. The less attention focused on me, the better. I don't need a title to do my job and earn money.

So far, Tucson has been safer longer than anywhere else. I don't yet know if it's because of the high concentration of vampires, shifters, and other miscellaneous supernatural oddballs who make the region their home, or some inherent power in the land itself, or my own extreme, rigorous caution this time in my personal habits, or what.

Don't know, and have stopped caring.

All I care about is that I'm safe.

I live downtown in an apartment building owned by Garrett Green. He's the Alpha of the Tucson werewolf pack, and a pretty nice dude, even if he looks scary as fuck. I do errands for them and for the vamps, and everyone gives me protection and leaves me alone. They pay me in cash, too, meaning I'm totally off-the-grid.

Well, I mean, off-the-grid with all the amenities I could ask for while living in a nice efficiency apartment in a high-rise in the middle of Tucson.

I also earn extra cash selling my blood to Lucius every few weeks. That part of our deal is secret. I don't want anyone knowing I am the source of the highly popular special vintage he sells as top-shelf, and the reason he makes a fuckton of money on that part of his operation.

What he's really doing is blending some of my blood with other blood to make it more desirable. I've never let a vamp feed directly from me. Lucius has honored our agreement and never told anyone who I am, other than Selene. Since she's the closest thing I have to a bestie, I'm fine with that.

I think it's also because Lucius doesn't know *what* I am any more than I know what I am, and that fascinates him. Besides, I don't challenge anyone for power or land or control, so no one sees me as a threat. Hell, I won't challenge anyone for a goddamned parking space. That kind of bull-shit will draw attention to me.

That's the last thing I need.

Not drawing attention of any kind is one of the reasons the various players in the area leave me alone and use my errand and courier services when needed. I'm neutral.

I mean, *completely* neutral. Including my scent, apparently. Lucius and Selene admit they can smell me, but sort of like you can smell rain, or a hot burner on an electric stove. It's there...but *not* there. Garrett Green said the same thing when I asked him.

During my period every month, which oddly lasts only three days and hits just like clockwork every four weeks, I take those days off from the club with Lucius' blessing. Last thing I need to be is advertising that in a fricking vampire club, right? More attention I do not want or need. I usually hit the grocery store the day before and don't set foot outside my apartment for those days.

The only time I step into a conflict and risk drawing attention to myself is when someone tries to fuck with me or one of my servers at Club Toxic. Apparently, I'm scary, according to the household humans who also work there. Especially if any of the vampire customers get a little too pushy with the humans upstairs at the club and try to coerce them downstairs to the dungeon against their will, or by using vamp powers on them instead of legitimately gaining their consent.

Although I've been in Tucson longer than anywhere else in my adult life and have put down what passes as roots for me, I suppose, I live light, a result of my nomadic existence for most of my life.

As I drive toward the club, my hand drifts to the front of my T-shirt, touching my father's ring, where it lays hidden underneath. I wear it on the same silver chain my mother used to wear it on.

It's literally all I have of his.

Mazbushka. That's what he and his friend Zuzu used to call me. They said it meant "sweet little angel," but I've yet to discover in what language.

Or maybe they made it up. Who knows?

The ring is my talisman now, I suppose. My good-luck charm. I touch it like this all the time without thinking about it. The only time I take it off is when I take a shower. It's a labradorite stone, dark grey with flashes of blue, green, yellow, and orange, depending on the kind of light it's in and how you tip it. The ring itself is gold, with symbols embossed on both sides and around the stone.

I haven't been able to decipher what they mean, even after years of research.

When I reach work, I park in my reserved spot and head inside, letting myself in the back entrance with my key.

I don't even need to look at the alarm panel to immediately know I'm the first and only one here. Being able to sense people around me—mortal or otherwise—is one of those weird little things I can do, and something I'm careful *not* to let others know I can.

Only two other human employees have keys and alarm codes, even though there are close to a dozen household humans who work here at the club full-time and even dozens more who are part-timers. None of the vampire employees will be in until after dark, obvs.

Lucius and Selene will arrive when he's damned good and ready. We all work on *his* schedule. Even the book-keeper works night hours. Theophilus, a vampire who works for Lucius and who is part of his inner circle, is actually the club's general manager. Buuut, he's a vampire. Meaning he can't be here during the day when we need to handle maintenance or repairs while we're closed.

Benny is one of the other humans who has a key, but he works directly for Lucius rather than the club. While he's not technically club staff, he frequently accepts shipments from suppliers, goes on shopping runs, deals with maintenance or repair issues, things like that. Sometimes, I'll come in on a day off and handle those tasks then take a night off later in the week, but it depends on the schedule. Lucius and Theophilus are very careful to not over-schedule me, since they know about my other part-time job.

I also keep Lucius apprised of any rumors I hear among shifters or other vamps in the area.

Heading upstairs to the second floor, I let myself into the office suite and make my way past the security console of video monitors to where my desk sits along the far wall behind a divider, giving me privacy. Most of the human staff aren't allowed up here unescorted and only come up here at the beginning and end of their shifts to count their tills. I have an actual desk in a private alcove at one end of the main outer office, with my own sofa.

When I lock my things in my desk, I retrieve my name tag. After I peel the masking tape off it, where it still says *PINK* in black marker from my last shift, I apply a new piece of tape and write *BLUE* on it, and then pin it to my shirt, over my left breast. When I wear one of my blonde wigs, I go by *Blondie*.

The employees and regular customers know to call me by whatever color wig I'm wearing on any given night. The name tag is for everyone else, and for my amusement when I'm feeling like fucking with someone. Only Lucius and Selene know my real name. They've promised never to use it, and to prevent anyone else from knowing it.

Helps that I'm paid in cash and have a good fake Arizona driver's license Lucius obtained for me. In the computer system, for the purpose of my security logins and the alarm, I'm known as Connie Doe, the same name on my fake ID.

Has a little more panache than Jane Smith, and my real name, Eilidh Connover, isn't anywhere in their system, where I can be tracked through it. I do have a passport and ID in that name, in case I ever need them.

With that completed, I boot the computer server that runs the club's POS payment system and make sure it's up and running. Then I lock the office behind me and head downstairs to the first floor. It's not unusual for me to end up in the office on my night off if I've been out running errands and I'm too far from home to make it there before dark. Plenty of times, I've spent the night sleeping up here curled on my couch, wrapped in a blanket, knowing I'm completely safe.

Lucius has issued standing orders to leave me alone and let me be, if that's the case.

Next, I go through the first floor, turning on lights, checking supplies, booting the POS terminals, and making

sure the closing crew from the night before cleaned everything, including the bathrooms. I don't bother going
through the small kitchen because that's not my domain. I
replenish anything behind the bar that wasn't restocked
before closing last night, make notes for Lucius and
Theophilus of anything we need—or things not properly
taken care of—and then take a deep breath before I head
downstairs, to the basement.

The private BDSM club area is accessed through a secret
passage of sorts, a staircase hidden behind the coat check
area near the front entrance. Access is for vampires and staff
only, and for any human guests the vampires bring downstairs. Most people don't even know there is a lower level.
The occasional shifter will go down, usually as a guest
Lucius has invited, but that is extremely rare.

Every once in a while, Lucius has a shifter who works for
him or who owes him a favor, and they'll show up at the
club. I don't get involved in any of that, because it's not my
business.

Minding my own business has kept me alive while
working with vampires, and I kind of want to continue that
trend.

I flip on the "ugly lights," the bright overhead fluores-
cents that starkly illuminate the space. The various pieces of
equipment, the curtained private alcoves—I check everything. Behind the bar down there, I see whoever closed last
night was on the ball, and I find nothing needing my
attention.

I don't work downstairs every night. In fact, I prefer not
to. Not that it bothers me what goes on—the sexy BDSM
play that can include full-on sex, and vampires feeding off
their willing partners and submissives.

It bothers me *I* can't partake of it.

Stupid, I know.

I won't let any of the vampires play with me or feed off me. Nothing personal, but I have trust issues.

Once I'm happy everything's taken care of downstairs, I turn off the work lights, which leaves the red mood lighting and the spotlights focused on some of the play equipment to illuminate the space, and I return to the office. I retrieve one of the tills from the safe, count it, and take it back down to the main bar in the nightclub area. In the quiet of the club, I hear the telltale *beep* from the back-door chime as someone lets themselves in.

My instincts tell me who it is. "Hey, Benny," I call out.

He laughs and walks into the main room. "That's fucking spooky when you do that...Blue." That last word he delivers once he gets a look at tonight's wig.

I smile. "Can't help it." I really can't. It's a blessing and a curse.

But even if it wasn't for my special little gifts, it was logic. Craig, the other human with a key, has tonight off, and it's still daylight out, meaning it was none of the vampires.

I look up and see Benny's dressed as handsomely as ever. Dark brown hair neatly coiffed, and he's wearing a suit and tie, the way Lucius prefers his men to dress. I've only ever seen Benny in jeans twice, and that was when the club was closed, and he was accepting a delivery from one of the beverage wholesalers.

If he wasn't so close to Lucius, I'd be damned tempted to pursue a relationship with him.

Problem is, he's too close to Lucius, and his allegiance is to the vampire king. Meaning if I'm ever forced to pack and leave in a hurry, I'd have to leave him behind.

No, thank you. I've said enough good-byes in my lifetime already. No reason to make it especially difficult on myself.

"Want me to leave the back door unlocked?" he asks.

"Please. House is ready."

"Cool." He returns to the back entrance and sets the door lock. Every employee has their own code to open the back door once we've "unlocked" it. Anyone else, if they don't have a key, needs to ring the bell. That way, we can tell who's coming and going from that entrance. It will open from the inside, of course, because it's also an emergency exit.

We just installed a new, enhanced security system, which includes IR night vision and FLIR thermal camera modes that now pick up the vamps, too. Expensive as fuck, and military-grade equipment, but Lucius wanted the extra security.

He survived an attempt to overthrow him not too long ago. Of course, the big showdown happened on my night off, because of *course* it did. Fortunately, he has Selene to protect him now. Then there was that recent business with a rogue vampire, Arthur, and his merry little band of miscreant thugs who blew into town, murdered the grandmother of a local coyote pack's Alpha—and a bunch of others—and nearly started a massive war between the shifters and vampires.

Benny and I are only two of a handful of humans allowed access to Lucius' home. I don't take that trust lightly. The reason I've been able to move between shifter and vampire communities is that they trust me and take me in. I've learned the politics between the packs and nests and always avoid entangling myself in anything that could make me an enemy of either side. Although it is unique for vampires and shifters to form such a close alliance the way they have here in Tucson.

I hope it's a sign of improving relations between the two factions.

Hey, a girl can dream.

Like I dream that, one day, maybe I'll meet someone who can give me some solid answers about who and what I really am.

3

D*exter*

I AWAKEN about four hours before safe twilight and spend the time handling work issues that arose before I did. Because of my age, it's rare I sleep from dawn to dusk anymore, unless I'm exceptionally tired. It's not unusual for me to stay up long past dawn, if I'm home.

The people working for me in New Jersey think I have a "sun allergy."

No, seriously, it's a thing. Look it up. Only six of my people know I'm a vampire, including John, my head of security, and Mark, my valet, both of who are with me on this trip and staying in adjacent suites.

Neither will accompany me to Club Toxic tonight. They're humans, and while quite capable of defending themselves—and me—under normal circumstances, I'd prefer they have little contact with Lucius' vampires, for now. They are too valuable to me to lose them in a misunderstanding, and I refuse to take unnecessary risks with their lives and safety. There will be plenty of time for them to become acquainted with the principals in the Tucson vampire nest once Lucius publicly announces our deal to his people. I prefer human employees to vampires simply because my experience is they're more loyal and less likely to want to "empire build." They're also more easily controlled, if need be.

My people who know I am a vampire come from families who have served me for nearly four centuries each and who I moved to America with me when I emigrated from the UK following World War II. They are sworn to protect my secret. I, in turn, make sure their families lack for nothing by paying them well.

No, I never feed from them.

Only one member in each generation knows my secret, usually the eldest son, although my current valet's mother was my previous valet. She was the only child her father— my valet before her—produced. I'm not being chauvinistic. I'm being *practical*. I would hate that a woman working for me might not be able to be home with her baby or toddler, and I definitely don't want to put her more at risk while she's pregnant.

I'm immortal, not evil.

I relegated Mark's mother to staying close to home when she was pregnant with him, only assisting me when I was in residence at the hotel. I wouldn't let her travel with me again until Mark started preschool. When he was a baby, after she returned from maternity leave, I let her bring him to work. I was "Uncle Dexter" to him and was careful to conceal my true nature from him until he was old enough to decide to work for me after he graduated from college. I would let him work part-time once he was a teenager, on weekends and during holidays, so he could earn his own spending money.

Since I avoid getting involved in anything illegal, which helps insulate me and my corporate interests, the other members of their families think that one of my forebears made a pact with one of their ancestors to work for me in exchange for lucrative pay and that I take those oaths seriously even to this day.

Yes, I guarantee each new generation's loyalty with a few mental nudges early on, but I treat them well and never need to compel them to work for me. One time, the eldest son in a generation had no desire to work for me, thinking it was "beneath" him. He obviously didn't know I was a vampire. So, the second oldest son gladly took the job and was thus initiated into the secret.

I don't need to have my own security tonight. Lucius knows better than to let anything happen to me while I am in his territory, just like I would protect him with my life were he in mine on announced business. I'm on amicable terms with him, and it's because I can afford to be. He might have the manpower, but I have the money and a corporate machine behind me, with plenty of safeguards in place that could ruin him—and many other vampires—should he ever try to fuck with me.

Which is another reason I've kept my distance from Lucius in recent years. Lately, he tends to attract the attention of law enforcement, due to some of his illegal enterprises, and I don't wish to draw similar attention to me and my business interests. It'd prove an annoyance.

As it is, it's difficult enough to ensure pictures of me aren't taken. I have three body doubles I employ full-time to make public appearances for me, none of whom know I am a vampire. Video cameras are prohibited in the elevators I use and on the floor where my suite is located, and we instead use infrared and thermal imaging cameras for security. That way, the security team never sees that I don't show up on regular cameras.

Yes, the personnel who monitor the feeds have also been given mental nudges to not think about why I don't show up on video. It's easier that way.

Except Lucius is the closest thing I have to family. I prefer the world with him in it, and thus we get along, even if we tend to have differences of opinion over certain topics, especially regarding humans. He tends to be overly lenient with his sired when they rebel and try to overthrow him.

Yet another reason I haven't pursued turning more people. It's difficult enough to maintain a normal life as it is. Bringing in someone who might want to overthrow me eventually?

No, thank you.

I, on the other hand, tend to view humans as commodities not for food, even though they are that, but for income opportunities. I have been virtually alone for so long that I don't know how to live any other way, to be honest.

Lucius, I believe, desperately wants to *not* be alone. I understand that because it *is* painful to watch the world spin on, to see humans pass and have no one to share those weighty emotions with, and to know that many who are like you have taken a very lackadaisical approach regarding humans. I mean, you normally don't mourn the passing of dairy cows, unless you have one particular pet cow you're fond of. They tend to blur together with little to distinguish one from another.

I, on the other hand, intently have focused on amassing wealth. Lucius focused on amassing a found family, of sorts.

Dysfunctional and toothy, but who am I to judge?

I don't know why I let Lucius talk me into going to his club tonight. The man really is a silver-tongued devil.

Oh, wait, I *do* know why.

It's the same reason I've struggled to stay focused on work issues today—the mystery supplier of that most delicious ambrosia I've ever sipped.

I *have* to meet whoever Lucius procures that blood from. If for no other reason than I want to sit down with them, talk to them, get to know them.

Get to know the person who awakened my senses like this. My cock stirs again as I think about it, and I resist the urge to stroke myself to completion like I did last night.

The first such reactions I've experienced in...too damned long. The closest analog I have is how I felt about Robert when I first met him and fed from him.

In fact, when I pour myself a large glass of purchased blood tonight from the supply Mark stocked for me in my suite, it tastes flat and bland. I find myself longing for what I had last night, which is even more reason I need to take my fill *now*.

Just in case.

I *must* remain in control.

I wait until a little before ten to leave for Club Toxic in the rented SUV. Yes, I'm driving myself tonight. I'm no stranger to blood clubs and have visited the best around the world. Never wanted to get involved with running one, though.

Attracts too many of the wrong kinds of people.

Human, and otherwise.

I prefer to buy blood for regular feeding. If I end up sleeping with someone, I'll feed off them, and then they think I simply got a little nippy during sex. I do get consent for biting, blood play, and "feral play." I never take more than a little from them if I feed from them.

Of course, I can't tell them I'm a vampire. Are you mad? I don't like to wipe minds more often than necessary. I always make sure I've fed well before being with someone I intend to play with, so I'm not hungry. I refuse to make mistakes.

Have I killed people?

Countless.

Wish I was kidding about that.

Most of them in battle, or people who deserved killing—the worst of humanity.

While I'm sure early on there are likely deaths of innocents on my conscience, in the last seven or eight hundred years, I have not killed anyone without clear cause.

Or, in some cases, to put them out of their misery. There were quite a few in World War II who met that standard, mortally wounded and suffering, and I hastened their departure while giving them pleasure in the process.

Unlike some vampires, I refuse to kill humans for sport.

But I require my sexual partners share my interest in kink. Even if all I do is spank them and give them rough sex, vanilla really doesn't do it for me anymore. I've been alive a long time. Missionary position gets awfully boring, after a while.

I've been to plenty of BDSM clubs around the world and have done far more in private. I especially love shibari, subduing a partner with intricate rope patterns, not even needing to use my powers on them to drop them into subspace and sweeten their blood—it's exhilarating.

My skills with other implements are equally adept.

I have a lot of time on my hands to practice.

Lucius has decided to pair a blood club with a BDSM club, to give his special clientele more fang for their buck, if you'll forgive the turn of phrase. They're willing to pay to access sweetbloods—humans drunk on the high of subspace, their veins coursing not just with blood but endorphins and dopamine and adrenaline, along with all the other lovely natural chemicals that are intoxicating to my kind.

Ingenious. It's a wonder more vampires don't open BDSM clubs. In the wake of popular fiction taking the *Fifty Shades* phenomenon mainstream, you'd think this kind of cash cow operation would be a draw for our kind. A lucrative business paired with nearly unlimited feeding opportunities.

Driving past the club first to appraise the location, I see a line for entry stringing halfway down the block. Lucius told me to walk up to the doorman, who would admit me immediately. Vampires never have to stand in line. But to also give my name, and one of his men would show me around.

Nightclubs like this aren't my preferred hunting grounds, but since my only chance to find out more about the source of that particular vintage Lucius teased me with last night is through attending tonight...

Well, here I am.

I find a parking spot for the Audi Q3 a block away and walk back. I opted to wear a suit and blazer tonight, and the collar and top button of my shirt lay open. When I walk up to the entrance, I'm barely given a glance by the vampire manning the door before the velvet rope is opened, and I'm waved in.

"Dexter Van Sussex," I say to another suit-clad vampire I assume is a bouncer, who stands in the entry to the coat check room.

"Yes, sir. You are expected. Please, follow me." I figured he'd lead me downstairs to the dungeon, but he doesn't.

Instead, he leads me inside, past the dance floor, which is teeming with humans who don't know they're being hunted by several vampires among them. The DJ has them bouncing around and the air is thick with sweat tinged with alcohol, desire, and hunger. We continue on past the bar, where a blue-haired waitress not dressed like the rest of the servers is currently taking care of customers, and into a back hallway.

There, he punches in a code to unlock a door to the stairwell, and I'm led upstairs, where he unlocks another door and leads me into an office suite. A faint, pleasant scent tickles my nose, but I don't have time to pause and savor it before I'm being led down another hallway and through another door into an office.

The vampire king, of course, occupies the largest office.

"Ah, there he is." Lucius stands and rounds the desk he was sitting behind to shake with me. No cheap IKEA flat-pack desk, either. This Brobdingnagian monstrosity is totally Lucius, easily six feet across, ornately carved mahogany and polished to a luxurious sheen. It's too large to fit up the stairwell I just ascended.

"How in holy hell did you even get this *up* here?"

He proudly smiles. "Do you like it?"

"It's...you."

He smirks. "They built the office around it. Literally. It was brought up and then the stairwell enclosed, and the walls built."

"You always were one to put on a show." The walls are ornate wood paneling with built-in bookshelves, making it look more like a study that belongs in a mansion instead of a nightclub office.

"What's the use of having this long life and all these funds if I can't be a showoff on occasion?"

I prefer my luxury more subtly stated and less likely to draw attention. "I am here." I don't want him to get sidetracked. "And you damn well know why."

He grins. "Thought about it all day, didn't you?"

"If I skip right to admitting you're right, will it earn me an introduction sooner?"

"Perhaps." The office door opens, and Selene enters. "Ah, my love. Is everything ready?"

"Yes." She's also smiling.

If this were any other vampire besides Lucius, I'd be expecting a trap, a betrayal. "Why are you so eager for me to meet the source?"

His smile fades. "Time and my recent change of circumstances has made me see things in ways I have not in centuries. Perhaps you are not as maudlin about humans as I once thought you to be. By that I mean the validity of your feelings about and toward them. Perhaps you were the one who was correct."

He holds out a hand to Selene, and she drifts over to him, where she curls against his side. The blatant love I see between them isn't something any vampire can fake.

It's also something I find myself envying in nearly painful ways right now.

"Love changes a man," he continues. "Had you not admitted the idea of greeting the sun, I likely would have kept our little secret to ourselves. However, even I know when there are things beyond my ken, both in knowledge as well as experience and abilities." He sighs. "Perhaps I'm simply being a romantic, and there won't be an attraction between you two. But...I can hope. While there is no immediate danger, you and I shall talk later. I want you to meet them first."

"They're...in danger?" The thought irrationally triggers something strongly protective within me.

"I do not know. And no," he quickly adds, "I'm not being deliberately cagey. There is a history I'm certain I do not know all the facts about." He slips his arm around Selene's waist and draws her closer. "Did you ever hear about the *gwyllgi*?"

I nod, and the way he asks it tickles something in my deepest, darkest memories. "Are...are we talking shifters again?"

He slowly shakes his head. "Just keep it in mind for later. I could be wrong, but it's what I thought of. Then again, I don't know all the details. There might be more facts surrounding this mystery than I am aware." He releases Selene and steps forward. "Come on. Let's see what happens."

We return downstairs to the ground floor level, which houses the nightclub. I follow Lucius and Selene as we make our way along the fringes of the dance floor, on the far side of the space from the bar. We aim for the lounge seating area, where one of his men holds a table open for us. I'm painfully aware of the prickling feeling in my mouth, the memory of last night's drink, and I fight the urge to beg Lucius to quit the games and introduce me.

We settle at the table and one of his household humans hurries over to take our order. The woman wears short black shorts, a perfectly pressed button-up dress shirt, and a black ribbon tied around her neck.

Lucius leans in and gives her our order, for alcoholic drinks, not "house specialties." She hurries away, heading to the bar.

She is not the special vintage—that much I can tell. She's been blooded before, by teeth, not a needle. The eager hunger she exuded as she looked me over tells me that much, and I'm certain if I untie the black ribbon around her throat, I'll find plenty of old fang marks on her.

Sensing Lucius' gaze on me, I watch the waitress as she leans over the bar and speaks to the blue-haired woman behind it.

Unlike the other servers, the blue-haired beauty wears a black Club Toxic T-shirt, and the neon pink logo across her round breasts lights up from the black lights scattered here and there.

No ribbon around her neck, no sign of a collar.

From the way both of them glance over at our table, I know the server has informed the bartender who the order is for. The bartender then sets about mixing our drinks.

Lucius leans in. "By the way, anything you order here is on my tab. I'll make sure the staff knows."

"Thank you," I idly say, still focused on the blue-haired woman behind the bar. "I appreciate that."

"Save your thanks, Dexter." He smiles. "I do so hate to make a man repeat himself."

4

E *ilidh*

IT'S A BUSY NIGHT, but then, all nights at Club Toxic are some varying degree of busy. Even Tuesdays, like tonight. We open at seven, and it's slow at first, until about eight. The floor starts to fill with eagerly gyrating, half-drunk, two-legged Lunchables, and there will soon be a line down the block of people waiting to get in.

I start out working the tables in the lounge, running back and forth to the bar with drink orders. I don't mind because some of the vamps are really good tippers, and every little bit counts.

Especially since I don't have to share tips. One of the special concessions Lucius gives me.

A little after nine, I've just delivered drinks to a table in the lounge when Augustus saunters my way with a vampire I've never seen before in tow. The new guy is a redhead, kind of thin, maybe around six feet tall, and looks like he was turned in his late forties. If he were human, I'd say his air is the kind of swagger a rich guy used to getting his way throws around a corporate boardroom before he fucks his secretary over his desk and then goes home to his trophy wife and kids whose names he can barely remember.

I instantly don't like him, but I don't fear him, either. He's definitely not dressed nearly as well as Lucius' men.

Augustus leans in. "This is Dagwood," he says.

Rolling my eyes, I slowly shake my head. "Seriously?"

Augustus grins. "It's as good a name as any. He wanted to meet you."

The guy has green eyes, and I look him dead in them. "Hiya," I say, holding my hand out. "Nice to meet you…" I wait for him to tell me his real name.

It takes him a moment. "Darren," he says, already thrown off his game as he hesitates before finally taking my hand.

Augustus stands there with his arms crossed over his chest, smiling, waiting for the show to begin.

Darren's gaze narrows as he studies me. "You're…human?"

"That's what they tell me." I hold my tray against me to hide my boobs. Force of habit, even though he's looking me right in the eyes and not eyeing my girls. "What can I do for you, Darren?"

He glances at my name tag. "Your name is Blue?"

Tiberius walks over. "Did she do it yet?"

"Not yet," Augustus says. Behind him, Maximus also walks up to listen in, as do a few of the human regulars. They've formed an impromptu circle around us, my back to the wall and Darren standing close, but not uncomfortably so.

I reach up and flick my blue tresses. "My name, tonight, is Blue."

"So...it's not your *real* name?"

He can't look away from my gaze now, and it's got to be freaking him out at least a little. "What's in a name, anyway?" I softly ask. "How old *are* you? *Really*?" As I ask that, I do my thing—which is basically think all this to him, in addition to saying it.

Compelling *him*.

"One hundred and thirty-four," he whispers back without hesitation, and I know I've got him. It works better sometimes than others, but this guy's not very strong. His sire was likely young, too. While I'm immune to vampires' thrall, I can't compel all of them like this, although I haven't yet met a human I haven't been able to use at least a little mojo on.

Between the music and the vamp bouncers doing crowd control around us, I know the humans paying attention only heard "thirty-four."

Oooh, this will freak the poor vamp out later, when he has time to think about it.

I narrow my gaze. "How badly do you want to know my name?"

One of the household humans giggles. She should be serving customers, but she'll also immediately spread the word that I played the name tag game, and that'll only help my cred around here.

"I'd...do anything to know it."

"Want to make a wager?"

He nods.

"I bet you're just *dying* to get me downstairs, aren't you?"

"I'd love for you to come downstairs with me."

Of course he would, the poor schmuck. "Got a C-note on you?"

He nods again, eagerly, and digs out his wallet. If he thinks he's getting off that easy, he's not, but at least he's got cash.

Booyah. There's my cell phone bill, paid for the month.

"Here are the rules: I will let you see the back of my name tag. My real name is on it. If you can pronounce it correctly, on the *first* try, I'll go downstairs with you. If you can't, I get the hundred. You never get another chance to play the game—just this once. You also can *never* reveal to anyone what it said. Deal?"

"Deal!"

"Now, when you try to pronounce it, keep your voice down." I wish I could say I know exactly what I do to them, but I don't. Except I know it's working, because his pupils have fully dilated, making his green eyes look nearly black in this light. It's a pretty neat party trick.

You know, among the fang-endowed crowd.

"Okay."

I cup my left hand over the front of my name tag. Holding my tray up so it hides both our faces and my name tag from those gathered around us, I tip my name tag forward enough that the writing on the back is visible.

But I'm still looking him in the eyes, and he's not looking away.

"Go ahead and try," I say, while I'm thinking to him that he has no clue how to say it.

Not that most people have a clue to start with. I have yet to meet anyone who does.

He glances at it, then immediately back to my eyes. "I... um..." I release my name tag and lower the tray as he stares into my eyes. "Uh... I... It's..." He swallows, and I pluck the hundred from his fingers.

"Thank you so much for playing," I sweetly say. I offer him a smile as cheers and laughter go up among the onlookers.

The guy looks dazed as I tuck my winnings into my sports bra. Augustus slaps the guy on the back, whacking him between the shoulder blades. Darren still looks stunned and probably will for a couple of minutes, if the past is any indicator.

"Come on, buddy," Augustus says. "I'll buy you a drink."

"I... Uh..."

When I head back toward the bar, I'm not surprised that Maximus sidles up alongside me. "One of these days, my dear, you will tell me how you do that trick of yours."

"That would spoil it, though," I remind him.

What I don't want to admit—and what only Selene and Lucius know—is that I have no *clue* how I do it.

Absolutely *none*.

As a human, when I look a vampire in the eyes, I should be completely in their thrall, and...I'm not. Quite the opposite.

I can't completely compel a vampire or a human the way a vampire can, but anyone who stares into my eyes like that, they usually end up...

Like Darren. Their wits get sort of knocked off-kilter for a moment, at the very least. I don't know if it's because I have powers, or I scramble their power and bounce it back to them, or what.

Oh, he'll be okay in a few minutes, but he'll have no fucking clue what my name tag said, and he'll be unable to remember it.

Like I said, I don't know how I do it. I just...*do* it. Lucius learned about my immunity to the thrall almost immediately when we first met and started talking. He didn't believe me when I told him about it, I guess. I discovered my secret talent by accident the first time I worked for a vampire, at a bar in Toronto. I was nineteen. By then, while I knew vampires and shifters supposedly existed, because of the fringe circles Mom and I lived and worked in while she was alive, I didn't realize they were...*real*.

The bar's owner, a vampire named Neimus, liked me because he didn't have to worry about the vampires trying to hit on me or get free drinks from me. From the second I met him, I knew exactly what he was when he tried to charm me and failed.

Fortunately, my stupidity—"Oh, my *god*! You *are* a vampire!"—didn't get me killed when I looked at him and accidentally did the scrambling thing on him. Neimus helped me realize exactly how different I was from other humans in terms of my abilities, and he helped me learn how to safely navigate a shadowy world that few humans are privileged enough to walk through, much less survive and thrive in.

I loved that job and my boss. I lasted there nearly two years before I had to go on the run again.

That's also where the name tag game first developed. Although, back then, I just went by Blondie, regardless of which wig I wore at the time. Then, I only had three from which to choose, two of them blonde and one black. And I took a twenty from my marks instead of a hundred.

I've gone up in the world.

And no, I don't use my power on Lucius and Selene beyond my initial demonstration of it. I'm not stupid. That'd be disrespectful. I try not to use it on any of his men because, again, respect. They won't harm a hair on my head with Lucius and Selene protecting me. They also won't allow any harm to come to me. That would sign anyone's death warrant, and they know it.

But humans and other vamps?

Fuck *yeah*, I do it.

It works on some shifters, a little, but not on others. I really don't push that, though. I don't want them knowing I can do it. I have everything with that situation balanced delicately enough as it is. I don't want them thinking I'm more on the vampires' side than on theirs. Garrett Green and his mate, Amber, know I am immune to the thrall, but they don't know the extent of what I can do. They've also agreed to keep that secret.

If Amber's seen what I can do in one of her visions, she hasn't admitted it to me.

A little after ten, I'm taking a turn behind the bar on the main floor when I do a double-take. Because, son of a bitch, it looks like Tiberius is leading actor Gareth David-Lloyd across the club and toward the back hallway.

Helloooo, Sweetie.

I mean, yeah, we've had VIPs in here before, even several A-list celebs. Ironically, Lucius doesn't want too many of them gracing the club's doorstep. He wants the place hopping every night, but on a local level and not attracting paparazzi or crazy crowds. A low-key, steady success that is sustainable and doesn't draw any of the bad kind of attention.

Also, Lucius doesn't want a celebrity accidentally getting harmed while or immediately after being here. Usually, he personally takes them in hand, and before they leave, they're given a gentle mental nudge not to return or talk about the club to people. Not a mind wipe, because in the case of a celebrity that might trigger more questions than can be comfortably dealt with.

But Ianto *fucking* Jones?

My heart skips a little. *Torchwood* is one of my favorite shows. Normally, I keep my chill, but I have *got* to meet that man before he leaves tonight, actor or not.

I quickly lose track of them because I take a couple of orders and start mixing drinks.

Since I'm focused, that's why I flinch when Selene suddenly whispers in my ear.

"Play the name tag game again. *He* wants to be amused."

The "who" wanting to be amused doesn't need clarification—her king. I also don't bother turning. I know she can hear me just fine, even as I whisper in reply, "Who with?"

"You'll know." By the time I glance behind me, she's little more than a white-haired blur heading for the back hallway.

I shiver. *Holy crap*, I'm going to meet Ianto *fucking* Jones!

And maybe make enough extra to pay my auto insurance early, too.

Maybe I can have him autograph the C-note I win from him and then get it framed.

Worth it!

Despite trying to pay attention and keep an eye on the opening to the hallway, a bachelorette party arrives, and I spend the next fifteen minutes mixing drinks for already drunk women. Several vampires mill around, sensing easy pickings, and I barely manage not to roll my eyes.

Lucius has a hard rule—no harming humans in the club, and no deaths in the club. Unless it comes from his hand or by his direction, of course.

But no *human* deaths on the premises. Or shifters, preferably. Not caused by vampires, anyway. Deaths mean possible attention from the police, and that's bad for business for a variety of reasons.

Once the drunk bachelorette party has their first round and is happy, I'm aware of being watched. Nothing unusual there because I get hit on several times a night, mostly by humans but also by the occasional vamp who doesn't know me.

This feels...*different*. Like a prickly feeling between my shoulder blades.

I turn and wipe down the bar, but what I'm really doing is sweeping the room with my gaze. The dance floor is hopping. The people at the bar are currently sated. The lounge...

There. I spot Lucius and Selene, and Ianto is with them. I wasn't paying super-close attention before. It can*not* really be the actor.

Can it?

I'm just gonna call him Ianto until I know his real name, and maybe even after.

The more I focus, disappointment trickles in. He probably can't be the actor because he's a vampire. I know that much now. Because as I remember the way he moved when he walked through the first time, and now from focusing on where he's sitting, I can isolate him.

No heartbeat, and he's not breathing when he's not talking. I was too gobsmacked earlier to let common sense take over.

The whole isolation thing is another talent that's not human that I can do quite well, but I'm not a vampire, and I'm not a shifter.

Maybe I'm the result of some mutant military research project, developed in a Data-X lab and then somehow got free. Maybe that's what my dad was. I always had the feeling there was plenty my mom didn't tell me about Dad's history. Whether because she thought she was keeping me safe, or because she didn't want me to know.

Or maybe she didn't even know.

Ianto's hunger makes everything else fade away around me, even as I turn to mix a gin and tonic for one of the slutty house elves, as I sometimes call them, to take to a customer.

Here, have a condom, Dobby.

Lucius is the most powerful and connected vamp I've ever hooked up working for. There are others out there even more powerful, but I avoid nests where the vamps are more interested in hunting than coexisting. Lucius and Selene both swore to protect me and my secret. He's the first one I've ever sold blood to, so I didn't realize how different I *really* was until he and Selene first sampled the test vial they drew on me.

Normally, someone would need to have a serious blooding fetish or be batcrap crazy to associate with vampires the way I do. I've always felt safest among them and shifters because most vampires have a serious sense of self-preservation and don't like to fuck with things stronger than them. Especially things that are day-walkers.

I'm not the average human. Could one of them snap my neck before I even realized they were behind me? Absolutely.

Which is why I play to my strengths as a curiosity, an enigma. The whole thing I can do influencing them and being immune to their influence might have helped a smidge, too.

Thank you, Neimus, my vampire sensei. He might have saved my life with his teachings.

Lucius is also the first vampire I've told as much of my backstory to as possible, and that's because of Selene.

Because if Lucius fell in love with a shifter and mated with her, he can't be soulless and evil.

So far, he's never let me down.

Which is why I'm a little pissed off that this strange vampire—hunky Ianto doppelgänger or not—is making fangy eyes at me.

He's still sitting there talking with Selene and Lucius, but his gaze never leaves me. When other vampires, or human males, come up to the bar to order something, it's like I feel a wave of possessive energy wash over me from him. Yes, all the way from the other end of the room.

Dang.

I shiver, and even my lady bits yawn and stir a little.

Nope. Not sleeping with a vampire, because sex *with* them leads to becoming dinner *for* them. I'm not stupid enough to let one do that to me, especially now that I know how desirable my blood is. I cannot get myself addicted to that and become a sweetblood. I'm protected by Lucius, and it's a death sentence to fuck with me without my consent.

Don't get me wrong, it's not that I'm frigid or anything. Every fanged hunkadoodle in this place who works for Lucius has made it clear they'd be happy to spank and fuck me even without blooding me, but I'm not about to risk my freedom that way. Even if I would like a Dom of my own to watch my back.

The vamps *are* hunky, for the most part. Yeah, I might have a suit fetish. Lucius knows what he's doing in the marketing department. It's not unusual for first-time vamps here to return on subsequent visits wearing a far better-quality outfit when Lucius' men snag all the prime Twat Pockets.

It's been a while since I've slept with anyone, though. Last guy was a couple of years ago, a cheetah shifter, Chad, passing through Tucson and visiting a cousin for a few days. I met him over at the shifter Fight Club when I was there running an errand for Garrett Green. He had no interest in a mate, so I knew he wouldn't be an asshole and try to mark me.

He was good. Speedy, but good. Excellent recovery time and long-term stamina, though, so I wasn't complaining.

When Mr. Dashing Ianto Wannabe gets up from the table and slowly starts making his way over, trailed by Selene and Lucius, I know I'm going to be playing the name tag game again here shortly. He looks like a vamp not used to hearing *no* for an answer, much less taking it for one.

Oh, goodie. This'll be interesting.

5

D*exter*

I FEEL like I'll crawl out of my damned skin watching others talk to her, especially other vampires.

I want to stake the ones who make her smile. Especially since I can sense the vampires' desire, how much they want to be the first to mark her unblemished throat.

Lucius leans in, dropping his voice so only Selene and I can hear. "Rule one—you do *not* violate consent while in my club. Rule two—you do *not* harm humans on my property. Rule three—*that* woman is under *my* protection. Harming her is an automatic death sentence, and any of my men will enforce it immediately, if Selene or I don't beat them to it. Do I make myself clear?"

"Crystal." I throw back the rest of my bourbon and slide out of the booth, so I can make my way over to the bar. I angle toward the far end, where it meets the wall, so I can hopefully have a private word with the woman.

I'm aware of Lucius and Selene following me, but I don't care. All I care about is remembering her taste, a taste that fills my senses even now.

I realize before I'm even halfway across the space that she's been watching me, aware of me. Whether because I'm sitting with Lucius and Selene or because she happened to notice me, I don't know.

Resisting the urge to puff and preen a little, I edge my way up to the end of the bar. She's currently filling another order, and once she cashes them out, she walks over.

"What can I get for you, stranger?"

Her handwritten name tag says *Blue*, and her hair's obviously a wig. Adorable, a bright blue pageboy cut that sweeps along her jawline, and I wonder what her real hair color is.

Except...

Even as I sniff, I realize I cannot smell...*her*.

Normally, someone's blood still holds at least part of their scent. Hell, humans are like three quarters water, so that makes sense.

But...

I glance back at Lucius, who lays a hand on my shoulder. "Blue, my dear, this is my nephew. Everything he orders is on my tab."

She props her hands on her shapely round hips. She's around five-five and has one hell of a gorgeously spankable ass. "Ianto Jones is your nephew, huh? Who'd a thunk?" But she's smirking, and Selene giggles behind me.

Finally, my irritation overrides my fascination and attraction. "All right, can someone *please* tell me who the hell this Ianto guy is?"

Selene and "Blue" both laugh. "From a TV show," Selene

says. "*Torchwood*. A *Doctor Who* spin-off. You've never heard of it?"

"No. I don't watch much television. I take it Ianto is an actor?"

"Character," Selene and Blue say in unison, making both women laugh. "Gareth David-Lloyd is the actor," Blue adds.

That's when I realize she's looking me *right* in the eyes.

I mean, dead-on.

And she's not...

Whoa.

I literally lean back.

"Problem?" Lucius softly asks, but make no mistake, he sounds amused.

I slowly shake my head even as I continue to stare into her beautiful violet eyes. Eyes I can tell are natural, not contacts, not fake, like her hair.

Violet eyes.

Eyes a very deep, rich violet that no human has.

Bewitching eyes.

Her smirk turns playful, sexy, even. "Hellooo, Sweetie," she says in a mock British accent.

"He won't get that reference, either," Selene says.

But I can't look away from Blue's eyes. "You're not a vampire?"

She tosses the bar towel in her hand over her right shoulder. "Nope."

"Not a shifter?"

She shakes her head.

Even as I try to compel her to tell me what she is, I realize it's useless. Meanwhile, I feel like I'm struggling not to fall into the depths of her gaze and totally lose myself there. "Dexter Van Sussex," I finally manage, extending my hand over the bar.

She cocks her head and appraises me for a moment before shaking with me. "Blue."

Lucius *snorts*.

Actually.

Fucking.

Snorts.

This is a set-up on multiple levels, and I'm not sure why.

I fully realize her name's not actually Blue. "And I can call you...?"

With a little flourish, she indicates her hand-written name tag, which identifies her as Blue.

"What do I have to do to learn your real name?" I'm...*desperate* for it.

And let's be clear that I am *never* desperate.

About *anything*.

She cocks her head the other way. "Why is that so important to you?"

"I don't know," I honestly answer. It's like I couldn't lie even if there were a stake pressed to my chest.

I watch as her gaze quickly sweeps me, and I feel my cock aching, throbbing in response. Her right eyebrow cockily arches, just a little. This woman is used to setting the terms of her interactions, and that turns me on even more.

I'd love to be the one who finally wins and tames her.

She moistens her lips with her tongue and I nearly come. "Then maybe once you can tell me why, we'll play a little game."

"A game?"

She's the only one behind the bar, and four people walk up to the far end of it, obviously wanting to place orders.

Blue glances at them, then Lucius.

He subtly tips his head, indicating for her to take care of them.

As she walks away, I want to go rip out the humans' throats for interrupting us...

That shocking mental image pulls me up short.

Holy shit.

Literally, this is a new reaction for me. My control is *never* tested like this.

Not in the better part of two thousand years.

Lucius' hand pats my shoulder. "Let me show you around downstairs, Dexter. Then you can come up and try again."

I'm still trying to keep my eyes on her even as I back up to follow him. Her gorgeous, rounded hips make that skirt and her hair sway with every step. I always thought heels were sexy, but she's rocking those Doc Martens boots and her subtle confidence is breathtaking.

Damn.

No one's ever affected me like this before.

Ever.

Not even Robert.

I finally turn and follow Lucius and Selene toward the front entrance, but we divert into the coat check area, where a concealed door leads to a stairwell taking us to the basement.

"And here we have the hidden gem of Club Toxic," Lucius says with all the unnecessary fanfare and pomp he's infamous for. He proceeds to drone on and on about various vampires, cites his reasoning for choosing certain pieces of equipment and their placement and points out some of the kinkier scenes going on. Like a pair of female and male vampires, who have a human male sandwiched between them, her impaled on the human's cock, and the male vampire's dick buried inside the human's ass, both of them snacking on the man.

The space is dim, with red mood lighting, spotlights highlighting pieces of dungeon equipment, naked people having kinky sex, yadda-yadda—

Yeah, yeah, I *get* it. It's a BDSM club for vampires.

Right now, I wouldn't care if it was a high school cafeteria on the fucking moon serving alien tartare as the daily special. "What's her name?" I ask Lucius as I trail behind them toward a pair of—oh, there they are—*literal* fucking thrones in the middle of the dungeon space.

"Selene and I swore never to reveal it. If you wish to know it, you'll have to ask her."

I grab his arm. "That's...*her*, though. Right?"

He smiles. "I'm certain you don't wish to talk about *that* in *this* space, do you, Dexter?" He glances around. There are at least fifteen other vampires down here, not counting his staff.

Infuriating. He really is. "You dropped this in my lap and don't want to follow through?" How cruel is he?

He sucks his lip for a moment, then smiles. "Go back up there and ask her if she'd like to accompany you down here."

"And if she says no, what, I'm supposed to scoop her up and carry her down here?" I already know trying to compel her won't work.

"I assure you, that won't be necessary." He flags down one of his men, whispers to him, and the guy heads upstairs.

"You'll order her down here?"

"No."

Desperation the likes of which I've never felt before rolls through me. "Then give me a hint, please?"

"She'll have someone else up at the bar to cover her in a moment or two. Go back up. *Ask* her." His smile widens.

It hits me. "This is more than a setup." A little common

sense tries to rein in my eager cock and aching fangs. "What's the deal with you? Why did you play me like this?"

"Dexter, my nephew. Yesterday, you revealed something rather...unsettling about your potential future plans." His smile fades. "I have lost too many over time. I would prefer not to lose you, too. But her story is not mine to tell. If my instincts are correct, I believe the two of you will hit it off swimmingly. As long as you don't fuck this part up." He waggles his fingers at me in a shooing motion. "Go win your prize and show me my faith in you isn't misplaced."

I fight the urge to blur back upstairs, but I do make haste. True to his word, there's now a second bartender behind the bar with Blue. I glare at two barely legal and overwhelmingly drunk human women who now stand where I previously stood, and they skedaddle.

Blue sees me, but she's serving a couple right now. As I watch her, I fight what feels like a losing war against my fangs. I know Blue is aware of me because even among the noise and distraction of the other patrons, I hear the way her pulse spikes every time she glances my way. Her gorgeous, smooth throat beckons to me and makes my mouth water. I can imagine my lips traveling up and down her flesh, how warm she'll feel, the sexy cries she'll give me as my fingers explore between her legs.

It feels like forever before she makes her way back down to me.

"What can I get for you, Not-Ianto?" She smiles.

"Your name, for starters." Gods, looking into her eyes... it's like I can reach out and touch the cosmos.

She looks down at her name tag and back up to me.

"Your *real* name. Come downstairs with me to talk. *Please*?"

Somehow, I feel like I just fell into a trap I'm helpless to extricate myself from, because her smile turns predatory and she cocks that eyebrow again. "You want me to go downstairs with you?"

I nod, well aware my erection is insistently pressing against the front of my slacks. Thankfully, the bar hides that from her.

"I don't play or do...other things. Especially not here."

I was right—her throat is unblemished. Certainly, it's possible she bears marks elsewhere, but Lucius said she's unblooded. "*Only* to talk. I give you my word." Not sure how I'll honor that vow, but I will damn sure try.

"Oh, I know it would only be to talk. Because if you tried something, I'd scream, and Lucius or one of his men would part your head from your shoulders before I even shut my mouth, if I didn't stake you myself first." She delivers that in a bright, playful tone, which chills me all the more but also makes my mouth water.

I hold up my hands. "Only to talk. I'll pay just to talk with you."

She pretends to evaluate me, but I can already tell I've walked into whatever trap this is.

Shockingly enough, I don't want to free myself.

"You want to put money on it? A little wager?"

I lean in, half over the bar. "Anything."

"Got a hundred on you?"

My wallet's already in my hand, and I withdraw not one but five hundred-dollar bills and hold them up. "There." If that's all it'll take, I'll give her my whole damn wallet.

She stares at them for a moment because, apparently, I've gone off-script.

"Oookaaaay." Her violet gaze meets mine again, and I feel...something.

My full, achingly hard cock throbs, demanding to be buried inside her.

She grabs one of the serving trays and props it sideways on the bar, to her right, so it blocks us from the view of other patrons. The wall is to her left. It unnerves me in good ways that she looks me in the eyes as she speaks, and yet I'm helpless to compel her.

"Let's play a game. Here's the rules: My real name's on the back of my name tag. I'll show you, and you get only *one* attempt to pronounce it correctly. You'll say it softly, so no one else can hear. You do *not* reveal to anyone what it says, win or lose. I win? *KA*-ching. You win? I'll go downstairs with you, *only* to talk. *Nothing* else. You also *never* get another chance to play this game."

"Do it."

Her right hand covers her name tag. "You sure?"

I nod.

I can already tell no one has ever won this game, even before I hear Lucius speak just behind me. "I do so *love* this game."

"Ready?" she asks.

I'm trying not to drool as I imagine how the glass of her blood tasted last night, I nod.

She leans closer, a victorious smile already curling those gorgeous lips of hers as she tugs on her name tag and flips it over, so I can read the back. I only glance away from her beautiful violet eyes just long enough to read the word written there in black marker.

Eilidh

VICTORY MAKES me want to cackle with glee, but I maintain my composure.

Maybe I'm not as ready to meet the sunrise as I thought.

"Hello, AY-lee," I whisper. "It's a pleasure to make your acquaintance."

I smile as her eyes go wide and her jaw drops open. Behind me, Lucius roars with laughter and slaps me between the shoulder blades.

6

E *ilidh*

MOTHERFUCKER.

Stunned, I stand there ready to lambaste Lucius, fricking vampire king or not, for telling the guy the answer.

Lucius holds up his hand. "I didn't tell him. I swear. Neither did Selene."

Not-Ianto smiles, and his Midwestern-blah accent turns into a sexy Scottish burr that makes my girly parts want to play his bagpipe. "He dinnae tell, me bonnie lass. Not his fault I grew up in that part o' the world." His smile fades, as does his accent, and his voice returns to a whisper. "My sister-in-law's name was Eilidh. It means 'sun' or 'radiant one,' depending who you ask."

Dammit. That figures.

"Take the rest of the night off, if you wish," Lucius tells me. "*Paid.*"

Dexter gently catches my hand before I can pull back, folds the five hundreds in half, and presses the wad into my palm, closing my fingers around them. "I still want you to have this."

I struggle against a wave of anger. "I'm not a whore," I grit through clenched teeth.

"I didn't say you were. All I wish to do is talk with you —*that* was the bet. I expect nothing more. But I can afford to be a gracious winner. Please?"

"Dexter is annoyingly chivalrous," Lucius volunteers. "His word is good." He drops his voice and addresses Dexter. "Do not *ever* speak her real name under this roof again without her permission."

I don't understand why Dexter's light blue eyes seem to affect me in a way no other vampire ever has. "Understood." I don't even mean he's compelling me. I mean...

They're just gorgeous. He's a gorgeous man. Not the fake kind of pretty man, like so many of the vamps. Real-world pretty, like he's not so far removed from the human race that he can't remember what it was like to be one.

There's a tiny yet noisy part of my soul begging me to let Dexter bend me over a spanking bench and have his way with me.

The rest of me quickly locks that part in a mental closet. I don't care how hunky he is or how chivalrous. He's a *vampire*. I don't shit where I eat. Or, in this case, I don't let them eat where I eat, so to speak.

I need to stand strong.

Don't I?

Besides, if he *did* know more about me, he'd likely run the other way. And I can't afford to lose my heart to a hunky guy who isn't interested in anything other than taking a few pints out of me and taking my pants off me while sticking his D into me.

Returning the tray to its place, I tuck the bills into my sports bra with the other hundred I earned earlier. Okay, so I made six hundred tonight, cash, on top of other tips and my pay. That's not a bad night at all. It means I can finally get new tires put on my SUV, which I've been putting off.

And all I have to do is talk to Not-Ianto?

I am nothing if not a realist. It's worth it, I suppose.

Even if that locked-away part of me is pounding on the closet door and begging me to give Dexter a chance.

I tell Carl, the other bartender, that Lucius needs me downstairs. That means Carl won't feel irritated that I'm bailing. Whatever Lucius wants, he gets. I feel Dexter's gaze heavy upon me as I walk all the way down and around the far end of the bar. I suspect if I tried to bolt for it that he would blur and appear right in front of me.

It's not worth embarrassing myself or Lucius like that. I'll be a gracious loser, even if I've never lost the name tag game before.

I walk over to where Dexter stands, waiting.

Dexter Van Sussex is handsome, yes.

The fact that I keep expecting Captain Jack Harkness to pop out of a nearby doorway and lay a sexy-ass kiss on his mouth doesn't hurt, either.

He offers his arm, and I take it. I'm not sure how I feel about the fact that he so easily beat me at my own game and doesn't seem the slightest bit interested in capitalizing on the bet the way any other vampire probably would.

Just wants to talk and not pop me open like a walking juice box? That's a true first. Every other vampire who's ever played the game wanted to get me downstairs to spank my ass and then feed on me.

Dexter also doesn't seem unnerved by me, despite realizing that he cannot control me the way vampires can control other humans and even weaker shifters.

I sense he's very old. Maybe not quite as old as Lucius, but at least as powerful. That's reinforced when every other vampire besides Lucius and Selene act differential toward him, tipping their heads to him as we pass.

My nipples tighten as my arm curls around his. I feel cool, firm muscles beneath the fabric of his blazer and shirt. He's around six-three, maybe two hundred and fifty pounds, and broad-shouldered.

What the hell *have I gotten myself into?*

And what harm would it be to let him—

NO. Absolutely not. Holding vampires at arms' length has kept me alive and unblooded, even if it has also kept me perpetually frustrated and feeling more than a little envious of some of the sweetbloods.

As we cross the room, I'm well aware of the hungry stares of the vampires who watch us depart. There's more than a little envy there because I've turned all of them down before—or they've seen me turn others down—and here's first-timer Dexter, getting me on his arm.

Not that they realize nothing more than talking will ensue between us.

Add in the evil gazes from mostly women patrons and a few men—humans—that Dexter chose *me*, and I'm in a no-win situation with pretty much everyone upstairs in terms of my guts being hated.

Wonderful.

We follow Lucius downstairs. Oh, yeah, *now* I remember the main reason I don't like coming down here any more than necessary when we're open. Because the endorphin soup smacks me in the face like a warm, soggy glove and tries to work a few fingers inside my cooter as we hit the bottom of the stairwell. I guess, in some ways, I'm an empath, and it's always overwhelming to me. Add in the fact that no, I can't engage in some kinky fun, and *yeah...* I *hate* it.

Lucius snaps his fingers, and one of the household humans, a man, steps forward. "Make sure the available suite's ready."

"*Whoa*," I say. "I told Not-Ianto here that I'd come down *only* to talk."

The household human hesitates, looking from me to Lucius. All the human staff, except maybe Benny, are terrified of me because they've seen me handle myself. Even the vampire staff are impressed by my skills, between my party trick and because they know I always carry a couple of wooden pencils on me. I nearly staked a vamp on the floor one night who was getting rowdy with one of the household humans.

Lucius arches an eyebrow at me. "The alcoves only have curtains. Do you *really* wish to have your private discussion where everyone else could possibly overhear? While Dexter was at our home last night, I allowed him to sample our *special* vintage." My stomach drops, but Lucius continues. "I personally guarantee Dexter will not do *anything* but talk with you, unless you first come out here and tell me you wish to do more with him. Otherwise, he will not leave this building alive." He looks at Dexter. "Will you?"

Dexter's gaze practically burns holes through me and has my clit throbbing in a way not even watching Captain Jack and Ianto making out on-screen usually causes. "I swear."

In the red lights down here, Dexter's blue eyes look more reddish grey, intense, but also restrained.

Yeah, I sense *that*. Restraint. This isn't some feral, newly turned schmuck without an ounce of willpower. This guy's old, cold, and controlled.

"Okay, fine." I point at Lucius. "Because *he* vouches for you."

The household human scurries off, and I focus on Selene.

She looks hopeful. "Your verdict?" I ask her.

Her smile is beautiful. "I really like him, Blue." She looks at Dexter. "Be honest with her and tell her what you told us last night."

Now they have my interest, even though that's the last thing I want to admit.

After giving Lucius stink-eye one more time, I head toward the available rear suite as Dexter falls into step behind me.

Not everyone gets to use these. The main vampire staff, like Maximus, Tiberius, Augustus, and others. Or VIPs Lucius okays.

Like Not-Ianto.

They have en suite bathrooms and secure interior locks. Every once in a while, a vampire will stay a few days if they're new in town and need a safe daytime sleeping spot before they acquire their own.

I stand in the doorway, waiting for the household human to finish checking everything. He pauses in the doorway, bowing his head to me. "It's ready, ma'am."

"Thank you."

He offers me a nervous smile and skitters back to the main part of the dungeon. Turning to Dexter, I hold out a hand, indicating for him to go. "And here we are."

"After you—ladies first."

"You have *no* idea how much of a lady I might or might

not be." I head inside, pausing so I can close and lock the door once he's inside.

His chuckle tightens my traitorous nipples even more. "You're absolutely right. I don't. But I am a man of my word."

There's the bed and a comfortable lounging chair, unless I want to sit on the dresser.

Which I don't.

I automatically take the chair. He can sit on the bed if he wants. "What are we talking about?" I ask.

He doesn't sit, at first. He slides his hands into his trouser pockets and studies his Berluti loafers for a moment. The guy's got style—I'll give him credit for that.

I mean, I expect him to be rich. That's not a shocker. Old, rich vampires are as much of a cliché as biker werewolves or cage-fighting bear shifters. In fact, if an older vampire isn't independently wealthy, I'd wonder what the hell is wrong with him. You have to be a special kind of stupid to be several hundred years old, or older, and *not* have at least a Swiss or Caymanian bank account or *something*.

"Where do you wish me to begin?" He finally looks into my eyes, and I can tell he feels as unnerved right now as I do.

I also see that's a considerable tent pole in his pants.

Yowza.

Nope, focus, *girlie.* That's a *vamp.* They're fine as employers and friends, but not for fucking, and *damn* sure not for fanging.

"What'd they mean about last night?" I ask. "Let's start there and work our way back. What'd you tell them?"

He lets out a sigh. "I'm in town on business. As you might guess, Lucius and I go back quite a distance in time. He and my sire shared the same sire, hence why he's my 'uncle.' After I admitted to him that I was considering greeting a sunrise, he asked Selene to bring out a special batch of blood and served it."

I feel a little bad for him. I don't think I've ever heard a vamp admit they're...

Wow.

His gaze drops to his loafers again. "He thought perhaps, if I met you, it might change my opinion about...that."

Okay, yeah, back to feeling pissed off at Lucius. I'm not a supernatural shrink. "Did he tell you I'm no sweetblood?"

I shove away more pounding coming from my mental closet. If I was going to break my personal rule, this would be the vamp to make me do it.

Which is all the more reason why I need to *not* do it.

"He did." His gaze angles up. In this light, his eyes once again look a beautiful light blue and are filled with ancient pain. "I'd like to know if I could take you out on a date."

"A *whut*?"

A smile plays at the corners of his handsome mouth. "You know, take you out to dinner. Or a movie, perhaps?"

"I kinda know of a nightclub in town."

He steadily meets my gaze. "Yes, but the owner can be a pretentious git sometimes."

Now I'm laughing. "Holy shit. *Dude*. You did *not* just call the king of the vampires a git."

"I believe I did." His lips give up their smile, and I hate that it does things to me no other vampire or man ever has before. He cocks his head. "I've known him long enough I can get away with it. He's not *my* king. He might as well have accepted a scimitar from a watery bint in some lake." I laugh again. Holy shit, he knows Monty Python. "I also noticed you weren't genuflecting or calling him 'sire.'"

I shrug. "I like to live dangerously."

"Nooo," he slowly said. "I don't think that's right at all. He hinted there was a story. While I can't read you, I'd be willing to bet you've stayed here under Lucius' protection because you are danger-averse."

I don't want to admit hammer just met nail, so I don't reply.

Stalemate. We study each other for a long moment before I finally speak. "So, you don't know *Torchwood* or *Doctor Who*, but you can sort of quote *Monty Python and the Holy Grail*?"

He shrugs. "It's my favorite movie. I saw it when it first came out, and it made me laugh. At that point, it'd been a long time since anything had made me laugh. It's one of the few movies I own."

"Ahh." Yep, this guy is really lonely and feeling it. Vamps usually don't allow others to see any hint of weakness on their part, especially loneliness.

He finally speaks again. "Anyway, you were..." Another sigh. "Delicious. Indescribable."

Of course, there's another little secret part deep inside me proudly preening over that. "Yeah, he makes a lot of money off me. Kind of creepy, though, when I'm working down here and describing the offerings and knowing some of them include some of *me*. I try not to think about anything but the cash Lucius hands me when he does it. I let him take a pint from me every so often. Pays me a grand for it."

"I don't suppose I could hire you away from him?"

"Uh, let's see. Let some rando vampire who just blew into town make me a bunch of big promises? That's a hard pass, sorry."

But he smiles again. "See? Risk-averse. Can I at least beg you for a strictly platonic and safe date? I'll even pay one of

Lucius' men to accompany us, if it'd make you feel better. You'd never have to be alone with me."

I hate to admit I'm finding myself liking him and getting a good feeling about him in a way I usually don't about vamps.

When I hear a muffled *see I told you so* from my mental closet, I kick the door, hard, to shut it up.

I inhale, and his scent reminds me of rich, sweet pipe tobacco and dark chocolate. "I don't know anything about you, for starters. Let's cover that ground."

He tugs on the perfect creases in his trousers as he settles on the edge of the bed. "Dexter Van Sussex. I currently run a hotel and casino in Atlantic City—"

I hold up a hand, feeling simultaneously relieved and disappointed. Of *course* he was too good to be true. "Stop right there. I'm out." I stand. "I don't get mixed up in organized crime."

"Neither do I. Ask Lucius, if you wish. I run an honest operation. I'm about to age out of the city and want to open a hotel and casino here in Tucson. I'm visiting here, speaking with Lucius to secure his agreement and arrange a meeting with the Tucson wolf pack Alpha through Lucius. I want to work with their pack, as well."

"Garrett Green?"

"Yes. You've heard of him?"

I snort. "*Dude*, he's my fricking *landlord*."

7

D *exter*

Now that I'm alone with Eilidh, I deeply inhale with every breath I take and realize...

I still cannot truly *smell* her.

She has an ephemeral scent—like rain, like a cool, spring breeze.

Like warm sunlight.

Definitely *not* like a human. Damn sure not like any shifter I've ever scented before.

Or...any other creature.

I have a feeling it will drive me mad before I figure it out.

That *she* will drive me to madness. I also belatedly realize it was probably her scent I detected upstairs in the office.

"He's your *landlord*?" I manage.

"Yeah. Don't let his biker exterior fool you, either. Guy's

smart and loaded. He and his crew started flipping houses, and it didn't take them long to own a goodly chunk of real estate in this city. Plus, his mate's an attorney. She's someone you don't fuck with, either."

"Oh."

"Exactly. She's also my friend."

I'm not exactly sure what I expected from the Tucson wolf pack Alpha, but it wasn't that. "Do you know him well enough to introduce me?"

"Dude, I don't know *you* well enough to introduce you. I might be talked into going with, depending when and where you do it, but as far as vouching? Nah, that'll have to be up to Lucius. I'm not putting myself or my rep on the line for you."

"Your...rep?"

"Yeah. Garrett Green's not only my landlord and my friend's mate—he also sends work my way."

"What kind of work?"

"I'm sort of a neutral-party errand girl. Courier service. I take on work for vampires that needs doing during daylight hours and handle tasks for the shifters that most humans can't be trusted with. I move between the nest and the various packs to pass messages, things like that. Nothing illegal," she quickly adds. "That's not my jam, and they all know it. But they also know I'm my own person."

I'm glad I'm sitting down because my cock's painfully hard right now. I love how snarky she is, love her fearlessness in this moment.

One of my deepest desires is to earn her trust, so I can play with her, perhaps even feed from her, if she allows it.

At the very least, I want to fuck her. I'd settle for that.

What I'd love to do is strip her naked, bind her in jute ropes, eat her pussy until she screams herself hoarse from orgasms, and then slowly lick my way over every inch of ligature marks left on her by my ropes while I untie her.

Or spank her. That'd be fun, too.

I am also willing to do whatever it takes to woo her. "May I ask you another question?"

She cocks her head at me again, her wig swishing a little, and settles back in the chair once more. "You can ask me anything. I won't promise to answer, though."

"Why the wig?"

Her smile now looks a little too tight, despite her attempt to exude cockiness. "Why not?"

"You match your name tag to your wig color, don't you?"

She shrugs, that adorable little smirk on her face.

I try a different tactic. "Lucius wouldn't even tell me last night if you were a man or a woman. He told me almost nothing about you."

"That's because I'm not one of his household humans, and I asked him to keep my secrets. The ones he knows. There are plenty of things he doesn't know about me."

"Why are you so afraid?"

She holds her hands up, indicating the building. "Did you notice I work for and with fricking vampires? A person would have to be an idiot not to show a healthy dose of fear."

She's got a valid point. "Would you like to know more about me?"

"It's your dime, dude. You can talk about whatever you'd like."

But I hear the way her pulse shifts a little at that, speeds up a tad. She's nervous, especially nervous about what I might ask her.

I want to wrap her in my arms and protect her, slay her dragons, buy her anyth—

Holy *fuck*, I'm already halfway in love with her, and I don't even know her full real name.

She watches me with an intensity I usually only see in vampires and shifters.

But the truth is now there. *Right* there.

I am completely enchanted by this woman.

Obsessed with her.

Whatever I have to do to earn her trust, I'll gladly do it.

"If I ask Lucius to arrange a meeting for me with Garrett Green, you would attend with us?"

"I might attend," she carefully says after considering. "The *with* part trips me up a little because, keep in mind, I won't put my neck on the line for you yet. I need to know you first before I'll risk my rep over you. Also depends when and where it is." I catch that repeated stipulation and wonder about it.

"Fair enough. May I ask Lucius to include you in the plans, then?"

She sucks on her teeth. "Why is this so important to you?"

Because you *are important to me.*

No, I don't say that. Are you mad? Don't want to scare her off.

I opt for the truth.

Sort of. "I am very drawn to you. Attracted to you."

I get a little snort in reply. "You want to buy the bottling source, is what you want. I *really* wish he hadn't given you an undiluted taste of me."

"Why not?"

She holds out her hand, indicating me.

Her meaning is clear.

"Blue, consent is *not* negotiable, for me. I insist upon it.

Would you do me the honor of a dinner date, at least? Please?"

Doubt darkens her violet eyes to the purple of an evening sky. "Where I'm *not* on the menu?"

"Exactly. I'll pay one of Lucius's men—hell, I'll pay *all* of them to come along."

"Greeeaat. More vampires. Perfect. That's not intimidating at alll."

I'm already making mental notes to find out from Lucius who I can talk to, a reliable realtor, to buy a house here. I want one in his neighborhood—a large, beautiful, palatial home. Blue deserves nothing less than that. I'll do anything to prove to her she can trust me.

"Have you ever actually *dated* anyone since you turned?" she asks. "Ever had a girlfriend who wasn't immortal, or non-human, or a snack?"

Inwardly, I cringe. I don't want to discuss Robert tonight. "It's been more years than I care to remember."

She leans forward in her chair. "You can't waltz your immortal ass into someone's life, turn it upside-down, and make a boatload of promises just because my vintage put some long-overdue starch in your shorts. I have a life, and it's a life I want to live."

I hate that she's effortlessly nailed me to a wall. Metaphorically speaking. "And what do you want to do with your life if not working in a vampire nightclub that's a secret BDSM blood club?"

I also hate that her voice turns sad and quiet. "Maybe if you stick around for a while, I'll come to trust you enough to tell you."

With all certainty, I know if I suddenly promise her the moon, she'll run. Not that I couldn't track or find her—in a vampire or human way—but I will forever ruin her trust.

I think that might kill me and drive me toward the dawn.

"I would really like that, Blue." Lightly rubbing my palms along the tops of my thighs, I can't think of a legitimate reason to keep her here right now, beyond my desire to do so. "Thank you for being a good sport and talking with me tonight. I appreciate it."

Another cock of her head. Every time she does that, I hear the way her wig whispers against her cheeks as it sways, the artificial hair sounding like a breeze to my sensitive hearing. "You're done talking to me?"

"Honestly? I could sit here all night talking with you, but I realize this isn't comfortable for you, and I apologize for that. I do not wish to make you feel uncomfortable. I've enjoyed this greatly, and I appreciate your time."

She studies me. "I don't mind hanging out for a while longer. You're not too bad to talk to, Not-Ianto."

First barrier—passed. "Thank you."

She shrugs like it's no big deal, but I feel something different. I hear her pulse thrumming, see the way her pupils dilate a little—she's intrigued by me and afraid to admit it. She's been hurt in some way in the past. She doesn't trust easily, or at all.

I wish I could fix every problem in her life for her, even if I never get to lay a finger or fang on her.

The thought of others getting to sample her, even from a glass, renders me nearly incoherent with rage. No one should be permitted to touch her, taste her.

I suspect the only reason she allows Lucius to take from her is the money, and that also enrages me, even as I admit he's being ethical about it.

It *personally* enrages me.

Mentally, I'm scrambling for something to talk about that isn't about blood, sex, or kink. The unholy trifecta. I want to get to know *her*—holy fuck, yeah, I'm obsessed, all right.

Lucius will laugh his ass off. The last thing on my mind now is meeting a sunrise.

"Tell me about that TV show," I say. "*Torchwood*, was it?"

Her violet eyes light up. "Oh, my god! It's fantastic..." But first, she has to give me an overview of *Doctor Who*, so I understand the context.

I'll admit I've heard of that show, but I've never seen it, either. Both shows feature long-lived, time-traveling adventurers who frequently have companions, as I understand it.

I can relate. I might find myself watching this show.

Her *voice*, though. I could easily listen to her all night. I've found something she's passionate about. Something she loves.

Something I can research and, hopefully, learn more about, so I can have a *thing* in common with her.

It's a desperate need within me, to have that.

To gently hold on to her, wind her around me, so she never wants to leave me.

If that means I've got to start watching fucking TV, then I guess I'm watching TV.

About an hour later, we reach a natural, comfortable lull in the conversation, and I receive another of those adorable head cocks from her.

"You know, I suppose if you wanted to have a dinner date, we could eat up in the conference room in the office tomorrow night. I wouldn't mind that. We could be alone up there. I wouldn't even make you bring one of Lucius' men with you."

If my heart still beat, it'd be pounding right now. "I wouldn't mind Lucius' men accompanying you to dinner. I'll take you anywhere you wish to go."

"No. Your choice of food, but we eat here." A cloud flits across her features. "I don't go out at night. If I'm not here at work, I'm home. That's a *me* rule."

"I swear I would make sure you're protected."

Her gaze drops for a moment. I suspect this is connected to what Lucius hinted at. "I don't go out," she repeats, her voice sounding a little duller, flatter. "At night, I'm almost always either at work or home. I'm *not* traveling after dark. That's all you need to know."

I hate that she feels unsafe. "Is someone bothering you? Please, I would be happy to pay for extra security and—"

She stays me with a hand and a wry smile. "You don't even *know* me. You don't know my situation. I'm giving you a concession. Take the offer or not, but it's not negotiable."

Fuck. I mentally smack myself and immediately retreat. "I will be happy to order food from whatever restaurant you'd like and have it delivered here tomorrow night."

"Send one of his guys out for it," she suggests. "We don't need anyone else here who didn't intend to be." She waggles her fingers at the walls. "Fricking vampires allll over the place."

I chuckle. "As you wish. Do you have a preference what food I order?"

"Surprise me."

I suspect this will be a test, and I'm desperate not to fuck it up. "What time?"

"Weeelll," she drawls, "I'm usually here before six, but I'm guessing you won't be here before dark. So, let's make it nine. That'll give you time to wake up and brush your fangs and get our food. Or would you prefer ten?"

I do quick mental calculations. "Ten might be safer."

"Ten it is." Her gaze lays heavy on me. My cock hasn't

gone soft yet, and I know I must return to my hotel and jerk off before dawn.

Not negotiable.

Her nostrils flare a little, just slightly, and I'm almost expecting her to comment on my state, but she doesn't. "What's your end game?" she quietly asks.

Slowly shaking my head, I speak the truth. "I don't know. You make me feel more alive than I have in..." I try not to think about Robert. A rush of shame and grief washes through me, and I shove it aside. "Even if all we do is talk and have dinner, I will be a better person for it and grateful for your presence in my life."

Her gaze darkens again. "I don't want to lead you on. I don't want you to assume you'll wear me down. Lucius knows the deal with me. One day, I might suddenly move on, and that's it."

Something painfully pulls in my chest at the thought of her leaving. "Then I'm truly honored you've agreed to let me have dinner with you tomorrow night."

I receive a brisk nod. When she stands, I stand with her. "I should go make sure they haven't burned the fricking place down upstairs. I've been down here longer than I like."

"With me?"

"No. I mean, down *here*." She waggles her fingers at the walls again. "In the basement. I don't mind when we're closed, but I prefer not pulling shifts down here. Earn my trust, and maybe I'll tell you why." She meets my gaze again, and the briefest trace of a luscious scent, like honey and vanilla, wafts to me. It's different than before, and distinctive. "Tomorrow, then."

"Tomorrow. Thank you, Blue, for tonight."

She pats her chest where the bills are tucked inside her sports bra. "Thank *you* for putting tires on my car."

That makes me want to buy her a brand-new car, one that's worthy of her, one that—

She turns and, in a speed that, for a moment, seems nearly vampiric, unlocks the door and leaves.

Leaving me standing there with my eyes dropping closed and deeply inhaling her lingering scent. Back to a rainy spring day.

There...and not.

"Enchanting, isn't she?" Lucius stands in the doorway. I can tell from his scent and the sound of his voice.

I open my eyes. "I need the best restaurant in Tucson," I tell him. "Where I can order food from, have one of your men pick up for me, and bring here tomorrow night. Obviously, I'll pay them for their time."

He smiles. "Done. She's offered to sup with you, then?"

"Tomorrow night, up in the office. In private. I offered to take her out—"

"She won't."

Unpacking his tone, to see if it's an order on his part or a statement of fact, I finally nod. "Yes. What do you know?"

He steps inside and pushes the door shut with a finger. "She won't," he says, and it's definitely a statement of fact. "What did she tell you?"

"Not very much, although I now know who Ianto is." I start to pull out my wallet when he stops me.

"*Tut.* I'll ask Selene to personally select something for tomorrow night, but we shall pay for it and make the arrangements. What time did you say?"

"We agreed upon ten. Up in your conference room."

"You realize she has the day off tomorrow, don't you?"

"No. She didn't tell me that. She said she's usually here before dark."

He shrugs. "She won't travel after dark. I mean, she has, but rarely, and only if unavoidable."

"She said that but wouldn't say why. Does that mean she's coming in...just for me?"

"I honestly cannot answer that question. Not 'will not' but cannot, because I do not know the full answer."

Something that's been pecking at my mind, something he said earlier up in the office, hits me. "You mentioned the *gwyllgi*."

He slowly nods. "I did."

"What did you mean by that?"

For a moment, he seems lost in concentration. "Let's get you through dinner tomorrow night. But suffice it to say it's wonderful to actually see her genuinely smile for the first time since I've known her."

That makes me puff up, and he notices. "Will you be spending more time in Tucson, then?" he asks.

I nod. "Can you arrange a meeting with Garrett Green?"

"To discuss the casino?"

"Yes. I'll work on that. Might take a few days to arrange. I'm not sure if he's in town right now or not."

"Understood. She said she knows him and is friends with his mate?"

"Yes. It's been a very helpful arrangement." He grins. I take it there are now no sunrises in your immediate future?"

I'm not too proud to admit it. "Yes, you were right. Yes, I have found a reason to stick around. Yes, I am infatuated with her. Happy?"

He chuckles. "Well, I'm not *un*happy."

I follow him out to the main play space, and he orders me a large glass of a "special house blend."

Before I even taste it, I know Blue's blood is mixed in with it. Now that I know what she smells like in person, I realize her taste is something completely different than anything I've ever experienced. It brightens and sharpens the other flavors like an enhancer.

I'm tempted to head upstairs and sit at the bar and watch her for what's left of the night, but Lucius has other ideas. "Can I perhaps interest you in one of our household humans for the night?"

Before meeting Blue in person—or tasting her—I might have been tempted.

Now?

The thought of touching someone other than her leaves me cold.

Cold*er*. "That's very kind of you, but—"

"Ah." His brows lift. "You *are* obsessed with her now, aren't you?"

Why deny it? "It would seem so."

Paternally, his hand grips my shoulder. "Take your time with her," he whispers. "Don't rush. You are the only one, besides myself and Selene, I would ever trust her with."

His words ring in my ears long after he's left to make rounds of the other guests. It's close to four a.m. when I finally emerge from the basement to leave, and I see that the nightclub is nearly deserted.

No Blue.

Theophilus, one of Lucius' men, walks over as I stand there feeling more than a little forlorn. "Can I help you, sir?"

"Blue's left already?"

From his slight scowl, I know she's still here. "She's not available, I'm sorry. Did you need us to call a car for you?"

I feel in my pocket for the key fob. "No, I have a rental."

"Ah."

He subtly shifts position, so he's standing between me

and a straight line toward the back hallway I know leads to the stairwell upstairs.

A locked stairwell.

I meet his gaze. "Promise me she'll be safe getting to her car."

"She never leaves before dawn, and she has a reserved staff spot near the back door, sir. She's safe." When I don't move, he adds, "I'm the general manager. She's under Lucius' personal protection. Believe me, she's safe."

It's the best I can ask for.

Nodding, I turn and leave, but outside I find myself hanging a right at the end of the building and walking down and around to the back. There are ten reserved parking spots, and seven are currently full. I can smell which car is Lucius' and Selene's. Five of the other cars—all of them ostentatiously expensive sports cars worth more than the average family home—are also owned by vampires.

The last vehicle looks like a pitiful interloper, the runt of the litter, sitting next to the others. An old, dark grey Toyota 4Runner SUV, with more than a few tiny door dings along both sides. It's at least fifteen years old. The tires' tread looks dangerously thin in places on all four tires. It's dusty, and the paint's shine has faded along the hood, more a matte finish than glossy. The front headlight housings are yellowed and hazy with time and wear.

Dammit.

The windows are tinted, but my eyes can easily see inside. It's neat and tidy, with no visible detritus like humans are prone to collecting. I notice it's a four-wheel drive and has a trailer hitch.

Before I can rethink, I snap a picture of the license plate, the VIN number plate visible on the dash, and a closeup of one of the tires, showing the wheel style and the tire size.

That done, I blur to my rental and climb in. Smiling to myself, I return to my hotel and securely lock myself in my suite, including placing the two wedge-shaped doorstops I always carry with me when traveling. One goes under the suite door and one under my bedroom door. Then I text instructions to my men and include the pictures. It might take a day or two to arrange the surprise for Eilidh.

I hope she takes it in the manner I mean it.

With that done, I retreat to my shower, close my eyes, and finally get to rub out a wholly satisfying orgasm while wishing my hand was Blue's mouth.

I couldn't even focus on watching the scenes going on around me downstairs without my mind returning to her violet eyes.

Violet.

A color that is not normally found in humans. Not like that.

They weren't contacts, either.

Amazing.

She's *amazing*.

And if it takes me the rest of my life, I *will* win her over and make her *mine*.

8

E *ilidh*

THEY DON'T NEED me on the floor tonight. After I change out the hundreds I received for twenties from the cash drawer behind the bar, I retreat upstairs to the office to handle paperwork. I don't want anyone seeing how rattled I feel right now.

Rattled because I *like* Dex.

I *reeeally* like him.

I cannot *like* anyone *like* him in *that* way. It's dangerous for me. Because for starters, what's he want with me, beyond being his fucktoy and perpetual Happy Meal?

Secondly, I'm a danger to him that he doesn't even know about. In ways he doesn't know about. Possibly not just him, but any like him. I won't risk someone else's life, immortal or not.

I know the shifters tend to call them "leeches," but I'm

not fond of that term. Sure, a few of them fit that stereotype, but they're trying to survive. Just like humans, there are plenty of them who are ethical and, while maybe not cuddly foo-foo with humans, they at least aren't murderous thugs. And look at the shifters—sometimes they'll kill humans who learn their secret. At least the vampires usually leave humans alive.

While I wouldn't think twice about staking a vicious asshole, vamps like Lucius, Selene, Dexter, and others are the good guys and should be protected.

I'm upstairs maybe fifteen minutes when I hear someone unlock the stairwell door. I know it's Theophilus before he makes it to the top of the stairs. Even if I hadn't heard the distinctive way the club manager always punches in his code, or the way he walks, his scent hits me before he makes it through the second door.

I haven't told Lucius and the others I can scent and hear them as easily as I do. I figure there are things best left back in case I need a tactical advantage.

He opens the main office suite door, concern on his face when he appears around the end of the divider that gives me privacy at my desk. I hold no illusions that if I wasn't under Lucius' personal protection, Theophilus wouldn't give an extra damn about me over the basic concern he shows any of the household humans for the extent they're working here.

But I'm in the "inner circle," so to speak. That elevates me to a higher level.

Thus, I matter.

"Are you all right? Lucius asked me to check on you."

Forcing a smile that probably doesn't fool him, I nod. "I'm fine. Is Dexter still here?"

"In the dungeon. If you want to remain up here, Lucius said you can take the rest of the night off. Paid."

"Thanks. I'll still do some work. I have enough paperwork to keep me busy."

He nods, hesitating.

"What?"

"Did Dexter upset you?"

"No, not at all. He was a perfect gentleman. All we did was talk, and Lucius was right that he didn't act improper in the slightest. He was very nice."

He doesn't look convinced. "I know you don't leave while it's dark, but if you'd like me to have people drive you home early, I will."

By people, he means vampires.

I'm actually touched, but small problem—I live in shifter territory, and them taking me home would violate the treaty. I won't let them get in trouble like that over me. "I'm good but thank you. Unless Dexter can't explode at dawn, I'm certain I'll be fine."

He chuffs with a laugh. "If you change your mind, let me know, and I'll arrange it."

"Thanks. Hey, I know I'm off tomorrow, but I'll unofficially be here. I told Dexter he and I can eat dinner up here in the conference room."

"Certainly. I'll keep everyone out, so you have privacy."

"Thanks."

He leaves me alone again. I pull out my phone and call up the Pluto TV app, tune it to the cat video channel, and prop it on my desk in its cradle charger while I work. It's a feel-good distraction that won't interrupt my concentration.

I've never allowed myself to have pets. We moved so often, it wouldn't have been practical. One more painful good-bye.

Instead, I have a stuffed dog and stuffed cat Dad and Zuzu bought for me when I was little. With the wholly original names of Cat and Dog, they've made every move with me and stay on my bed at night and on my nightstand during the day.

It's not long before I know I'm alone in the club, and when I check the time, I find it's nearly six.

Past dawn.

Yawning, I shut off my computer, gather my things, and head downstairs.

I smell stale human sex and sweat and alcohol, but also the sharp, artificial aroma of pine in the cleaner we use in the mop water and the bleach solution we use on the tables and chairs and the bar.

Likely, humans would only smell the barest traces of piney bleach. The ventilation system will have it cleared out long before the first vampire arrives later this evening.

I don't bother going downstairs. Technically, not my shift tomorrow. If someone fucked up, they'll hear about it from Theophilus, if they're lucky, and Lucius, if they aren't. I check the front door, find it secure, then head to the back and set the alarm, locking that door behind me. I'm in my old 4Runner seconds later despite knowing how silly my reaction is.

It's morning. Daylight.

Nothing bad ever happens to me in daylight. That's always reserved for darkness.

Still, I'm wary as I leave the club and randomly pick a direction. I never drive straight home. It's stupid, I guess, because if someone's determined to figure out where I live, all they'd have to do is run my license plate. It's registered under my fake ID, but I used my apartment address because I needed paperwork proving where I lived, like utility bills and my lease.

But not being predictable is something Mom drilled into my head, and old habits die hard. It's weird having what amounts to roots in the Tucson area. Not a bad-weird, either.

Almost enough to make me want to hope this will be my home.

Once I reach my apartment building, I scurry across the parking lot and manage to catch the elevator with perfect timing as people are exiting to start their day. I'm so used to living a swing-shift lifestyle that it doesn't bother me. I've lived this way for years, even before Mom died. I was home-schooled and earned my GED when I was fifteen.

I take the elevator up to the floor above mine and then descend via the stairs. Not that it would matter, I suppose. I'm one of many humans in a building whose population is tilted heavily with both shifters and non-shifting shifter races.

No vamps. Even if Garrett would approve a vampire living here—which he wouldn't, because of safety issues and because of the treaty—they like having houses where they can install subterranean crypts and Fort Knox-level security systems.

I'm thirty-five and blessed—or cursed, depending on how you view it—to look like I'm barely nineteen. It's one reason I rarely buy alcohol, because I hate getting carded. Not because it's a pain, but I want few people knowing any name attached to me.

You'd think I'd have settled down by now. That I'd have figured shit out instead of staying on the run.

Except you'd be wrong.

Safely locked in my apartment, I immediately dig out the box of tampons under the bathroom sink, dump the contents, and then carefully remove the fake bottom inside.

There, where I have nearly six thousand in cash stored, I tuck another three hundred from my tips and winnings and replace everything. Then I pull out the package of pads and dig out the fake wrapper in the middle, where another growing bundle resides. All but two hundred in cash goes in there.

On my way to the club later, I'll stop by a convenience store and buy another pre-paid credit card. I have a stash of them hidden in a fake deodorant container in my medicine cabinet, with about eight thousand dollars on them. Those are my bug-out cards. I rotate through them every so often, so they don't expire. I always keep enough on them that, if I ever have to leave, I have the means to do so without needing a lot of cash. I have two other good burner phones, too, stashed inside the false bottoms of two other boxes of tampons, and five cheap burner phones, flip phones, stashed in shoes in my closet. I've had this phone number the longest and really don't want to change it if I don't have to, although I can always route it through Google Voice to ring to one of the other burners, once I'm forced to change it.

And I'm always forced to change it sooner or later.

It used to be easier to get around without credit cards and bank accounts, which is why I stick to waitressing and bartending jobs. Vampires and shifters are willing to work with me on a cash basis. I file my taxes every year, under my real name, using a rented box at a UPS Store up in Mesa, which I check every few weeks.

Lucius gives me fake tax forms tied to one of his shell companies. The only reason I do that is so I don't trip any computer systems in case I have to bug out and leave the country. I don't want my passport to get flagged because I have a tax evasion warrant out on me or something stupid like that. Plus, it's getting harder and harder to use fake passports. I have my US one, and my UK one, since I hold dual citizenship. While I can use those, I would prefer to save them as an emergency last resort because it then pins an electronic paper trail to my ass.

Lucius offered to create me an entire new persona that would pass Homeland Security and Interpol computer systems, not just the fake ID, but I declined. Getting that kind of replacement identity, one that will withstand scrutiny with modern global immigration systems, is super-pricey, takes a long time, and is not the kind of indebtedness I want to owe to the "vampire king."

The shifters can get me one if I need it, but if Lucius hears I did that, it might offend his sensibilities. I might not call Lucius "sire," but I won't disrespect the man, either. Not when he's treated me damned well and has entrusted me with secrets. He's always insisted I can call him Lucius at work, but in front of customers and staff, I insist on calling him Mr. Frangelico or Mr. F, depending on the circumstances. Sometimes, I'll refer to him as "sir," with a lower-case *s*.

Right now, I'm okay. I still have connections in several areas of the country where I could ask for help, if I was in trouble. The rented box looks like a regular street address, not a PO Box, meaning I can receive deliveries there, if necessary.

I realized about ten years ago that whatever it is doggedly searching for me isn't...*normal*. By that I mean it's not human, or vamp, or shifter.

It's *other*worldly, as stupid as that sounds.

Shivering at the thought, I remove my wig and brush out my hair before I climb into the shower. My whole apartment is flooded with bright early morning light, including the bathroom. It filters through the small, opaque bathroom window as I take my shower and let the water sluice over me and wash away the residual vampiric and human funk from Club Toxic.

Dexter likely has a lot more money than Lucius. I guess if I end up needing to move and I'm really desperate, I could always ask Dexter to allow me to relocate to Atlantic City and work for him there.

As long as he's not the reason I'm running.

Except I've run from New York City, and that's pretty close. I thought of all the places in the world, that would be the safest city for me to get lost in. Yet one brutally cold December morning, I ended up running for my life. That was a year after I'd fled Toronto.

Almost like I'd summoned my nightmare into being by thinking too hard about my parents. I'd left work early that day because we were dead, and I didn't have a good excuse to hang around until dawn. Plus, I thought I was being silly. I'd lived in New York for a year at that point, with no sign of problems. So, I'd spent the twilight just before dawn walking along the waterfront as I headed toward my subway station, my breath frosting in the air. I'd paused to look at the Hudson River and think about Mom and Dad and Zuzu and was missing them horribly. The water reminded me of walking along the beach in Cardiff with them. It was close to Christmas, and I'd stopped and fished the ring out from under my shirt, staring at the labradorite stone and how it flashed in the streetlights.

I used to be fascinated by it when Dad was alive. As I remembered his accent, I slipped the ring on my ring finger, where even with it on the chain, it was still large on me.

Then I'd heard a loud chuffing behind me and saw...*it*.

My nightmare come to life, not twenty yards away, starting to fade into being.

The large, black form, the red eyes, looking around as if trying to home in on me.

Panicked, I yanked the ring off my finger and ran, jumped on a bus, and quickly made my way away from there.

It didn't follow.

I stayed on the bus until it was full light, then ended up taking the subway to my usual stop and ran home to my tiny efficiency apartment.

I packed and left. Back then, I didn't have a car, just two large rolling suitcases, a duffle bag, and a backpack. The 4Runner came after I ended up in Alexandria for a year.

I've crisscrossed the country since then, before settling here.

Is Dexter a sign I'm where I finally should be? The poor guy spent our entire talk hard as a rock. I could smell his arousal, which is a funny plot twist. Usually, the vamps can easily smell if humans are aroused or not. Kinda part of their whole schtick in Club Toxic, sweetening a human's blood with their BDSM play.

Unfortunately, I have no idea what it is that pursues me. I only know that if it wasn't for the witnesses saying it looked like a man who killed Mom, I would've assumed that the thing did.

She warned me we always had to run. Keep to ourselves. I'd never seen it myself until after she died.

I get the feeling whatever it is also killed Dad.

Like I could *seriously* go to the cops and tell them. Tell them *what*, exactly? That something—I don't know what—comes after me...sometimes? But I can't really describe it or tell them when or where?

Yeah, no.

It's easier to live my life on the fringes.

One day, my luck will run out. When it does...I guess I'll deal with it then.

I finish my shower while trying to not think about the sexy vampire whose light blue eyes I can't get out of my mind. Or about his hands and those long, elegant fingers, which would probably feel fandamntastic spanking me and doing...other things to me.

Sigh.

I throw on an oversized T-shirt, grab my sleep mask, and pull down my Murphy bed. The small efficiency apartment is perfect for me and came with the bed. All I had to do was buy a new mattress for it. As far as furniture, I have a comfy chair, a matching hassock, a nightstand, and an old, wooden coffee table. It's all I need, not that there's room for much else. If I want to lounge, I pull down the bed.

I put my phone in *Do Not Disturb* mode and plug it into the charger. Then I climb between my sheets, grab Cat and Dog, and pull down my sleep mask.

Eilidh Connover, you are most definitely not *going to think about hunky, fangy Dexter Van Sussex.*

Nope, not at all.

Much.

9

E *ilidh*

I SLEEP until one in the afternoon, and the first thought on my mind when I awaken is Dexter.

Mostly because I spent the morning dreaming about the sinful things he could probably do to my body.

Goddammit.

Why do vampires have to be so fricking *sexy*? Especially him? I've never seriously lusted after one of them before. Not that most of them aren't practically angelic in their beauty, because *damn*.

Yeah, fine, I'll admit the biggest reason I don't like working downstairs is because of all the hunky vampire dick being freely passed around, and knowing I'm not partaking of it since that will end my freedom in more than one way.

Although Dexter Van Sussex might prove dangerous to

my resolve in that area. Especially after the dreams I had of him taking charge of me.

I close my eyes and my fingers creep between my legs as I think about him. He's a handsome guy, and he's definitely into me.

Or, I should say, definitely wants to be *inside* me.

As I finger myself, it's too damn easy to get lost in a fantasy of Dexter tying me to a St. Andrew's cross and flogging me or laying cane stripes across my ass and thighs before sliding what I assume is a nice-sized cock inside me.

With my clit aching over that image, it's not long before I come to the thought of Dexter being the first vamp I ever let open my tap, so to speak.

I need to get laid.

It's been way too long since me and the cheetah shifter did our thing. Maybe I should take a stroll through the wolves' Fight Club and pick me up another friend for a night. Sure, some vamps hang out there, but there are shifters aplenty. I don't usually like strings-free sex because on the back end of things, I feel sort of empty and lonely.

But I've got an itch to scratch now that needs more than a few C-cell batteries' worth of buzzing.

Stupid vampires and their sex appeal, anyway.

I'm tempted to cancel dinner, but that would be shitty. I don't like to be shitty to people who don't deserve it. Yes, I consider the vampires "people."

And I do want to spend more time with Dexter.

There's also the bonus that I can put new tires on my SUV next week, thanks to Dexter. The old 4Runner is reliable, runs great, and isn't flashy. It doesn't draw attention to me. It's practical. I can get parts for it in nearly every area of the country. It can hold all my important shit when I move.

It's also nondescript and blends in, its own subtle camouflage.

Could I have afforded tires a long time ago? Yes, but I'm very tight with my budgeting. I'm actually building up my funds because I splurged to have the engine and transmission overhauled on the 4Runner last year, meaning it'll last me several more years into the future.

I don't like to spend money when I can squirrel it away in case I have to run. I spent way too many years lean and practically starving—financially speaking—to blow it. I remember the perpetual stress on Mom's face, how she had to literally fight to feed us sometimes.

When waitressing wasn't paying the bills, and she couldn't find a job teaching a flavor of martial arts that she was skilled in, she'd pick up quick cash in underground fight clubs. Not difficult for a woman who was an expert mixed martial arts fighter and a trained stuntwoman.

When I was little, I used to think it was badass that my mom could do that. The older I got, the more I realized it sucked that she couldn't be a normal mom. It was why I worked my ass off to get my GED so early, meaning I was one less stress on her plate, and I could usually pick up cash to help us out by waiting tables or washing dishes at the same places she worked.

I grab my cell phone on my way to the bathroom. As I'm sitting there, I take it out of *Do Not Disturb* mode and find I have a text from Garrett Green.

LUCIUS CALLED ME. *Can we talk? Call me when you wake up.*

. . .

MY STOMACH TIGHTENS. He knows I work nights and sleep mornings. Might as well do this now. When I call, he answers almost immediately.

"Hey, Connie." It's what I told him he and the other wolves can call me, just like Lucius' inner circle thinks my name's Connie Doe. It's what's on my fake ID.

It was easier than trying to have them remember the wig rule, and I wasn't going to tell them my full, real name. It's close enough to "Connover" that I can remember to respond when addressed like that.

"Garrett. What's up?"

He plunges right into the topic. "I talked to Lucius overnight. Said he's got someone he'd like me to talk to. Leech from Atlantic City who's looking to relocate to Tucson. Guy named Dexter Van Sussex."

My heart sinks. "I only met him last night." I don't lie to shifters or vamps. I either tell them the truth or keep my mouth shut. Besides, in person, they can both tell I'm lying, so it'd be stupid. Makes it easy to keep my story straight if I don't have to remember a lie. They know this about me, so it helps with them trusting me.

"What's your impression of him?"

I relax. Lucius didn't throw me to the wolves in a literal way. "He didn't get handsy with me. Wasn't improper with me. Seems like a decent guy, but I'm not risking my reputation vouching for him when I just met him."

"I told Lucius I'd meet with Van Sussex, if you came with."

Well, fuck. I close my eyes and rub my forehead. "How'd I end up in the middle of a casino deal? I'm just a bartender and errand girl."

He snorts, sounding every bit like the Alpha wolf he is.

"That's bullshit, and you and I both know it. You're way more than that. Amber even says so."

My eyes pop open. Sometimes, Amber *sees* things. Yes, like a psychic. Next to Selene, she's also my best friend.

One of my only friends. "What'd she say?"

"That you're a good person I can always trust. So, will you?"

"Garrett, I'm honored, seriously. But I cannot and will not vouch for him." I'm desperate not to go out after dark, either.

"Not asking you to vouch for him. I'll make the decision or not, and nothing will splash back on you. I just want to see how he acts with you."

Huh? "Why?"

"Because I know Lucius' men are terrified of crossing you since you're Lucius' and Selene's favorite feral human." He lets out a throaty, rumbly chuckle. "Can't call you a pet, since you aren't. Lucius said Van Sussex showed up already prepared to talk to me. He didn't assume he could just clear it with Lucius and move into the area. I like that show of respect, and as much as I hate Lucius, I like that he's looping me in. I'm not eager about more leeches moving into the area, but if Van Sussex wants to throw my pack some cash and make assurances, I'm willing to listen. I'd be a stupid businessman not to."

"Even though you don't like Lucius?"

"I don't have to like him. I do trust Selene. Amber told me this morning that the future of not only our pack, but of all packs, and the leeches, depends on whether or not Lucius and I can maintain this truce and work together. As much as I hate to admit it, that's way bigger than both of us."

"She had a vision about it?"

"Yeah."

Wow. "Did you tell Lucius that?"

"I did. He agrees it's better for business for all of us to work together."

Now that Garrett and Lucius are on the same page, if I refuse the Alpha's request, I'm placed in a very untenable position.

Fuck.

"Then there's the fact that I know you are immune to the leeches' thrall," he adds. "I want you there when I talk to him, just in case."

Double fuck. Guess that settles it. "When and where?"

"Tomorrow night at Fight Club. Ten?"

My heart sinks. Again, this isn't something negotiable. His tone tells me that. I can't ask him to go to Club Toxic without clearing that with Lucius first. Even if I did, I suspect Garrett's answer would be no.

Dexter's coming to him—that means it happens on Garrett's turf.

So to speak. Technically, Fight Club is in neutral territory. It's run by one of Garrett's pack but technically not on pack land, so they have plausible deniability should anything happen.

I know I won't be able to go there before dark and spend all night there. I don't want the wolves knowing more of my secrets than necessary. "Sure. Just to be clear, this is *you* asking me and not Lucius or Dexter asking you to ask me, right?"

"Right."

Well, damn. "All right. I guess we'll see you there."

"Excellent. If anything changes between now and then, please let me know. Oh, hold on. Amber wants to say hi." He passes the phone to her.

"Hey, girl!" Amber sounds way too chipper for this time of morning. Until I remember it's after lunch for everyone not on the same schedule I am.

"Hey. What's up?"

She laughs. "Have fun at dinner tonight."

I suppress a groan. "Did you see it?"

"Sure did. Look, let this play out. I don't know more than that. Trust him, and trust yourself. I don't see anything bad for you with this guy."

My heart races. "You...don't?"

"No. I mean, I can't tell yet if you two end up together, but he's not going to harm you. I get a sort of chivalrous knight vibe from him. Oh, and enjoy the tires."

I laugh. Being friends with someone who's psychically endowed can be trippy. "Thanks, I will, once I get them."

She giggles. "Suuure. *That*. Your instincts about him are right. Trust them. Here's Garrett."

Trying not to get my hopes up over her words, I push past them as Garrett speaks again. "Connie?"

"Yeah."

"So, I'll see you both at ten tomorrow night at Fight Club?"

He can't order me around because I'm not in his pack, but I know an Alpha order when I hear it. "Yeah. Please warn your guys, so they don't get pissed off at me for showing up with him, okay?" I don't want to ruin my rep with them.

"We allow leeches. You know that. Just not in the cage."

"Yeah, but I don't want them thinking I'm suddenly more on one side than the other."

"Ah, gotcha. I'll tell everyone I asked you to accompany him as a personal favor to me. No worries."

"Thanks."

"Do you want an escort here tomorrow and home?"

I ponder that and then opt for the obvious. "What's Amber say?"

Without hesitation, I hear him pull the phone from his face and ask. Then he's back. "She says you're supposed to ride with Dexter. That it's safe."

Terrific. "Then...I guess that's what I'll do. Thanks." Once the call ends, I finish what I was doing and get up to wash my hands.

Then I look in the mirror.

Hell.

My hair, which hangs past my shoulders, is now a solid black so deep and rich it practically shimmers with blue undertones in the bright sunlight streaming through my bathroom window. My hair hasn't turned this color in a while. My eyebrows match.

You'd think I'd be used to this by now, but no.

I'm sure it's also one of the reasons Mom homeschooled me, even if I didn't realize it at the time, and she always downplayed it.

The fact that she told me never to tell anyone it happened only reinforces that belief.

I run my fingers through it, holding locks up in front of my eyes.

Hell, I even give it a tug, just in case.

Ow. Fucker.

Okay, then. Definitely *not* imagining it.

If my hair stays this color, I won't have to wear a wig tomorrow night. For tonight, I'll be Blue again. What I really should do right now, though, is laundry. I throw on clothes, strip my bed, grab the towels out of the bathroom and everything else from the hamper, and carry the basket downstairs to the laundry room. A benefit of my oddball schedule is that during weekdays, I practically have the laundry room to myself.

I start two loads—towels and sheets in one, and clothes in the other because everything's dark anyway—and set a timer on my phone before I head upstairs.

Another benefit of having a shifter landlord and having plenty of them in residence in the building is it's probably the safest building anywhere around. No one would dare steal someone's clothes from the laundry room. Even the clueless humans who live here who don't know about shifters know better than to step a toe out of line.

It's nice.

It's safe.

Yeah, I know. Don't get my hopes up, right?

I spend a few minutes tidying my bedroom-slash-living room-slash-dining room, including running my Dustbuster after I sweep the floor to pick up anything I might have missed. Then I grab myself a yogurt for breakfast and walk over to the windows to stand there to eat.

I love the view. The previous tenant apparently used a free-standing room divider screen in front of the windows to shade the bed from morning sun on the weekends. Garrett told me I could hang curtains or shades if I wanted, but no.

I *want* the morning daylight. The price on the tiny apartment was right, too. No one from the club's ever been to my apartment, human or vampire. Not that vampires could come over because of the treaty, but I'm not stupid enough to invite any vampires in, not even Lucius and Selene.

Trust...but verify.

Or, in my case, trust but take no chances.

Trust comes hard for me. Damned hard.

I clean my bathroom and then head back to the laundry room to move my clothes into the dryer. In my apartment, while I'm waiting, I decide to do a little snooping of my own and open my laptop.

There's not a lot of info available about Dexter Van Sussex. He runs a casino in Atlantic City. There are some pictures of him, which confuses me until I look closer and realize he's using a body double.

Not unheard of for vamps to do that when they have to be in the public eye.

I mean, come on, no reflection. Vampires will show up on IR and FLIR and trigger motion sensors. Regular video and photos? Nope. Sometimes, you'll get an unrecognizable blur but never a clear picture. And the mirror thing? Totes true. That's why the only two mirrors in Club Toxic are in the nightclub bathrooms on the ground floor. Mostly because it'd be weird if they didn't have mirrors in there.

I head down to the exercise room and run a couple of miles on the treadmill. I hate to exercise, and I'm usually on my feet during a shift at work, but I don't want to lose my edge. I frequently spar and train with a bear shifter over at Fight Club when it's closed, but right now, he's out of town. I don't like to spar with humans because even with guys bigger than me, I tend to overwhelm them and freak them out.

It's a reasonably safe bet some of the shifters who know I can physically take care of myself are hoping I'll one day go rogue and stake every vamp in Club Toxic.

No, that won't happen. Live and let live.

Believe me, I *get* it. I understand *why* there are plenty of shifters who don't like vampires. There are a lot of vampires I don't like, either. But we have to build bridges somewhere.

Maybe Tucson will one day be seen as the start of a new era of cooperation.

When I finish my workout, I grab my clean laundry from the dryer, fold everything, and head upstairs to take a shower and start getting ready. It's not even four yet, but I always have something to do at the club. Might as well arrive early.

Before dark.

After my shower, I get dressed and decide to put on heavier makeup than I usually wear when I'm working, followed by my wig. One final check in the mirror, and "Blue" is ready. I grab a comfy pair of PJ pants and flip-flops and tuck them into a duffel bag, along with a light blanket and a pillow.

I gave serious thought to dressing up for Dexter. I have a pair of black Jimmy Choo pumps in my closet, shoes I hardly ever get to wear. I honestly don't even know why I still have them. They were given to me a few years ago as a gift, and I haven't been able to bring myself to sell them. Hell, they literally look brand new.

It's not like I date. I don't dress up for work because the last thing I want to do is draw too much attention from vampires. But sometimes, for my errands, it requires I wear a cocktail dress or other formal attire to fit in, and the shoes come in handy. I've also been known to occasionally play a girlfriend for a shifter who needs a date to a family wedding or other event and who wants to keep their family off their back. Safer than bringing a clueless human with them, and I can play the role.

Not tonight, though. I'm wearing jeans tonight—my Docs and a black Club Toxic tee with a neon blue logo. I thought about wearing a skirt, but I'd rather have the extra protection.

Of course, a layer of stone-washed denim won't stop a determined vampire any more than garlic and a silver crucifix, but it makes *me* feel better.

Grabbing my stuff, I lock my apartment door and head downstairs. I'm busy paying attention to my surroundings as I leave the building and cross the sunbaked parking lot, angling toward my Toyota. Which is why I pull up short when I'm a few feet away, the smell of fresh rubber wrinkling my nose. And...

What.

The.

Actual.

Fuuuck?

There are four new tires on my 4Runner.

I'm legit having trouble processing this, which is why it takes me a moment to snap back into awareness. I glance around, but there's no sign of a mechanic, or AAA dude, or...

Shitballs.

They're Pirellis, too, which are *hella* expensive.

Reaching out with my right foot, I toe the rear driver's tire with my Docs and confirm the new rubber isn't an illusion. I circle my SUV—yep, all four tires—five, counting the spare mounted on the back—are new.

That's when I realize it's also been detailed on the outside, including waxed as best it can be given the condition of the paint in places. And my headlamp housings, which were all hazy and yellowed, have been treated and polished and practically look like new.

There aren't any cars on either side of me, and weren't when I parked, so it would've been easy to accomplish without moving my 4Runner.

Dexter.

It *has* to be him.

I can't imagine Lucius would invade my privacy like this. For starters, if he was going to have it done, he'd tell me. He'd also have it done while I was at the club, or tell me to take my car in to a garage.

He wouldn't just…

I shiver, and I'm not sure if it's from the creep factor or the fact that hunky Dexter cared enough to do this for me.

Or is obsessed enough to do this for me.

Now Amber's comment about the tires makes sense.

Climbing into my 4Runner, I lock myself inside, crank it, and turn the AC on full blast before calling Amber's cell.

She answers on the first ring, giggling. "Well?"

"This was Dexter?"

"Uh, *duh*. He likes you."

"Let's not buy me flowers. Nooo, let's buy me a set of tires *literally* worth more than twice what my ride's worth." Hell, he probably spent more on the tires than I did on my engine and transmission overhaul. "Should I be creeped out?"

"No. Hey, you needed tires. Right?"

I grumble. "Yes."

"Say, 'Thank you, Dexter. That was very thoughtful of you. I appreciate it.' Go ahead and practice it now, so you know how to say it later."

Ugh! "Smart-ass."

She giggles again. "Better than a dumb-ass. Enjoy dinner!"

My attorney bestie hangs up on me.

Okay, then.

On my way to the club, I stop and buy another prepaid credit card with the extra cash I held back last night. As I'm waiting for the clerk to activate it, I wonder what it must be like to be Dexter Van Sussex. He's probably rich enough to never think about how much something costs. Probably plops down a black AmEx and pays it off every month.

Must be nice.

His little purchase on my behalf probably didn't even blip on his radar in terms of expense. Which was spendy, no doubt, considering how much I know those tires cost. Between the price of the tires themselves and then getting them so fast—and paying someone to do a record-fast tire change on my car, without my keys, in the parking lot of my apartment building...

Well, you can't snag a Groupon for that kind of service.

No matter what Amber says, I don't know if that makes me feel good or not. He can buy whatever he wants, whenever he wants.

I wonder if he thinks *I* can be bought?

Guess we'll find out.

The reserved staff parking area behind Club Toxic is empty when I pull into my spot. Another reason I like arriving first and leaving last is that I don't have to look at the other cars parked around mine. How pitiful mine looks in comparison. The runt of the litter next to Bugattis and Mercedes and Ferraris and Lambos or whatever exotic flavor of metal the staff vamps decide to roll up in on any given night. Several of them have multiple cars. Lucius usually has a driver and security for him and Selene, but every once in a while, he'll drive.

Why do I do this to myself? Why do I choose to live like this?

I could walk down to the basement tonight, stroll up to one of Lucius' hunky men, let them taste me, and be set for *life*. I've heard how they talk about my blood, not that they know it's mine. Every last one of them are hunks in suits, rich—*loaded*.

They'd be territorial and not share me.

For the rest of my life, however long it is, I could be taken care of, kept happy.

Have my ass spanked every night. Get all the vamp D I want, whenever I want it. Whatever it takes to keep me a subby little sweetblood. Be a pampered pet human.

That could all be...mine.

Dexter Van Sussex could be mine. Or, rather, I'd be his.

Because you can't *really* ever own a vampire's heart, can you?

Except for my secret occasional supernatural stalker. I won't put someone else in jeopardy. My left hand touches the ring on the chain through my shirt.

Pain blossoms in my right hand, and I realize I punched my steering wheel.

Flexing my fingers, I study my short, unpainted nails. I keep them trimmed. I don't bother getting manicures. I don't waste money on that. Besides, having long claws makes it tougher to do my fricking job.

Hurts more if I have to punch someone.

Not like I'm the prettiest waitress here, or the sexiest.

I'm basically the human housemother. Especially since I'm older than most of the humans here.

I stare out at the sunbaked streets around me. Waves of heat shimmer off the sidewalks and pavement. I never see the city at night, unless I'm staring at it through my apartment window. Most nights, I'm inside Club Toxic.

Sort of ironic. The mirror image of the vampires.

I head inside, disarm the alarm, and set about my usual routine, including getting my name tag.

Nothing's going to happen tonight beyond having dinner and curling up on the office couch to sleep once Dexter's left.

I'm not banging a hot vamp who bought me freaking expensive tires and had my ride detailed.

Nope.

Not doing it.

Definitely *not*.

Even if he does look like Ianto.

10

D *exter*

JOHN AND MARK came through for me. They used the private jet to fetch the tires from LA early this morning. When I awaken late that afternoon, I find confirmation, including photos, that Eilidh's SUV now has new top-of-the-line tires, and it's been detailed for her, including cleaning the headlamps so she can actually freaking see the road at night.

I hope she likes it.

Smiling, I get out of bed early. After using the bathroom, I crawl back into bed with my laptop and all the episodes of *Torchwood* purchased through Amazon Prime.

Yep. I'm going to start watching them.

This must be obsession, right? Especially since I would normally start working on e-mails and phone calls whenever I awaken this early.

I mean, that's what I've always done in the past. Made use of daylight hours when I'm conscious, which also helps keep my clueless human staff from getting suspicious about my unusual hours.

Not today.

Vacation day.

A *me* day ahead of a *me* night with Eilidh.

Lying in bed, I prop my laptop on my chest and start watching. I looked up pictures of the show's cast. If Eilidh thinks I resemble this Ianto guy, I can live with that. I'm flattered, even. It's been so damned long since I've seen my own face that I couldn't pick myself out of a police lineup if someone had a stake pressed against my chest at five seconds before sunrise. I've never been vain enough to have my portrait painted, much less patient enough to sit for one.

Plus, that usually requires daylight, and that is an uncomfortable conversation that could possibly raise someone's suspicions. Vampire mental mojo powers or not, I prefer not taking unnecessary chances.

It's nearly seven when my phone buzzes with another text. This time from Selene.

DONE. *Enjoy! :) I think you two will be great together.*

I CAN ONLY HOPE Selene's enthusiasm is a good portent of my future. She goes on to detail the arrangements. Augustus is bringing everything and will help me set up our private dinner in the conference room upstairs.

I'm to see Theophilus when I arrive tonight, and he will escort me upstairs.

I stare at Selene's messages for a long moment. She's

barely a couple of years old in vampire years. She's still easily able to remember what it felt like being a human.

I envy her that.

For the first time in as long as I can remember, I truly feel hopeful about something.

THANK *you so much for your help. You and Lucius both. I am indebted to you.*

SHE RESPONDS A MOMENT LATER.

JUST DON'T SCREW *this up! I'd love to see both of you happy.*

I SMILE and set my phone aside. *That makes two of us.*

EVENTUALLY, I force myself to put my computer away, and I call in John and Mark to see if there's anything I need to handle today. They've been in touch with the office and know when to kick ass for me, so I'm not forced to.

Because when I'm forced to, heads roll.

Eh, metaphorically speaking. Meaning people are fired. Jeez, what kind of monster do you think I am?

Wait, please don't answer that.

Lucius has also talked to Garrett Green, and I have a personal meeting with him tomorrow night, which Green is arranging through Eilidh. Or, Connie, as the shifters apparently know her, another assumed name I'm not to reveal at the club.

I struggle against the urge to leave my room as soon as it's safely dark outside. Now that I have a reason to want to live again, it's like Eilidh's soaked into every cell of my body and drawing me to her.

Or, maybe I'm a crazy, old fool. Obsessed.

Even if I could overpower her with my mind, I wouldn't. I want enthusiastic consent. Here's to hoping she wasn't creeped out by my gesture.

Although, yes, it was sooo tempting to buy her a car and have the dealership drop the keys off with her.

That would be overkill.

Maybe on date number three I can upgrade her ride for her.

Or...not.

We'll see how this one goes. I'm not guaranteed anything.

I drive to the club and park close to where I did the night before. It's almost a quarter 'til ten, and there's a line to get in. I head straight to the entrance, where one of Lucius' men admits me.

"I'm supposed to see Theophilus," I tell the bouncer.

He points, and I spot Theophilus near the lounge area, talking with a couple of humans. It takes every ounce of self-control I have not to blur over to him.

When he spots me, he wraps up his conversation with the humans and joins me. "Augustus just took everything upstairs." He leads me to the back hallway and punches in his code to the stairwell door. Upstairs, he lets us into the office, and immediately, I scent her.

And food.

I hear her and a male's throaty laugh. Territoriality rolls

through me, and it's all I can do not to race around my guide to find her.

Except that'd be bad form, and I'm trying to make a good impression.

He leads me to the conference room, where Eilidh and Augustus are unpacking the food. The aroma says chicken piccata, most likely. Vampires don't have to eat or drink anything but blood, but we can and do enjoy it.

"Hello, Blue," I say.

I love that a sweet, pink blush fills her cheeks. "Hey. Let me guess—"

"Selene and Lucius offered to help when I asked for information about arranging this. I hope that was all right?" Not going to start off trying to lie to her about it or take credit for something I didn't do.

She shrugs, but she looks pleased. "Good choice."

The other two vampires have paused and are looking to her for guidance. Eilidh takes a deep breath and smiles again before turning to them. "Thank you for the help, guys. We'll be all right."

"Lucius told us to hang out up here, if you want us to," Theophilus says.

She meets my gaze with a steady one of her own. "I appreciate it, but I don't think that'll be necessary. *Will* it?" she asks me, but I also know it's a statement.

I shake my head. "On my life, I swear it."

"We'll hold you to that," Augustus growls, but the two of them retreat.

Once we're alone, I help her finish unpacking and plating our meals. "They'll have someone stationed downstairs, won't they?" I ask.

She snorts. "Oooh, yeah. Probably in the stairwell. Lucius won't take a chance with me." She blows out a breath. "Thanks for the tires. And the detail job. That was endearingly stalky and unexpected, but thoughtful, and greatly appreciated."

I love her sense of humor and her fearlessness around me. "Your tires were a death trap. And so were those head-lights. And no," I quickly add, "I don't expect anything in return. I had a lovely time chatting with you, and you agreed to give me more of your time on your night off. It's the least I could do."

We're eating at one end of a large conference table. Real wood, not some cheap-ass thing. Lucius doesn't skimp. Once our food is arranged, I hold Eilidh's chair for her and help her scoot it in. There are crystal wine goblets, but she's drinking water.

I have a goblet of water and one of blood.

I pick up my water glass and raise it in a toast. "To new friends."

Her gaze narrows a little, but she clinks glasses with me. "To new friends." It's uncanny how her gaze holds mine as she sips. "Why do I get the feeling you're now obsessed with me?"

Several options flash through my mind, but I once again settle on the truth. "I suppose I am. But that's my problem, not yours."

"If I'm the obsessee, it sort of makes it my problem by default, doesn't it?"

"No. Because I'm not an idiot, and I have self-control."

She studies me. "I'm debating how to handle tomorrow night."

"What do you mean?"

"If I should let your men pick me up at home or meet you here and ride together. Or meet you there." She scowls, her gaze briefly unfocusing. "Not happy about traveling at night, but there's no other option."

I want to pick her up and drive her, but I didn't get to be my age by being impetuous. "Your decision. Even if you wish to change your mind at the last minute. Or, you could meet me at my hotel. You could arrive before dark, if you wish. If that helps?"

"I'll let you know." She cocks her head again. "You're not like other vampires, and I don't know why."

"Not many as old as I am."

She takes a bite of, yes, her chicken piccata, and happily sighs. "Selene has an excellent memory." She takes another bite. "For my birthday last year, she and Lucius gave me a gift card to this place. I don't eat out very often."

I want to memorize every line on her face, every whisper of her breath, every beat of her pulse. It's tempting to quiz her about not traveling at night, but I resist. "I appreciate you accompanying me tomorrow."

"Yeah, well, Garrett likes that you can't mojo me. He wants me there as backup. He doesn't stay Alpha by taking stupid risks."

"I don't understand. Backup?"

"I'm a secret weapon. You don't think I survived this long working at Club Toxic and not being blooded by being a pushover, did you?" She points at her eyes with two fingers, then to me and back again. "The whole 'can't be mojoed' thing."

"Lucius hinted that you are very...special. That's all he would tell me. That I needed to ask you directly."

"Are you asking?"

I pick up the glass of blood and sip to buy myself a moment. It's a blend, but she's in it.

Oh, I should mention my cock's been hard ever since I

sat down, and the taste of her rolling along my tongue only amplifies my condition.

"I understand trust is built over time, and that there are things you will not wish to tell me. I'm content to accept whatever you want to reveal to me, on your timeframe. I also know Lucius didn't get as old as he is by not being very careful and following his instincts. If he considers you part of his inner circle, that's a sign of his trust and his faith in you. I have nothing but time, in abundance. That means I'll wait."

"I'm not looking forward to tomorrow night. Not because of you, but because of the time of day."

I slowly nod. "I understand, and I appreciate it greatly."

She takes a bite of her green beans. They were prepared perfectly, with just the right amount of tenderness to them, and naturally sweet. "If I tell you something, anything, I expect you to hold my secrets the way I'd hold yours."

"Absolutely."

I can tell she's weighing a decision quite heavily, and I resist the urge to make her any promise I can about keeping her safe.

This has to be in her time, not mine.

"So...here's the thing. Tomorrow, when we're there, you need to drop whatever bullshit vampire machismo instincts you have and follow my lead. Do what I say. If you can't do that, tell me now."

"I won't let anyone hurt you, though."

"Yeah, see, that's not a concern. Not while we're there. Not a single shifter in that place will hurt me. It's *you* who needs to worry."

"Me?"

"Yeah. You stay with me, and you don't look them in the eyes and challenge them. Some of them might try to bait you. There might be other vampires there, too. Some of them Lucius' men, some not. You ignore them, too. If any of them make comments to me, you *ignore* them. You don't have a right to be territorial about me. You want me to help you with this introduction, then you do this *my* way."

I nod, as much as it grates on me. "Understood."

"See, I do errands for them. For Lucius and his men, too. I know things about some of the vampires in this area that not even their frequent booty calls know. I know where crypts are. I have alarm codes and access that some of their human employees don't have.

"But with the shifters, I also have access. I've helped out in emergencies as a babysitter. I've run errands between shifter groups when neither trusted the other. I've been a go-between when shifters needed to do business with vampires for whatever reason. Yes, I'm on Lucius' payroll for the club, but everyone knows I'm my own person and a free-lancer. I live in Garrett Green's building, for crying out loud. I'm friends with both his mate and with Lucius' mate.

"I can tell you've figured part of it out, between the taste of my blood and what you don't smell." She takes another bite of her chicken. "So, go ahead and ask it."

I do. "What are you?"

She shrugs. "I wish I could tell you. Lucius and Garrett can't tell me, either. Garrett and his pack helped shut down a secret program called Data-X. Government black ops labs. Trying to experiment on shifters, captive breeding, shit like that. Sanctioned torture is what it was. My mom's stepfather was in the military. Maybe she or my father were experimented on. I don't know. I never will know. I don't even think I have my father's real first name, and I don't know his true last name."

She sits back, as if realizing she just said more than she

meant to. "Or, I might be some sort of human hybrid with a shifter no one else has encountered. I could have a funky gene mutation and coincidentally crossed paths with the supernatural beings walking our world. I have no idea."

"What does that have to do with why you won't go out at night?"

She looks grim. "Because I wanted you to know how unusual my very existence is when I warn you that being with me at night might endanger your life."

11

E *ilidh*

DEXTER STUDIES ME. "Not from the shifters?"

"No." I wish I'd waited to have this discussion because now my appetite's fled, and that's a damned shame.

Still, I take another tiny bite of heavenly chicken while he waits for me to continue.

"I'm going to gloss over my past," I say. "Maybe if whatever this is between us develops, then I'll tell you all the deets." Except...he's a vampire. So...it can't develop. Right? "Mom and I were on the run for a lot of years after we left Cardiff. I didn't know what from, until after I'd lost her. I still don't know exactly what from. Or if it's the same reason."

I realize I'm reaching up with my left hand and touching the ring through my shirt. "There's also no pattern for when it happens. Maybe everything will be fine tomorrow night. That's also possible. In fact, odds tell me it's likely. I just want you to know what might happen, for the sake of transparency. You and Lucius and Garrett have placed a lot of trust in me, and I don't want you to think I held information back."

"I appreciate that and will take it under advisement."

I shift in my chair a little and sip my water. "Sometimes, at night, this...*thing* tries to show up. Only at night. Right now, it's been the longest stretch of time since I've seen it. Several years. Whenever I see it, that's when I bolt to a new location. It never comes in the daytime."

He waits me out while I take another bite of chicken. "It has never fully materialized, so I don't know what it'll do if it ever does. I don't stick around long enough to find out. It looks black, kind of like a dog, but huge. *Way* larger. Like, I'm talking grizzly bear-large. And it has red eyes. I don't think it's from this world. Because, as you proved today, it'd be stupid easy to track me down if it was." I shiver. "It's terrifying."

Looking thoughtful, he studies me. "*Gwyllgi.*"

"What?"

He picks up his water glass and sips. "There's a legend in Wales about a gigantic ghost dog, or wolf. Huge, black thing, with red eyes. They call it *gwyllgi,* but it's got other names, too. Sometimes known to stalk and attack travelers at night. Other cultures have similar creatures in their mythology, but I find it incomprehensibly coincidental that you and your mother lived in Cardiff, and you're seeing something straight from Welsh mythos."

My heart races, pounds so hard I can barely speak. "Are...are you *kidding* me?"

"I am not." His expression is serious, too. "I'd like to offer my help."

"Is there a way to get rid of it? To predict when or where

it'll show up? To protect myself from it? To know what it wants?"

"That I don't know. I'd have to research it. There's no pattern to when it appears?"

"Only that it happens at night." Now he's intently watching me, and I realize that while we're talking, I've fished the chain out from under my shirt and I'm playing with the ring. "Sorry. Nervous habit."

"What is that?"

"It was my dad's. It's all I have of his." I look at it. "I don't know what the symbols on it mean. Mom used to wear it on this chain, but the night she died, the ring was on her finger. I think someone tried to mug her for it and she fought them, but they still managed to kill her. Which..." I realize that's a story for another night. "It's a long story. But Mom was a badass, and I guess he caught her by surprise. Normally, she could've held her own."

He intently stares at it. "May I?"

I finally lift the chain over my head and pass it to him, being careful not to touch his hand as I set the ring in his palm and then lower the rest of the chain, releasing it.

He carefully examines it, studying the sides of it. "You don't know what the markings mean?"

"No. They're not any writing or runes I can discover. I showed it to Lucius, and he didn't know either."

A handsome eyebrow arches. "Then he's seen this?"

"Yeah. And he knows about my...what'd you call it?"

"*Gwyllgi.*" He's focused on the ring, turning it around, looking inside it for any inscriptions. "Labradorite is known as a stone of transformation, by some. Some think it's a shield. Others believe it can protect against negativity."

"So, you're a gemologist, too?"

He smirks. "I have my hobbies." His smile fades. "I've

had a lot of them over the years. Sometimes, hobbies were the only things that kept me sane." His focus is still on the ring, and he even breaks out his cell phone and takes several closeup pictures of it. "The writing isn't any language I understand, but there is something very familiar about it."

Hope explodes inside me. "Yeah?"

Then hope recedes equally fast when he holds the chain to set the ring back in my hand almost exactly as I put it in his. "I think so. It looks like something I've seen before, but it's not any kind of runic language I'm familiar with. It's definitely not Ogham or Futhark. I'd have to research it, though. Believe me, I know most of the old and modern languages from the UK, and more than a few from elsewhere in the world. It's highly unlikely I *wouldn't* know what it says, if it originated in that region. But there is...*something*."

I don't get the feeling he's just humoring me, either. From the way he's studying the pictures on his phone, I can tell this is something he wants to help me with.

"Oh." I pull the chain over my head and tuck the ring under my shirt. "Thanks, anyway." It shouldn't bother me so much that he doesn't know. No one else has known, either.

"I will look into it for you. It feels like it's something I should know but have forgotten."

I am touched he's willing to try. "I appreciate it." Nope, won't get my hopes up.

I mean, I'll try not to.

"Why not get it resized and wear it on your hand?"

A shiver washes through me, a memory of Mom answering that same question for me once, not long after Dad's death. "Can't ruin the magick," I softly reply.

"I'm sorry?"

I blink, pulling myself back to the present. "Mom never would. That's what she said, but I think she meant that metaphorically. She always wore it on the chain. Labradorite shouldn't be immersed in water for long. I think she was worried about damaging or losing it. Having it on a chain was safer."

"Ah."

We continue eating. "I have to say, other than Lucius and Selene, you aren't like any other vampire I've ever met."

"Thank...you?" He smiles, and it makes my nipples tighten and my lady bits flutter. "I think?"

"Yeah, that is a compliment." I study him and try not to focus on how gorgeous not-Ianto is. "What's your endgame, here?"

"Regarding...?"

"Me."

He dabs at his handsome lips with the linen napkin and takes another sip of water. "I have no expectations except, hopefully, friendship." He's looking me in the eyes as he says it.

"That's it?" That's sweet, but it's almost a...let-down.

His right eyebrow slowly arches. "That's not to say I don't have...hopes."

"Hopes?"

He shrugs, but his gaze burns into mine. "I don't wish to overwhelm you."

My breath catches at the intensity in his voice. "Try me," I say. "I want to hear it. Give me your worst."

He leans forward and his voice drops to a sexier, deeper rumble that soaks my panties. "Not my worst, but you'd be wearing my cuffs and collar and tied to my spanking bench. I'd spend hours teasing you with my hands and my mouth. I'd flog you, introduce you to my canes, spank that gorgeous ass of yours until you're begging to come."

Fuuuuck me. I fight the urge to squirm in my chair, but he's not done.

"Then I'd bury my cock inside you and fuck you until you screamed my name." He smiles. "After that, we could really have some fun."

Part of me wants to beg him to do that right now because my clit's throbbing.

The other part of me is a buzzkill realist. It's a good thing he can't force me, because it wouldn't take much for me to drop my panties for him, anyway. "Guess you don't have trouble getting people to agree with that, since you're a vamp."

His smile fades. "I never use my thrall to force people to sleep with me. I'm not a predator. Not a sexual one, anyway."

"Honestly?" He certainly sounds genuine.

"Honestly. I have no desire to force anyone like that. I certainly wouldn't want to attempt to force you, even if you weren't immune to my powers."

"Sounds like there's a story behind that decision."

He slowly nods. "There is." His quiet tone hints at centuries or more of deep pain.

"If you feel like talking about it, I promise to keep your secrets. And no, Lucius doesn't have the place bugged. One of the reasons I have the trust of so many is that they know I will keep their secrets."

Something deep inside me almost painfully twists when the dark cloud fills his expression. He continues eating. "Lucius and my sire shared the same sire." He takes another bite, chewing thoughtfully, his gaze unfocused for a moment. "I don't know how much of his history Lucius has shared with you, so I will avoid telling as much of that as possible."

I nod, and he continues. "My sire was older than Lucius. Apparently, he wanted to create a nest of his own, a powerful army. But turning humans and siring vampires is not a simple process, contrary to Hollywood stories. Especially back then, when finding a safe daytime hiding place was far more difficult. I wasn't the first he sired, and I wasn't the last, unfortunately for him. Had he stopped with me, he might still be...alive."

When his scent changes slightly, I realize the almost perpetual arousal I smelled on him since his arrival has fled. This is a painful subject for him to discuss.

I regret asking him, but also, kinda not.

Because it's exceedingly rare for a vampire to let down their guard like this around anyone.

Especially a human.

Doubly especially a human who can't be kept under their firm control.

"I honestly can't tell you how old I was. Two thousand years ago, we weren't keeping tabs on things like that, where I was from. I was raised in the region that is close to what's now known as Dumfries, Scotland. Wasn't called that back then, obviously. I was a little old for my time, so the best I can remember, I was probably thirty-two, thirty-three, maybe. Certainly, no older than forty. We were farmers and shepherds and fished.

"Now, keep in mind the times. I'd already been a widow once. A girl my father picked for me to wed, the daughter of a cousin of his. I didn't really love her. I met her maybe once before we were married. But our families insisted on the union. She wasn't much happier with me, but we didn't hate each other, and we even came to tolerate and like each other. We made a good team, even if we weren't exactly setting the world on fire with romance.

"Unfortunately, she died in childbirth with our fifth child. A girl, after four boys." When his eyes unfocus, I realize he's not staring at me but at sad memories in the past. "I had hoped for a little girl. Only two of our sons made it past infancy, Eochaidh and Sealbhach."

I feel horrible for him. "Yikes. I'm sorry."

"It happened far too often then. Fortunately, I wasn't pressed into service as a groom after that. I had help raising my children from others in our community. But, back to my turning. I had traveled with a cousin to a neighboring village to trade, and we were spending a few nights there. I'd left the children behind. We'd had a larger meal than we were used to, and excellent ale, and it was nice weather out. It was dark, and I wandered a little from where we were staying with the intention to find a soft place to lie down and pleasure myself. That's when a man appeared out of the darkness."

"Uh-oh."

"Exactly." He takes another bite of chicken. "There was something bewitching about him. He was gorgeous, strange, and while he knew a little of my language, he also spoke languages I had never heard before."

"Uh-oh, again."

"Yes. He fed from me that night and exchanged blood with me, although I didn't know this until later."

"Later?"

"Yes. He told me later, after I survived the turning. He returned the following two nights. On the third night, he killed me after exchanging blood with me."

"Oh, shit."

"Yes. Fortunately, he spirited me away from there before he did, or I might have been buried or cremated. He had a hiding place in an old underground burial cairn. He left behind my tunic, ripped and covered in blood, to make it look like an attack by a wild animal."

Dread fills his tone. "Feeding from me wasn't the only thing he did to me those three nights, or in the weeks and months after he successfully turned and sired me." His light blue gaze looks more grey now, darker, as he meets my gaze. "He *used* me. Sexually."

My stomach rolls. "I'm so sorry."

"It seems he had a pattern. He would leave the nest safely sequestered, go out in search of a new prospect, and then turn them. After they had survived the initial turning and could be safely moved, he'd rejoin the nest with the newest member.

"For every one he turned, he probably killed at least thirty more. Once his sired were strong enough to resist him, he would then attempt to sire another. So that usually took a while to happen—a rebellion—because being sired is a powerful experience. There's a codependency, physically, emotionally, and psychically. It was a time of fear and survival instincts.

"It might have been a supernatural existence, but I still had a very strong survival instinct. He deliberately withheld many facts for as long as possible, to keep us dependent as long as possible. For example, he never revealed to us how to turn someone. Back then, there was much we didn't know about what we were, unless you met an older vampire who told you. This was also before Christianity existed in our region. Even the Romans were newcomers. So much, obviously, was unknown.

"For example, now we know it's a virus, even if we don't understand it and cannot yet treat it. Back then, it was evil spirits and dark magick and..." He sighs. "So even though we all hated our sire, it was unthinkable to us to consider destroying him. We didn't know what information he might take with him if we did, information we needed for our very survival. We didn't know for sure if destroying him might not kill us, too. Plus, there was a certain safety in numbers. Until, one day, he picked someone who was far stronger than he realized. Once they were through the initial turning process, they destroyed him and then awaited the sunrise."

He sadly smiles and picks up the goblet of blood. "And that," he quietly says, "is why, to this day, I do not violate consent." He sips, staring me in the eyes. "Because I know what it feels like to have agency ripped away and to feel utterly violated and helpless."

12

D *exter*

WHY DID I reveal my most intimate pain to her, pain that's chased and haunted me throughout the millennia?

Pain I've only shared with one other in my life?

Maybe because, as I stare into her violet eyes, eyes surely not wholly of this world, I realize I am not merely obsessed with her—I feel about her something I haven't felt since losing Robert. That is a sensation I desperately don't want to lose.

And I am so very, very alone.

I remember Robert, loving him, how in many ways his love allowed me to sleep in peace for the first time since my hellish rebirth. This thing I feel inside me now, for Eilidh, this warmth brightly blooming within my soul, is something I haven't felt since consigning my love to his tomb from which he would never arise.

Not even Lucius knows all of that about me, even though he knows what an evil bastard my sire was and no doubt suspects what I might have endured at his hands.

Something about Eilidh makes me want to open up to her. It's said that shifters know who their true mates are.

Perhaps this could be the case for me, as well. Could I be so lucky a second time in my un-life?

Maybe if I can keep from scaring her off, I'll be able to find out.

"But you've killed people?" she asks.

"I have."

"Recently?"

Of course, she wishes to know this. Despite my reluctance to speak about it, she deserves answers. "Not to sound pedantic, but define recently. To me, it feels like World War II was only a few years ago."

"I mean, you don't kill for sport? For fun?"

"No. I never have done that. I've killed in battle and in self-defense. I've released people from suffering, and I've been an executioner for those deserving death. Not once have I ever killed for sport. Although, I would be lying if I said I never took pleasure in it."

"Like when?"

I really didn't mean for our first deeply intimate conversation to take such a dark turn, but I suppose it is inevitable if I wish to earn her trust. "Murderers. Rapists. Child abusers."

She doesn't look horrified by that admission, so I suppose it's a good thing. "How'd you know they were guilty?"

"Well, you are literally the first human I haven't been able to charm, so..." I shrug. "I would simply ask them to tell me the truth. If they were innocent, I did my best to help bring the truth to light and the guilty to justice. Countless times, I've hunted down the truly guilty and forced them to publicly admit their sins to exonerate the innocent and then face their own punishment."

I chuckle. "Once, I even rescued a woman who was falsely accused of murder through witchcraft. I put her younger sister in the cell in her place. She'd poisoned her brother-in-law because she was jealous of her older sister's true love. I deposited the innocent with the local priest, told him I was an angel, and the facts of the story—which I'd already gotten from the true murderess, obviously, and then sat back to watch."

"She was exonerated?"

"Yes. They hung the guilty woman the next day, just after sunset, as the 'angel' ordered. No way was I missing *that* one. Before they hung her, she actually confessed to several murders that others had already been brought to justice for. She wanted to 'cleanse her soul.'" I take another sip of blood. "In that case, as you can imagine, I did thoroughly relish that justice was truly served."

"Oh. That's...I probably would have done the same thing." She takes another bite of her dinner. "Did you ever torture anyone? Like, I mean, the bad kind of torture. *Not* BDSM."

"Only someone deserving. And perhaps a handful of times. I don't have a stomach for that kind of sadism, ironically enough. It's something my sire used to berate me for, that I didn't have bloodlust within me beyond sating my basic hunger. Brutality for brutality's sake. Merely to sweeten the blood. If it wasn't enjoyable to the person I was feeding from, I certainly couldn't enjoy partaking of it when I fed from them. Unless, of course, they were cruel, and I was their retribution."

"Doesn't exactly sound like a bad thing."

"I'd like to think it's not." I smile and touch a finger to my lips. "*Shh.* Don't tell anyone I'm a big softy."

She giggles. The sound makes me happily sigh. As I take another drink of blood, I realize I have now become a willing pet vampire to a very unusual human.

I hope she's ready to learn what it's like to be the focus of loving obsession.

ONCE WE FINISH EATING around eleven, I help her clean up the dishes and carry everything downstairs to the small kitchen they have on-site. They only serve things like appetizers, bar snacks—nothing complicated.

Augustus had been hovering around the back hallway near the door to the stairs. She whispers in his ear and then flashes me another smile.

The club is busy. Now that we're down here and I'm paying attention, I realize *how* busy it is. I'm about to suggest we return to the office where it's quieter, private, and we don't have to raise our voices to have what I hope will be an intimate conversation, when she darts away and onto the crowded dance floor.

Apparently, her actions take Augustus by surprise because he blurs after her. As if by magick, the crowd parts, and there's my blue-haired goddess with a male vampire face down on the dance floor, his right arm wrenched what looks painfully high, her knee planted in the small of his back, and...

Is that a pencil?

It's in her other fist and looks like she's about to jab him through the ribs with it and—

Oh, shit! I hurry over.

"Look, dirtbag," she growls in his ear. "You were told last week that was your second strike. I come in here and see you trying it *again*? You're *done*, Tonio."

The vampire must be really young because he's literally crying. "I'm sorry, Blue! I just wanted to—"

Lucius blurs out of nowhere, looking furious and dressed in his shirtsleeves, which I know is rare. "What happened? What's going on?"

"Oh, you're really in trouble now," she tells the young vampire. "You pissed off the big guy."

Tonio *literally* squeals in fear. "I'm sorry, Blue! I'm sorry!"

Theophilus, Augustus, and another of Lucius' men grab the guy's arms, and once Eilidh is safely back on her feet again, they roughly jerk the vampire upright.

"Take him upstairs," Lucius coldly says. "*Now*."

The vampire's struggling, but Eilidh jogs ahead, opening the bottom door for them and bolting up the stairs to get the next one. I bring up the rear. As I'm pulling the bottom door shut behind me, Lucius turns and smiles.

"And how was dinner?"

"Excellent and amazing. I wasn't expecting a floor show with it."

His smile widens. "You haven't seen anything yet, dear nephew. But you are about to."

They drag the vampire into a small, bare office just down from the conference room we ate in. Lucius unbuttons his cuffs and starts slowly rolling up his sleeves.

Eilidh's wearing a dark glare and stands with her arms crossed over her chest, the pencil still in her fist. "We told you that you're not allowed down in the basement for a month because of your bullshit, Tonio," she scolds. "Then I catch you trying to mojo one of our household humans out the fucking *door*? You're *done*."

"Yeeesss," Lucius drawls. "That *is* rather bad form." The young vampire yelps as Lucius grabs him by the jaw. "You interrupted Blue's date night, young man. It is her night off, and yet still she must deal with the likes of you? Not to mention, I had to leave my own queen's side, just as things were getting interesting. Do you have *any* idea the levels of utter *hell* I wish to unleash upon you in this moment?"

"I'm sorry, Sire! I didn't mean to—OOOWWWWW!" He's screaming because Lucius digs his fingers in around the guy's lower jaw, piercing his cheeks with his nails on either side and squeezing with an audible *crack* of popping bone and teeth.

I mean, Tonio is a vampire. He will heal.

Unless Lucius rips his lower jaw right off him. He'll still heal, but that won't grow back.

Lucius, however, must be feeling generous. He releases the man's jaw and wipes the blood off his hand onto the guy's shirt.

"Despite my better instincts, I felt pity for you and I allowed you to settle in Tucson because you swore allegiance to me. That means abiding by *my* rules. If you think I will let infractions slide simply because you shed some tears, you are sadly mistaken. Blue, my dear, what do we do to people who refuse to honor their commitments to me?"

Me and Lucius' three men all flinch when her hand snaps out, almost a blur, and she plunges the pencil into Tonio's right chest, making him scream as she snaps it off about an inch from the eraser. "We don't fricking like it, Mr. Frangelico. We attempt reasonable behavior modification first. We also take it *personally* when someone disrespects you by not fulfilling their basic obligations to you."

"Yes, that's exactly right, my dear." He leans in toward the sobbing vampire, who's likely upright only because of the men holding his arms. "Tonio, there are no other chances. You may remain in Tucson, but if you ever set foot inside this club again, it is your death sentence. If you feed from humans, you'd better master self-control quickly. If I hear of any humans coming to harm anywhere close to your proximity, it is a death sentence."

He points to Blue. "Remember, she is human. If you don't wish for the last sight you ever see to be her face as she gleefully drags you out of your crypt and into the sunlight, you'd do well to heed me more carefully this time."

Lucius steps back. "Take him out the back way, bind and blindfold him, drop him somewhere inconvenient, and take his keys from him. Make him work to return to safety and perhaps he'll appreciate it more once he achieves it. *If* he achieves it."

The men hustle him out while Eilidh follows, but she turns and heads deeper into the office suite. I hear a sink running seconds later.

Lucius examines his hands. "Good thing he didn't get his blood all over this shirt," he muses. "It's brand-new. Selene would eviscerate him." He smiles, his voice dropping to a whisper. "So, how are you liking our sweet Blue?"

I'm too fucking turned on to lie. "I think I'm in love with her," I breathe so only Lucius can hear me.

ONCE LUCIUS WASHES HIS HANDS, he leaves us alone in the office suite. Eilidh returns from the bathroom and looks a little abashed.

"Sorry," she mumbles.

"Why are you apologizing? That was...I've *never* seen anything like that. That was *incredible*."

Her tight, nervous smile makes me want to lean in and kiss her, but I resist. "Like I said, Mom was a badass." She looks up at me through her lashes, the closest expression to vulnerability I think I've seen her show yet. "I didn't...freak you out?"

I open my arms to her, offering a hug and pleasantly surprised when she steps in and wraps her arms around me. I'm careful not to grind on her—you have no idea how difficult that restraint is—and gently close my embrace, letting her dictate how long.

Then she presses herself against me, her warmth along the length of my body, and I know she has to be feeling how aroused I am.

We stand there for a long moment, with me deeply inhaling her scent. She feels perfect pressed against me. Then she tips her head back, her gaze searching my face.

"No, I'm not freaked out." I smile. "I'm turned on. As if you couldn't tell."

Her hesitant smile in return fills with confidence, but she doesn't move to step away, so I hold still, drinking in her sweet warmth. When was the last time I really hugged someone?

I can't even remember. "Do you have to intervene often?"

"Not like that. Not with vampires. Humans, yeah. When I'm handy, the guys will frequently let me throw a scare into the human instead of mojoing them, just to prove a point, and because it amuses them."

She shrugs, like it's no big deal that she *literally* took down a vampire, by herself. "Usually, the guys are on it when it comes to the vamps, but I just happened to see him and realized exactly what he was up to. Guy's fucking dangerous. He's not careful. He's only been a vampire for a couple of years. Really poor impulse control."

Fuck, I could stand here all night doing nothing but holding her like this, and it'd still rank up there in one of my top memories. "What happened to his sire? Nestmates?"

"Dead. Territory war this guy wasn't a part of. Lucius felt sorry for him and let him pledge his loyalty." She stares at her hands. "Bet he thinks twice before doing that again. If he even makes it back from the desert."

"The pencil thing was brilliant."

"Mini-stake. Has to be a real wooden pencil, though." She grins. "First vampire I worked for taught me that. Guy owned a bar in Toronto. Told me to always keep at least one tucked behind my ear, or in my hair, a few in my apron, back pocket. No one notices them until it's snapped off inside their chest. Right side to send a message, left to stake." With her right index finger, she barely touches my chest. "Right there, or through the side, or back. Depending on the circumstance and what they're wearing. In a pinch, through the neck to distract them, then a second to the left chest."

"A *vampire* taught you that trick? Seriously?"

She shrugs, like it's no big deal. "He was cool. He liked that I couldn't be controlled. Put me in charge of afternoon and early evening shifts, so he could stay open longer."

"Wow." She's a treasure of amazing experiences.

"Soooo." She sucks air through her teeth as she plays with the buttons on my shirt. "How was *that* for a first date?"

Laughing feels *so* damned good. The things this woman does to me. "I think we're still on it. I mean, I hope we are. And it's been brilliant."

"I wouldn't mind talking some more. If you'd like to. Or, I'm open to suggestions."

Of course, I won't ask her to go downstairs to the

dungeon, even though I really want to. I could tell from the way her scent changed earlier that my honesty about some of what I wanted to do to her aroused her. Notes of honey and apricot sprang up in her scent, strongly present in a way they usually aren't.

I wonder if that's the same luscious scent I would smell if I have my face buried between her gorgeous thighs while I lap up every drop of her juices.

It's a question I can't wait to answer for myself. Which is why I want her consent—so I know she's really into it because she *wants* to be, not because I've forced her to.

This is the kind of hunt I truly enjoy—an honest pursuit, winning someone over, earning their trust. Any lazy asshole can compel someone to spread their legs.

I *want* to work for it. "Well, if we're being completely honest, then I'm curious to know what it is *you'd* like to do right now."

I love her adorable surprise at my answer. "Really?"

I nod. "Yes. Total freebie."

"*Anything* I want?"

"Anything you want."

"Okay." She looks me in the eyes. "Let's go cuddle," she quietly says. "If I haven't totally freaked you out and scared you off. I'll set up my phone so we can watch a movie and cuddle. I have a couch by my desk."

"You do?"

I allow her to step out of my embrace and she leads me back toward the main office entrance and around a divider. I realize this is her desk.

Her scent subtly floats in the air, notes of honey and apricot back again. Combined with the way her pulse races, I force myself not to grin. My balls might be unhappy with this choice, but *she's* happy.

That's what's important. And, yes, she has a couch just behind her desk and against the wall.

I walk over and sit at the far end. "What movie would you like to watch?"

"Seriously?"

"Seriously. It's what you asked for." And while she may not realize it, this will be the toughest test of my self-control in my very long life.

"But..." She looks like she can't believe I actually agreed to it. "No negotiation?"

"To watch a movie? I mean, all right." I think about it. "I'm not really a Hallmark kind of guy. While I don't mind foreign films, you might find it tedious to read the subtitles on a phone screen. I don't enjoy gory horror movies, but I like old classic Hollywood monster movies."

She bursts out laughing, and my cock surges, throbbing. I barely restrain myself from reaching down and adjusting myself. I love the sound of her laugh, and if I won't get laid tonight, at least I will have *this* memory—of her laughter and her smile—to sustain me when I return to my hotel later and jerk off.

"How about *Monty Python and the Holy Grail*?"

My heart *truly* feels light for the first time since losing Robert. "Perfect."

After digging out her phone, she sets it up in the charging cradle, so we can watch it. Then she settles next to me on the couch, and when I raise my arm so she can snuggle against me, she surprises me by curling up on her side with her head in my lap.

Okay, I'm not only hard, I'm hard in a way I didn't think was possible to achieve. Painfully so.

There will be a very long masturbation session in my immediate future, or I'll never get to sleep, dawn or not.

As the opening credits roll, she wiggles around a little, getting comfortable, and pulls my arm around her so she can hold my hand. Her flesh feels warm against me, and while I wish we were naked, this is an almost perfect moment. It's the sweetest torture imaginable, and I don't ever wish to escape it.

Then she looks up. "Thank you."

She sounds relieved and lost...and like she's feeling as terrified as I am. "No, thank *you*."

13

E *ilidh*

I CAN IMAGINE TRYING to tell someone this story, being asked about it.

You work at a nightclub with a secret BDSM club in the basement, surrounded by suit-clad hunks, and had dinner with yet another hunk who seems to be into you. That's really neat, huh? So, what'd you do tonight?

Well, me and a very old, very rich, and *very* freaking handsome vampire cuddled on my office couch and watched *Monty Python and the Holy Grail* on my phone. *That's* what we did.

And then we watched the first three episodes of *Cowboy Bebop.*

Yeah, I'm not even sure *I* believe it.

We cuddled, and we watched my phone, and not once did Dexter try to pressure me for more despite the scent of his arousal returning stronger than ever and me occasionally brushing up against what feels like a freaking telephone pole in his perfectly tailored slacks.

Okay, so yeah, I was a little mean and deliberately shifted positions a few times to gauge his interest.

Apparently, he's *very* interested.

How much self-control he has was evident by how he didn't simply grab me and kiss me.

Although, by the time we knew he'd have to leave, I was *really* hoping he'd lean in and kiss me as I laid in his lap.

I get the impression his self-control is boss-level good, and it wasn't abject terror from watching me snap a pencil off in that vamp's chest, either.

He drove himself, and he has to leave before me. The nightclub is closed, even though I know from the faint sound of music in the basement that there are still some vamps down there.

I walk Dexter down to the door at the bottom of the stairs, where I hesitate. "About tomorrow night. I mean, tonight. I mean—"

"I know." He smiles. "Tomorrow night, relatively speaking. The meeting."

"Yeah." I take a deep breath. "If you want to send your guy to pick me up at my place before dark and take me back to your hotel, then you and I can ride together to the meeting. We'll figure it out from there, what to do...after. Maybe your guy can take me back to my place, once you go to bed."

I like that he doesn't make a joke about taking me himself and me inviting him in. He knows damned well he can't enter if I don't invite him.

"I like that plan very much, thank you. And if you wish to change it, I'm fine with that, too. I'd like to buy you dinner tomorrow, if you'd be comfortable with that. My hotel has an excellent restaurant. Or we can ask for room service."

"Okay. Cool. We'll decide that tomorrow night. Have him pick me up by five, please. That'll give us plenty of time."

"I will."

We quickly exchange cell phone numbers. Then, nervous, I step close to him and drape my arms around his neck again.

Just a test, you know.

Um...research.

Yeah, that's it.

Fuck, he's tall. Six-three is taller than five-five, and he's a *very* hunky six-three.

With my pulse racing, I rise up on my toes and kiss him as his arms gently close around me, the way he hugged me earlier. I know he could literally crush me if he wanted to, but his hands barely touch me as my lips brush his.

I've never kissed a vampire before. His lips feel soft and cool, and there's that thick, sweet aroma surrounding him.

Yeah, I'll be firing up my B.O.B. when I get home. My panties are probably soaked, and I'm certain he can smell that. Yet he was a man of his word and didn't try to make me do more.

He doesn't move after that kiss, waiting on me.

What the hell? Why not?

I kiss him again.

This one I deepen as I press myself against his body as we kiss. There's a dusting of scruff on his cheeks and chin, and I like the way it gently rasps against my flesh. He also has a very firm, fit, strong body.

Yep, he's *hard*.

Haaarrrrd.

I wiggle my hips against him and feel the rush of air from him as he softly gasps.

I only feel a little bad about that.

His embrace tightens around me, but still gentle, and I reeeally like that he seems to be a man of his word about not rushing me. That's sexy as hell, because I hope it means I can drop my guard around him at some point.

That's when something hits me. "Where are your fangs?" I ask, staring into those blue eyes.

He smiles, drawing back his upper lip to show me his teeth.

Normal-looking teeth. No...fangs. "Only when I feed or bite. Like shifters, we can control them."

Before I even realize what I'm doing, I reach up and touch his left canine. Feels like a normal tooth, maybe a little pointier.

Honestly? I've never asked about that before. I've also never been this close to a vampire for this long. Not like...*this*. "I guess I didn't know that. Learned my new thing for the day, thanks."

He reaches up and plays with my hair then brushes the backs of his fingers along my jaw. I shiver, but it's not fear—it's the good kind of panty-dampening shiver.

"That's fair, since you've taught me a lot in a short few hours."

I don't want to let him go, even though I know I need to. "Sorry about the raging case of blue balls I've given you."

#notsorry

He smiles and lightly flicks my hair again, playfully. "Apropos, *Blue*." He sighs. "I'll return to my hotel and think about you while I'm taking care of that." Heat darkens his eyes again. "Seems like I'm not the only one tonight had an effect on." His gaze flicks down just long enough I know I was right—he can smell me. "I hope you have enough batteries."

I snort. He's got a great sense of humor and a gorgeous smile.

Fuck me, why's he got to be immortal?

Why's he got to be a *vampire*?

I limit myself to one last kiss. "Uncle Lucius and Auntie Selene are very protective of me. Did I mention that?"

"Memo received loud and clear." This smile, however, is definitely reaching his eyes. God, I love making him smile like that. Like it's been too damned long since he's felt like smiling in this way.

I know the feeling.

I mean, sort of. Relatively speaking. "Drive safe," I say. "Have your guy text me when he's at my place, and I'll come down."

"I'd rather he come up and escort you to the car."

"Yeah, well, a strange human smelling like a strange vamp, wandering around alone in a building full of shifters..."

"Ah, got it."

"Exactly. He's human, so him being there isn't a territory violation, but I don't want to push it." In fact, while we could have this meeting at my apartment, which would solve my traveling at night problem, Garrett likely doesn't want the vampire in his building, where he lives, where his own mate and packmates and clueless humans live.

Doesn't want the vampire having permission to enter his "home."

I can totally respect and understand that.

He also doesn't want to have to justify to his pack why he allowed a vamp to wander into shifter territory without retribution.

And having the meet in neutral territory, at Fight Club, with lots of pack members around, is a safety factor, too.

After a long, tight hug, I finally release him so he can depart. Once it's dawn, I race home, shower, and climb into bed with my rabbit vibrator. Of course, Dexter is the star of my fantasies. As I slide the toy inside me, I close my eyes and pretend it's his cock. Although, from what I felt tonight, I'm reasonably certain his cock is larger than this toy.

Yowza.

Rolling onto my stomach, I hike my hips up and stroke the toy inside me, imagining it's him fucking me, his lips kissing the back of my shoulder, his voice whispering in my ear as he thrusts. I think about what his body would feel like rubbing against my freshly spanked ass, how it would feel surrendering to him.

Because I *wanted* to, not because he compelled me.

Dexter's the first man—immortal or not—who I've seriously considered taking that leap of faith with.

I even—fates help me—imagine what it'd feel like if he bit me as I come, and it's that thought that trips me over the edge and has me moaning into my pillow.

After I flip over and pull the toy out and turn it off, I lie there for a moment, thinking about Dexter. Why him, and why now? Why does he do things to me no one else has?

No offense to Chad the cheetah shifter, but even his decent skills drop to nothing when I think about Dexter, and all I've done is kiss the vamp!

Once I clean up the toy—and me—and return to bed, I settle in. Still, it takes me way longer to fall asleep than I thought it would. I can't stop thinking about Dexter and the things he admitted to me tonight.

I've never had a vampire open up to me like that before.

Hell, while I am a keeper of secrets, I've never had

anyone open up to me like that before, in such a personal way, and about something so...intimate and traumatic.

Mostly because I've never *had* anyone.

Yes, I'm nearly certain he's not bullshitting me. It was almost like he felt relieved to be able to be honest with me.

Then, there was the cuddling.

Holy *shit*. The *cuddling*.

We...*cuddled*!

I literally haven't been able to do that in...ever. Not even with the cheetah shifter that time. We were both horny and not looking for anything other than sex.

At some point, apparently, I drift to sleep. I awaken at my usual time to several texts, from Selene, Amber, and from Dexter's man, John, who will be picking me up and wants to confirm my address and the time.

First, the bathroom. Hair's still black, so...yay. I handle business and then return to sit on my bed.

I answer John first, to get that out of the way.

Then I reply to Selene, knowing it'll be awhile before she responds. *Duh*, she's asleep.

I leave Amber for last, because I know what will happen. As soon as I reply, less than thirty seconds later, she's calling me.

"Well? How'd it go?"

"You know exactly how it went." I flop back onto my unmade bed. "It went *amazing*. I didn't even scare him off when I had to stab a vamp with a pencil."

"You can trust him, honey. He's so into you, it's nearly painful. He's your future."

I try not to get my hopes up over that. "Will you be there tonight? I'd like for you to meet him."

"Unfortunately, no. I've got a charity auction I'm running. Otherwise, I would."

"Is there anything else you see?"

She goes quiet for a moment, and I wait her out. "*Mazbushka*."

Feels like my heart stutters. "What?" It comes out a whisper.

"It's what your father calls you."

I swallow hard. I've seen her make some pretty freaky predictions that were dead-on. "*Called*," I sadly correct. "He's dead."

"No. *Calls*. He's *not* dead." Her firm tone brooks no resistance. "He's not dead. He's... *hiding*. Although that doesn't feel exactly right. He is concealed, somehow."

I've never had an in-depth conversation with her about my parents. "That's...that's impossible."

"I know what I see."

I'm glad I'm already lying down. "But he's *dead*. Mom wouldn't have lied to me about that!"

Another pause. "She didn't lie to you. That's what she suspected. She didn't know for sure. She assumed he was dead, because he never... *returned*."

It takes me a moment to find my voice. "Where the *hell* is he then?"

"I..." Another pause. "I can't see that. It's like it's fuzzy. Like there's something in the way. All I know is he is alive, and he misses you and your mom." She blows out a breath. "That's all. That's all I see about him right now." I hear the exhaustion in her tone. I know the visions sometimes take a lot out of her physically as well as emotionally.

"What about Dexter?"

"*Trust* him, honey. Seriously. He's a soul in pain equal to yours. You're each other's remedies."

"He's a vampire."

"I know. But he's still a man. And he's a damned good man."

I'm still trying to process everything she just told me. "Please don't tell anyone else about what you said about my dad. Not even Garrett. Not yet."

"Maybe we could help you search—"

"No." I feel...numb. "Mom died loving him. If you're right, and he is still alive, why didn't he find us?" Mom never changed her name or used fake names for me. If he is alive, and he'd really wanted to, he could've found us.

If Amber's even right.

Maybe she's not.

"Okay. I promise I won't tell Garrett. *Yet.*"

"Thanks. I-I'll talk to you later."

I lie there, staring out my wall of windows looking out over Tucson. I wish I could say it's Amber's prediction about Dexter that has me shook, but no.

Not today.

I don't want to get my hopes up, either. Because if my father is alive...why wouldn't Dad come find us?

Now I wish I hadn't agreed to facilitate this meeting tonight. What I want to do is...

What, *exactly*?

All I have is a sorta-psychic saying he's alive. Not where he is. Hell, I don't even have a picture of him.

I realize the ring's in my hand, but I have no conscious memory of pulling it out from under the T-shirt I slept in last night.

The only three people I would feel reasonably comfortable talking to about this are all, ironically, asleep until sunset.

Now what do I do?

I've never felt more alone and adrift than I do at this

moment. I should get up and decide what to wear, not that I have a lot of choices.

Then...

Hmm.

Maybe tonight would be a good night to break out the Jimmy Choos. They aren't called fuck-me pumps without good reason.

Because maybe I would like to see what it feels like to get laid by a vampire. And spanked by one. At least once in my life, I'd like to try it. Especially with one I know I can trust not to overpower me or violate my limits.

A handsome one full of heartbreak.

I damned sure need *something* to take my mind off the revelation Amber dropped into my lap.

I think Dexter Van Sussex could be the perfect something.

14

D *exter*

I HATE LEAVING the club Thursday morning, but it's not like I can stay there with Eilidh. She has a life outside of me that, for now, I have no access to and no right to demand to be a part of.

Time. It's something I have in abundance, unfortunately.

It's the one thing I can freely offer her without restrictions or hesitation because I know it's the one thing she'll accept from me without reservation. I'm simply glad I didn't scare her off with my grand gesture.

Stepping into the shower, I lean against the wall, close my eyes, and take my erection in hand. There won't be any sleep in my future if I don't relieve some tension. Whatever special perfection exists within Eilidh, it has an effect on me I didn't realize I'd been missing so much.

Everything about her speaks to me, weaves a spell around me. I've spent so many centuries reinforcing walls around me just to have this sweet, perfect woman walk right through them.

Imagining it's her mouth around my cock and her violet eyes staring up at me, I stroke myself, not dragging it out this morning. Tipping my head back, a fantasy of gathering her hair in my hands and using it to fuck her mouth takes over. Even as my balls tighten and pleasure snaps, and I spend all over my hand and the shower, I feel a shadow of guilt try to root itself in my soul. She's no sweetblood. She's no eager slut willing to let a vampire flog or spank her to chase the high she wants.

And I'm not a good man. I'm not even sure I'm worthy of her. The darkness within me and that I am consigned to taints everything in my existence.

Just like it tainted my love with Robert.

Finally, I finish and dry off. I deal with a couple of minor tasks before stretching out in bed naked just before dawn. I send a few final texts to John and Mark and then close my eyes. As the daily stupor creeps over me, I sense the sun's presence outside, even though all the windows in my suite have been prepared. John and Mark have taped a heavy tarp inside each window, as well as affixed clips to the blackout curtains, so they cannot drift open, even a little.

The only light in my room comes from the LEDs on the TV and DVD player and the digital clock on the nightstand, but to me, I can see as well as if it were daylight.

I miss my sun like a phantom ache. Robert used to love the sun.

I miss how Robert used to walk outside and lie in the sun, completely warm his body, and then immediately return to me, so I could hold him, bury my face in his hair, and inhale its scent.

He was my sun, and I orbited around him.

In many ways, I still do.

I haven't allowed myself to love anyone since losing him, although there have been some humans I grew fond of. I always sent them away before I could become too attached, used my powers to make them think they left me.

Made it my fault. Always my fault, and sent them away with plenty of funds, so they could make it on their own.

Always wished them well.

But no one ever dug under my skin and embedded themselves in my soul the way Robert did.

I never loved anyone since losing him.

I didn't think it was even possible.

I remember how in the mornings after I fed from him, or he'd tried yet another vampiric "cure" on me, he used to pluck a couple of hairs from me and lay them on the windowsill, hoping beyond hope.

His devastation every time to see them turned to ash used to gut me.

How he begged me to turn him, so he wouldn't lose me. I wanted to. Oh, how I wanted to. Terror filled me, though, because I was already afraid he wouldn't survive the process. Once I felt certain what he was sick with, I was even more convinced he might not survive. Yes, it was selfish on my part, not wanting to speed his departure.

I tried healing him with my blood. Letting him feed from me. If nothing else, I thought certainly the more he fed from me, the better his chances once I did turn him.

He would have done any- and everything I asked of him. He wasn't just my love, he was my willing submissive, my slave. I met him in a small pub on the outskirts of London and knew from the moment I laid eyes on him that he was mine. I didn't have to thrall him.

I didn't have to compel him.

I feel about Eilidh the way I felt about him, and it terrifies me all the more, knowing how that story ended, even though the bacteria that eventually stole him from me had already invaded his body before I met him.

Except this is the twenty-first century. They have drugs now that can kill all but the most tenacious strains of TB. I know more than I did back then. I have more resources.

I have Lucius and others to consult with.

Yet I also have my old fears. Plus, Eilidh's so young! I haven't asked that, but she looks barely nineteen, so she can't be more than twenty-three or -four. Even if she does come to love me, what right do I have to turn her, willing or not? What right do I have to deny her the sun?

What if she wants children? That's not something I could ever give her. I mean, we could visit a fertility clinic, of course. But then she would need to raise our children. I couldn't turn her before they were grown and deny them their mother.

Children are the most beautiful, breathtaking heartache. I was present when my two remaining children died, the first in his forties or so, after an injury turned gangrenous. I came to Eochaidh in the night even as the infection ravaged his body. I told him who I was, and that I loved him, and then released him from his pain as I cried. He'd already fathered five children, three of whom survived to adulthood.

My other son, Sealbhach, survived to a rare old age back then, when he finally succumbed to what I suspect now was cancer. He died peacefully and naturally in my arms, slipping away in the middle of the night with me whispering my love.

For centuries, I lingered in that area, keeping watch over my family line, helping when I could, in the ways that I could, without exposing myself. Hiring humans to help me.

Protecting them as best I could.

I finally sleep, my thoughts filled with Eilidh. When was the last time I thought about anything but Robert or work when lying in my daily imprisonment?

Her sweet rounded curves, how her body fit perfectly against mine—when was the last time I was blessed with pure contact like that?

Cuddling.

I'd thought there was no greater thirst to be had than when I'm overdue to feed, but it turns out there is one even worse.

Skin hunger.

It's tempting to beg her to come work for me. To tell her that her only job is to stay alive, and healthy, and snuggle with me.

That would be enough.

Of course, I would want more, but even if that is all she ever gave me, I would gladly take it, without question.

If asked about my fantasies?

Oh, I imagine her in my collar and cuffs and nothing else, kneeling on the floor in front of me, her spine perfectly rounded as her forehead touches my feet.

My hands leaving pink marks on her ass, enjoying every gasp she lets out as my flogger kisses her flesh.

Rubbing away the sting of a cane slicing across the backs of her thighs.

Sliding my cock inside her as my teeth pierce her neck—

Fuck. Now I'm hard again. And I wake up way too early and alone in that dark room and fist my cock, stroking, unable to help myself. This orgasm is totally unsatisfying because my fangs have also extended, hunger breaking through.

Once I've spilled all over myself, I go clean up and then retrieve a bag of blood from the small refrigerator in the bedroom. Ripping the corner of the bag with my teeth, I drink it cold, straight from the bag, like an animal.

It's barely satisfying.

Dammit.

I desperately want *her*, and that means I must be even more careful. I don't know why her and why now, but if I ever hurt her, I'd rather walk into the sunrise than live another minute.

SOMEHOW, I manage to go back to sleep, even though it took a second bag of blood and another orgasm to fill my stomach and drain my balls.

When I finally awaken a little after four, I check my phone and find that John has sent me a text telling me he's on his way to pick her up.

Moving carefully, I kick the doorstop out of the way and ease the bedroom door open, just a little. The suite's living room is still safely dark. I walk over to the door, remove the doorstop and unfasten the safety bar and deadbolt, then retreat to the bedroom and replace the doorstop.

That done, I text instructions to Mark, confirm what I want him to get us for dinner, and that Connie, as she's asked me to refer to her, is to be escorted into the suite's living room and left alone after instructing her not to touch the windows or open the curtains.

I'm literally humming as I take my shower. Shaving is

always interesting, since I can't see my reflection, but electric razors make that chore much easier.

There's an inner light growing within me. Even if tonight's meeting ends with no deal being struck, I'll be happy just to have spent it with Eilidh.

I'm hoping she'll want to return here after the meeting to at least talk some more.

Yes, I know exactly when John and Mark escort her to my suite, and it takes every ounce of self-control I have not to dash out there wet and butt-naked to greet her.

Smooth, Van Sussex. Very smooth.

I down another bag of blood, cold, as I decide what to wear. Three-piece suit tonight, no tie. I finally settle on a charcoal blazer, slacks, and vest, with a midnight blue shirt, open at the collar.

I don't care what the werewolves think of my appearance. I know they belittle Lucius' men and think them too "perfect," too "fake." Too "pretty." It's a common complaint shifters make about vampires.

Shifters have all these blessings of power, combined with the best of humanity in their veins, the ability to run in the sun and have *children*, yet they can't get past petty jealousy.

I'm aware of her out there, sitting in the living room and awaiting me. They'll have dinner up for us shortly.

I'm actually hoping I can talk her into ice cream or coffee after the meeting. Doing something...mundane.

Once I've dressed and realize I am only stalling because I'm nervous, I finally nudge the doorstop out of the way and open the bedroom door.

Her scent hits me first—light, sweet, with a hint of apricot spice. She stands and...

My cock immediately hardens. Without thinking, I reach down and adjust myself because I just cannot *even*...

She's gorgeous. Black hair flowing loose just past her shoulders, the barest hints of makeup, and a simple but elegant knee-length black dress with a black embroidered wrap over her bare shoulders...

Oh, fates help me, the three-inch black pumps expose her calves and make me drool.

"Well? How do I look?" she finally asks, and I realize how nervous she feels.

Even more than me.

"Breathtaking. Simply...perfect." I force myself across the room and hold out my hand to her. "May I?"

She nods and places her hand in mine.

With my gaze on hers, I brush my lips over the back of her hand, lingering there, deeply inhaling her scent. "You look amazing."

Her mouth quirks in a lopsided smile. "Thanks. I didn't think you could look hotter, but you do."

"Thank you." I open my arms to her and she steps in, tense at first, but then relaxes against me. I bury my face in *her* hair and inhale again. No wig this time. "Your hair is beautiful. Thank you for not wearing a wig tonight."

"Yeah, well, don't get used to it," she mutters against me.

"What?" I look down at her. "Why?"

She sighs. "It's a...story. Part of my story. The bitch of it is, I don't *know* why, but it is why I wear wigs to work."

"I don't understand."

"Yeah, well, neither do I."

There's a knock on the door, and I know it's Mark. I release Eilidh and answer it, and he rolls in the cart with our dinner. I escort Eilidh over to the table, holding her chair for her and then help Mark set everything out. Once we're alone again, I take my seat.

"I hope this is all right?" I opted for lasagna as our main course because Selene told me it was one of Eilidh's favorites.

"It's wonderful, thank you."

Even if the meeting tonight fails, I've already succeeded in making Eilidh smile, so it's a win. "What would you like to talk about?"

She takes a deep breath. "I guess I really owe you the full story about me. Because I have to be honest, I'm tempted to ask you later if you'd like to scene with me. It's also not fair to do that to you before you know everything about me."

Her violet gaze meets mine, and I read a heady mix of desire and fear there. "You're not the only one who believes in informed consent. And I couldn't live with myself if I'm the reason something bad happens to you."

15

E *ilidh*

I MEAN, obviously Dexter's attracted to me. I got that message loud and clear even before he had to reach down and adjust the boys. The jaw-drop when he saw me standing there in my dress and the Jimmy Choos would've been a clue if I hadn't already spent last night with my head in his lap.

Tonight, he's got a glass of water and a glass of bourbon. I settled for just water. "I can't imagine that there's anything you could say that would shock me or make me not want to take things to a more intimate level with you," he says. "And I've gotten pretty adept at taking care of myself over the years."

I think about my phone call with Amber today. "Oooh, you might not want to say that until you hear my story." The lasagna's fantastic. I make a mental note to send Selene a thank-you gift for giving Dexter great advice. "See, I learned something today I'm still trying to...process."

"What?"

"Let me tell you the story as it stood *before* I woke up."

His brows knit. "I don't understand."

"Neither do I," I snark. "But please, bear with me."

"Does what I witnessed last night have to do with it?"

"Kind of."

When he shifts position in his chair, I fight the urge to crawl into his lap. "Where did you pick up your fighting skills?" he asks.

"Mom. She was a stuntwoman and underground cage-fighter."

I get why his brow furrows again. "That's...not a very common occupation for a woman."

"No, it's not. She was American. Her mom and stepfather were in the Air Force and stationed at a post in Wales when she was in high school. Mom was nineteen when her parents were going to change posts again, and she left home and stayed behind. I guess her stepfather had her enrolled in martial arts classes from when she was little, and her four stepbrothers taught her how to fight dirty.

"She lived outside Cardiff, and, somehow, she got hooked up with the BBC and started working on shows as a stuntwoman. That's when she first met my father, I guess."

"Lived with your father?"

Here's where it gets tricky. I'm still trying to...reconcile what Amber told me. "She really didn't talk about him a lot. I was only eight when he died. I guess when he died, it scared her. That's when we started moving all over the world. Because I had dual citizenship, we were able to come to the States. They homeschooled me even before he died. She worked a lot of waitressing jobs under the table, got hooked into fights that way. Sometimes as a ringer working with the organizer. Get some guy in the cage with her who looked like he could mop the floor with her, and she'd take him out in under fifteen seconds. Usually a knockout."

His gaze widens. "Wow."

"Exactly." I lift my glass in salute to her. "As I said, Mom was a badass."

"How did your father die?"

I take a deep breath. "Pin an asterisk in this part of the convo because we'll double back shortly." He nods, and I continue. "Mom wouldn't talk about it. I remember her coming home in tears that day, with her arms and face all bruised up, her hands kind of cut up, like she'd been in a fight, and saying Dad was gone and not coming back."

I couldn't forget that day if I tried, even though adult me realizes there is probably more than a little distortion in my memory due to my age and the intense emotions surrounding the events. I remember her coming home wearing my father's ring on her finger.

A ring he only wore when he was getting ready to leave "for work." When he'd be gone days at a time. Otherwise, he kept it on a silver chain he wore around his neck.

He'd been wearing the ring the last time I saw him.

She dug the silver chain out of her jewelry box, threaded the ring on it, and never took it off after that, except to shower.

"What happened?" he asks.

"I don't know, for sure. I get the feeling someone attacked them. We moved that night, and never stopped moving."

"Where is he buried?"

"I don't know. I don't remember a funeral. She didn't have

his ashes, so I honestly don't know. I don't have a death certificate or anything." I shove away the familiar grief. "I don't even know his birthday, or the exact date he died. I just remember we'd celebrated my eighth birthday not long before, and it was only Mom and me when I celebrated my ninth."

"And you still move?"

"Yeah. Tucson's been safest by far. I've been here the longest." My left hand reaches up and touches the ring through my dress. "I'm scared to let my guard down. Every time I do, I end up needing to move again."

"You said your mother was killed?"

"She was mugged. Fell and sustained a severe head injury. There were two couples who witnessed it and tried to help her, but it happened so fast. They said it was like the guy appeared out of nowhere, tried to grab her, but she screamed and fought. Then she fell and hit her head. The guy disappeared before the bystanders could stop him. They were too worried about Mom to see which way the guy ran, and there wasn't any video to go by. They never caught the guy."

I remember standing next to her bed in the ICU, stunned, and the nurse handing me the bag with her possessions in it.

How the ring had been with her things, but not on the chain, like she usually wore it. She normally wore it around her neck. They told me she'd had it on her finger when she was brought in. I'd immediately strung the ring on the necklace and put it on, not wanting to risk losing it.

I remember the way the monitors slowed and eventually flat-lined after they disconnected her life support.

I remember how I felt, a new, unfamiliar rage deep within me, burning so white-hot I was terrified to express any emotions for fear of rampaging through the hospital and killing people just to be put out of my own misery.

"I'm sorry," he says, snapping my focus back to the present. "How old were you?"

"Seventeen. Three months shy of eighteen. I'm lucky our neighbor let me stay with her, so I didn't have to go into foster care. From the day I turned eighteen, I've been on my own."

"What about your father's family?"

"I don't know anything about them. I'm not even sure if my father's real name is on my birth certificate."

"You have uncles, though. Right?"

"Step-uncles. My mom wasn't close to them and lost contact with them. I don't even know if they're alive or where they are. I know her mother, father, and step-father all died when I was still a kid." I sip my tea. "I'm a family of one. Except for 'Uncle' Lucius and 'Auntie' Selene. And Garrett and Amber. Found family, for the win."

"Have you ever tried running one of those DNA kits?"

I shudder. "No. Because maybe it's best some things stay in the past. If someone did kill him, maybe I don't want them to have a way to track me." I point at my hair. "This is my natural hair, but remember how I said don't get used to it?"

"Yes?"

"It...changes."

"What do you mean?"

"I mean the other day when we first met, my hair was sort of golden blonde. Then, the morning after I met you, when I woke up, it was..." I point. "*This*. It's done this all my life. It might stay the same color for weeks or even months. Then I'll wake up one morning, and it'll be a different color. Eyebrows, too. I can't tell you if the carpet matches the drapes because the floors are bare, if you get my drift."

Yeah, I see the way his gaze quickly sweeps me, like he's already picturing *that*. I won't deny it fills me with more than a little heat, that I know I'm having an effect on him.

The long silence grows nearly uncomfortable. "That's why you wear wigs to work?"

"That's why I wear wigs to work. Because I don't want people asking questions about my hair."

"Why does it do that?"

I wave my fork at him. "Good question. No freaking clue."

"None?"

"Nope. That's not all that's different about me. I can hear and smell and sense things in a way like vampires and shifters can. I probably couldn't track someone by scent, but I can tell your scent from another vampire's, from a human, from a shifter. Can hear the difference, too. Vampires sound different because they only breathe for talking, not because they, you know, actually *need* to. Ditto their pulse." I decide to toss another nugget out there. "I can even smell arousal." I let my gaze briefly drop to his lap and force myself not to giggle when his eyes widen, and he clears his throat.

I see the wheels turning in his head and I hope my chances of getting spanked and spooned aren't heading into the crapper because of my honesty. "That's...unusual."

"No shit."

"Do you think it's tied to why you are immune to a vampire's powers?"

"I don't know. It might be. But know how I said stick a pin in the part about my dad's death?"

"Yeah?"

"I talked to Amber earlier." I explain who she is, her

abilities, and then relate our conversation as I watch his expression.

He's good, I'll give him that much. Perfect poker face, even by vampire standards. "And you don't think she's wrong?"

"Not about something like this, no."

"You can't be half vampire," he finally says. "It's impossible for vampires to father children or get pregnant."

"Right."

He takes a bite of his dinner and slowly chews. "Most shifters are immune, at least to a certain extent, from a vampire's powers. Strong shifters are. Sometimes, non-shifters are susceptible."

"Yep."

"I have met dozens of shifters from diverse species over the years," he says. "You do not smell like any shifter race I've ever net."

"That's what other shifters have told me, too. And Lucius told me. There are fae, though, right?"

"Yes, but I have little experience with them." He studies me. "If I'm not mistaken, Lucius has had more experience with them than I. If he recognized you as such, he would have said so."

"Oh." So, no help there.

"How can I help with the search for your father?"

How, indeed? "I can't think that far ahead. I want to get through tonight first." I poke at my food. "I'd understand if you would rather tap out now instead of taking things further with me. I don't want to do anything that might draw attention to you. Being with me could get...weird."

Dexter reaches over, his touch feather-light as he strokes the backs of his fingers along my cheek the way he did last night. "I've survived a lot in my life, including heartbreak the likes of which I never imagined possible. I'm not going anywhere, unless you tell me to."

I dare to meet his gaze again. Those light blue eyes steadily looking at me turn my insides to liquid and not because of vampire powers.

That has to mean something, right? Maybe Amber's correct.

Because inside this man's cool facade lies a decent, caring soul. "You can't control me," I quietly say. "Your powers don't work on me. You saw what I did to Tonio. And now...*new* insanity could be on the horizon. I'm still processing and don't even know where to start looking for him."

"Please, at least let me help you. I can hire detectives, I can pay—"

"No." I can't believe I said it, either. "I know how this works. What if I find him and it turns out he's part of some vampire-hunting family? Like what happened to Selene. What if everything I know is a lie? What if I'm being manipulated, and I don't even know it?"

"What if you aren't, and you're forcing yourself to do things the hard way out of fear? There is no power any vampire has that can make a human immune to vampire powers. Selene's memory was wiped and manipulated."

"What if mine was?"

"They can't fake your abilities and resistance." He cups my cheek, and I lean into his touch. "There's no way to fake your taste. *Nothing* exists like that. If so, some enterprising vampire would've mass-produced it decades ago. Lucius damn sure would have. Whether you're a hybrid by natural mutation or because your father is something we don't yet understand, you are *you*."

I desperately want that to be true. "Could you be with me if I never want to be turned?"

He smiles. "You haven't yet agreed to be with me. I think that conversation is premature. But I would never turn a human against their will. So, yes, I would gladly spend the rest of your life with you."

"Have you turned many humans?"

He sits back and resumes eating as a weighty sigh breathes free—ironic, I know, because he doesn't actually... you know...breathe. "Rarely, and not for centuries."

"Why not?"

Dex picks up his bourbon and swirls the amber liquid before sipping. "Because the first human I tried to turn, I killed. I was deeply in love and was talked into it despite my misgivings and knowing the risks. Completely shattered my heart."

Yikes. Now I feel like a total shit. "I'm so sorry. What was her name?"

The left corner of his mouth turns up in a smirk. "Robert."

"That's...not a woman's name."

"No, it's not." He arches an eyebrow at me. "I guess in modern parlance I'm called 'pansexual.' I am attracted to a person, not a gender. Even before I was wed, I was attracted to men and women. I've had lovers across the gender spectrum throughout my life. As old as I am, sticking to one gender would get rather dull. Is that an issue for you?"

Fuck. No, he just got about a thousand times hotter, in my head.

Shallow, I know. Fricking sue me. "No. I'm really sorry. You tried to turn him because you loved him?"

His low, velvety voice bears hints of unbearable personal pain. "That, and he was dying. Tuberculosis is my best guess, based on what I know now. I don't know if he died because he was already weakened from the disease or due to what I did. Perhaps a combination. He was still early in the disease. He likely would have lived several more years had I not attempted to turn him. Every time I let him feed from me, it strengthened him, but never completely eradicated the disease from his system.

"Back then, I was younger, not as strong, and my blood couldn't cure him. He endured it for several years. Letting him feed from me kept him alive and strong, albeit every time the disease reasserted itself within him, it came back stronger, like it was growing immune to my blood."

He takes another drink. "Turning a human is very risky under the best of circumstances. You have to take them to the point of death so that the virus that makes us what we are can infect their system and kill them. Then, if they survive that process, you have to work with them. Feed them. Wean them off your blood so they can survive on their own. Most who survived the initial turning die somewhere within that process. Frequently, because they go mad and do something that gets them killed. Only the most powerful vampires can successfully accomplish turnings. Like Lucius. And only the most powerful turned vampires can survive it."

Yikes. "I'm so sorry." This man's still waters truly run deep. "And you? Are you powerful now?"

He shrugs. "I suppose. Then again, I thought I was back then. But I was less than five hundred years old, at the time. At that time, I did not even know what I did not know. My ignorance and arrogance were completely inverted to their proportions now."

"Did you ever turn anyone else?"

"I did, but I wasn't in love with them. It was one of my

great-great-great grandsons. Toss a few more greats in there. Last of the family line."

"You kept track of your family?"

"Yes, in a fashion. Once my children and their children passed, I traveled a lot, but I paid people to watch over them. I always returned to that area. It was part of my heart and my soul, you see. Part of *me*. Where I owned property, even still to this day. And where I laid Robert to rest when I lost him."

"You weren't afraid of your grandson dying during the turning?"

"I was, but he was a bit of a wanker." He smirks. "It would not have shattered my heart had he not survived, as cold as that might sound. It was two hundred years or so after I lost Robert when I attempted to turn him. I'd learned far more by then. I guess I wanted to see if it was possible. I thought if my sire could be such a bastard and do it in such a haphazard way, why couldn't I do it if I were careful and deliberate?"

Surprisingly enough, it doesn't sound cold to me, it sounds...practical.

"What happened to him? Is he still...around?" Because I guess, technically, he's not "alive."

"He was eventually killed during the night attack at Nairn in 1746. I wasn't there, but a friend of his, another vampire, later brought word to me. Felled by a spear and a lucky strike."

"So, your family knew you were a vampire?"

"Only him. I was very, very careful who I brought into my inner circle. Unlike some, I didn't go on murderous rampages. I settled in one place for years and treated those around me quite well, so that they had every reason to protect me, feel loyal to me, and not fear me. I was careful to treat them kindly and generously. Also, I might have... persuaded them with my powers to assure their silence. How do you think I've stayed alive so long?"

"Alive?" Yes, I'm snarky.

He shrugs. "*Ish*. I haven't made many enemies. The few I have, I've taken care of. I don't leave loose ends."

"Am I a loose end, now that I know about you and you can't compel me?"

He smiles. "Only a very beautiful one. You're an enigma. You make me...curious. I'm not bored anymore."

"Does that mean you're going to kill me off once I bore you?" I'm just yanking his chain, but I am curious about his answer. If I seriously thought I was in danger, I'd talk to Lucius and Garrett and let them deal with Dexter.

"Absolutely not." He sighs, but it sounds weighted with lead and concrete. "You've kept me wanting to remain in this world. If I grow bored again, the only danger is to myself, not to you."

I shiver. I don't want to think about a world without him in it.

"Besides," he adds, "you are under Lucius' protection. I've managed to exist this many centuries without making an enemy of my 'uncle.' I prefer the world order as it currently stands, thank you very much."

"I have to say, for an old vamp, you sure are...chill."

"Is that a pun?"

"I mean literally. Most of the older ones like Lucius are..."

"Greedy? Power-hungry? Megalomaniacal?" He smirks.

"I was going to say borderline or outright douchebags, but yeah, those work, too."

I love the sound of his laughter. "I'm guessing you don't feel like that about Lucius?"

"No. I mean, he can be a dick when someone pisses him off, but I get it. If you treat him courteously, respectfully, he gives it in return. I've never had a problem with him. I consider Selene one of my best friends. He's crazy over her. She's got that dom wrapped around her paws, and they both know it."

"You interest him, too."

"I guess. I make him money. A *lot* of money. That doesn't hurt."

He studies me for a moment. "Do you think he'd let you leave?"

"I have the freedom to come and go as I please. The deal was always that I'd move on if I needed to and no hard feelings about it. I told him about my little night visitor when he hired me. I didn't want that coming out of nowhere and him thinking I lied to him when I suddenly left."

I study my water glass, unable to look Dex in the eyes right now. "I know he researched the hell out of my story when I first arrived. I'm still alive, so obviously I passed the sniff test."

"So to speak."

"Yeah." I shrug and finally look up again. "Like you said, I don't bore him. And I'm useful, to him and to the shifters. I can move among them." Of course, now I'm once again thinking about Amber's certainty regarding her vision. "I need to update Lucius and tell him what Amber said. And... everything else. He doesn't know the full story."

"The hair?"

I shake my head. "I could be bald under those wigs for all he knows. I know Lucius gets a bad rap sometimes, but he's kept order. Is he ruthless? Well, *duh*. Fricking *vampires*. Kinda goes with the territory."

He smiles. "Are you jealous of Selene? That she's his queen?"

"Nooo." I take another sip of water. "Look, I'd be lying if I said Lucius and his men are fugly grunts. They're gorgeous. So are you. When I first let Lucius sample me...I gotta be honest, I nearly bolted then, after he told me what I tasted like. I was afraid he might try to keep me prisoner."

"Why didn't you?"

Why, indeed? Dexter doesn't interrupt me as I think about it. "I guess because I sensed I could trust him. That, and I'm thirty-five, and I'm sick of being alone. No family—"

Shock widens his eyes. He'd been in the process of taking a drink of bourbon, and he literally spit-takes back into his glass, choking on his liquor. "You're *thirty-five*?" he asks once he stops coughing.

"Yeah, I know, I know. I look younger." He continues staring at me in obvious disbelief. "Wait, you can accept that you can't mojo me, my blood's a funky and addictive flavor, my hair has a life of its own—and did you notice I have fricking *violet* eyes?—I have superpowers with my senses of hearing and smell, I can stake a vamp with a number-two pencil and my snark, I'm being stalked by a supernatural Cujo, and oh, add in that my dad's apparently *not* dead after all if my psychic friend's correct...but you can't believe I'm thirty-five? *That's* the line? *Seriously*?"

"It's just...I mean..." He grabs his napkin and pats the liquor off his lips. "I wasn't expecting *that* revelation, is all."

"Nooooobody expects it," I tease, hoping he gets the reference.

He smiles. "If only the Spanish Inquisition had been as enchanting as you, I might have actually enjoyed it."

16

D*exter*

Yes, I know. Eilidh is absolutely right that it's ludicrous her *age* is what's tripping me.

"If it's any consolation, Lucius didn't believe my age at first, either," she adds.

"How'd you prove it to him?"

"I showed him my birth certificate and let him research. Plus, I gave him plenty of references."

"You...did?"

"Yeah. I was never fired or left on bad terms. There were plenty of vampires who could vouch for me. Shifters, too."

"Then why did you move on?"

"Uh, my little intermittent stalker?"

"Oh, right."

A comfortable silence descends over us for several

minutes while we eat before she next speaks. "Not freaked out?"

The last thing I want to do is lie to her or scare her off. She could turn out to be a secret kind of shifter sent to kill me, and, fates help me, I'd still want her.

"I want to help you unravel this mystery," I finally say. "And no, I'm not freaked out."

I sense she's trying to build up to an ask—a pretty big one—so I let the silence between us play out again. Her cheeks flush a little, a delightful shade of pink that enchants me.

"You're not scared of me?" This is the voice of a vulnerable woman, not the feisty fighter I watched with my own two eyes as she took down a vampire.

Slowly shaking my head, I sit back. "Not in the slightest."

"I don't know if that should scare *me*," she mutters before nervously taking a drink of water. After a deep, shaky breath, she bites her lower lip and my cock throbs in response. "After the meeting...maybe we could do more than just cuddle? But no feeding," she quickly adds. "If you can't promise that, I understand. No harm, no foul."

Forcing myself to remain still, I take a breath. "If you mean having sex without feeding, yes. I'm perfectly capable of that. Besides, I've already fed today."

"Yeah, this lasagna's gr—*oh*." She blinks. "You mean... you *fed*."

"I have a mini fridge in the bedroom full of blood." I point. "You may go look, if you wish."

Her relieved breath tells me yes, the sudden spike in her pulse meant jealousy.

That pleases me more than I care to admit.

"No, I believe you."

"Is there anything else you'd wish to do tonight?" I'm

already struggling to shove back a wave of dirty, sexy things I long to do to and with her. I need my focus tonight, and fantasizing about tying her up and ravishing her pussy with my mouth isn't helping me.

Yes, I can smell her arousal, and it's making it difficult to think. What I *want* to do is drop to my knees before her, shove her thighs apart, and bury my face between them, so I can spend the whole evening tasting and pleasuring her.

I want her addicted to me the way I already am to her.

That she doesn't realize the depths of my obsession with her makes *me* very vulnerable, and she doesn't even know it.

The pink tip of her tongue flicks out and she licks her lips. "Spanking and orgasms sounds...fun."

"Yes, it does." In a way, I'm glad I can't compel her. It means she's asking this because she *wants* it. *Really* wants it.

Wants it in a way that forces her to push past her fear.

"So...not that I don't want to do that here. Just not...yet?" I let her finish. "There's the suite at Club Toxic, where we talked. We could lock ourselves in. And it's safe, if we play too late for you to come back. It's okay for you to stay over there."

"To be clear, I don't think I'd want to play in the main dungeon our first time playing," I admit. "I might never be okay playing with you in front of other vampires like that. I'm...territorial."

Her lips part, her pulse now thrumming as a soft gasp escapes her. "You are?"

"Yes. I don't share well." I reach out and lightly trail one finger along the back of her hand. "I damn sure don't want any of them catching scent of your blood."

"No?"

"No. Because I'd kill anyone who thought they were entitled enough to so much as ask to taste you. Even Lucius."

She nervously swallows, her gaze now following the path of my finger as I slowly draw lazy swirls across her flesh. From the way her pulse suddenly thrums, I know she's turned on. "Um, okay." She nods. "Maybe alone would be best, then."

She took a huge risk, so maybe it is time I take one of my own. "Eilidh." I wait until she looks up and meets my gaze again. There's full comprehension and awareness in her eyes, and it totally hardens my cock, knowing I don't have to hold back with her in that way, at least.

It hits me she's lived most of her life relying on herself and not having a protector.

A partner.

Someone to watch her back.

At least I've been able to afford to buy protection and help.

"I'm never letting you go. Even if I have to spend the rest of my life watching and protecting you from afar because you don't want me directly in your life, I will. But while you are *in* my presence? I *will* defend you to the death, and you cannot stop me from doing that. That is *my* choice."

Her lips part again. "Oh!" I smell a renewed wave of her arousal scenting the air and it nearly makes me drool.

"How about this proposal—whatever you feel like doing after the meeting, that's what we'll do. No pressure. Anything from crazy, wild sex and play, all the way to sharing a table in a cafe and sipping frappes and talking."

"Really?"

"Really. I refuse to rush this and make a mistake with you. Days, months—years. I'll be here patiently waiting on you."

I wait as she takes a deep, relieved breath and nods. "Deal."

"Thank you for trusting me." I want to amend something to that comment—*pet*, *girl*, *sweetheart*.

Love.

She smiles. "Yeah, well, it's kind of funny how in my life it's been the apex predators I could always trust the most. At least they're...predictable."

I TEXT my men before I head out with Eilidh. Mark calls down to the front desk, and I find my rental waiting for us at the front entrance when we emerge from the lobby. I hold the passenger door open for her and wait until she's tucked in to close it and round the SUV to slide behind the wheel.

"I have to say, I'm a little surprised," she admits as we pull away. "An Audi Q3? That's practically slumming it."

"Why?"

"It's not something sporty and Italian."

"It's practical and comfortable."

"How many Bugattis do you own?" From her teasing tone, I can tell she's loosening up again.

"Not a one. No Ferraris, no Lambos, no McLarens, no Paganis."

"*Wow*. I kind of thought that was a vampire requirement. Better not let Lucius hear that. He might try to revoke your cool vamp club membership card."

She makes me *laugh*. How long has it been since I really felt like laughing?

Forever, it seems. "I have a Ford Mustang and a Honda Pilot back in Atlantic City. In Scotland and London, I have Land Rovers. At my other houses, I have cars I can easily get serviced locally. Exotic cars are a pain in the ass and draw too much attention from bystanders and the IRS. Not to mention, they attract crime. Good luck trying to find someone who will change the oil for you if you want to take a road trip."

"You take road trips?"

"On occasion. Well-planned, obviously, for stops and logistics. Hence why an SUV is a smarter choice. I can carry supplies with me to make a room safe. Vampire equivalent of roughing it."

"I am pleasantly surprised. I don't think I've ever met a vampire who doesn't think roughing it is drinking bagged blood, much less driving somewhere."

"I've rented RVs, on occasion. Sometimes, I need to get away from the city and be alone but can't go to Scotland. Not to mention, you have to remember the time I grew up in. Anything approaching 'roughing it,' to me, is still a luxury compared to back then. I refuse to lose sight of that."

Her hand comes to rest on my right thigh. "I can honestly say I've never met a vampire like you before."

I take the chance to let my hand rest on top of hers, lacing fingers with her. "And I can honestly say I've never met another human like you before."

Fight Club is located in a neutral zone of sorts, as laid out by the treaty Lucius struck with Garrett Green of the Tucson werewolves. It's in an industrial area, a large, nondescript warehouse building. The parking lot is maybe three-quarters full.

I normally would drop her by the door and go park, but I refuse to let her wait alone. Especially since a large, muscle-bound guy stands watch outside the door. Probably a shifter.

I park. Before I get out to open her door for her, she stays me with her hand. "Let me lead, please? I know the guy at the door. He's one of the wolves. No pissing contests. Right?"

"He's not the first shifter I've dealt with, and he won't be the last."

"Is that a yes? My rep is on the line, here." I sense her anxiety isn't just because of me but because we're out at night. I didn't miss how her head was on a swivel as we drove, and several times she reached over to confirm the door was locked.

"Yes, of course, I'll behave." I get out and open her door for her, holding my arm out for her the way I did that first night. I love the warmth from her touch and slow my strides, so she doesn't have any trouble keeping up with me across the parking lot.

From the way the bouncer's nose wrinkles and how his stance tenses, I know he's already scented me.

"Hey, Perry," she calls out.

That apparently throws him off-balance, and he scowls. "*Connie*? Is that you?"

"Yeah, this is Dexter. We have an appointment with Alpha Green. He's expecting us. He asked me to bring Dexter and said he'd leave word."

He still regards me warily, but he nods. "Boss said you were coming." He opens the door for us, but I suspect if he had his preference, he'd stake me.

"Thanks!" she brightly says and leads the way in, releasing my arm once we're inside.

I fight the urge to grab her hand and pull her back against my side. All eyes momentarily turn, taking her in, and I could easily murder every last one of them before the first one even hit the floor.

Shit. I do have it bad for her.

She walks over to the bar. "Hey, Alpha Green's expecting us," she says to the bartender.

He nods and picks up a phone, even as his wary gaze remains on me.

I get it, why she's using his title. Trying to soothe ruffled scruffs and warn people that it's official business, not a social call.

Eventually, attention turns away from us and to a fight getting ready to happen in the cage farther back in the space.

While we wait, I glance around at the gathered crowd. There are shifters of various species, mostly wolves and coyotes, but at least one bear and a cat of some sort. Panther, perhaps? Humans, too. I sense no other vampires here tonight, although I smell the occasional hint of previous visits. The dingy warehouse's exterior belies the feel of the bar's interior. Like it's deliberately spartan and industrial, designed for a rougher crowd not looking for or needing a manufactured grungy hipster vibe to assuage their egos. But it's clean and looks like there was care taken to choosing the tables, chairs, high-tops—the bar itself. It's not a haphazard dumpster-diving mishmash.

I lean in so I can speak in her ear. "You know, I could hire several of Garrett's men to protect you."

"Yeah, like *that's* not overkill? I go from an overprotective vampire to several overprotective wolves? That won't draw the slightest bit of attention to me. Not at allll."

"I sense sarcasm."

"You sense right." She turns to me. "I don't want bodyguards."

I can tell there will be plenty of times, just like now, when I'll want to flip her over my knee and spank her until she agrees to let me take care of her. "You'll take them if I tell you to."

She plants her hands on her shapely hips, the hem of

her dress swirling around her knees and distracting me. "You and what fricking army, dude?"

We have a stare-down that ends with me literally blinking first. "Why the *hell* doesn't that work on you?" I mutter.

She grins. "I don't know, but it's annoying, isn't it? At least you don't have to worry about some other vamp staking a claim on me like that."

"Can we use another word?"

"What word, vamp?"

"No—staking."

"No. That word amuses me. Oh, there he is. That's him." She points. I spot Garrett Green emerging from an office in the back of the building. The Alpha immediately heads our way, three large guys shadowing him. "Stay cool and *please* let me do the talking, huh? Remember, he's my friend, my best friend's mate, *and* he's my landlord."

"I could buy that building for pocket change and give it to you," I mutter.

"Shut up, and do *not* get into a pissing contest with him, or any other shifter."

"Yes, dear."

Garrett walks up and shakes hands with her, but his intense gaze remains on me. His men view me with undisguised loathing. "Connie. Thanks for coming. I know you don't like to travel at night. I appreciate you being here."

I hate that she tips her chin to him, exposing her throat in the wolves' tradition, denoting submission.

Even though she's not a wolf, and she is most definitely *not* his. "Alpha Green. This is Dexter Van Sussex."

I don't give a fuck who he is—I'm *not* showing him my throat. I do extend my hand as I keep my gaze no higher than his nose. No, I likely couldn't compel him, but that is the level of respect and deference I will give him. Courtesy.

Despite wanting to throw him across the fucking building because Eilidh showed him her throat. "Nice to meet you, Alpha Green. Connie and Lucius have both spoken quite well of you."

One of the men behind him lets out a low growl and spits on the floor at the mention of Lucius' name, but Green holds up a hand to stay him. "She showed me her throat," Green says. "But I've never seen her in a dress before, like this. I can *smell* the two of you, like honey and syrup together. Yet her throat's not marked, and I can tell she's never been blooded or drank from a leech, either. So...what the fuck's up with *that*?" He tosses a glare her way. "Did you suddenly pick a team to be more loyal to?"

I keep my hand extended. This is dominance posturing on his part, and I won't budge. I keep my voice low enough only Eilidh, Green, and the men with him can hear. "I'm here to form a lucrative alliance with you, not piss on fence posts. If it were up to me, the *only* person she would ever show her throat to would be *me*, and my fist would now be halfway down *your* throat for disrespecting her by talking to her like that. But she's your mate's best friend, she actually said you're her friend, and you know *damn* well what's going on. I am a man of my word. You'll either do business with me, or you won't, but we'll do it as equals. And you *will* apologize to her right *now* for the disrespect, after she came here tonight, in good faith, at *your* specific request. Not because she had to, but because she considers you a friend."

Finally, a smile breaks free and he shakes with me as his men relax. "Amber was right about you." He makes a point of looking at Eilidh. "My apologies, Connie. You know I had to test him."

"Not a problem, Garrett." She glances around, at all the eyes on us. "Can we go talk now? Or would you two like to go pee on a few tires in the parking lot first to celebrate not killing each other?"

The Alpha's laugh sounds like a choked howl, and even his men snicker. "Let's go back to the office where we can have some privacy."

I let Eilidh follow Green, and I stay close behind her, throwing warning glares at anyone who so much as looks at her in more than a passing way. Green has his men wait outside the office door. He settles behind the desk, and I do wait until he sits first before I take my seat.

He leans back, beefy hands laced behind his head. "So, Mr. Dexter Van Sussex. What are your intentions with my mate's best friend?"

"Garrett!" she snaps.

He grins. "What? You're wearing a dress, hon."

"You've *seen* me in a dress before. What was *that* bullshit?"

"Uh, I've never seen you in a dress *here*. At a wedding or cocktail party, yeah. Outside that, no. I figured you'd show up in your shit-kickers and jeans, not walk in here all hot and looking like I need to have my guys guard you to protect your honor." He chuckles. "A little warning would've been nice."

Well, he earns more respect from me for that. "We're in discussions," I say, interrupting this interplay before it derails the purpose of us being here tonight. "And it's our *personal* business. Nothing will happen unless she wants it to. I've already told her that, and I mean it."

"Garrett, we're cool," she says. "Seriously. Dexter's been very sweet, and a gentleman." I notice her hand automatically plays with the ring, where it hangs from the chain.

A silver chain.

Well, hopefully that means no shifters will be trying to sneak a quick bite of her neck tonight. I'd hate to start a war during a business trip because I had to kill a shifter for trying to snipe her out from under me.

His smile fades, and his attention stays on her. "No offense, but I don't trust leeches."

She groans. "*Garrett.* Be my friend, that's fine, but you *don't* get to insult him like that. *Especially* not when he's sitting right *here.*"

He shifts his focus to me. Even though his hands are laced behind his head, I can tell he could easily leap over the desk and try to kill me. He's an animal, a wolf, and it's right there, just below the surface and barely constrained.

Instead, he blows out a long breath. "Sorry," he says. "That'll take some getting used to. But Amber's right—there's crazy chemistry between you two." He sits forward and clasps his hands on the desk, and I see his wolf sink back down as the man takes over. "What are we discussing tonight?"

I get to the crux of my offer and outline the main points. Then, moving slowly, I pull a thumb drive out of my jacket and hand it to him. "There are PDFs on there with more details."

He studies it in his hand, then grabs a laptop and plugs the drive in.

I wait while he skims through the information, feeling a little satisfaction when his brow furrows then rises as he processes what I'm offering.

As he reads, I hold my hand out to Eilidh.

I'm pleased that she takes it and wraps her fingers around it, so I offer her a playful smile.

After ten minutes, he sits back, relaxed and thoughtful.

"I'll admit when Lucius called me, I was skeptical. I wondered what the catch was. This looks...doable."

"I'll tell you the same thing I told him—I won't pay tribute. We're businessmen, and a *legal* enterprise like this, a *lucrative* legal enterprise, only helps all of us. I'll sweeten the pot a little. I know your pack recently helped resettle a large group of shifter refugees rescued from one of those secret labs."

He scowls. "Who told you that?"

"I have sources even Lucius doesn't know about. But you and I are absolutely in agreement those labs must be destroyed. Create a legal nonprofit I can funnel a considerable donation into every year to help fund those efforts. Or some other legal entity I can fund, however it needs to be handled to keep the IRS out of it. With the goal being the destruction of any other labs you locate and to care for shifters displaced by them. We can even create a program to integrate them as employees at the hotel and casino, provide immediate emergency housing, all of that."

I don't blame him for his skepticism. "Why do you care?"

"Programs like that threaten *all* of us, not just shifters. Do you *really* want the government—any government—making shifter-vampire hybrids?" I take a risk. "Lucius' decision to turn Selene was completely based on his love for her, but he made some enemies by doing so. Fortunately, she's a good person with a good heart, and has no desire to take over. Lucius has her well in hand. I say this as a friend to them both, by the way. Keeping both your and Lucius' operations strong here in Tucson means taking power away from rogue vampires who want to sow mayhem, and from rogue shifters who want nothing but war."

He rocks back in his chair, which groans and creaks a little in protest under his bulk. "Connie? Thoughts?"

She's watching me. "I don't know the details of the business proposal. I can't give you an opinion."

"About him." He points at me.

"You know me," she says. "I stay neutral. But..." She smiles. "I like him. So far, he hasn't done or said anything to make me not like or trust him. If he does, you'll be the first to know."

"All right then." Back to me. "You know I own the piece of land you're looking at buying."

"I do. That was a deliberate choice on my part after researching several options. And as a show of good faith, Lucius is willing to convert some of his territory to neutral territory, provided the shifters don't antagonize vampires at night in those territories. A day/night usage split. He'd also be willing to introduce you to some of his contacts about maybe expanding Fight Club's operations. And both of us will help fund your preferred local political campaigns and issues, as well as apply our special kind of...*influence*, when necessary, to protect all our interests."

"You'll pay full market value for the land?"

"It's all there in my proposal."

He takes the thumb drive out and tucks it in his pocket. Then he offers me his hand. I shake with him.

"We have a deal, Dexter. I'll get with my attorney to go over this in detail, and we'll set up an official meeting in a couple of weeks to handle the sale and get things rolling."

"Thank you, Alpha Green. All my contact info is in the PDF."

"Garrett." He smiles but displays his canines. "You break her heart, I'll kill you myself."

"I think you'd have to get in line behind Lucius and Selene, and your own mate, but point taken."

"Oh, good grief," she mutters.

17

E *ilidh*

MY NERVES ARE SHOT by the time we leave Fight Club a little after two a.m. after the two of them finally finish talking.

One bonus?

Garrett gives Dexter and his men a permanent conditional exemption to be in their territory, as long as they're there to see me or going to see Garrett. Garrett, Dexter, and Lucius will sit down and work on revising the treaty deets in a couple of weeks, once Dexter and Garrett close the deal for the land.

"I think that went rather well," he says once we're back in the Audi and heading away from Fight Club. "What would you like to do now?"

It's a nearly full moon, and it hangs in the gorgeous, desert sky where it lights the landscape with a silver, shimmering glow. "Well, it's going to be dawn in just under three hours. As much as I'd like to do something, it's late, and I'm tired, and I don't want our first time together to be rushed." That's disappointing as freaking hell, though, because I was reeeally looking forward to getting boned tonight.

After several years, I can wait one more day, I suppose.

"What *is* that?" He points to Sentinel Peak, where the large *A* is visible in the daytime.

"That's 'A' Mountain." I start to explain what little history I know about it when I realize he's changing direction, heading toward it. "Where are we going?"

"I want to see it."

"Well, the park's closed, but we can drive up there."

"Why drive?" He smiles and pulls into a street parking spot across from the hospital just north of the peak. "Trust me?"

In this moment...yes, I do. He looks happy, and for some stupid reason, I can't bear to tell him no.

Mostly because I've heard some of his history, and I personally understand how grief and loss can change a person for the worse. I saw Mom mourn my father, and if he's really not dead...

I stare into Dexter's eyes, which look dark grey in the dim light. "Yes. I do trust you."

I can only hope that won't be my undoing.

His smile does things to my lady parts in a way no other vampire—or human or shifter, quite honestly—ever has.

He gets out and comes around to my door, helping me out. "Leave your purse and wear your wrap." I do, and he locks the car and puts the fob in his pocket. Then he scoops me into his arms. "Hold on, sweetheart."

I drape my arms around his neck. "What are we go —*HOOOOOLY SHIIIIT!*"

The crazy fucker actually *laughs* as he blurs, racing up

the side.

Of the.

Freaking.

MOUNTAIN.

I mean, yeah, it's not Everest, and it's not like it's heavily forested, like in the Pacific Northwest or something, but *damn*. I've seen vamps blur before, but I've never been held by one during the process or seen it happen over such long distances.

I close my eyes and press my face to the side of his neck as we race through the desert night, deftly avoiding cactuses. After what feels like forever, but is probably less than twenty seconds, I feel the breeze ease up as he comes to a stop.

He chuckles, the sound rumbling through his chest and warming my girlie parts. "You can look."

"No," I mumble against his shoulder. "I'm not sure I can."

He chuckles and continues holding me. "It is a beautiful view. Such a shame not to look."

Finally, I peek.

We are on *top* of the freaking mountain.

Took him seconds. *Seconds!*

"Why do you even bother driving?" I tighten my grip around his neck just in case he was thinking about putting me down. I don't want to get left up here and have to hike back down in my Jimmy Choos.

Not that I think he'd leave me.

Come to think of it, I suspect he's never going to leave me.

How weird is it that I'm increasingly okay with that idea?

The other reason I don't want to get down is I kind of like being held in his arms. It's...comforting.

Sexy.

Below us, Tucson and the valley glitter with lights.

"I like driving," he says. "And a car is—"

"Practical. Yeah."

"Well, you can't haul luggage very effectively like this."

"True."

"And, eventually, even vampires tire. We might have better stamina and strength, but it is finite."

It is a gorgeous view. I've hiked up here before. It's kind of a touristy thing to do. Some locals will come up here, but there are prettier hikes in the area. Never been up here at night, though.

"I'm going to buy you a proper house," he softly says, his breath cool against the top of my head. "Anywhere you want. Whatever house you want. I'll pay for it all." He stares into my eyes. "I don't want you living in a building with a bunch of other people. I want you safe. Where I can make sure you're protected. A place that suits you. Go house shopping, please? Preferably one with a pool and a very tall fence, a secure gate, a large garage, and maybe a dark basement for the occasional guest." He smiles.

Wait, what? "What about you? You won't live with me there?" That disappoints me waaay more than it should, considering I just fricking met the vamp.

And yet, I've also imagined what it'd be like if I let him play with me in the club's dungeon.

Definitely a line of thought that dampens my panties.

"I'm talking about *you*." He looks out over the city. "*If* you decide you want me permanently in your life, we can talk about that then. I am not going to assume you will desire to have a long-term relationship with me. Even if you don't want to be with me, this is something I still want to do for you. No strings."

I know I could say no, but I already see how that plays out. He'll buy it, put it in my name, and all my shit will be moved there for me while I'm gone. I'll try to go home from work one morning, and his guys will be waiting to drive me to the new house.

I can see it all as if it's already happened. Because he's already warned me he's never letting me go.

And I know Garrett and Amber would probably let him and the movers into my apartment to help them do it, too.

The bills would automatically get paid every month, no matter what. The taxes paid every year. Insurance. Full state-of-the-art security system. A number to call if anything breaks or needs maintenance.

He won't let me refuse him doing anything for me—I feel it to my core.

Fates help me, I don't think I want to refuse him, either. "Why?"

His focus returns to me and he studies my face for several long minutes. "Because for the first time in too damned long, I actually give a damn about someone else. And it's terrifying, but it feels good, too. I'd forgotten what it feels like to not feel alone. To feel *alive*. I have felt dead inside since losing Robert. For that, if for no other reason, I want to do *this* for you, if you'll let me."

WE STAY UP THERE for longer than we probably should, but he's a big boy. I'm ready this time and close my eyes when he blurs us back down the mountain.

"We're here." When he carefully sets me on my feet, I risk opening my eyes again.

We're by the car. I turn, and next thing I know, I'm kissing him.

Yep, it was definitely me kissing him, even as my heart races and the last things on my mind are my apparently not-dead dad and my mystery whatever-he-called-it dog thing.

This is a *kiss*, a deep, slow one I savor and relish. He turns, his back against the Audi to cushion me, and yep—he's hard.

Poor bastard.

I playfully grind against him, which backfires when my nipples tighten at the sexy friction between us, sending jolts of need straight to my lady bits. "Did you rub one out before bed last night?" I playfully ask.

He growls, but it only turns me on more. "Yes. Many. Including I woke up in the middle of the day horny and had to jerk off. That hasn't happened to me in literally centuries."

I'm still grinding on him. "I have to work tomorrow night, but come to the club as soon as it's dark and bring me dinner, please? I'll hold one of the rooms downstairs, and we'll play whenever I can. Or, if it's busy, once we've closed. We can stay there through the day, and I'll tell everyone to leave us alone. It's safe. I'll even pack an overnight bag."

He kisses me this time, his fingers threading through my hair and gently cupping my head. "I understand why you wear a wig for work. But when we're alone in the room, no wig. I want to feel *your* hair in my hands. Deal?"

Oh, so we're making rules? Okay. "Only if you don't feed off of or have sex with anyone there but *me*."

"I'm not feeding off of you yet, if ever. I promised you that. I won't violate a hard limit. I can buy blood."

I realize what I said, and thank fates he's watching out for me. "You're not the only territorial one. I mean, you get blood from the tap only, or a bag, not from the source. I'm not sharing you with the house Dobbys and crew for fangs *or* fucking."

He smiles. "Deal." We kiss again, and I'm wondering how severe the charge would be for getting caught fucking in public.

With one hand still cupping my head, he slides his other hand along my ass, cupping it, fingers digging in and squeezing, allowing him to grind back as he smiles down at me. "The first time you let me fuck you, I will apologize in advance if I get off quickly. I suspect I won't be able to hold back. I will make it up to you immediately after."

"It's been a couple of years for me, so forgive me if I ride you like a stolen pony." I can already tell he's hung better than the cheetah shifter was.

Far better.

He smirks. "Who says I won't have you tied up so I can spend hours eating that delicious pussy of yours that I'm smelling right now? It's making my mouth water."

Fates, the things this man does to me. I kiss him again, loving the low rumble vibrating from him into me. I hook one leg around his and really go to town grinding against his thigh. Then he shifts position, cradling me in one arm, his other reaching under my dress and easing inside my panties.

"*Mmm*," he whispers. "Someone feels very wet." When he slides not one but two cool fingers inside me, I see stars, and I'm glad he's holding me up. I fist his hair and yank his lips back down over mine to help muffle my moans.

He slowly fingers me, dragging them over my swollen clit with every stroke. I don't care if all of Tucson is watching us, it feels like the world ends just outside his arms, and it's only the two of us. He takes his time building me up, our tongues dueling as he plays my body. If he's this damned good and still has his clothes on, I can only imagine how fantastic he'll be when we're naked and horizontal and alone in a secure room.

The risks this man inspires me to take—I don't understand why he makes me feel this way.

Why he blows through my defenses without even trying.

We kiss, and I completely lose track of time and space as he finally builds me up to the best orgasm I think I've ever experienced. It leaves me shaky and weak and satisfied like never before.

He finally breaks our kiss, smiling down at me as he brings his hand up to his mouth. Looking into my eyes, he slowly licks every finger clean. My brains are barely starting to fall back into my head when he says, "I'd love to fuck you over the hood of this car right now."

I'm sure I squeaked in fear because he laughs and pulls me in for a hug. "No, sweetheart. The first time I fuck you, I want to be in a comfortable bed, so we can curl up together and go to sleep after."

"Really?" I feel like I could happily get lost within the safety of his arms.

"Really."

Now that I can actually think again, I feel a little guilty. "But you're... This isn't fair to you."

"I can take care of myself later." He sighs as he stares down into my eyes. "I will *not* be rushed when I finally get to claim you. My beautiful, feisty, territorial Eilidh," he says, and the sound of my name spilling from his tongue is like sunlight in my ears. His whole energy feels...*lighter* than it did when we first met. "My sunshine. My radiant one. I'm so glad I didn't give up before I met you."

"Me, too, Dex. Me, too."

18

E*ilidh*

WE MAKE it back into the Audi without a public indecency charge—*nertz*—and he drives me home.

Yes, he walks with me up to my apartment. Then he stands there, hands in his pockets, as I unlock the door and step through.

I put my purse down and stand inside the door, just out of reach.

He waits.

Not that he has a choice.

"Can we please hold off on the whole buying me a house thing? Let me get used to having a boyfriend first. Okay?"

He smiles, looking incredibly smug and pleased with himself. "You want me to be your boyfriend?"

"Yeah. I'd like to try that label on for a while. If you're okay with that? I'm not looking for a sugar...vampy."

He slides his hands from his pockets, bracing them on the door jamb and those sexy as fuck fingers curling around it—Did I mention he's six-three?—leaning in as far as he can. I literally see the way an invisible force presses back, a resistance, against his forehead and hair.

"Please be my girlfriend, Eilidh," he whispers. "Please, be *mine*."

I smile, stepping back, out of the way. "Come on in and let's talk about it, big guy."

I wish I could describe the look of shock on his face as he falls into my apartment and hits the floor, landing on my soft, fluffy pink faux fur area rug that I picked up at a yard sale for five dollars.

Laughing, I hold out a hand to help him up, but he kicks my door shut and pulls me down on top of him, where I sit up, straddling him.

Ooooh, yeah. Dude's getting ridden *hard* the first time we do it.

Or, would that be ridden soft?

He's getting rode—ridden?—until he can't get it up again, and *that's* the important thing.

"I *will* win you over, sweetheart." He cups my hands in his and kisses them, then presses them against his chest. "As long as it takes. I'm patient and persistent. But once you're mine? You're *mine*. I will *never* let anything happen to you. I'll protect you and keep you happy, whatever you need from me."

"Doesn't sound very sadistic and domly," I tease.

He smiles. "Maybe I'm a sensual sadist." His eyes widen. "A Daddy Dom!" I'm reminded of my talk with Amber, and I guess that translates to my face because he quickly adds, "But you can call me Sir or Master, not Daddy. We won't do that."

"Thank fates."

"Provided I don't scare you off by then." I can tell he's joking because of the sexy smile he's wearing, but I spot the fear in his eyes.

Fear I feel, too.

Kind of makes me feel better to know he's just as scared as I am. That this guy who can live forever and easily kill me if he wanted to—and who just gave me the best orgasm I've ever had—is worried that he might not be able to win me over.

"Haven't scared me off yet, buddy."

Chuckling, he pulls me in for a hug, rolling us to our sides so my head's cradled on his arm. If you'd told me a week ago I'd be canoodling with a hunky, fanged DILFy dude who can be on the receiving end of the *Okay, Boomer* game with Jesus freaking Christ, I'd have called you nuts.

Seriously.

Now?

I have to say, I think maybe I could get used to this.

That's when it hits me...

He's a vampire.

—followed by—

3...2...1....

And he's in my apartment.

He freezes. "Am I moving too fast for you?"

"It's spooky that you can do that." I sit up despite my nipples begging to rub against him again.

Against that firm chest of his. I let my fingers play with the buttons on his shirt. Hell, this suit he's wearing, and his shoes, are probably worth more than my 4Runner.

Minus the new tires, obvs.

"The sudden, abject panic in your eyes was a clue," he softly says.

"Sorry."

"Please don't apologize." He sits up. "I had the best night in decades tonight. And I thought last night was fantastic." He smiles. "The night before was pretty wonderful, too."

"Maybe you can actually get past third base tomorrow night."

He tucks a strand of my hair behind my ear. "I wish I could tell you how much I appreciate you giving me this chance."

"You can have anyone you want. Literally. *Why* are you fixated on the *one* woman you have to work your ass off for?"

"Because I want someone who wants me because *they* want me, not just because *I* want them."

This is getting a little too real a little too quickly.

I climb to my feet and kick off the Jimmy Choos, tossing them into my closet.

Then I can wiggle my toes. *Oh, that's better.* "I have to hit the little girl's room. 'Scuse me for just a minute."

"Of course."

After I take care of business, I look at myself in the mirror. My cheeks are flushed—my hair looks good, at least —and the girls are shown off nicely in this dress.

Fuck. I invited *a fricking* vampire *into my* apartment.

After he fingered me on the side of the road.

What the *hell* am I doing? Have I lost all common sense?

I return to find him sitting exactly where I left him. When he looks up at me...

Yeah. He's hot. Hunky.

And sad.

Lonely.

Kinda like me.

A lot like me, in some ways.

I return to sit in front of him on the area rug.

He glances around. "May I ask a stupid question?"

"Because it's a very small apartment, and it's just me. I never have visitors. And I only get what I need because I leave it behind when I bug out, if it won't fit in my car."

He smirks. "*Now* who's psychic?"

I shrug. "You had a 'look'. Call it abject curiosity."

He holds out his hands, wiggling his fingers at me, and I lay mine in his. "Ask me anything," he says.

"Right now, I'm still in the processing stage." He starts massaging my hands. "You're not allowed to kill anyone at the club tomorrow. Even if they flirt with me."

He growls. "Why not?"

"Murder's bad. Lucius forbids it on the premises, unless he's ordered it. Besides, sometimes the tips are better if I pretend to flirt a little. Especially if it's a newer vamp who doesn't yet know I'm immune to their charms."

His growl deepens, and my clit flutters in response. "Yeah, I'll need some of those pencils of yours." But I see the hint of the smirk, the way one corner of his kissable lips is twitching a little.

We start talking again, and *talking*.

And taaalllking.

And, before long, we've totally lost track of time. "When do you need to head back to your hotel?" I ask.

"I'm sure I have plenty of time."

"What time is it?"

"I'm not sure."

That's when I take a look out the windows, at the way the eastern sky is turning deep purple beyond the mountains. "Oh, crap!" I jump up.

"What?"

"You realize you should have been out of here about twenty minutes ago, right?"

He stands. "What? Why? I'm sorry, did I say something wrong? I thought we were having a lovely conversation."

I point at the wall of windows in my apartment. "It's close to dawn. You gotta *go*!"

"So?" He shrugs. "You know what I am now. I'll simply go to sleep. Draw the curtains. I promise, I'll keep my clothes on and my hands to myself. You won't even know I'm here."

"Believe me, I'd love to take you up on that, buuuut got a slight problem."

"What?"

I walk over to my fricking.

Wall.

Of.

Windows.

And hold out my hands. "Ta-da, dumbass. Do you *see* any fricking curtains? Kind of the *point*. I have window film, so people can't see inside them at night, not that there's much chance of that, anyway. But the windows flooding the room with light were a selling point when I signed the lease because I sort of have a problem with the dark."

His brow furrows. "What about your bedroom? We can close the curtains and wrap me in a blanket. I'll be fine. I've done it before, in a pinch."

I stomp my foot and make the same two-handed wave at the rest of the room. "This *is* my bedroom. Murphy bed. It's an *efficiency* apartment. One room, no waiting. *That's* where the 'efficient' part of 'efficiency apartment' comes into play."

His eyes widen as the severity of the problem seems to finally—*finally*—sink in. "Oh, shit!"

"*Exactly* what I've been trying to *tell* you, genius. With traffic, you won't be able to make it back to your hotel in time. Even if you try running, you'll be cutting it dangerously close. Not that I haven't enjoyed our evening—because I have—but I *really* don't want to have to go back to my boss and explain his old friend, guest, and nephew turned into a used piece of charcoal in my fucking. Living. Room. Oh, in a building owned by the Tucson pack Alpha. Who is expecting to ink a *very* lucrative real estate deal with you!"

Now he *finally*—thankfully—looks like he's starting to worry. "What about your bathroom?"

"Has a window. Frosted glass, but still, we're facing east. I don't have any way of blocking the window. For someone as old as you are, you're *really* bad at this vampire stuff, you know that?"

Now his composure cracks. "How can you *not* have *any* curtains?"

"How can you *not* have an app on your phone to tell you the times of sundown and sunrise based on a GPS fix of your current location, and which sets off an alarm to let you know it's close to fricking *sunrise*?"

"They have those?"

O. M. Fricking GEE. I'm losing my shit. The guy's adorable, but how the *hell* can he be so damned old and rich if he's *this* fucking *stupid*?

I guess the old adage of guys getting stupider when they think with the little brain even applies to vamps.

"My closet." I walk over and yank the door open to my large walk-in closet. "*In.*" I turn on the light and grab a T-shirt to sleep in, and clothes to wear for my shift later, so I'm not waiting for Fangster Hunkadoofalus to wake up from his beauty nap before I can start getting ready for work.

I turn, and he's standing in the closet doorway and evaluating it. "Is it light-proof?"

"It will be when I give you a blanket to wrap yourself in

and shove towels under the door so there's no light leaking in that way. It's either this, or you curl up in the cabinet under my kitchen sink. Personally, I think this'll be more comfortable."

"Right." He tucks his hands into his pockets and seems to consider his lack of other options.

"And go use the bathroom. No peeing in my closet."

"Ah. Good idea." He does. When he returns, he's carrying his blazer, leaving him in his vest and shirt.

I still can't get over how he looks like Ianto.

Le sigh.

Why's he got to look so fricking yummy? And in such a delicious way?

Why do I have to feel...*attracted* to him?

I've never felt *attracted* to one of the vamps before, or the shifters. Not like this. I mean, yeah, I banged the cheetah shifter, but he wasn't really even boyfriend material. And, yes, the vamps are fucking hot.

I can think they look hot and not have my lady bits sudsing up like a freaking junior varsity cheerleader car wash.

But Dexter Van Sussex is different.

Why'd he have to be so damned different in such a good way?

I grab the blanket for him and give him a healthy shove. "Inside. You said you're used to roughing it. Think of it like camping."

He turns, holding the blanket. "Other than my unfortunate logistical snafu, how was our second date?"

I start laughing when he smiles. "Dude, I don't know what to think about you." I brush a kiss across his lips. "You need a keeper."

"Interested in the position?" He waggles his eyebrows at me.

"I'm sure I'll be interested in a lot of positions with you, if you keep up the good work with me, and you remember to not burn to ashes."

I step back and grab a couple of towels. While I'm thinking about it, I snag a pair of shorts and a tank top from the closet, to wear before I have to get dressed for work. At least the closet door is on the same wall as the bathroom door, meaning perpendicular to the big fricking wall of windows. By eleven or so, this wall will lie in shadows.

I start to close the door. "Hey, do me a favor."

"Yes?"

"Please text your guys, so they don't think I killed you or something. Let them know what's going on." Left unsaid, in case the worst-case happens and he does die.

When his smile fades, I sense he knows exactly what I mean. "I will." He drops his blazer on the closet floor and leans in for a kiss. "Oh, here." He hands me the key fob to the Audi, his hotel key card, and his wallet. "Please, do me a favor and pick me up a few things for tomorrow night, so I don't have to go back to my room later."

I stare at the items. "You...just handed me your *wallet*."

"Yes, I did." He smirks, toes off his loafers, and starts to unfasten his cuffs so he can roll up his sleeves. Holy *fuck*, that's sexy, watching him do that. "I trust you."

"This is...your *wallet*."

"Yes." His smile widens. "Use the black Amex. It's a corporate card. Buy yourself something pretty, sweetheart. Anything you wish. Dress, shoes, engagement ring, Porsche, a house."

He's smiling, but his eyes have darkened in his intensity.

I smile. "Nice try. Mojoing doesn't work on me, buddy."

"*Dammit*," he mutters. Then he sighs. "Can't blame me for trying."

I chuckle and lean in for yet another kiss. "I'll go after I've slept. Tell them it'll be probably one or two in the afternoon." What I leave unsaid is that I want to stay here this morning and pray my walk-in closet is safe enough.

Because it'll fucking destroy my heart if it's not, and I don't even know when he slipped in there.

Into my heart, that is.

Sneaky, fanged fuck.

He nods. "I will." We stare at each other for a long moment as the sky continues to lighten. "Please, don't panic when I stop responding. I can usually stay up a while after dawn, but eventually, I do succumb and have to sleep."

"Like the dead."

"Yes." He unbuttons his vest. "I'm sorry I miscalculated." He smirks and starts unbuttoning his shirt. "I actually carry a black body bag when I go on road trips, just in case."

"Just in case?"

"It's a heavy, rubber one. Light proof. In case there are any light leaks in my hotel room. Unfortunately, I don't have one in the Audi." He nods to the key fob in my hand. "Please, drive that today."

"You're dying to buy me a new car, aren't you?"

"Duh."

I take a deep breath. I *really* need to close the door. "I did have a good night. Thank you."

"Here's hoping I make it to date number three."

"And a home run." I smile, earning me one in return. This kiss sweetly lingers and is filled with longing.

It'd be so easy to try to blame this on him using his thrall on me, except that's not the case.

He can't.

This is *me*, and *him*, and it's scary as fricking *hell* because it's *real*.

Nothing ever works out for me. Why should this?

Why *can't* this?

I shut the door, make sure it's securely closed, and then stuff towels all along the bottom of the door. I don't even have tape or anything I can run along the doorjamb.

Please let it be enough.

I stand there with my forehead resting against the door. I hear him texting, the little *tic-tic-tic* keyboard sound, the sound of texts being sent and received, and then it goes quiet.

"I told them." It sounds like he's standing right there, on the other side of the door. I mean, *right* there.

"Don't lean on the inside of the door," I warn. "Don't accidentally push it open."

"I'm not."

I lay my hand on the door and I instinctively know his hand is *right* there, opposite mine.

Blinking back tears, I try to focus. I *really* want this to work. A relationship, I mean.

Well, and him hopefully not dying.

I don't know how this is supposed to work, but it's like he gets me. There's no braggadocio, no bullshit posturing, no assholish arrogance on his part.

I *want* to hope things work out between us.

Except I learned a long time ago that I don't get a happily ever after.

"Sleep well, love," he says.

He called me love. "Yeah." I sniffle. "You, too. Sorry it's not better."

"It's better than dying. And it smells like you in here, too, so that's a lovely benefit."

Aww. "What do you want me to bring you to wear?"

"Whatever you select for me. Surprise me. My shower kit's in the bathroom. My phone charger's on the nightstand."

I sit down, leaning against the door. I know he just did the same thing, except for not leaning.

I *know* it.

Our heads are separated by nothing but the wooden door. "Sounds like Robert was blessed to have you in his life."

There's a pause. "I was the blessed one. He brought sunlight into my life. He would stay in bed with me in the morning and hold me. Then he would arise later. He would tell me about his day, sometimes come back to bed and join me after he'd been outside, if he knew I was awake, so I could smell the heat on him. He knew how much I missed sunlight. He always tried to find little ways to bring joy and warmth into my life, any way that he could, to make up for that."

Dammit, my heart's breaking for him. "It sounds like he loved you very much."

"I honestly never knew true, romantic love, until I met him. He fell in love with me honestly. I didn't compel him when we first met—he was instantly attracted to me as a man, not because I made him feel it. I never had to compel him to do anything. *Ever.* Never wanted to, either. I only wish I could have saved him. I feel like I failed him."

"Were you there when he died?"

"I held him in my arms the whole time. Even long after I knew turning him hadn't worked and he wasn't coming back to me. I couldn't let him go. I laid there with him for three days, crying, begging him to return to me. I didn't eat. I slept wrapped around him, in case he awakened. Until I was forced to accept the truth. Then, I dug his grave with my own hands and buried him. I almost sat there and greeted the sun, until I remembered that he wouldn't have wanted me to do that."

Even through the door, I hear his weighty sigh. "I take comfort knowing the last thing he heard was me telling him how much I loved him. And he told me how much he loved me. That if it didn't work, he didn't blame me. That he wanted me to go on and be happy."

When my vision blurs, I realize I'm blinking back tears. "Did he suffer?"

"Not from what I did, no. His body was apparently too weak from the disease, or my blood wasn't powerful enough at that time, or maybe both, for the virus to fully take hold and turn him. I held the disease at bay for years longer than he could have ever survived otherwise. We made love one last time, I fed him again...and then I did it. He simply slipped away. It didn't hurt. I made it feel pleasurable. For him, anyway. It felt like my soul was ripped from my body."

I wipe the tears from my cheeks. "Still say it doesn't sound like you're a sadist. He sounds like he was a very lucky guy."

"Sadism and pleasure and pain and love are not mutually exclusive, sweetheart."

I sniffle again. I feel his grief, just below the surface, still bubbling even this long since. "You've never loved anyone else?"

"I...don't know how you want me to answer that."

My pulse skips. "Honestly."

"It might frighten you."

"Try me."

There's a long pause, and I'm starting to wonder if he fell

asleep when he finally answers. "I didn't think it *was* possible, until I met you."

I close my eyes, willing my pulse to slow because I know he can hear it, hear the way I'm breathing. Hell, he can sense me crying.

"I can't make you any promises, Dex, except that I'll try. I'm scared."

"I know, love. All I ask is a chance."

"I'm trying."

"I know. And I appreciate it." I hear him moving around inside the closet. "I'm going to settle in. Please, try to get some sleep."

"Sleep tight."

"You, too."

I look down and spy a couple of his hairs on my dress. It's silly, but I smile and pluck them off, carrying them over to the windowsill, where I carefully lay them. At least part of him can experience the sun.

The sun hasn't quite peeped over the top of the mountains yet when my cell phone rings.

Amber.

"Hey, chica," I answer. I know why she's calling this insanely early.

"Soooo? How'd things go last night?"

"Long story." I don't want to admit he's in my closet. I know shifters can scent him, but why possibly invite trouble? He has Garrett's permission to be here. That's all that matters. "Was *very* promising. We're getting together again tonight at the club."

"Excellent. Did he upgrade your ride?"

"What do you mean? Besides the tires?"

"No, silly. The Audi."

My face heats. "It's a rental. He asked me to drive it

today." None of that, *technically*, is a lie. "How'd you know about the Audi?"

"I wanted to cook breakfast. Garrett ran out to buy us eggs because I fumbled the dang carton getting it out of the fridge and dropped and broke them all. He saw it parked out there."

Well, scented it, is more likely. He probably picked up Dex's scent in the elevator or lobby and tracked it back to the vehicle. "Things are going well between me and Dex." I remember he's in the closet, and I don't know if he's still awake or not and can hear me. "Anything else about my father?"

Okay, that's playing dirty, distracting her like that, and I know it.

She goes quiet for a moment. "No, sorry. I just *know* he's alive."

Greeting the sunrise is something I've done frequently since living here. I glance down just as the sun peeks over the...well, peaks to the east. As the brilliant orange rays cascade into my apartment and over my skin, my focus is on the hairs.

Which promptly incinerate with soft, audible *poofs* as the light hits them, making me gasp.

"Connie? Are you all right?"

"I-I'm fine, sorry." My pulse pounds. "Just heard a door shut across the hall, and it startled me, that's all. I'm tired." There are two fine lines of ash, barely dust, where the hairs were.

Shhiiit!

"Garrett said, and I quote, 'For a leech, Dexter seems okay. I won't stake him. Yet.'" She giggles.

"Thanks." I blink, but the two lines of ash are still there. "Hey, listen, I'm exhausted, and I need to get to bed. I have errands to do later before work. Please tell Garrett I appreciate him extending an exemption to Dex and his guys for territory access."

"Sure thing, hon. I'm looking forward to meeting him."

"Yeah, he's looking forward to meeting you, too. Maybe we can go out to dinner together one night this week."

She laughs. "*You* wanting to go out to *dinner*? Holy hellballs, he really *is* a good influence on you."

I blink—the ash is still there. "I trust him." That's absolutely the truth. "I've never met anyone like him." I hope he can still hear me. "He hasn't lost his humanity, like so many of them do. He's not interested in doing anything except living his life and getting along. He's a good man with a good heart."

"I know, sweetie," she gently says. "I already told you—I see you two together. Go get some sleep."

"Thanks." I end the call and slowly squat to get a better look at the ash, but just that simple act creates enough of a draft that it blows it away.

Squinting against the sunlight, I stand and turn, staring at my closet door. I don't know what to do with him beyond just getting through today.

He gave me his danged wallet. The key fob to his rental.

His hotel room key.

He trusts me.

He's a vampire, and I'm at a crossroads in my life. I don't want his life endangered because of my crazy shit—including oh, now it looks like my dad's still alive—but I don't know how to *not* be afraid or how to accept this chance that he's freely offering. He literally has everything to lose, including his life.

I have...well, nothing. Just me.

Forcing myself away from the window, I grab my clothes

and head to the bathroom to change and brush my teeth. Unlike after a shift at work, I don't want to take a shower.

I don't want to wash his scent off me.

Once I've changed, I stop by the closet door. "Dex?" I softly call. "Are you all right?"

I hear nothing in reply.

Please let him be okay.

19

E *ilidh*

I SLEEP LIKE SHIT.

My dreams are filled with nightmares. Of Dex bursting into ash in my living room. Of the massive dog-phantom attacking him and rending him into pieces. Of a band of renegade shifters bursting in and staking him while I beg them to leave him alone.

I startle awake several times in terror, gasping for air, my heart pounding.

Around 11:30 a.m. I give up trying to sleep and walk over to the closet. "Dex? How are you doing?"

Nothing.

No, I am *not* tempted to peek. After that little example of what could happen, he'll be lucky if I don't wedge my comfy chair under the doorknob and keep him hostage until it's well past dark, just to be on the safe side. I mean, I'm certain he's plenty strong enough to punch through the door like it's tissue paper, but I don't want to take a risk with his safety.

Oh, and my hair's still black. So, I have that going for me, at least.

I have two texts on my phone, from Dexter's guys John and Mark, making sure I have their room numbers and both their cell numbers, in case I have any questions or can't find something. And they both assure me it's okay to call them and wake them up. They're in the same larger suite Dex is, comprised of several suites behind a main door. Apparently, he has that whole section of the floor to himself.

I reply to both of them and then debate taking a shower. I kind of want to wait until Dex is up.

I can still faintly smell him on me.

Except, I *really* need a shower.

Hell, I can always take another one with him.

I shower quickly and send Dexter a text that I'm going to go run errands, just in case he wakes up. I opt for the shorts and tank top because it's fricking hot as balls. I mean, it *is* Tucson. And I don't want to get my jeans and T-shirt all sweaty and have to do laundry early next week. Plus, I don't like to wear my Club Toxic shirts when I'm not on my way to work.

I wonder what the weather's like in Atlantic City?

Stop. Bad girl. Don't get your hopes up.

I'm already nervous thinking about driving the Audi. After I crank it to get the AC going, I have to slide the seat forward because Dex's legs are *way* fricking longer than mine. Then I need to adjust the steering wheel and all the mirrors. But I have to admit it is kind of fun to have it to—

He can't see himself in the rearview mirror when he looks in it.

That thought punches me in the gut.

I sit there for a moment, hands fisting the steering wheel, just...breathing.

Deep breaths.

Which is why I fucking scream like a girl—*hello*—and nearly piss myself when Garrett raps on the driver's side window with the back of his fingers. He snuck up on me, and that just flat does *not* happen to me, usually.

He's wearing mirrored shades and I can tell he's...concerned.

I finally figure out which button puts the window down. "Um, heeeey, Garrett."

"Hi." He studies me for a moment. "You all right?"

"Yeah. Please take your glasses off. You know that weirds me out."

He chuffs the way wolves do, but he takes them off. Yep, he's looking at my neck and arms.

"He hasn't bit me, Garrett. We haven't even had sex. Hell, he hasn't made it past third base yet."

He scowls. "Why not? What the hell's wrong with him?"

"Nothing! We just...got distracted last night talking and ran out of time."

"Ran out of ti—*ohhh*."

"Yeah. He turns into a pumpkin. Killer curfew."

Literally.

He leans against the side of the car, bracing his bare forearm against the top of the door, and I know *exactly* what he's doing.

If he didn't think people would look at him weird, he'd be rubbing himself all over the car and then would probably *literally* piss on the tires.

It's a wolf thing.

And they know vampires can scent them, so he wants to make a statement.

Add one car wash to my fricking list of things to do...

"So, funny thing, Connie." He levels his gaze at me and, while he's not even close to shifting, it's like I can *see* his dang wolf, right *there*, shimmering near the surface. "I know Dexter walked into the building and up to your apartment with you, but I didn't scent a second trail leaving."

I stare at him, and he waits me out.

Minutes tick by.

He's good at this Alpha shit. I obviously crack first. "What do you want me to say?" I finally ask.

"I want you to tell me where he is."

My pulse spikes. "Why?" Mentally, I'm already running through a list of Lucius' human guys I can call who might stand a chance helping me hold the shifters off, and—

He takes a deep breath and slowly lets it out, like he's trying to stay patient. "I'm *not* going to hurt him. We have *shifters* living in the building, and maybe not all of them have gotten the message yet. I don't want anyone freaking out."

"Why should they freak out? He can't enter an apartment if he's not invited."

"Work with me here, *please*? I'll have one of my guys stand guard outside your door while you're gone. Because he's in your freaking *closet*, isn't he? Your apartment is an east-facing efficiency apartment. That's not exactly secure, and frankly, the pack stands to make a lot of damn money off him. I'd kinda like to keep him alive."

"Oh."

"Yeah, oh. Can I put my glasses back on now? It's bright out here."

"Sure. Sorry." I release the steering wheel and shake out my hands. "We literally sat there talking on my fuzzy pink rug and lost track of time." I think about the pain and loss and grief in his voice as he told me about his love. "He's a good guy."

He smiles and waves at a couple who park a few spots away, waits for them to head inside, then glances around. He ducks his head into the window and drops his voice to a whisper.

"I *know*, Connie. I'm not happy about this weird little business merger, except Amber says it's what has to happen for the good of everyone. I might not trust leeches, but I trust *her*. And she says we can trust him. Because of you, if nothing else. So, I'll put a guy in front of your door."

"He won't go inside?"

"No, he won't go inside, I swear. He'll also make sure no one else does until you return. But word of advice? *Please* don't make this a regular occurrence, okay? Fuck him here, if you want, but have daytime sleepovers at his place or at Club Toxic. I don't want people freaked out. And make sure Lucius knows and passes the word that it's a special, *conditional* exemption for Dexter and his two men *only*. It's *not* a new free pass for everyone."

"I will. Thank you."

He nods and pats the roof of the Audi. "You look good in this. Should have him buy you one of these. That 4Runner of yours is a death trap."

"It is not, and you know it. Your guy did the work on it and said it's in great shape now."

He grins. "Van Sussex is rich. He should buy you pretty things. He can afford it."

I roll my eyes. "Gotta go, Garrett. Thank you for looking out for me."

He pats the roof again, in a different spot. *Fricking hell.* Like he thinks I don't know what he's doing. "Well, you're pack, sort of. Adopted. You ever get tired of working for that leech, I'll put you in Eclipse, or at Fight Club. We could use someone like you full time. Management, even."

I think about my mom, how she sometimes fought. How the smells in Fight Club are very much what she smelled like sometimes when she came home from a fight, bruised and sore, but usually having made rent money in just one night's fight.

How I *hated* that she was forced to do that for us.

For *me*.

Because she had to raise *me*.

I think I instinctively knew the reason we were on the run—why I couldn't go to regular school—was because of *me*.

"I don't know if I could work at Fight Club," I quietly say.

He cocks his head. "I-I'm sorry, hon. I didn't mean to hit a nerve."

"No, I know. It's...a long story." I force a smile I know doesn't fool him.

But he doesn't move. "Tell me the truth—do you think he's the one?"

"I don't know. I'd like him to be. But I also don't want to endanger his life."

"I told you—"

"I meant because of me and my...shit. What happens the day that *thing* comes back, huh?"

"We stand shoulder to shoulder *with* him and fight it *for* you," he says, his voice full of certainty. "*That's* what we do."

"I don't know if it's something that *can* be fought."

"Maybe it's time for you to stop running and find out."

"But I don't want to find out at the expense of *anyone's* life—shifter or vampire or human."

He grumbles some. I can tell he wants to argue this point with me, and I *get* it. I appreciate it—I *do*. But he's already conflicted enough. If it was up to him, the shifters would wipe out all the vampires.

I *get* it.

I also understand why the vampires do their thing. Some of them are pretty shitty, some are great, and most are average. Like shifters.

Like humans. I mean, humans can be *massively* shitty to each other.

But, hey, it's the *vampires* the shifters will call on to wipe human minds, so they don't have to freaking *kill* them because of their bullshit secrecy codes, sooo...

Who's the "worst" one of the two? Well, three, counting humans.

It's a draw.

"Be safe, Connie." He steps back and pats the side of the Audi—*motherfucker*—and smiles. "Let him buy you stuff. You deserve it." He strides back toward the building and is already pulling his cell out.

It's tempting to race back inside, but I have to trust Garrett. He's a wolf of his word.

Besides, he's a fricking wolf. He could practically walk through my door and rip the closet open before I could even get halfway up the stairs.

I roll the window up, make a final check of the mirrors and everything, and fasten my seat belt.

This will be a *long* freaking afternoon.

20

E *ilidh*

THE FIRST STOP I make is at a full-service car wash, except I pay for it myself with cash.

I mean, *seriously*. Garrett did everything but drop his jeans and rub his junk on the Audi.

Relatively speaking.

Once the car is de-wolfed, I head to the hotel. I have Dex's wallet in my purse. I bypass valet parking and self-park in the lot. When I head inside, I fight the urge to run.

This isn't a walk of shame.

There's nothing wrong with what I'm doing.

Hell, the people here don't even know Dex is a vampire. They don't know about shifters or vampires, unless they're part of either world. They're clueless humans who go about their lives happily unaware of the danger living among them.

They don't know I'm attracted to Dexter in a way I've never felt about anyone before, and all the conflicting feelings I can't process.

I'm sweating fricking bullets as I ride the elevator up to his floor and then get my bearings. The main suite door opens with the key, and I head down the hall. At his room door, I swipe the key, and the lock turns green and clicks open.

Okay, here we go.

The suite is still and dark, except for a table lamp in the living room that's on. The air smells like him.

I close the door behind me and stand there with my eyes closed, deeply inhaling.

No, I can't ignore the way my soul keens for him. The way my body longs for him.

I think about how it felt being carried up the mountain by him.

The way he kisses.

The sexy things he did to me, and we were both still fully clothed.

The grief in his voice as he told me about Robert.

These men are, around others, stoic and strong and seemingly invincible.

Except in daylight.

That's why they have to be such fucking bastards sometimes, or at the very least tend to come off as massively cold assholes. Because they can't afford to show weakness. They're vulnerable in the daylight, and have to make others fear them enough to avoid them.

But they're even more vulnerable when they love.

Being in Lucius' inner circle allows me access few others get, humans or vampires. I've been lucky enough to see Lucius with Selene in private. He would sacrifice himself without hesitation to protect her. He loves her with everything he is and has. She is his biggest weakness. I've seen other vampires pair off and find forever love and have the same reaction.

Wolves mate for life, when they find and mark their true mate. The wolf who marks their mate will forever follow their mate and try to protect them, achingly long to be with them if circumstances force them apart.

Can never love another. And the one who's marked will forever bear the scent of that wolf in them, meaning no other wolves will touch them.

The wolves and vampires really aren't that different, when you get right down to it. Different sides of the same coin.

I know I can't stand here all day and should get moving. Even though I've been—*ha ha*—invited in here, I feel like I'm an interloper in Dex's private albeit temporary domain.

I walk into the bedroom. The small mini fridge must be his personal one because it doesn't look like the one out in the small kitchenette, and it's plugged into an extension cord.

Steeling myself, I open it. Yep, full of bags of blood. There are also some of those freezer packs in the, you know, freezer portion. And a soft-sided cooler sitting on top of it. So, I grab it and the freezer packs and pack two bags of blood.

Thinking about it, I add two more bags of blood. Hell, might as well. I don't know how many he'll need. Better to have extra he can store in my fridge.

On to the bathroom, where I find his shower kit and grab everything I can think of that he might need, including checking the shower for anything he left in there.

His clothes are actually unpacked—into the dresser and closet.

Really? I mean...*wow*. I don't think I've ever done that. I've used a hotel closet before, but never unpacked my suitcases into the dresser, even when I've stayed in one for more than a few days.

I open the closet and find several suits hanging in there.

Rawr. Helloooo, Sweetie.

I most *def* have a suit fetish.

Then I see he also brought a couple pairs of jeans, and a hunky pair of black leather harness motorcycle boots. *Sploosh.*

Fuck.

Me.

I grab a pair of jeans, the boots, socks for the boots, and now to decide what shirt. Henley, or button-up?

Hmm. Decisions, decisions.

I think about Lucius' men, and I opt for both. He can put the Henley on later. But a button-up shirt and a vest to start the evening.

Ohhh, yeah.

And he wears boxer briefs that probably make his ass look sexy as fuck.

Nom!

Two pairs go into the pile, along with a black leather belt that matches the boots. Grabbing his charger cord from the nightstand, I pause and press my face into his pillow and deeply inhale, nearly bursting into tears as his scent fills my lungs.

Yeah, I've got it bad for Fangster Hunkadoofalus.

Please let him be okay!

I find a carryon and pack everything in it except the cooler full of blood bags and the button-up and vest. The latter two items I tuck into his zippered garment bag that I located in his closet.

Where I also spot a plastic storage tub on the floor, tucked into the back. I missed it there earlier.

Opening it, I find supplies—rolls of duct tape, rolls of wide, blue painter's tape, a couple of tarps, and...

A body bag.

I grab the painter's tape, a tarp, and the body bag. It's a little after-the-fact, but maybe they'll come in handy.

If I'm going to have a pet vampire—or, rather, be the pet of a vampire—I need to stay prepared. I won't get caught off-guard again.

I stow them in the carryon and head out, making sure both his room door and the outer suite door are pulled tightly shut behind me.

ONCE I'M BACK in the Audi, I text both John and Mark and let them know mission accomplished. Then I stop by the grocery store to grab a couple of things for us for dinner. Back at my apartment building, I remember to slide the seat all the way back, so Dexter doesn't get kneecapped when he drives it next. Somehow, I manage to carry everything inside in one trip, although my heart's in my throat when the elevator doors slide open on my floor.

I spot one of Garret's men, Cairo—"*It's KAY-roh, like the syrup,*" he'll tell you—by my apartment door, leaning against the wall, his cell phone in hand and looking like he's playing a game on it or something.

When he sees me, he pushes away from the wall, stows his phone in his back pocket, and covers the distance in several quick strides before I'm even all the way out of the elevator. When he reaches to take things from me to carry them for me, I let him.

"Hey, Cairo," I nervously say.

He nods. "Hey, Connie." He lives in the building, too. He's one of Garrett's cousins or something, a wolf shifter, and just moved to Tucson not too long ago. Single and hunky, I've had some pleasant interactions with him. Last time, he tried to offer to take me out to lunch. That was a few weeks ago, and I almost said yes.

I wish I had, now.

Or, do I?

I don't know.

I notice he starts to reach for the cooler with the blood in it, then apparently realizes what it is and bypasses that, letting me carry it.

I drop my voice to barely a whisper, knowing the wolf can hear me as we walk to my door. "Thank you for this. I'm sorry."

He tersely nods. "Boss said it's okay, but if you want my opinion? Don't let it happen again." He tips his head down the hall. "Johnsons in the last apartment down there have three pups, you know."

My stomach sinks. They're a super nice family, a wolf shifter family. I've babysat for them before when their usual shifter sitter couldn't make it. "Are they upset?" I fit the key in the lock to open the door.

He snorts. "They ain't happy. Pretty freaked out, if you ask me. Alpha talked to them, but my advice would be to keep this on the down-low. I would also suggest getting him out of here as soon as possible this evening."

Shit. My life's impacting others in a negative way. Exactly what I *didn't* want to happen. "I'm sorry. We literally lost track of time. I couldn't exactly stash him in a stairwell or something. I swear, he would *never* harm someone here, or an innocent anywhere else, either. He's not like other vampires. I will put my own reputation on the line to vouch for him."

Funny how I went from not sticking my neck out to throwing myself in front of him as a *literal* human shield in under twenty-four hours.

Cairo sets the things he carried for me just inside my apartment door without stepping inside. "Alpha's taking a big risk by not throwing you and him out of here, Connie. I hope you know what you're doing."

So do I.

There's barely constrained anger, and resentment, and maybe even a tinge of grief in his energy as he walks away.

A missed opportunity there, I'm certain. I'd had paid errands to run that afternoon for Theophilus, and always meant to take Cairo up on his rain check, but never got around to it.

I hope I didn't screw up.

As I step inside and close and lock my apartment door, I take a deep breath.

Please let my chosen path be the right one.

I QUICKLY UNPACK EVERYTHING—GROCERIES and blood into the fridge, his shower kit on my bathroom counter, and I hang his garment bag on my shower curtain rod, because, well, *duh.*

I'd left my bed open earlier, so I set his other things on that. Digging out the painter's tape, I quickly run a strip of it around the door seam and hope this isn't too little too late.

Please *don't let it be too little too late.*

There are still several hours between now and dark. I'm not even sure what's "safe" dark for him. I mean, does it have to be twilight? Is dusk okay? Is there some sort of light meter for safe levels?

Is there a freaking *app* for that?

Come *on*, there has to be some bored, rich vamp app dev somewhere who knows *all* the programming languages—because of *course* they would—who could develop something like that.

Right?

I grab my phone and send Dexter a text, deleting and typing probably a dozen or more times before I finally settle on something I hope isn't totally inane.

I'M BACK. *I'll keep my phone close.*

AS THE HOURS TICK BY, I fight the urge to pace. Every noise out in the hall makes me jump, and I double and triple and quadruple check my deadbolt and lock and chain, staring through the fish-eye viewfinder in the door to make sure there's not an angry horde outside my door.

I drag the comfy chair in front of the door.

Again, I *know* it won't stop a shifter, but it makes me feel a little better.

During this wait, my mind fucks with me, too. It tells me what a fucking dumbass I am to put my neck on the line for a vampire I've only known a short amount of time.

Tries to convince me that vampires are masters of manipulation. Sure, he can't pull me into his thrall with his powers, but maybe he's still trying to control me in more mundane ways.

I wouldn't be the first woman to fall for a sob story spun by a hunky guy, or mistake really great sex for something more than that. He's lived a *long* freaking time. Plenty of time to learn exactly what to say, to hone the sob story, to refine the details for maximum effect with minimum effort. Maybe he's a sociopath, or a psychopath, or an emotional sadist.

Even trying to convince myself Lucius vouching for him is a good thing leads me down darker paths.

I've witnessed firsthand what Lucius and other vampires can do to others, not to mention each other. As long as his human staff don't betray him—meaning try to kill him or get him killed—Lucius honestly treats them like anyone else would. I'm truly *not* afraid of him, because he could have killed me at any time and hasn't. I'm more valuable to him alive than dead. Most of the vampires who know me are wary of me. Because besides my protection from Lucius and Selene, while they could easily kill me, they know that unless they sneak up on me, I'll probably put a hurting on them in the process, and that juice just ain't worth the squeeze.

Literally.

Eh, juice meaning blood, obvs.

Yeah, being honest with myself, it's another reason if I'm not at work at night I like to be home, in my apartment.

Where vampires can't get in unless I invite them, and sonofabitch, looky what I freaking did?

I don't want to die, but I'm not afraid of it, either. Living's a pain in the ass. Seriously.

Except...

Amber.

What if my father's alive?

What if he's out there?

Why didn't he search for us?

Do I really *want* to find him?

I draw in shaky breaths, but I've done such a mindfuck on myself over the past several hours that I don't even *know* what I want anymore. If I choose Dexter and effectively isolate myself from the shifters, what then? I'll be ostracized if shit goes south.

How can I stay neutral if I'm getting a dose of Vitamin D —for *Dick*—from Dexter every night?

The answer, for those of you still uncertain—I *can't*. I won't be allowed to be neutral at that point. It's impossible.

I'll lose the trust of the Tucson pack and other shifters, because I'll have made my coffin and will be told it's time for me to lie in it.

I've been alone for nearly twenty years. On my own.

Never let anyone in.

Survival mode.

Never allowed myself to think of anywhere as "home," because I knew I could be bugging out the next day.

Tucson is the first place I was *really* starting to hope could be that home for me. Where it felt like my terrified roots were *finally* starting to tentatively spread out a little.

I have a small photo album, one of those single-photos to a page size. Those are all the photos I have of Mom and me together because back then, she'd always have the cheapest cell phone possible, usually without a camera, or it had a crappy camera.

One of my favorites was taken when I was sixteen, and we were at a park with neighbors. The mom of that family took it with her phone and printed it out and gave us a copy. Mom looked tired but happy. My hair was reddish blonde then, matching hers, and you can see how much we look alike with our smiles. We were both wearing tank tops because, luckily, we were the same size and could share clothes.

It was a good day. One of the last truly "good" days I can remember, where my soul actually felt *lighter*, before she died the next year.

I drop the album on the bed and hurry to the bathroom, where I shut myself inside, turn on the sink in case Dexter's listening, and softly cry.

I'M HOPING the fact that I don't smell any smoke or charbroiled Dexter is a good sign. At 6:18, I'm obsessively trying to vacuum up the nonexistent dust on my windowsill—

ash

—with the Dustbuster—

ash from his hair because he's a

—when I hear a noise—

fricking vampire and might be dead-dead now because of me

—that startles me.

Wheeling around, I see the closet door open as the blue painter's tape gives way with a startled *buuurrrrp* that yanks a hysterical bray of laughter from me.

I step toward the closet and belatedly realize I'm holding the Dustbuster out in front of me.

Dexter's alive and apparently uncharred, thank fates, sitting there with the blanket down around his armpits.

One hunky eyebrow slides up. "What is that?" He nods toward my hand.

"Um, it's a Dustbuster."

He blinks. "A vacuum cleaner?"

"Yeah. Duh." I resort to snark when I'm nervous, and I

know it. Defense mechanism. I can't help it. Snark, and sharp number-two pencils.

"And were you going to attack me with it? Your broom handle would make a far better improvised stake."

I'm so wound up I totally ignore the handsome smirk on his face and realize I'm an idiot to think I could ever have happiness, rich hunky vamp or not. "I wasn't going to attack you with it, asshole." Yes, I know he's trying to deflect with humor because he probably senses how stressed and upset I am.

"Then what were you doing?"

I feel my face redden and, for the first time in my dealings with vampires, I outright lie to one. "I wasn't sure what I'd find when I opened the door. Don't I get brownie points for *not* opening the door early?"

He studies me for a moment. I know *he* knows I just lied. "You wanted it in case I burned up." He states it in an annoyingly amused tone.

"Hey, I have a pair of Jimmy Choos in there, jerkface. They're worth a lot of damn money to have your icky, ashy self dusted all over them, all right?"

"I'm flattered." He pulls the blanket off. At some point, he shed his vest, and his shirt's unbuttoned, exposing his firm, hunky chest and abs. He's also barefoot, which is unexpectedly sexy and I don't know why. "You could have bought new ones with my credit cards, though." He smiles. "I wouldn't have minded you modeling them for me. Or did you buy some?" His smile widens.

I step back, ignoring his last comment. "Yeah, well, they're not only the best pair of shoes I own, they're probably the most expensive thing I own. Except the tires on my 4Runner, thanks."

His gaze pointedly drops to where the ring hangs on its silver chain under my shirt.

"That doesn't count," I quietly say.

He stands, unfolding his body and reminding me how tall he is. I take a step back, still brandishing the Dustbuster between us. I don't know what I expect to do with it.

"Why on earth doesn't it count?" He starts to fold the blanket with precision. "Is it not far more precious than those 'chew shoes'?"

"They're Jimmy Choos, and you damn well know it." I hate that he's trying to be dryly witty and charming. "Because I don't own...*it*." I take a breath. "I sometimes feel like it owns *me*." Holy *hell*, why did I admit that? The things he does to me.

"Did you ever stop to think perhaps you should rid yourself of it?"

"Why?" One hand protectively flies up to cover it through my shirt while I step back and hold the Dustbuster out in front of me as menacingly as possible.

"Because perhaps it's how you're being tracked."

"What? It's not a damned GPS. It's a ring. It's a very old ring that belonged to my father. It's all I have left of him. I'm not getting rid of it. My mom probably died trying to protect this ring."

He finishes folding the blanket, and I hate that he gives me a look that's three parts pity and one part smoldering, sexy heat.

Not the bad kind of smoldering, either.

"I've been thinking," he says. "If it's a magickal artifact, it could very well be a supernatural GPS, in a manner of speaking."

I stare at him. "Go on. Pull the other one."

He holds out the blanket, and I finally take it from him

with the hand not brandishing the Dustbuster, being careful not to touch him when I do.

"I'm serious." He glances at the windows. "Don't you have to be at work?"

"I do." I'd been growing increasingly worried about that, too, adding to all my stress. "I need a shower. Your stuff's here. I'll text Theophilus that I'm running late."

He studies me for a long and uncomfortable moment. "What happened, Eilidh?" he softly asks. The concern in his tone nearly undoes me.

"Nothing." Ooh, second lie in under five minutes. I'm on a roll. "I should get ready and head out."

"Aren't we riding together?"

"I'll drive, thanks. That way, you're not stuck there if you decide you want to leave and return to your hotel."

I guess in my head I've already decided no, not doing this tonight. Or...ever.

Even though I reeeally want to do this.

Wanted to.

Before the reality of the repercussions started sinking in.

He draws in what sounds like one of those annoying kinds of breaths people take when they're trying to stay patient. "I have a car. I can drive you. If you're really in danger, wouldn't it make sense to let me take you to work? I can protect you."

"How do I know I'm not in danger from *you*?"

"That would be bad form, wouldn't it?" He smirks. "To harm the woman who allowed me to hide in her closet?" I sense he wants to say more, but he's treading lightly.

I finally turn, so I can put the Dustbuster and blanket away. "I can't wait to tell Lucius you came out of the closet."

"Yes, well, I can see where that would be amusing."

21

D*exter*

I STEP into the bathroom to relieve myself and to have a moment alone to think while I do.

Something happened while I was asleep. Maybe I can't thrall Eilidh, but she just lied to me twice, and I don't understand why.

She *never* lies. Mostly because she's an honest person, according to Lucius, but also because she knows it's pointless to lie to a vampire or a shifter. We can hear the way a human's pulse spikes, how their breathing changes when they lie. We can practically *taste* a lie.

She *knows* this.

Meaning *something* happened, and I need to find out what. Just the fact that she's shoved her chair in front of the apartment's door tells me something happened while I was asleep.

Then there's the fact that I heard her crying in the bathroom earlier. It took everything in me not to burst through the closet door to find out who'd upset her, so I could rip their throat out.

Only reminding myself that me dying wouldn't help her in the least kept me in place.

I sense a darkening dread within her far beyond mere trepidation. I'm afraid if I don't get to the bottom of this *right* now, I might not get another chance with her. That she's quickly clamping down, trying to rebuild her mental and emotional defenses against me, shutting me out.

Meaning I also can't simply grab her and spank the truth out of her, which is absolutely what I'd be doing right now if I'd already negotiated a relationship with her.

When I emerge from the bathroom, I'm convinced that this is something we need to settle without delay. "I'm going to call Lucius."

She flinches. "Why?"

"Because I need to tell him something." I pull out my phone and dial Lucius' number as I watch her.

He picks up almost immediately. "Dexter, nephew. How are you?"

"I'm fine, but I seem to have absconded with your club's assistant manager. We're running a bit late. It's totally my fault for losing track of time, and I apologize, but can I get Connie to work later than usual? Or will that put you in a bind? I know it's Friday night and you'll be busy."

Her eyes widen as she realizes what I'm doing, and she starts making hand gestures, trying to stop me. I smile and turn away from her as she circles me and stays in my field of vision, gently warding her off with one hand as I hold my phone in the other.

"I think we can get through opening just fine," he says.

"We always overstaff Fridays and Saturdays. Plus, Selene and I will be there. Will you be coming with her, then?"

"Yes, I was hoping I could impose on you and use that suite again tonight and through tomorrow night?"

"Oh, absolutely. That'll be fine. I'll tell Theophilus and the staff. Things are going well between you, I take it?"

"I believe so."

"And last night's meeting with Garrett Green?"

"I'm satisfied, and I'll fill you in later, at the club."

"Excellent. Shall we expect you before ten?"

"Yes, that should be doable. I'll drive her. May I park in her spot? I have a rental, an Audi SUV."

"Absolutely. So glad things are working out."

"Me, too."

As I hang up, I see her fury building, like a beautiful storm billowing in off the Atlantic. She plants her hands on her hips. "You had no right to do that!"

"I believe I did." I refuse to rise to the bait. Instead, I slip my phone into my pocket and stand there, hands in my pockets, staring down at her for a long moment. "Why did you just lie to me *twice*, Eilidh? If I already had a negotiated relationship with you, lying to me—*twice*—would earn you a very hard spanking over my lap. A spanking which *certainly* would *not* be conducted for your enjoyment but to punish you."

That's an extremely calculated risk on my part. I know it could send her running, and I'd be forced to chase and rebuild her trust from scratch.

But I hear a dry *click* as she nervously swallows, her gorgeous throat working, and the way her pulse spikes. A beautiful flush rises in her chest and cheeks.

Therefore, I stand, waiting, coolly staring down at her

with a practiced expression I've used on plenty of submissives before.

She finally cracks, her gaze dropping. "This can't work."

Her strained whisper isn't one of someone convinced of that. More, it's the tone of someone who very much *wants* this to work, yet who feels terrified it won't due to past events in their life.

Someone conditioned by circumstance to expect no good thing can ever be theirs.

It breaks my heart.

"It *can*, sweetheart. What I can't do to directly protect you myself, I can buy that protection. I'll put people in place to run the Tucson property, and you and I will live anywhere you wish. We can move every day, if you want. I am *that* wealthy. There is nothing I cannot give to or do for you, if you'll simply *let* me."

She gazes up at me through her lashes. "Garrett knows you spent the day here."

"So? He gave me an exemption to be here."

"It freaked out some people in the building. Including a shifter family on this floor. They have young pups, and I sometimes babysit for them."

Ahh. This sounds like the truth. "Is that why you moved the chair in front of the door? You were worried someone might try to break in and hurt me?"

"Garrett caught me downstairs when I was leaving to get your things. He had one of his guys stand guard outside the apartment while I was gone. He didn't want anyone trying to break in."

I make a mental note to both thank and apologize to Garrett for the imposition. "I'm sorry, sweetheart. We'll spend days at the club or at my hotel, your choice. Until you let me buy you a house." But that's only part of it, I sense.

"What else happened?" Because there *has* to be more. She's still too upset.

Her gaze drops again. I risk stepping in close, so I can tip her chin with one finger, until she's looking up at me. "Please tell me."

Tears well in her eyes, breaking my heart and shattering it to absolute pieces. "I found a couple of your hairs on my dress after you were in the closet. I put them on the windowsill. I thought... I thought at least you could have that little bit of sunlight..." Her voice chokes.

And *now* everything makes sense—why there was a frantic air to her actions when I emerged. Why I'd heard her moving around the tiny, spotless apartment, and why I heard her obsessively vacuuming for the past thirty minutes while I was texting with Mark and John, along with handling a few work e-mails on my phone while I still had a charge. I was waiting for John to give me the all-clear to emerge.

"Oh, sweetheart." I fold her into my arms as she starts sobbing. Truth be told, tears prickle my eyes, too. "Robert used to do the same thing. He would try various 'remedies' on me and then test them out like that. He hoped beyond hope one day to see them remain intact past dawn." I gently rock her in my embrace as she cries, and I bury my face in her hair while breathing her intoxicating scent.

Did I think she barely had a scent before?

No, now I could easily recognize her scent even amongst a sea of sweaty, unwashed, weekend music festival goers high on stinky weed and bathing in patchouli. "I see you found my supply bin in the closet. I do appreciate the tape."

"You're in danger with me," she chokes out. "How does this even *work*? What if I don't ever want to be turned? So, you just live with me and watch me grow old and die one day, and I break your heart again? I can't do that to you."

"Love, that is *my* choice, and one that I make without hesitation or reservation when it comes to you." I rub my cheek against the top of her head. I desperately want to turn her thoughts away from that darkness. "I'm curious to see what I'm wearing tonight."

She tips her head back and meets my gaze, my attempt to cajole her with a little humor falling pitifully flat. I can't help cupping her cheeks in my hands, so I can brush her tears away with my thumbs.

"I will *not* rush you. Tonight, tomorrow, next year, ten years from now—I will be *right* here, waiting, hoping. But I will *not* walk away from you or allow you to let fear make this decision for you. I am stronger than anything that will ever threaten you. It is *my* decision to fight for you. We *will* figure out what it is, and we'll take care of it *together*."

She nods, and I brush a kiss across her lips.

"Good girl. Let's take a shower, and you will need some food before we leave, and I'll have to feed."

"I brought four bags of blood for you. I hope that was enough."

"More than, thank you." I don't add that I can drink more at the club later, if I'm still hungry.

I turn to retrieve my things from the closet and peel the remaining tape off the doorframe for her when I spot the open photo album on her bed. I pause, studying it. "Love, is this your mother?"

She glances over. "Yeah. That was me and Mom when I was sixteen."

"May I?"

She nods.

I pick up the album, my gaze drawn not to how much

they look alike, with the same hair and the same beautiful smiles, but to the faint marks on the top of her mother's left shoulder. Very faint, near the curve of her neck, visible thanks to the tank top.

"She was beautiful," I honestly say. "And you look so much like her."

"Mom always said I have Dad's eyes."

Interesting. Violet eyes are rare in humans, and they are never the brilliant, clear color of Eilidh's. If her father had the same color eyes...

If I didn't know any better, I'd say the mark on her mother's shoulder was a mating mark. "Did your mother ever have another husband, or boyfriend, or anyone like that in her life?"

She shakes her head. "Never even dated. Even when I was older and told her she should try going out and meeting guys. She loved Dad too much. I honestly think if it hadn't been for me, she might have given up on life. Those first years were really rough. Countless times, I remember hearing her cry at night, when she thought I was asleep."

Ahhh.

My sweet Eilidh's enigma grows even more complex.

When she steps into the bathroom, I pull out my phone and snap two photos of that picture, one at regular size and one zoomed in on the marks. They don't look exactly like a wolf's mark, but it can't be anything *but* a mating mark. I'd stake my life on it.

Literally.

By the time she emerges from the bathroom with my garment bag, I'm peeling the tape from around the closet door. Then I retrieve my blazer, vest, shoes, and socks from the closet.

She shows me what she selected for me to wear and I can't help but smile. "Jeans and boots, hmm?"

"I hope that was okay."

"It's brilliant, love. I'll wear whatever makes you happy."

It feels damned perfect, calling her that. *Love.*

Unless she asks me not to, I will.

I plug my nearly dead phone into its charger and then gently tug Eilidh into my arms again. "Don't forget to pack for tonight. If you still wish to stay with me, that is."

Her pulse thrums in a delicious flutter of need and desire that confirms this is the truth, even if she is scared. "I do."

"Even if all we do is snuggle and watch movies and talk," I add. "If you would rather shower alone, I understand and will not take offense."

It's adorable, the way she bites on her lower lip as she stares up at me. Her fingers play with the front placket on my shirt, fingering the buttons and stitching before lightly brushing over my bare abs. "I'd like to shower together."

"*You* set the pace of this."

She nods, then looks up again. "Would you really spank me for lying?"

"Absolutely, I would. I still might. I reserve the right to give you a punishment spanking for that. You do *not* lie to me. Ever. I will *never* lie to you. In the future, be advised lying to me *will* earn you a spanking."

She blushes again. "I'm sorry I lied."

"You even knew I'd know."

"Yeah."

I tuck her hair behind her ears and cradle her face in my hands. "Love, I am the *one* person you never need lie to. I'll always be honest with you. Trust flows both ways, and I need the truth from you, even if you think it'll hurt me."

She bounces up on her toes and kisses me, her arms wrapping around me. I linger, savoring the sweet taste of her.

Please, don't let me fuck this up.

Her lashes flutter. "How about that shower?"

"Sounds great."

I swear I had honorable intentions.

I really, truly did.

Except when we reach the bathroom, she grabs me by the front of my shirt and pulls me in for another kiss that heats up...

Fast.

A supernova hits a fuel tanker leaking gasoline all over a dynamite factory kind of fast *fast.*

She backs me against the wall and, as we kiss, she shoves my shirt down and off my shoulders. I shrug out of it and discard it while she's already working on my belt and slacks.

She's wearing a tank top and shorts, and her hair's still that lovely shade of black. I cup the back of her head to take control of our kiss, or she won't end up at work tonight, and I'll be spending another night in her closet rather than leave her.

Because if this woman takes a leap of faith with me, I'm damned sure going to catch her.

Every time.

22

D *exter*

I SLOW DOWN OUR KISS—I know, I *know*. But I'm a gentleman.

Except being a gentleman still gets me stripped to my boxer briefs with a raging hardon that I can't disguise, and I'm trying to help Eilidh out of her clothes.

Her violet eyes darken into gorgeous, sparkling nebulas I'd love to spend eternity swimming through. Spending all day today surrounded by her scent...

Despite the circumstances, I think today was the deepest, soundest sleep I've had in what feels like forever. It felt like being hugged by her while the darkness and oblivion took me. I didn't have any nightmares.

For once, I awoke feeling refreshed instead of resigned.

I haven't slept with anyone—I mean, gone to *sleep* with anyone—since I lost Robert.

There's never been someone I trusted enough or felt even remotely like sharing my bed with in such an intimate way.

Sex with someone? Sure.

Spank them? Eat their pussy? Tie them up? Feed from them?

Yeah.

Curl up next to them when I'm forced to succumb to the sun's powers every day and allow them to hold me?

To see me at my weakest?

To make myself vulnerable to them?

My sweet Robert was the last. It doesn't matter that I could have easily compelled anyone else to behave themselves while I slept. I never had to compel my sweet boy to love me or to hold my secrets and carefully tend my trust.

Never.

I don't want a partner forced to comply.

I want one I know does it out of pure desire, of love.

God, my life's pathetic, when I look back on it.

I peel Eilidh's top off over her head, and then we're racing to finish stripping. She's gorgeous, her beautiful, rounded curves no longer hidden from my hungry gaze. I'm tempted to cup her breasts and run my tongue over her dusky, pebbled nipples, but first I want as much of her flesh pressed against mine as I can feel.

Her warmth.

My mouth crashes over hers again, hunger rolling through me. Thirst.

Not for blood, or wine, or water, but for *her*.

I'm *starving* for the way her hands stroke my body, the way her curves fit against me, the way my cold, still heart struggles to beat in time with hers.

I'm famished, and she's my endless, bountiful feast.

When her fingers close around my cock, I moan into her mouth, practically a roar, making her flinch.

I cup her ass with my other hand and pull her body tight against mine. "Anytime I'm too much for you," I rumble against her lips, "anytime you need me to stop or slow down, whether it's in play, or in bed, or even in a deep conversation about us, you tell me *red* or *yellow*."

Her eyes are hooded, pupils large, lips sweetly swollen and red already from our kisses. "What if I don't want you to stop?"

"Then you tell me *green*, baby."

Her fingers tighten around my cock and she slowly slides her hand down my shaft, easing my foreskin away from the head and making me growl. I draw my head back just enough I can look down at her. "Are you teasing me, baby?"

She bites her lower lip again, slowly shakes her head, and I nearly explode in her hand. Her flesh practically scorches me as a flood of memories wash in and threaten to take my knees out.

I've never had this reaction to any other since losing my Robert. *Ever*. This visceral, primal *need* that can only be satiated by her body being wrapped around mine.

After Robert and before Eilidh, humans were mostly all the same to me. A means to an end. Even with sex. While I usually could get off, mostly I had sex with them to keep from feeling guilty about feeding on them.

No reason for both of us to be miserable.

Although, lately, it's been far easier to buy blood than to go looking for it fresh from the source. Even with my powers, I haven't wanted to be bothered going through the motions and expending the energy. It's just...too much work.

Yes, even with my powers. I could barely force myself to

go in search of someone appropriate. Someone I knew I could make myself perform with.

But Eilidh...

My soul's been...renewed. Restored. Rain falling in the desert.

It's a struggle to keep my voice low, so I don't scare her, but I haven't felt desire like this since my loss. "Tell me what you want, Eilidh. *Say* it."

"You. I want *you*."

I spin us around and dip so I can hoist her up, wrap her legs around my waist, and pin her against the wall while I kiss her. The scent of her arousal thickly filling the bathroom makes my fangs ache and I struggle to keep from sinking them into her sweet flesh.

Which means I keep kissing her, devouring her mouth. Her arms drape around my neck, and her fingers plunge into my hair. Every nerve ending in my body feels like it's truly alive, on fire.

She's fire.

She's sunlight and passion and warmth, all right here in my arms.

Enough to work its way through my cold, dark soul and bring it back to radiant life.

When I lick along the seam of her lips, they part for me, and then her tongue and mine duel while she grinds against me. I keep one hand on her ass, supporting her, preventing her from impaling herself on me yet. I know if I let her do that, I'll be completely lost.

I want it to be her decision, but I also want it to be one she won't regret, not one she made because she was so horny she couldn't help herself.

She tastes of springtime and honey. I'm addicted to her,

even without drinking a drop of blood directly from her sweet, perfect veins.

I can already hear Lucius laughing as I realize I will be dropping a very pretty penny with him to buy every last drop of her blood—straight or blended—in his possession. Because like holy fucking *hell* will I share her in any way with others.

No one gets her but *me*.

Here's hoping she'll have me for life, because I won't stop until I convince her she's *mine*.

Letting her lean against the wall for support, I move the hand cupping her head and use my thumb to play with her clit. There she goes, biting down on her lip again—fates help me, she's perfection personified. A luscious, spankable ass, with curves I can actually hold on to.

Staring into her eyes anchors me to her. I fear I'll be lost if I let go. Her clit swells as I play with her, making her moan and gasp and rock against me. Her nipples are pebbled into tight peaks, and I know at some future point I'll be leaving my marks all over her breasts, not just her throat and mons.

"Play with your nipples, love," I whisper, and she does. She tips her head back against the wall, her gaze locked on mine. Every gasping breath rushing from her fills my ears, and I have no other desire than to make her come.

In my arms, with my strength, she weighs practically nothing. My stiff cock waves in the air, occasionally bumping against her rounded ass as I focus solely on her and her pleasure. Her heels dig into my ass as she rocks against me, and her sweet nectar coats my fingers.

And when her eyes start to unfocus, and her lips part, I know I have her close to the edge. It'd be so easy to notch myself between her thighs and press in just as she's orgasming, but I won't do that to her yet.

It matters. Her trust in me matters.

I never want it in the back of her mind that I might one day violate her consent, whether it's for sex or play or blooding.

I need her to trust me. I *need* this bond with her.

I lean in until my mouth hovers over hers. "Give it to me, love. I want to hear you cry for me."

She tips over the edge, every muscle in her body tensing and then uncoiling with a snap that makes my dick twitch and throb.

I don't stop what I'm doing, though. I keep my thumb right there, still playing with her, her mons and clit and my fingers slick with her juices and making it that much better for her. It takes me a few minutes, but I get her over a second time, swallowing her cries with a deep kiss that tastes better than anything I've ever sampled.

As she sits there catching her breath, I'm looking into her eyes while I bring my hand to my mouth and slowly lick my fingers clean, just like I did last night.

Fates! In this way, she tastes even better than her blood.

"What about you?" she whispers, breathless.

I smile. "What about me, love?" Yes, there is absolutely more than a little smug pride coursing through me, that I got her over honestly, without needing to mentally tip her over the edge with my powers.

Allll me.

She drapes her arms around my neck again and kisses me, wiggling against me. "Fuck me, please?"

"I don't have any condoms."

"You're a fricking vampire. You can't get me pregnant, and unless there's something new about vamp biology no one told me, you're clear of all STIs. So *please* fuck me."

She has a point. I smile, sucking on her lower lip. "Ask me *properly*, love."

Either she will, or she'll resist, and I can back up, without having pushed her too far in a bad way.

Her lips crash over mine and she grinds on me again. "Please fuck me, *Sir*."

I'm lost. I'm absolutely, completely lost. Either she's mine forever, or she'll spend forever with me silently shadowing and protecting her, but there is no one else for me.

There *cannot* be anyone else for me.

I lift her enough I can reach down and line myself up, then slowly lower her onto my dick. All that sweetly scorching heat clenches around me. Once I'm fully seated inside her, I hold her ass in both hands and kiss her. She tries to rock against me, but I remain steadfast, wanting to savor this.

Pressing her against the wall, I nuzzle my nose against hers. "You're getting a spanking tonight," I say. "For lying to me. I'm going to use my bare hand and redden that gorgeous ass of yours, and then I'm going to put you on your hands and knees and fuck you until you've come so hard and so many times that you're too hoarse to scream anymore."

She whimpers and tries to rock against me again. I think she's beyond coherent thought at this point.

I lick along her jaw, to her ear. "Then I'm going to tie you up and bury my face in that sweet pussy of yours and make you come some more. Until *I'm* ready to stop. I hope you're good with that, love."

"Yes, Sir!"

I nip her earlobe, not with my fangs, and not nearly hard enough to break the skin. "I know I can't compel you, love, but I will spend every second we're together proving to you I can take care of you in any way you need, satisfying your every need." I take a slow thrust out and back in, deeply seating myself within her slick pussy and drawing a needy moan from her. "Give me your trust, and I will give you everything I am in return, forever."

23

E *ilidh*

I GOTTA ADMIT, that doesn't sound like a bad deal at all. Especially when I have what feels like the better part of nine thick inches of vampire cock sliding up my cooter after experiencing two of *the* best orgasms I think I've ever had in my life. Even better than last night.

Yes, I was a little perturbed that Dexter called Lucius and just took over like that, telling my boss I'd be late.

Except I'm not nearly as mad as I thought I was.

In fact...I'm kind of wishing I didn't have to go to work at all tonight.

I realize if I just ask Dexter to take over and take care of me, I'd never have to work again.

Ever.

That's my lady bits and my stupid, weak heart speaking.

The rest of me has pulled hard enough on the emergency brake to keep those words from tumbling out of my mouth, though. Because, let's be honest, crazy-hot chemistry aside, I *barely* know the guy.

Every slow thrust he takes makes me try to grind against him, but he's got a firm grip on my ass and I don't have any leverage. All I can do is hold on and kiss him, which isn't a bad option, either.

I mean, he's fucking *hot*.

Relatively speaking, because the sensation of his cool cock fucking me only makes it all feel sexier.

Then, he stops. At this point I'm pretty much beyond doing anything except begging. But he smiles and slips a hand between us again, his magic thumb doing its thing on my clit, and I moan, shamelessly begging for more.

My body clenches around his hard cock and I'm sooo glad he can't compel me.

That means he's *really* this good in bed.

Fuuuuuck me.

"Do you want to come again, love?" he softly teases.

"Yes, Sir!" Yep, those two words are already engraved in my brain. The first time I said them sounded so damned perfect that I can't help doing it now. He absolutely has my trust. He could've already had his fangs buried in my flesh and I wouldn't have stopped him.

Who'd a thunk my perfect guy would be Fangster Hunkadoofalus?

My objections to why this can't work have mostly dissolved. He's old and smart—minus the time management snafu earlier—and rich and powerful. There's got to be a way to make this work.

I can't imagine not having him in my life. I want to keep making him smile like this. I want to be the reason he wants to stay alive and stay safe.

I want to be his, and I want him to be mine.

I want this to last, so I can get to know him and silence the remaining doubts in my brain for good.

My gaze locks on his. "I can't share you. Please don't do this to me and ask me to share you."

He leans in and kisses me again, which presses his thumb against me and his cock farther inside me, making my clit flutter with pleasure. "Only you. I can buy what I need to feed."

"I mean...you know... Bad guys, okay. Waste not, want not. Drain them dry, but that's—"

He silences me with a long, deep kiss and pistons his cock inside me several times, shoving all my cares out of my brain.

Who says he can't compel me? Maybe not the usual way, but this is a damn good method of shutting down my brain.

Every thrust he takes drags his cock along my G-spot, until I'm coming again, and the feel of my body clamping down on him as the orgasm slams home only makes it that much stronger.

With his arms around me he speeds up, thrusting deep and fast inside me until he explodes, groaning with pleasure as he falls still buried within me after a last, deep stroke. His lips close over mine, tender and gentle this time, his tongue flicking against my teeth, zooming in on my canines, running the tip over them.

That's when I realize his teeth are a little sharper than they were.

Where that might have terrified me before,...not now.

I force my eyes open to find him looking at me, waiting.

"Do you want to feed from me?" I whisper.

He smiles. "Yes, but I will not do that here and now. Not like this. I want us stretched out in a bed without worrying about the neighbors overhearing you scream my name. There's plenty of time for that, sweetheart. Doesn't have to happen now. Doesn't even have to happen this month or this year." He nips my bottom lip. "Then again, I'd planned to make love to you for the first time in a bed, too. You have a way of making me discard my best-laid plans."

He holds me as I unwind my legs from around him, his arms caging me until he's certain I can support my own weight.

Which is iffy, to be honest.

All I want to do is go to bed and cuddle with him. But if I do that, we're back to square one in the closet game, because I could probably sleep most of the night, at this point.

"Shower, Sir?" I ask.

His face glows with a radiant joy I never imagined possible for any being to express. Leaning in, he nuzzles noses with me. "Shower, love."

I take off the necklace holding the ring and leave it on the counter. Once we're in the shower, he takes the scrubby from me and washes my back. "So why were you crying earlier? Because of what we already discussed, or something else?"

I lean back against him, pulling his arms around me. "Because of the hairs. Because I guess that's when it hit me how freaking dangerous it was for you here."

He nuzzles the side of my neck. I can almost imagine what it'll feel like the first time he feeds from me.

I want that.

How'd I get *here*? In just a couple of days?

He washes me, washes my hair for me, and then I wash him. Now that my brain isn't totally shut down with pleasure, I can explore and appreciate what a freaking hunk he is. Firm chest and abs, hard, lean muscles. I can imagine

him running wild on the Scottish moors, his hair long and...
Did they have kilts back then?

Whatever.

He turns to face me again, staring down at me with pure adoration in his blue eyes.

Not-Ianto wants me. Fuck me, I'm so screwed.

Especially when he drops to his knees with a very wicked grin and licks between my thighs, nudging my legs apart and bracing me with his hands.

Ooohhhh mmmmyyyy!

The way he drags his tongue over my sensitive clit makes me see stars well before he has me coming all over his face. I'm barely coherent and only his hand pinning me to the shower wall is keeping me upright by the time he's finally satisfied I've had enough, and he stands.

His cock's hard again, too.

"How was that, love?"

I pull him in for a long kiss, tasting myself on him, loving his unabashedly carnal grin. Like he's happy just because I got me some.

As if his needs are secondary.

"That was fricking amazing. But what about you?"

He continues smiling as he slowly shakes his head. "I'll wait until later."

I reach down and palm his hard cock. *Hello, friend.* "But that's kind of mean, making you wait."

"You're not 'making' me do anything, love." He backs me against the wall again, his hands braced against it and caging my head. "Anything I do like this is because I *want* to, not because I feel obligated. Taking care of what's *mine* is, believe me, *exactly* what I want to be doing."

I swallow hard. I guess I am his now, huh?

I mean, my body and lady parts and heart are all on-board with that plan. Completely.

When we finish our shower, I wrap a towel around my hair and grab my robe. He ties a towel low around his hips and I want to lick along where his abs form a *V* that points to Happy Land, now concealed by a layer of cheap grey terrycloth. I want to bite his tight, gorgeous ass.

Guess that's irony, huh?

He picks up the chain and studies the ring. "I'm sorry I haven't had the opportunity yet to research this for you. I promise I'll do that this week."

"Thank you."

"May I try it on?"

I nod.

I hold my breath as he unfastens the chain's clasp and slides it free from the ring, then fits the ring on his left ring finger.

It fits him perfectly.

Don't know what I was expecting to happen, but I suck in a relieved breath as the world doesn't end. Smiling, he removes the ring from his finger and hands it back to me. He watches as I thread it onto the chain and then drape it around my neck again.

It's a comfort having it back where it belongs.

"What?"

He smiles. "Nothing, love." He leans in for a kiss. "I suppose we should eat."

"Yeah. Got it covered." First, I need to get the food cook-ing. I head to the kitchen, where I grab my electric skillet and dump in the frozen dinner kit I picked up earlier. It'll cook in about twenty minutes while I return to the bath-room and dry my hair.

I'm used to making do with a small microwave, an electric skillet, and a slow cooker. I do have a single-burner hot plate, too. All things that easily fit in my vehicle, and it means I can live in a hotel room for weeks at a time, if I need to. I have a tiny mini fridge stowed in the closet with the rest of my things. I don't need it in the apartment, obviously, but as long as I have access to electricity, I'm good. I rarely use my apartment's stove, unless I'm boiling eggs or cooking pasta or something like that.

While I'm doing that, Dex retrieves a bag of blood from the fridge, and I show him where I keep the four plain coffee mugs I own. Hey, they're multitaskers. Not like I entertain guests. I have two large refillable water bottles, and the coffee mugs. It's all I need. Plus, they're microwaveable. You can also drink wine or liquor from a coffee mug just as well as you can from a fancy glass.

Hey, don't judge.

I return to the bathroom so I can finish drying my hair. I'll still need to put my wig on, but I'll do that after we eat. By the time I emerge from the bathroom with my hair blown dry, he's finished off three of the bags of blood and is dressed in his jeans, no shirt, and barefoot.

My clit waves her hand in the air, signaling that she hasn't tapped out yet.

And the church said, "Amen." I didn't think he could look any hotter than he did last night in his suit, but I was wrong.

So, soooo wrong. Once he dons the boots, button-up, and vest, he's going to be lighting fires in lady parts all around Tucson just from spontaneous combustion.

Maybe this was a miscalculation on my part. He's going to have every goddamned het woman, and more than a few gay men—maybe even some of the straight ones—wanting him tonight.

Except...

I take a deep breath. He agreed not to have sex with or feed off anyone.

I've got to trust him, since he hasn't given me any reason not to trust him.

I receive another of "those" looks from him. "What?" I ask.

"I might not be able to read you, or compel you, but I can sense when something troubles you, love."

"It's nothing. You promised you wouldn't do anything with anyone else tonight, and I need to trust you."

His expression softens and he walks over to me. When he pulls me against him, that lickable bare chest of his...

Mmmm. Yeah.

"If you would prefer, I can take you to work, speak with Lucius, and then leave and return in plenty of time to pick you up, and we can return to my hotel. Or, I can have John wait for you and drive you, once your shift ends. Then there's no reason for you to have any concerns."

I tighten my grip around him. "Yeah, but then you won't be there, and I won't be able to walk up to you and kiss you in front of everyone and stake *my* claim on *you*." I tip my head back and stare into his eyes. "It's silly to do that. We'll lose more time. Let's stick to the plan of staying at the club."

"Are you certain?"

"Yeah." I rise onto my toes and kiss him. "But bonus boyfriend points to you for making the offer and meaning it. *Sir*," I belatedly add.

He smiles. "I can't wait until the day I hear you upgrade that descriptor."

"Which one?"

"Boyfriend." He kisses me again. "Maybe to dominant. Master. *Husband.*"

That last one makes me gasp, because I both want it, and yet I can't imagine I'll ever be that lucky.

He nuzzles the side of my neck—holy *hellballs*, when did I suddenly become so *sensitive* there? "The day you decide you wish to call me the last one will be one of the happiest days of my exceedingly long life."

24

E *ilidh*

IT'S ALMOST nine p.m. by the time we're ready to leave. I feel guilty that I'm not already at work. Friday and Saturday are the two busiest nights of the week.

Except seeing Dexter dressed, and wearing those boots —and that leather belt—nearly makes me want to quit right then. I was right—he looks hot as fuck.

Watching him roll up his shirtsleeves to just below his elbows is a borderline religious experience.

Can I get a hallelujah?

Dexter offers to carry everything downstairs and have the Audi waiting for me at the entrance to my building, so I don't have to walk across the parking lot in the dark, but I nix that idea.

I don't need anyone trying to give him shit in the elevator or lobby. It's best if I'm with him. Besides, nothing happened last night while we were out. And any time I've ever seen my phantom doggo, I've been alone.

Of course, I'm usually alone, but still.

I've *got* this. I will put my trust in Dexter.

I pack a tote bag with everything I'm going to need for an overnight, and he refuses to let me carry anything other than my purse. Fortunately, we don't run into anyone in the elevator or lobby, and we quickly cross the parking lot to where I parked the Audi. The sound his boots make as he crosses the parking lot makes my lady parts throb in time with his steps.

Yeah, suit fetish just dropped to second place.

He frowns as he stows everything in the back hatch. "Did you get this washed, love?"

My face heats. "Yeah," I mutter. "Garrett was being a wolf when he was talking to me. Leaned on it, put his hands all over it. Marking it, sort of. At least he didn't lick it, or pee on it."

Dexter starts laughing. "You are an amazing woman, love."

He opens my door for me. Once he's behind the wheel, I ask, "Why do you say that?"

"Say what?"

"That I'm amazing. You barely know me." *Oh, hello, self-doubt and fear. I wondered where you went.*

He turns to me. "You *are* amazing, and I don't simply mean your special abilities. You're a survivor. You're funny and intelligent. You're obviously capable, because Lucius wouldn't have entrusted you with as much responsibility as he has if you weren't. He isn't very forgiving of avoidable mistakes, and that you are a human who's earned his trust means a lot. I might not agree with my 'uncle' in many ways, but that doesn't mean I don't trust him in others. That he thinks as highly of you as he does, as do his men, is very telling. Then there's the way the shifters trust you, too."

My face heats and I turn forward. "Yeah, well, I'm just lucky."

"It's not merely luck. You and I both know that. And there's another point—you eschew self-aggrandizement. You don't pat yourself on the back or look for outside validation."

"We really need to go," I quietly say.

"*Eilidh.*"

Something about his tone makes me turn back to him. He leans in and kisses me. "I promised never to lie to you. One day, I hope you'll grow comfortable with me paying you compliments."

"Yeah, but today is *not* that day," I mutter.

He smiles. "And there's the wit I love so desperately." Fortunately, he lets me off the hook. He quickly adjusts the mirrors and seat and everything, and off we go.

Love.

I think he's in love with me.

He hasn't exactly said those three little words in that particular order, but I *know* it.

I also know if I told him no and walked away from him, he'd likely pursue me anywhere I went. Maybe not trying to force me to be with him, but he'd shadow me.

As we drive, I can see it play out. Walking away from him means a life of my rent and bills mysteriously being paid. Eating out just to find the tab's already settled. My car's gas tank is always full every morning, and the tires never get more than half-worn. If I ever break down, a tow truck will show up before I could even call for it. Guys who I'm not interested in will leave me alone.

Guys who are?

He'd probably screen the hell out of them and make sure they were who they said they were. I would never know who wasn't influenced by him in some way—thrall, money, or just old-fashioned intimidation.

Why would I *not* give this a chance?

I keep an eye out as he drives. All I see are the normal views of Tucson at night, something I rarely see.

Here I am, two nights in a row, I'm out and about in it.

With a guy I barely know.

With a *vampire* I'm already falling in love with.

"You've already bought a house, haven't you?" I ask without looking.

A pleased tone fills his voice. "An apartment building with an appropriate penthouse. It's a sound business investment. I'll buy a house eventually, but I want to see them in person before I make a choice. John and Mark know my preferences for accommodations and can have the arrangements made to convert the penthouse. It already has a safe room. It just needs to be expanded to the full bedroom and en suite."

I should have known. I look over at him. "I know it's not my building, because it doesn't have a penthouse, and it's in Garrett's territory."

"Just on the edge of it," he admits. He can't hide his pleased smile. "Not far from the property I'm buying for the resort. I'll be able to directly oversee the construction that way."

"How long will it take to fix up the penthouse?"

"They can install temporary shades by the end of the week, but I would not be living there during the actual renovation. There's an apartment just one floor down they will prepare for me to live in, and it will be ready by next Wednesday. We're in the process of buying out the other residents on that floor so my people can live there." He glances my way with a playful smirk. "Even has a west-facing balcony."

"Meaning slightly later mornings, but longer days."

"Once the sun's behind the mountains to the west, it's safe for me."

It's...overwhelming. "How can you just uproot yourself like this over *me*?"

"Not just over you, love. Now that I've found a reason to continue living, I realize how much fun it is. And the casino project will go on."

"Don't you have to get permitting permissions for that? Gaming license?"

This smile is the hard, cold one of a businessman. I've seen Lucius wear a similar smile countless times when discussing negotiations that impact his bottom line. "Those will not be obstacles."

It smacks me in the head what he means. "Because you're a vampire and can compel them, or because you're rich enough to buy them?"

"Yes."

Ah... I face forward, my mind once again swinging back to totally freaked out.

This is moving way too fast. Isn't it? Is it me, or my blood, that he's falling for? He hadn't even *fucked* me yet before he bought an entire apartment *building*?

How does he go from wanting to die to wanting...*me*?

I'm not just freaked out—I'm *terrified*. Because this feels like it could go atomic-bomb levels of bad if it explodes.

~

Dexter

. . .

"It's a very beneficial deal for Green's pack," I add. "Immediate employment for any who need it. Safe emergency housing. Assistance ferreting out any other Data-X labs and destroying them. Not to mention, providing a lucrative contract for Wolf Ridge Brewery."

That's run by Garrett Green's father, Phoenix pack Alpha Emmett Green. We will prominently feature their products, which will help smooth any ruffled fur Garrett's father might have regarding my project.

It also means that, yes, I *am* choosing to support the younger Alpha, even though the two cities are separate packs. Garrett Green is the future of wolves and only wants what's best for them—protection and survival.

I can help him provide that.

It also means I can help prevent challenges to his position as Alpha before they even happen. We're not so different. Garrett has already proven himself an intelligent and wily businessman. He's hungry in a smart way, without being greedy.

That he feels concern for Eilidh as a friend and as an Alpha means I wish to keep him as happy as a vampire can keep a reluctant business partner.

The world is quickly moving on in a way that makes it increasingly difficult for either of our races to remain hidden and threatens the existence of all of us. Banding together is a logical and necessary next step.

I've had limited success making contacts and alliances with shifters from my base in Atlantic City. The wolves long ago abandoned the urban canyons for more rural areas.

There are other shifters who sometimes hide within the cities to stay lost, their scent overwhelmed by the sheer numbers of humanity, and vehicle emissions, and other incidental sensory camouflage. But other than a few rare exceptions, lone shifters never seek me out.

Not that I blame them. I certainly wouldn't, if I were them.

The cities are usually the domain of the vampires. Except for Philadelphia.

They'd planned a war against humans, and an informant let me know. My people eradicated all fifteen members of their nest in a surgical strike of military precision. To the informant, I provided safe passage out of the United States and adequate resources for them to start over in South America.

That was twenty-eight years ago, and no other vampires have settled in Philadelphia since.

I have business interests all over the world, especially in the UK. I have secure residences all over the world, too, but Scotland will always hold a fond place in my heart. It's also where I visit Robert's grave, take him his favorite wildflowers, talk about my life, reminisce about our adventures. We only had twenty years together, but they were magic, and breathtaking, and the only reason I've held on as long as I have was my promise to him to do so.

It wouldn't have been a Tucson sunrise I greeted. It would've been a Scottish one. My plan was to get the Tucson project up and running as one last personal victory, put principal players into position to keep my empire running, and then return to Scotland. After drinking one last toast to my love, I would have lain on his grave and awaited sunrise.

But now...

I am so glad I waited. No, Eilidh's not guaranteed to be mine, but as long as she's alive, I now have a purpose, a mission.

A renewed sense of wonder about the world.

My beautiful enigma.

At Club Toxic, she directs me around back and into her reserved spot, which is the only one open. The Audi is still the least expensive vehicle there, but it can hold its own in appearance.

I open her door for her and help her out. The blue wig again tonight, and a black Club Toxic tee with the logo in neon green, and black jeans that hug her rounded curves and make me seriously wonder how I'll keep my hands off her.

Or keep from murdering anyone who looks at her too long and hard.

I grab my things, but she takes her tote bag from me. "I'll stash this upstairs at my desk for now."

I follow her to the back door, where she punches in her code. I open the door for her, though, and the one at the base of the stairs, after she punches in her code there, too.

She moves through the space comfortably, without worries about the predators she works for and with. I know she might not fully realize just how rare she truly is.

I wait for her while she stows her things and dons her name tag and apron. Then she gives me a kiss. "I need to get to work."

I kiss her one last time, taking my time and making sure she's nearly melted by the time I finally release her. I want my girl's mind on me while she's working.

She wobbles a little as I smile. "Enjoy your shift, love."

"That was mean," she whispers.

I smile. "I know." Downstairs, the nightclub is packed, the dance floor crowded, the air warm and full of sweat and lust and barely constrained hunger. I find myself averting my gaze as nearly every human woman I pass turns toward me with blatant invitations in their eyes.

On another night, I might have picked the first one and gotten things over with, just to satiate my basic hunger.

Not tonight.

Eilidh peels off to head to the bar while I make my way to the coat check room. Maximus is standing guard and steps aside to let me pass with a respectful nod.

When I head down to the dungeon, I see a few vampires are already playing with their selected dinners. There's a male vampire fucking a male human in a sex swing while a female vampire feeds from the human's neck. Next to them, a shirtless male vampire is flogging a female human against a St. Andrew's cross. I hear a soft female moan from one of the curtained alcoves and realize more play is going on there, too.

No, the first time I scene with my girl, it'll be in private, so I can focus on and savor her, and not worry about anyone else lusting after her. I want her in cuffs and my collar, to make her crawl naked across the floor as I watch her willingly come to me. I want to feel the heat of her forehead through the top of my boot as she formally bows in front of me.

There's an entire encyclopedia of kinky things I want to do to and with her, and I absolutely will *not* share her with anyone.

I spot Lucius and Selene standing by the bar and talking with Theophilus, so I walk over.

"Ah, there he is!" Lucius says. "Come, let us go talk."

He leads the way back to the suite Eilidh and I used the other night. It's just the two of us, and I set my things down next to the dresser as he closes the door behind us.

"And how is Alpha Green?" he asks as he sits in the chair.

I get right to the point and summarize the meeting. "Everything looks good," I say in conclusion.

"I appreciate you doing this. With the eyes of law enforcement on me, it's far better coming from you and keeping me as a silent partner."

"You need to tightly control your nest," I caution. "And operate your businesses beyond reproach, from a legal standpoint. We cannot have scrutiny from the authorities."

He waves away my objections. "California was an aberration."

I arch an eyebrow at him.

"An aberration in the *past*," he says. "I have no interest in drawing scrutiny." He picks an imaginary piece of fluff off his slacks. "It is getting more difficult to remain undetected. While I will admit to past business practices that skirted the edges of legality, this modern age has made that untenable, at best. Damned computers and the Internet, anyway. Cell phones. Things I thought would make life and communication so much simpler have completely complicated and threatened our very existence." He sighs. "I do not wish a repeat of Philadelphia. I feel somewhat responsible."

"You should. You sired the idiot."

He waves that away, too. "He was young, only two hundred, or so. I never should have allowed him to fledge from the nest and go out on his own when I did. It's difficult to find the kind of loyalty such as I have with my other sired."

I snort. "You were the victim of an attempted coup."

"*Attempted* being the keyword. Far from the first, as you well know. Which is why I forbid my sired from turning anyone without express permission. If anything, I wish to thin the herd, as it were. I want only a trusted core group surrounding me."

"And as more vampires move to the area?"

He grimly smiles. "As you saw with Tonio the other night, they either pledge allegiance and act accordingly, or they can burn. Tucson can become a safe haven for vampires and shifters, if we play this right. The vampire capital of North America. We can weed out violent, predatory humans, dropping the crime rates and making it a destination spot, a developer's wet-dream."

"That's the hope."

"I heard you made another real estate purchase. An apartment building."

"News travels fast in this town."

He smiles. "Remember the old days? Running through battles and ripping out throats? Drinking our fill under smoky skies as villages burned around us?" He sighs. "Easier, simpler times, then. We quietly ruled the world without worries, save the sun, and those of our kind who had delusions of grandeur."

A sour taste hits the back of my tongue. "I prefer *not* to remember. I never had a love for the kill the way you and my sire did."

"No, you did not." He sighs. "I always disagreed with your sire's particular...predilections." He shifts position and leans forward. "Do not let your immutable past color your potential future too darkly, nephew. Claim her quickly. You know this is right. If you wish to turn her, I'll even help, if you'd like. Do not lose her. Not when you don't have to."

My stomach rolls and it takes me a moment to calm it before I feel safe enough to quietly speak. "I appreciate the offer, Lucius, but we are not at that stage yet, if ever. I will let her set the pace." The thought of losing her to time and age guts me, but if I were to participate in her dying far younger simply to satisfy my selfish need to keep her...

It would drive me utterly and completely mad, I know it would.

"Oh, there is one more matter," I say. "I want to buy the entire supply you have."

He arches an eyebrow. "Of?"

"You know what of."

That would fetch a considerable sum."

"Then give me the friends and family discount. You know my deal will make you a lot of money with zero risk and outlay on your part. And no more bleeding her, even if she asks."

He studies me for a moment. "Five hundred thousand. Even though I could easily make twice that selling it by the glass."

"Done. Take it off-tap tonight. Immediately. Except for me."

"And how do you plan on storing it?"

"As soon as my apartment is ready here, I'll be in touch."

He tips his head to me. "Very well."

"Oh, I will need to borrow some implements and rope."

He points to a closet. "You should find everything in there that you'll likely need."

"Thanks."

We return to the dungeon, where the scent of human arousal and blood are much stronger down here, to the point I can't help the way my mouth sharply waters. I follow him over to the bar, where he speaks to the bartender. The man nods and glances my way.

Lucius smiles at me. "Would you like a glass of your particular vintage now?"

"Yes," I practically growl.

Once I have a glass, and Lucius has a glass of red wine, we walk over to the thrones, where Selene is currently perched and watching a knife play scene. It's just for sensation, not cutting, but the male bottom smells thick of subspace and need as the male vampire traces intricate Celtic designs across his back.

It triggers...something in my brain, a memory that teases close to the surface before diving away again.

"Dexter?" Lucius asks.

I pull my thoughts to the present. "Nothing. I have a puzzle I'm working on and haven't untangled yet."

"Her ring?"

I glare at him. "What do you know of it?"

"That it feels like I should know what it says, and I do not, and it irritates me." He sips his wine. "I think it's a clue to her...issue."

"We're in agreement." I want to go up to the nightclub, but I know if I do, I'll be at risk of causing a scene. The last thing I wish to do is interfere with her working.

I mean, since I haven't convinced her to let me totally take care of her yet. Once I do, she will not have to sling drinks for humans and vampires.

She will rule my empire beside me, and she'll never want for anything again in her life.

25

D*exter*

LUCIUS HAS a chair brought over for me to sit on the platform with him and Selene, and we talk. Maybe an hour after our arrival at the club, Eilidh makes her way downstairs.

As soon as the door from the stairwell opens, I know she is there.

I sense her energy, her presence.

When I turn, her gaze immediately meets mine. Every human escorted down here tonight since my arrival, and many of the household humans, have eyed me with longing invitations in their gazes, and I've ignored all of them, save the server who brought me another glass of my now private vintage.

I feel borderline drunk and wonder if this is what it'll feel like when I feed from her. I've had more blood tonight than I have in a while, but I feel like I could drink her taste forever and never fully satiate my thirst.

I climb down from the platform when she walks over. Then I pull her into my arms and kiss her, leaving no doubts to anyone who she belongs to. Or who I belong to, either. I grab her ass and pull her hips against mine, letting her feel how ready I am for her.

"Staying out of trouble?" she breathlessly teases once I finally end our kiss.

"Of course. Just waiting for you to finish so we can play." With my bulge notched between her thighs, I grind against her again and love the way she bites down on her lower lip.

"I've had four different requests to come downstairs with vamps."

The growl rumbles free before I can stop it. "*Who* are they?"

She snorts. "Yeah, like I'm telling you. *Sir*," she adds, bouncing onto her toes to kiss me again. "I'm no idiot."

"You aren't available for that."

"I know, but I've made over two hundred in tips so far tonight." She taps a pencil tucked behind her right ear. "Don't worry. I got this."

"She really is amazing," Lucius says from his throne. "Blue, my dear, can they spare you for the rest of the evening upstairs?"

"Not really, Mr. Frangelico," she says. "The line's all the way down the block, and we're hopping upstairs. I was asked how busy it was down here, so thought I'd take a minute to check in." Her gaze returns to me. "And say hi."

"She is adorable, is she not?" Lucius says. "Blue, you may call me Lucius while you're working, if you wish. I've told you that."

"Thank you, Mr. F, but I'd rather set a good example for the staff and customers."

He looks at me. "Nephew, help?"

I grin. "I'm the only one she has to call Sir, and even that's by *her* choice."

Lucius sighs melodramatically and looks to Selene. "Any advice, dear?"

She grins. "Blue's got a point, Sir. Sorry."

Lucius looks at me and shrugs with a *what can you do?* kind of resignation, making me chuckle. "I have to say, uncle, I like this new, mellower you. It suits you."

He reaches over and squeezes Selene's hand. "My queen has been a rather interesting influence on me. Ironically, I can afford to embrace a softer stance with her by my side. Mostly because she's terrifying as fuck, as they say."

After one last kiss, Eilidh returns to the nightclub and I retake my seat. Tonight, I don't mind watching people playing or having sex, because I no longer feel the familiar, painful emptiness. There's no twisting pang in my soul.

I'm no longer alone.

Throughout the night, the dungeon picks up and the debauchery intensifies. I watch two of Lucius' men, Augustus and Tiberius, sandwich a young man between them and DP him as they each feed from his neck. I watch Theophilus fuck a young woman into bliss as he snacks on her, and then passes her off to Maximus, who has a turn fucking her face before getting his own taste. There are mostly male vampires, with a mix of male and female bottoms, and two different female vampires, who are definitely tops.

It's lustful carnality and something that, only a week ago, I would have been unable to stand by and observe so placidly without feeling grief.

At home, I have a special hotel suite right off the casino floor where I can take people, quickly feed and fuck them, and then they can awaken there later, courtesy of the house, their bill completely paid if they're a hotel guest, or sent away after a fresh breakfast if they're just there for the casino.

I never leave them with a memory of who they were with—I always plant in their mind before leaving them that they are very, very drunk, and while they will remember they had a fantastic time, they will have no memory of who that someone was. I also never take someone who isn't single, unless their partner is with them and also attracts me, and I can take them both.

Lately, the suite's remained unused, my needs most easily sated with bagged blood and my own right hand.

Tonight, as the clock closes in on two a.m., which is last call in the nightclub, a few more vampires make their way downstairs with the last of their nightly chosen. When Eilidh returns to the dungeon at 2:17, my cock's hard and my need is high. I've already been back to the suite and confirmed everything I wanted is there. I take her hand in mine and bid Lucius and Selene a good night as I lead her to our awaiting sanctuary. I'll have approximately three solid hours before sunrise, and maybe another hour or two after that before I'll be forced to close my eyes.

I want to make full use of every second I'll have, showing her how I feel.

Once we're locked inside, I smile and pull her into my arms. "Where are your things?"

"I'll grab them later once we're alone. They're counting tills and tips up in the office. I didn't want to get roped into closing procedures. Theophilus shooed me down here."

I kiss her, savoring her. "Remind me to thank him later."

"I will." Another kiss, with her delicious body pressed along mine and setting my soul aflame once more. I am a better man with her in my arms and no one can convince me otherwise. I want to be the best I can for her.

"Seems like someone got left hanging earlier," she teases as I back her toward the bed.

"We will remedy that, eventually." I kiss my way along her jaw, to the sensitive spot I found behind her ear earlier, and she shivers in my arms. "Right now, I want to keep that one promise to you."

"Which one?"

I smile down at her. "To tie you up and spend as long as I want eating you."

~

Eilidh

Heat fills my face and my pulse spikes. I know he can tell it does, because his smile darkens, widens, pure desire.

"You are, huh?"

He arches his eyebrow at me. "Yeesss. I want another taste of that sweet pussy. That tease earlier wasn't nearly enough to satiate me."

Gulp!

When the backs of my knees hit the bed, he eases me down onto it, following me and kissing me until I pretty much forget my own name, assumed or otherwise. Before I know it, I'm helping him strip me, until I'm lying there naked before him, except for the ring on the chain, and he's still fully clothed.

"One last thing," he says, pointing to my wig.

I quickly remove the hair pins, pull the wig and wig cap off, and then take out the hair bands and pins holding my braids in place.

He takes it all from me and puts it on the dresser, then uses his fingers to comb out my tresses. "Perfect. Don't move, sweetheart." He retrieves something from the closet—a few things, it turns out—and holds up a coil of rope to start with.

"What are your safewords?"

I swallow. "*Red* and *yellow*."

"And where are we right now?"

"*Green*, Sir."

He holds up a sleep mask, dangling it from his finger. "Yes, or no?"

All the times I've watched people submitting to the vampires and longed to experience it come flooding to mind.

All the times I've denied myself, refused invitations to scene. Even from Lucius' men, who promised not to feed from me or thrall me, if I'd just submit to them.

All the fantasies that have filled my dreams for years.

"Yes, Sir."

That gorgeous smile widens, and my personal Not-Ianto leans in and kisses me. "Good girl," he whispers. He kisses me again and eases the blindfold over my head, fitting it in place. "How's that?"

"*Green*."

I hear and feel him step away for just a moment, like he's getting something else from the closet. "I will not feed from you tonight," he says. "I swear. I doubt anything I do tonight will accidentally draw blood, either. I want that clear. Understand?"

"Yes, Sir."

I feel the bed sink next to me. Then I hear the whisper of rope as he uncoils it, the soft *thump* as the loose end lands next to me on the mattress, and then his hands are back, at my right wrist.

Working quickly, he binds my wrist, pushes my thighs open, and bends my knees up and back. My right knee is quickly lashed to my wrist, and then that to somewhere else, I'm assuming an underbed restraint point, because it has several. He repeats it with my left wrist and knee, and I'm lying there spread open for him.

"Wonderful," he whispers.

My breath comes in quick, shallow gasps as anticipation wrenches sky-high. I do trust him.

And I want this.

More than anything.

I want *him*.

He's still dressed when he leans in and I feel his cool breath against my exposed pussy. I'm wet, and he damn well knows it. My nipples have tightly pebbled, and I'm eager to feel his hands on me again.

I jump when the tip of his tongue lightly traces around my clit, slow, lazy circles that immediately have me whining and rocking against his mouth, wanting and needing more.

His hands close around my breasts, thumb and fore-finger gently rolling my nipples and adding to my hunger as he continues teasing me.

"*Mmm*, sweetheart. I might spend the rest of the night doing nothing but sampling you like this." He slowly swipes the length of his tongue along my clit, making me moan. "Get comfortable, because you'll be here for a while."

Honestly? That's the last coherent thought I have for... well, a *while*. He makes me come almost immediately, plunging his tongue deep inside me and tasting me after he does. Then he uses his fingers on me, slipping them inside me and finding my G-spot while lightly sucking on my clit. He even ends up donning gloves and slipping a lubed finger up my ass while making me come—helloooo, there!—and sending me over the damned moon.

By the time he finally removes my blindfold, I'm spent and trembling and soooo damned glad I don't have to leave him tonight.

No kidding—best orgasms of my *life*. I totally lost count.

He keeps raising the bar, somehow.

He smiles as he unfastens his belt and slowly slides it out of his jeans. "I had planned to use a multitude of implements on you tonight, love, but the hour grows late, and perhaps the first thing I use on you should be something that actually belongs to *me*. Something you can see and blush over as I thread it through my belt loops."

Motherfucker, he's absolutely right. I'm already eagerly nodding as he holds the buckle and winds the rest of the belt around his hand, leaving a tail maybe twelve inches.

Smiling, he holds it out to me. "Kiss it, sweetheart."

I do, my gaze locked with his as I kiss and lick the soft, supple leather. Heat turns his blue eyes dark grey, and I can see the way his cock presses against the front of his jeans. He unties the ropes where they're attached to the bed and closes my thighs, turning me toward the left.

Faster than I can follow the movement, his hand flicks out and the leather belt kisses my ass, making me yelp more from shock than pain, because it didn't hurt.

But he smiles. "Color?"

"*Green*."

Again and again he uses the belt on me as he slowly increases the intensity. He turns me back and forth, evenly coating my ass and the backs of my thighs with marks, until my mind has once again sailed off into a sweet, happy oblivion I know all too well is subspace. Still, every impact is a little harder, a little more time between them, until I'm wincing and yelping and just about to call *yellow* when he stops.

"Goooood girl."

Holy shitballs, I'm *flying*.

He sets the belt aside, unties me, and starts undressing. All while his hungry gaze devours me. He looks at me the way Captain Jack looks at Ianto, and I'm starting to think maybe I'm going to get a happily ever after of my own. Finally.

I mean, I hope so, because things didn't end so well for Jack and Ianto.

I'm still salty about that, by the way.

Once he's naked, he stalks up the bed, covering me, staring down at me. "You realize you're *mine*, don't you?"

I pull him in for a kiss. "Two-way street, buster."

"Absolutely, love." He notches his cock against me and easily slides deep inside, both of us moaning at the sensation.

I wouldn't have blamed him if he used this time to ride me like he stole me and get off, but he takes his time, adjusting position and angle, until I realize what he's doing when his cock perfectly glides across my clit on the withdrawal, and along my G-spot as he thrusts.

Holy.

Shit.

My toes curl. His gaze narrows and he grabs my wrists, pinning them as he keeps it up. Now that he's got my number, I realize he's not stopping until he gets one out of me like this. It takes a little while, but when I feel the climb start, he senses it.

"That's it, love," he whispers. "*Everything* is mine, *including* this."

I would argue that we need a little more time together before orgasm control becomes a thing between us, except I tip over the edge and start to come.

"There you are." He picks up the pace, prolonging my own release, until he catches up with me and finishes deep inside me, his lips on mine, my arms and legs wrapped around him.

My heart wrapped around his.

Fuck, I'm falling in love with him. When the *hell* did *that* happen?

26

E *ilidh*

WE CURL up together and doze off. It's just before dawn Saturday morning when I remember I still haven't grabbed my stuff from upstairs in the office. If I don't do it now, I won't want to do it later, and I *reeeally* don't want to do a walk of shame in front of Benny or anyone else just so I can take a shower before working my shift.

I start to extricate myself from Dex's embrace and he pulls me back. "Where are you going, love?" he mumbles.

He must be exhausted. He couldn't have been comfortable sleeping in my closet last night. "I need to go upstairs and get my stuff from the office."

He pulls me in for a kiss. "Hurry back, sweetheart. I'll miss you"

My heart pounds, because for a second there, I thought he was going somewhere else with that. I'm not sure if I'm disappointed or not that he didn't. "Miss you, too," I whisper back, terrified to admit what I just thought.

That maybe he really is *the* one. Not sure how to wrap my head around that.

He peels open one blue eye. "I'm afraid the sun will catch me earlier than I'd hoped today, but we *are* having a long and deep talk about our future together when I awaken. You're *mine*, and I'm *not* letting you go. Understand?"

I nod.

"Good girl." A handsome, sleepy smile fills his face and he makes adorable fish lips at me.

I lean in for one more kiss. "Sleep well, Sir. I might have to get up before you do to get ready for work, so don't panic if I'm not here when you wake up."

He mumbles something, but from the way all the tension flows from his body, I can tell he's already out like a light.

I do a quick clean-up in the bathroom and pull my clothes on. I don't bother taking the wig with me, because I'll just be putting it on again down here before my shift.

Well, I'll be putting it on up in the nightclub bathroom, because there aren't any mirrors down here, even in the private suites.

The suite automatically locks behind me, but I have the other key. Humming lightly to myself, I make my way upstairs to the nightclub and don't even bother checking behind the bar to see if the closing procedures were done correctly. That can wait.

Yay, me! Look at me, putting myself first, for a change.

I just want to grab my things and get back to Dex. We're totally alone in the club—I can feel it. Just me and Dex.

That's kinda cool, in a way. Having it all to our lonesome.

Too bad he can't be awake longer to enjoy more of it.

I'm hoping we can use the cross or spanking bench that's in the suite tonight.

My ass is pleasantly sore, not much, just enough to make me want more.

A *lot* more.

Okay, I want *everything* with him. If he was some rando vampire from nowhere, I wouldn't be having this reaction, I'm sure. But Lucius knows him, and while Lucius might not be a stellar being in terms of ethics and morals, he doesn't lie to the people he considers within his trusted inner circle, including humans. I've never seen him do that. If anything, it would behoove him to warn me off Dexter, because I know Dex won't let me sell blood to Lucius now. So, Lucius is actually losing money.

Meaning he must really believe Dexter is a good guy.

I head upstairs to the second floor. When I enter the main office suite, on my way to my desk I walk past the security console, where all the CCTV and security camera feeds are displayed on monitors. That's when movement on one of them catches my eye.

I back up and stare, horror washing through me.

It's one of the cameras focused on the private employee parking area directly behind the club, which currently shows the Audi is the only vehicle parked there.

Standing *right* there is my phantom dog creature, more solid than I've ever seen him looking before. I flip camera modes. He's appearing on the IR feed, too, and when I flip it to FLIR, while he's not clear, you can see a faint blob a slightly different temperature.

Meaning he has form, substance.

The scream locks in my throat, cold chills rooting me in place. I watch as it circles the car several times. Then, just as it's about to head toward the club's back door, the sun's rays break over the tops of buildings to the east and illuminate the parking area, and the phantom fades from sight as if it was never there.

I gasp for air and only then realize I'd been holding my breath.

Fuuuuck!

When I run the feed back—yep, there it is. I most certainly did NOT imagine it. And it looks like it came from the direction we drove.

Like it was scenting the Audi.

Tracking *me*.

Without thinking, I grab my phone and snap a few pics of the image. I want proof I can look at later just to prove to myself and anyone else that I am *not* fucking insane.

Well, I mean, I *might* be insane, but I'm *not* imagining this thing, or making it up.

I'm on autopilot now. I grab all my things from behind my desk and bolt downstairs, heading to the front door. A well-honed checklist is already rolling through my mind as I feel a familiar, cool detachment settling within me.

Money stash... Cat and Dog... Burner phones... Clothes... Bathroom stuff... Bedding... Load the microwave and mini fridge first, what I can fit in the cooler and load it, pack everything around them...

The logistics are the only thing in my head as I ease the front door open to see the brightly sun-lit sidewalk in front of the club, then lock the door behind me.

I'm already halfway down the block before I flag a cab.

I have it drop me one building over from my apartment building and let myself in the rear entrance instead of the front. I don't want to risk running into Garrett or Amber. Then I scamper up the stairs, because ditto the elevators.

I'm nearly panicked by the time I finally reach my apartment. I wish I could say good-bye to Dexter...

But he's already safely locked away in the suite for the day, and I need to get the *fuck* out of Tucson so that thing doesn't home in on him.

Now.

Unfortunately, this is an operation I know how to do all too well. I grab my suitcases and dump them in the middle of the floor, wide open and ready. I also grab the box of contractor's bags from under the kitchen sink. I've learned to keep my life limited to what I can carry in them and fit in my car. I'll lose the furniture, but that's easily replaced.

If I can't load it in the car, it's not going. And as of right now, everything in the apartment, other than the furniture, will fit in my car.

Marie Kondo has *nothing* on me.

More items filter through my mind.

Go through Mesa and check the mailbox... File a mail hold online for here...

The adrenaline spike doesn't ease up as the morning rolls on. By ten a.m., I'm ten miles northwest of Tucson before the crash finally hits me.

Dex.

I pull over into a truck stop and park, drop my head onto the steering wheel, and sob.

This isn't fucking fair!

Why *now*? He just told me he wanted to discuss the future, that he wouldn't let me go!

And...I love him.

But...

The memory of my mom's bruised and battered face as they pulled her life support haunts me now.

The memory of her injuries that day when she came home and told me Dad died, and that we had to move.

The years of running, of early morning dashes from wherever we were living. Literally waking up in a new city.

I cannot have someone else's death be on my conscience. Not when I'm certain Mom was killed because of me.

We ran because of *me*.

Because she was trying to keep *me* safe.

And I'm now convinced it killed her, or had something to do with her death. It's obviously more than just a ghost, because the FLIR feed showed a heat signature. Maybe the dog thing found her, and its owner followed and was the one who killed her. Funny that the police couldn't find any kind of evidence on her. They said the DNA didn't even make sense. That it was a contaminated sample.

Shit. I'm still in my Club Toxic tee and jeans.

I dig a plain black tank top out of my overnight bag and swap it out. Then I pull my hair into a ponytail and don a baseball cap I've had since Toronto before I top off my gas tank using one of the prepaid cards. After a quick stop in the bathroom, I buy a bag of ice for the cooler, two large, strong black coffees, a couple of cheese sticks, and three large bottles of water. I plug one of the backup burner phones into my car charger and let it start powering up. Twenty minutes after I arrive, I'm back in my SUV and ready to leave.

Except...

Dex.

I didn't even turn in my keys. To the club or my apartment. I just...

Ran.

I grab my phone and create a new text message to Dex,

except nothing comes to mind. How do I distill my feelings and fears into a text?

I can't. Not really.

But I cannot expose him, or the shifters, or anyone else to that...*thing*. Whatever it is. It's fine for Garrett to say they'd stand shoulder-to-shoulder with Dexter to fight it, but what if it can't be fought?

What if they all uselessly die because of me?

What if kids are put at risk because of me? What if it tracks me to my apartment building and hurts someone there?

I can't risk it.

I *won't* risk it.

Dragging in a shaky breath, I type.

IT'S BACK. *I'm so sorry, but I won't put you or anyone else at risk.*

I STUDY it before finally hitting send. I want to add more, but maybe it's better that I didn't.

Good-byes hurt enough without adding an *I love you* to it that he might or might not really feel.

I send Lucius a quick text as well.

I SAW *it outside the club this morning. Dex was already asleep. I'm so sorry, but I have to leave. I won't put you all at risk. Thank you and Selene for everything, and for your kindness to me. I'll miss all of you.*

. . .

TEARS ROLL DOWN my face as I power off my phone and stick it in my overnight bag. I'm not stupid enough to text Garrett or Amber right now. They're both awake, and it wouldn't surprise me if Garrett sent men out looking for me, or phoned ahead to his dad in Phoenix and asked him to send men to Mesa to intercept me when I hit my PO Box. One of his dad's pack runs the place.

No, messaging them can wait until I'm far enough away from the area that my trail will be cold and slow them down.

Then I pull out of the truck stop and head toward Mesa. Where I'll go from there...

I don't know yet.

I wish there was a way to track down my father, if he really is alive. Maybe he has answers to my questions.

All I know is that, right now, I need to put as much distance as I can between me and Tucson before dark, so that thing hopefully leaves Dex and everyone else alone.

Please *let it leave them alone.*

DEXTER

I AM VAGUELY aware of Eilidh moving around the room when she says she needs to retrieve her things from upstairs. I guess I'm far more exhausted than I thought, because I crash hard and sleep far longer than I usually do anymore.

Except when I awaken a little after six that evening, I stupidly realize I forgot to put my phone on its charger, and it's dead.

I also realize I am alone in the suite.

Hmm.

Oh, wait, it's Saturday. Of course. And Eilidh did warn me she might have to get up before me to go to work. The club opens at seven, and she's management. Obviously, she's already working.

I use the restroom and then put my phone on its charger. It didn't receive a full charge yesterday, and I drained it nearly dead while in the closet.

No worries about that today, at least.

At some point this evening, I'll need to return to my hotel for fresh clothes. Meanwhile, I'll grab a quick shower and freshen up. I opt for the same jeans I wore, but I don the Henley. I can't wait to wrap my arms around my girl and hold her, give her a kiss.

I will take her away from having to work like this for a living. If she wants to work, I can help her do whatever it is she wishes to achieve. She can go to school, if she wants. She can learn my business and help me manage the new Tucson casino. She can open her own business. Anything.

The possibilities are *literally* endless.

A borderline giddiness I haven't felt in centuries fills me. I feel...*alive.*

I know, I know.

I'm nearly ready to emerge from the suite when there's a knock on the door. Looking through the viewfinder shows Lucius standing there, looking grim.

I open the door. "Hey. What's wrong?"

He rushes in. "You're not answering your phone."

"Sorry, it went dead during the day. I've got it on the charger now." Dread fills me. "What's going on? What happened?"

He swipes into a message and hands me his phone, so I can read it. "I've tried calling her several times," he says as I read, "and left voicemails, sent her texts. She's not responding. I believe she's turned her phone off."

I read it several times, just to make sure. "That...that can't be right." I return his phone and check mine, but it still won't power up.

I resist the urge to crush it in my hand, because that won't help a damn thing.

Then I see her wig.

It's still on the dresser, where it ended up earlier.

She never goes to work without a wig.

A mix of terror-filled rage washes through me. "What the *hell* happened?"

"That's what we're going to find out. I just arrived. Come on."

He blurs, and I follow. Seconds later, we're upstairs in the office suite and looking over Theophilus' shoulder as he runs back video surveillance from this morning. He uses alarm logs to find out when the last time the door to the office stairs was opened this morning, and works back from there to isolate the time.

Just before dawn.

We start with the video feed from in front of the nightclub, and then from the parking area in the back. We see when Eilidh left through the front door and start backtracking from there.

All three of us draw back, stunned, at the sight of the gigantic phantom dog walking up to the parking lot and sniffing around the Audi as if it tracked it there.

Theophilus freezes the video on a frame clearly showing the beast looking up at the camera, a faint red glow visible in its eyes. "What in the great muppety *fucking* Odin is *that* shit, boss?"

"*Gwyllgi*," I whisper, stunned.

Because that's *exactly* what it looks like. I've never seen one, but of course I've heard the old myths.

Lucius glances around and drops his voice. "Do *not* say a *word* of this to *anyone*. I will inform the others." By "others" I know he means his vampire men.

The beast also faintly shows up in the IR night vision and FLIR views. It's definitely...real. She wasn't imagining it.

That relieves me on one level, because it means she's telling the truth.

But it certainly terrifies me on others, because what the *hell* is it?

Lucius' voice sounds calm, yet I can tell he's anything but. "Can you isolate that entire section of feed in all three views and save it, as well as get me some clear screenshots?"

"Sure thing."

"E-mail them to me."

"Send it to me, too, please," I say.

Lucius nods and pats me on the shoulder. He motions for me to follow him. I do, and we head downstairs and out the back door, to the Audi, where Lucius squats low to the ground and I follow suit.

"I don't smell anything," he says. "Nothing unusual, I mean."

I sniff. "Neither do I." Although the faint traces of Eilidh's scent flip my switch into wanting to rage and howl at the sky. I've never wanted to be a shifter more than I do right now, so that I can shift and rage and pounce on something and rip it to shreds with teeth and claws in a primal, visceral way to protect my girl.

I *need* to find her.

Now.

I left my phone and the key fob for the Audi downstairs. Lucius lets me back inside the club, and I blur downstairs to grab my things, including her wig. The scent of her clinging to it makes my heart keen with nearly painful agony.

I need her.

He catches up with me. "If there's anything you need, please, let me know. Men, resources—*anything*."

"Thank you. Maybe she's still at her apartment." That's the only thing I can hope for.

"I doubt it, and she's got a twelve-hour head start on us. I will call around to others I know she's had contact with in other areas and see if perhaps she's reached out for leads on jobs."

"Thanks."

"We *will* find her," he says.

"Yeah, but will we find her before that...*thing* finds her?"

"I'll work on researching that angle as well. Perhaps there is help in old mythology we can glean insight from."

"Thanks."

I rush out to the Audi and put my phone on the charger there. It finally has enough juice I can power it up. My first call is to Garrett Green, and I use handsfree mode while racing through Tucson traffic.

"This is Dexter Van Sussex," I say as soon as he answers. "Have you seen Eilidh today?"

"Who?"

I want to smack myself in the head. "Sorry. Connie. Have you seen Connie? Can you *please* check her apartment for me? See if she's there? And *keep* her there, if she is, until I arrive."

I don't blame him for his growly tone. "*What* happened?"

"She saw the thing that's been chasing her. It showed up this morning just before dawn. We have video proof. The club's security system caught it on its cameras."

"*What*?"

"Yeah. And she left."

"What is it?"

"It's..." My phone dings. I look, and it's a message from Lucius with attachments. "Better shown than explained. Please, go look. Now."

"I'm already on my way downstairs. Hang on." Come to think of it, it does sound like he's running.

Then I hear the sound of a series of booming knocks, like he's going to kick the door down. "*Connie! Open* up! *Now!*" Another series of knocks. "I don't think she's here. I can't scent her, nothing recent. Nothing warm." I hear him running again, the sound of a stairwell door slamming open, and more running. Finally, another door opening. "Her 'Yota's gone, Dexter. Any idea where she headed?"

"No. Lucius will make some calls and see if she reached out to anyone." I slide to a stop at a light and take a moment to flip to my messages and scan them.

That's when I find the one from her, sent around the time she sent the one to Lucius.

Fuck.

I resist the urge to fling the phone through my windshield.

"I'll pull the CCTV films for today in the lobby and find out when she bugged out, exactly. Maybe we can get some clues from that."

"Thank you. I owe you. It would have been just around sunrise. Not long after."

"I'll meet you in the lobby as soon as you get here."

"Thanks." I hang up and, minutes later, I'm wheeling the Audi into the parking lot. I grab my charger cord and jump out.

Garrett's already standing there, holding the door open

as I race inside. He leads me down to the management office, where he unlocks the door and I follow him in. "What *is* this fucking thing?"

I show him the videos and images on my phone and it pulls him up short. His eyes widen. "Fuuuuuck me. I've never seen anything like that."

"We think it's a *gwyllgi*."

"A what the fuck?"

I quickly explain the myths.

"Okay. So, we're looking for a thing that's never been captured on video before, and supposedly doesn't exist. *Terrific*." He sits at a computer console. "We keep a month's worth of feed on the hard drive."

"Can Amber maybe see anything?"

"She's already working on it. I got the master key and let her into the apartment. She thought maybe being alone there would help."

I nod. "Thanks."

He's scrolling through the video feeds. "What did you call Connie earlier? Hayley?"

"Eilidh. That's not to be repeated, either. It's her real first name. Connie Doe is an alias. I'm sorry, I shouldn't have let it slip like that."

"We'll need to know her real name and info, so I can get people looking for her. If she crosses the border anywhere and goes through passport control, we'll have an idea where she's heading next. Jackson King's mate, Kylie, is a hacker extraordinaire. And we've got a former CIA spook in our pack, too."

He turns to me. "We *will* find her, Dexter. You've got the manpower behind you, and you damn sure have the money. I can't believe I'm saying this, but I'll closely coordinate directly with Frangelico, so we're not duplicating efforts."

"Thanks." Cold dread fills me. "I really appreciate this."

"Hey, she's pack. Sort of." He looks up at me. "Or is she part of a nest now?"

"I haven't fed from her yet. If your question is have we had sex, yes, we have. We haven't yet had discussions about our future. Between you and me, frankly, I don't want to turn her. I'm terrified of her not surviving the process. But she's *mine*. And if she never lets me feed from her, I'm fine with that."

He turns to me. "How can *that* be possible?"

"Contrary to popular belief, it's not required. Just like marking a mate isn't a requirement among shifters to love them and be with them."

"Touché." He focuses on the feed and finds her. Fast-forwarding through the lobby camera feeds, we locate when she finished and drove away. "Looks like maybe she headed west."

"But that doesn't mean it's her final direction."

"No, but I'll bet she headed up to Mesa, to close out her box there." He places a phone call and, moments later, has confirmation. "One of my dad's pack owns the store. He confirmed she came in this morning and closed it out, but no idea what way she headed. She didn't leave a forwarding. He'll keep an eye out for anything coming through from the official USPS system about a change of address or forwarding. We've got her license plate, too. If she tries to change that, it'll ping the system. She'll have to use her Connie Doe name for that, because that's the paperwork she has for it."

"Thanks." I slump against the wall, my phone in my hand and feeling...

Useless.

I feel like I should be doing something, anything.

"Let's go see if Amber's picked up anything."

We take the stairs, and the only reason I don't blur and beat him up there is because I don't want to freak out Amber, or any other residents we might encounter, by racing ahead.

Amber's sitting on the bed, which is unfolded, with her eyes closed and hands flat on the mattress on either side of her. Eilidh's furniture is still here, but everything else is gone and it feels empty.

Worse, I can smell the terror Eilidh felt as she hurriedly packed.

We don't interrupt Amber.

Finally, after several minutes, she opens her eyes and sadly shakes her head. "Nothing. She doesn't even know where she's heading yet. All I'm getting is panic. I'll try again later. Maybe by then she'll know, and I can see it."

"How far could she make it in twelve hours?" I ask. "We know what time she left the mailbox store, right? Can we mark an obvious radius and start there?"

Garrett runs a hand through his hair. "Let me call Jackson and Kylie and get that started from our end. You call Lucius and see what he's learned."

I plug my phone into the charger and call Lucius to update him.

"I haven't learned anything yet," he says. "But I've started making calls and will continue to do so. Please, tell Garrett he can give Jackson King my information, so we can coordinate."

Swallowing the choked terror wanting to rise in my throat, I nod, even though he can't see me. "Thanks."

"We *will* find her, Dexter. I must admit, I owe her an apology."

"Why?"

"Because I honestly thought perhaps she was imagining

things, or overstating her terror. Now..." He sighs. "Let's just say I can now fully understand why she runs. Were I a human, I probably would do the same."

"Ditto," Garrett says from where he's on the phone. I turn and find he's looking at me. I realize his sensitive shifter hearing, like my vampire hearing, heard Lucius clearly.

I have no idea what to do now, but Lucius speaks. "Go to your hotel, check in with your men, regroup, then return here. Park in the back again, and use code 1852 to enter the back door and the office stairs. We'll use the office as our war room. Please feel free to share that code with Garrett. That is for the use of him and his mate while this is ongoing. I will inform my people to make sure they both have safe passage. I personally guarantee their safety while in our territory."

"Yeah, I heard him," Garrett says to me as he ends the call he was on. "Thanks, Frangelico," he calls out. I switch the phone to speaker mode.

Lucius chuckles. "Who would have thought it would take a special little human to so utterly unite our two factions with a cooperative and singular purpose of brotherhood?"

"You ain't kidding," Garrett says.

"Once she's safely back with Dexter," Lucius says, "I shall buy you a drink. Your choice."

Garrett looks me in the eyes. "We'll hold off on the toasts until that happens. Then we have another problem to deal with, anyway."

"The casino project?"

"No," Garrett says. "I want to know what the *fuck* that thing is, and how the *hell* we send it the fuck away, so it doesn't come back."

27

E *ilidh*

I CLEAN out my mailbox and put a hold on my mail. I don't bother filing a forwarding address because—spoiler alert—not only do I not have one, I'm *not* stupid.

Dexter or Garrett, or one of their men, would no doubt be sitting there waiting for me the first time I showed up to get my mail.

I'll have to invest in a mail forwarding service at some point. For now, the only mail I receive there relates to my income taxes, and that's easily changed by logging in online and doing it myself.

After I clean out the mailbox, I book it away from that area and grab gas and lunch in Scottsdale, as well as a brand-new trucker's road atlas of North America.

The problem with being from this region is knowing you can't easily get *there* from *here*. Between the desert and the mountains, there aren't a lot of major arteries out of the area. I know it'd be too easy for the wolves to send their bikers out on the main arteries, looking for me. And they'd likely catch up with me, too, if I stayed on them.

The only advantage I have right now is time. Lucius and Dexter most likely haven't received my texts yet, meaning Garrett doesn't know.

But why make things easier on them?

I immediately scratch the obvious choices—I-10 west, or I-17 north, or US93 to the northwest. I have no desire to head to Los Angeles, Las Vegas, Flagstaff, or south into Mexico. On the last point, for starters, my Spanish muy sucks ballsackos.

As I drink my coffee, I start looking at other options and settle, for now, on northeast. I'll cut up to I-40 and arrive in Albuquerque just around dark. That's about a seven-hour drive.

From there?

Well, I'll be able to make a few phone calls to decide my next step. But Albuquerque is large enough I should be able to hide out overnight. As far as I know, there aren't any vampire nests there. I'm sure the wolves likely have people they know there, but I don't know any personally.

With a game plan now, I take one last bathroom break, buy a couple of gallons of antifreeze, just in case, and a couple of gallons of drinking water, some snacks, and head out.

Despite my nerves, the drive goes without a hitch. I quickly find a hotel room in a busy section of town far enough from the interstate that I feel comfortable stopping for the night.

And I have to stop for the night. I'm exhausted. I can't keep my eyes open.

I don't even bother turning on my phone, either. I know it'll be full of texts from Dexter, Lucius, Garrett, and others. I want to text Garrett and Amber, but if Dexter hasn't already told them what's going on, I damn sure don't want to admit it yet. I also don't want there to be any way to ping the phone and locate me.

Fortunately for me, I'm smarter than the average bear, and I save my contacts in Google Contacts so I can retrieve them.

Which is where I refer to, via my laptop, to find a few numbers I need. I sync one of the cheap burners to my contacts and, ten minutes later, I know what my plan will be. But I'll need to get up before dawn to make some late phone calls. If I reach out too soon, someone might tip off Lucius and Dexter, and give them time to mobilize people to look for me.

Thus, I take a shower, set every alarm I can, and, after bracing the door with a chair, I reluctantly fall asleep.

Unfortunately, my dreams are filled with a mix of nightmares about losing Dexter to my phantom dog, and it attacking Lucius and the others, and Garrett and Amber, and—

I sit bolt upright as the first of my alarms goes off.

Fuckballs.

It's 3:27 a.m., and time for me to get ready.

I use the room's crappy single-serve coffeemaker to brew me a cup while I grab a wake-up shower. Then, after I'm safely in my 4Runner, I make the first of my calls.

The first two people had already heard from Lucius. So I kindly thank them and hang up without asking for help. They were longshots, but my third should be a safer option.

I power down that burner and set it aside. I'm certain

Lucius or Garrett will try to track me through the burner number and find out I'm here.

That's okay, because by the time they do, I'll be far from here.

I break out the next burner phone, which I charged while I slept, turn it on, and import my contacts into it. All I need to do is stay one step ahead of everyone, reach my destination, and stay there until Dexter and Lucius and Garrett all forget about me and go on with their lives.

The third phone call I make...

As I predicted, Neimus has not heard from Lucius. He hasn't heard from Dexter, either.

Or Garrett.

And, thankfully, Neimus has a lead for me and promises to not tell anyone I called, should they call looking for me. He agrees to me using a different alias for reference for the next call I need to make, so Lucius and Dexter won't track me, should their inquiries lead that far.

One more phone call, and I now have a destination and a lead on a job.

Doesn't matter I've ripped my own heart out in the process, or that I was finally starting to feel like I was home and had an extended family, of sorts.

The important thing is that I can protect them all by getting the fuck away from them as quickly as possible.

I start crying as I start driving. Because every mile I drive is another mile further from Dexter.

And I sense it's another mile further from the only man I'll ever really love.

A man whose heart I'm likely breaking right now, and I hate myself for that.

❧

DEXTER

EILIDH WON'T RESPOND to my texts or answer my phone calls. Her voice mail quickly fills up.

It's likely she's turned off the phone and won't turn it on again.

She doesn't even have a bank account. Who doesn't have a bank account? Credit cards? How does she survive? She must have a heck of a stash of cash and pre-paid cards to make it this long.

I *will* spank her for that when I find her. For making it harder for me to find her.

Three days after Eilidh's disappearance from Tucson, and I'm not sure if Lucius or Garrett wish me dead more, because I'm constantly asking for updates. I can't think straight not knowing if she's safe or not.

There's been no sign of her at all in the past forty-eight hours, other than two of Lucius' contacts reporting back to him that she called them, but as soon as they admitted Lucius had called looking for her, she thanked them and hung up.

From a burner phone. Which she's already stopped using, because it can't be tracked any further than Albuquerque. Garrett sent men out looking for her, but she had too much of a head start on them. I've got men looking for her. We all have people looking for her.

Even Jackson King's mate and her hacker friends haven't located so much as a hint of Eilidh's whereabouts. The e-mail address Lucius and Garrett had for Eilidh hasn't been logged into in over a week. It is likely a throwaway account. There were no contacts associated with it that Kylie could sort through.

My beautiful, brilliant girl is adept at hiding her trail, unfortunately.

Meanwhile, I spend my nights heading to Club Toxic, up to the office, to go over any information we're able to glean. Lucius' conference room is now my base of operations.

That's where I'm sitting, my eyes closed and trying to think, when Lucius once again tries to be helpful.

"What if she decided to return to the UK? Perhaps she feels she would be safe there? Maybe she's gone to Wales?"

I start to argue with him when something pings my memory, making my eyes pop open. "*Shit!*"

"What?"

I open my laptop and use Google Earth to do some searching. Once I've confirmed the spelling, I run a search...

And then I stupidly have one answer that I have no idea how it fits in with the rest of the puzzle. "That's it!"

Lucius arches an eyebrow at me from across the conference table. "What? Do you know where she is?"

"No! I know what the symbols on her ring are!" I spin my laptop around and show him. "They're the same symbols etched in rocks on an old ring of standing stones in Wales!"

Lucius' brow furrows, a deep scowl making him frown. "Well, that *is* interesting, but I don't understand how it's relative to locating her."

"You and I are in agreement that damned thing is a *gwyllgi*, right?"

"I mean, I don't know what it is, but that certainly fits."

"*Gwyllgi* originated in Wales. Maybe if I can figure out where the hell that thing is coming from, it might be another way of locating *her*. And maybe it has something to do with her ring." I grab my phone and call John and Mark to get the jet ready to leave for Wales ASAP.

When I end that call, I start gathering my things, but

Lucius stops me. "Are you sure you want to do this? Shouldn't you stay close by for when we locate her?"

"Look, this *is* important. If I find her, it's not like I can compel her and drag her back. She'll just run away again if this thing shows up. *Stopping* whatever this is, finding out if it can even hurt us, is every bit as important as *finding* her. Right?"

He doesn't look convinced, but he finally nods. "I suppose you are correct."

As I return to my hotel to join up with my men, I pray I'm right about this. Because I have to find her.

But even more importantly, once I do find her, I have to be able to hold on to her.

And that won't be possible until we figure out *this* part once and for all.

28

D exter

I HAVE plenty of time shut up in the private cabin of my jet to contemplate my situation. Returning to the UK is always a melancholy experience for me, even in the best of times and under the best of circumstances. It's yet another reason I decided to relocate to the US when I knew it was time to move on.

The irony isn't lost on me that, less than two weeks ago, I thought my last time traveling to the UK would be to say good-bye to my old love and greet the sunrise.

But then, I thought I'd be able to bring Eilidh here to see where she grew up in Cardiff and show her around Scotland.

Now?

I come seeking answers, and I *will* have them.

I have people on the ground in the UK scouring libraries

and museums and universities for more information on the standing stone ring in question. There are two similar ones with similar markings, but of the three, that one in particular is the only one with those exact markings, matching the ones on Eilidh's ring.

It's not a language, per se, and no one's ever figured out what the symbols mean. Like so many symbols from this period in history, the meanings were lost to the mists of time.

The other two stone rings, the markings are similar, but slightly different. No one knows what they mean. No one knows for sure what the stone rings were used for, although working hypotheses are, as always, some sort of ritual space.

Still say it cannot be a coincidence that the only time I've found those markings replicated is on this stone ring, and she is from Wales.

Twenty-four hours after my departure from Tucson, I'm standing with John and Mark at the stone ring in Wales, not far from Cardiff, and staring at markings that exactly match the ones on Eilidh's ring. There's *something* about this place, but I don't know what.

And we're still no closer to locating Eilidh, puzzling out what is pursuing her, or how it figures in with this stone ring.

Mark kneels next to one of the stones and traces the symbols with his fingers. "Perhaps the ring is part of a ritual they conducted here?"

"What was the moon phase the night she saw the thing?" John asks as he thumbs through information on his tablet. "Standing stones were frequently aligned to solstices and equinoxes. Maybe it's a moon phase trigger?"

I dig out my phone and look. "Night of the full moon."

"Do we know any of the other times she saw the thing?" Mark asks.

"No." I walk through the center of the ring of stones and...

I drop to my hands and knees and lower my face, until it's nearly at the ground.

It's as if I can smell the faintest traces of...*something*.

Not her, but...something *odd*.

Something maybe not of this world.

Gooseflesh rises all over my body, and that's damn sure something that hasn't happened for well over a thousand years.

"What is it, sir?" Mark asks.

"I don't know. Maybe nothing." I stand and look up at the waning moon.

Give me your secrets, damn you.

Before dawn the next morning, I am safely in my estate in Scotland and falling asleep in a bed I never dreamed I'd ever sleep in alone again.

Not once I met Eilidh.

Still no sign of her, and I'm trying to convince myself it's just because she's *that* good at staying hidden, and not because something's happened to her.

No record of either of her passports being used to leave the country. No record of her on any flights, or trains, or buses.

Nothing.

Like she's disappeared from the face of the planet. She could give classes on it. Even the former CIA spook who's joined Garrett's pack gave her disappearing skills high praise.

Maybe, once I find her, one of her "things" she can do is give new vampires lessons on how to stay off the grid.

I, on the other hand, am going to give her one *hell* of a fucking spanking when I finally get my hands on her again.

Then I'm going to spend an entire night with her tied up and squirming under my hands and making her beg to come.

Then another spanking.

I *have* to believe she's safe. If I allow my mind to drift to dark places, it's too easy to sink into depression, and I don't want to do that.

I *need* her to be safe.

I need *her*.

Kylie and her hacker friends have started sorting through traffic camera images in and around Albuquerque, trying to use image recognition software to see if they can find her license plate in any images to get a hint of what direction she headed.

But it's a big fucking country.

We have flags out for the two phone numbers we know about—the one she used to use and the one she made the two phone calls on. No doubt she had more than one burner with her and switched phones as soon as she knew Lucius had already spoken to both of the people she called.

Clever, clever girl.

Emmett Green, Garrett's father, offered to call in favors and have law enforcement issue a BOLO for her and her vehicle, but that's only as a last resort. I'd rather Eilidh not end up on any official radar like that, if possible. It could come back to impact us in unexpected ways later.

Besides, she's broken no laws. Technically. I mean, using the fake ID and having her license plate issued to it *is* against the law, yes, but it's a victimless crime.

Or maybe she didn't really love you, asshole.

There is that possibility. That I moved too fast, she got scared, and this was the perfect timing for her to leave.

I've paid Garrett to hold Eilidh's apartment, as-is, so Amber can keep trying to see her.

So far, no luck.

She insists that Eilidh's father *is* alive, however. And that Eilidh and I will end up together.

That she is alive and safe.

There are no secrets to be learned at the stone ring tonight. I'll keep people here, watching the ring and monitoring it with remote cameras. Maybe if they pick up something, it'll provide a clue.

The only thing I can do now is wait until we have some hint of where Eilidh is, unless we uncover more evidence about the stone ring.

Unfortunately, waiting is a skill I've had a lot of practice at.

Doesn't make it any easier. Especially when my soulmate is somewhere, out there, and I have no idea where, or if she's in danger.

ONE NIGHT SIX WEEKS LATER, I'm sitting on the ground in Scotland, outside the third of the three standing stone rings, when my cell rings.

My hope soars when I see it's a Tucson number that's not Lucius' or Garrett's numbers.

"Dexter Van Sussex."

"Hiya. It's Kylie."

Kylie King, hacker extraordinaire. If my heart were beating, it'd be racing right now. "*Please* tell me you have something."

"I have something."

I jump to my feet. "Really?"

"Really. I just verified thirty minutes ago that she boarded a ferry in Bellingham, Washington, and took it to Whittier, Alaska. I confirmed her license plate and everything. She used an assumed name, but she transported her Toyota, so she still has it."

"What? Seriously? She's just boarded a ferry to Alaska?"

"Oh, sorry, no. I mean, I just *confirmed* it. She actually *took* the ferry weeks ago. My bad. Sorry, dude."

My hope sinks. "*Weeks* ago?"

"Yes. Frangelico is working his sources who know the vampires in that region, trying to learn who the wholesale blood suppliers are, and running down leads that way. If we can track who receives shipments of blood on the regular, that'll give him a starting point to ask for assistance locating her. Garrett's talking to shifters up there, too. Trying to locate the shifter bars, fight clubs—anywhere she might feel right at home and able to do her thing."

I groan. "Alaska is a big place. It's enormous and remote."

"Don't worry—we're working on it. I would suggest making your way to Anchorage. They have larger hotels there. Chances are, she's still on the Kenai Peninsula. Or possibly up in Mat-Su, just to the north. Once we find out where she went from Whittier, or if she's still in Whittier, we'll be able to let you know where to go. It's doubtful she's still in Whittier, though."

"Why can't I just fly into Whittier, then?"

"For starters, it's tiny. I don't know what you're flying on, but your pilot needs to check if their airfield can even handle your plane. Secondly, Whittier is *tiny*. Did I mention it's tiny? You kind of need a specialized type of quarters to—"

"Okay, I *get* it," I wearily say. "It's a small town lacking in vampire-friendly accommodations. I'll fly into Anchorage."

"Excellent. We'll keep working on this and hope to have more news for you within twenty-four hours. I'll call you back from this number as soon as we know anything."

"Thanks."

I hang up and blur the mile back to where my pilot is waiting with a helicopter. I make a couple of quick phone calls to start preparations to move me, and then sit back as we take off to return to my estate. I've scoured every inch of the three standing rings multiple times over these past six weeks and have yet to find any answers.

The general consensus is perhaps the stone ring activates the apparition somehow, maybe in conjunction with the ring Eilidh has.

The last full moon, John, Mark, and I were standing at the stone ring outside of Cardiff and waiting for something, *anything* to happen.

Nothing happened, except I think I got another whiff of that scent, sort of like Eilidh, but kind of not. Then it was gone again so quickly, it might have simply been my wishful thinking.

We've just landed at my estate when my phone rings. Garrett Green.

I answer. "Please give me more good news."

"Nothing solid yet, beyond Kylie's lead, but I've got people heading there now. Boots on the ground. I'm going to put you in touch with my cousin, Noah. He's agreed to help you and work closely with you. He's not normally a vampire fan, but he said since I vouch for you, he'll help. Keep in touch with me and let me know when you arrive, and you all can coordinate."

I nearly weep with gratitude. "I cannot tell you how much I appreciate all you and your pack have done for me."

"Yeah, well, like I said, she's pack. And *our* fucking deal won't happen until we find her." He snorts. "I mean, that's not my *main* consideration, but I'd be lying if I said it isn't one."

I chuckle. "I apologize for the delay. As soon as my girl is safely in my arms again, we *will* push that deal through as quickly as possible."

"Yeah, well, item number one better be one hell of a spanking. For her," he clarifies.

"Oh, believe me, that tops my list."

Boy, does it.

Less than an hour later, my jet is in the air with me on board. I hate last-minute travel. I much prefer to fly at night, but now in the space of two months, I've made two last-minute air flights.

Because of *her*.

Yes, she's damned well worth it. She's my heart and soul, of this I'm convinced.

And yes, there is one *hell* of a spanking in her future.

29

E *ilidh*

THEY SAY your blood thins when you move somewhere warm.

#irony

Three-plus years in Tucson made me learn to hate humidity and damp, cold weather.

In other news, I hate Alaska.

Fuck my life.

I've been here nearly six weeks, and it's seven weeks since I fled Tucson.

I dream about Dexter every night and miss him like fucking crazy.

In my sleep, my mind takes me back to Club Toxic's dungeon, where Dexter and I engage in pretty much every kind of kinky fun two people can have together. Last night he wore jeans and a black Henley, and those boots, and he tied me up, flogged me, and fucked my brains out before biting me.

I awoke alone in my room with my fingers jammed in my cooter, while the echoes of an orgasm faded.

It's almost enough to make me want to try to contact him, except I know what will happen. He'll show up, do his fangy white knight act, wanting to fix my fucking life. Then what am I supposed to do?

I'm in fucking *Alaska*. There's not much farther I can run unless I try to *Dukes of Hazzard* jump my fricking 4Runner to Russia from the goddamned backyard.

I am *not* looking forward to an Alaskan winter. Maybe I'll make my way to Florida before the days shorten too much.

Arizona is *right* out.

I can't go back there, even though the thought of never seeing Dexter again makes me want to climb down the switchback path winding along the bluff's face, plunge my head into the frigid waters of Kachemak Bay just off the beach, and stay there until death takes me.

What's the point of life? I mean, seriously? What's the point of staying alive if I'm going to feel *this* freaking miserable?

The only good thing about Alaska right now is that nights are only about four hours long.

Yeah, that's right, baby. Land of the Midnight fricking Sun. Which is why, along with the low population densities, vampires as a general rule tend to avoid Alaska.

Unfortunately, those short nights don't last forever. Eventually, it changes to months when the days are barely that long.

Dexter might think he can protect me, but the truth is, he can't. I think that was made perfectly clear in Tucson.

Finally having proof—the FLIR was pretty conclusive—that the dog-thing is real shook my faith in anyone being able to help me.

The last thing I want to do is draw attention to myself, because I'll not only have the vampires after me, but shifters, as well. I'm...different in a way that doesn't fit in. If I'm a liability. I'm dead. That's how it works, and I know that all too well.

I mean, this thing tracked me to outside Lucius Frangelico's nightclub. If Lucius doesn't want humans getting harmed or killed on the premises so it doesn't draw attention, he *damn* sure doesn't want huge phantom dog-thingies sniffing around his staff parking lot for the same reason.

The vampires and shifters can't risk humans finding out about them. They also can't risk attracting government attention. The shifters have already shut down several Data-X labs, but it's possible there might be more, or other secret programs out there, trying to snatch shifters and vampires and breed super-beings for war. Selene's hybrid status makes her a particularly high-value target, should the wrong people learn about her existence.

No, best I completely disappear before I make the bad kind of name for myself with any of them.

I'm lucky my very first vampire boss, Neimus, the one in Toronto, likes me and gave me this job lead. Chaldis Bianchi is a very old vampire—nearly as old as Lucius and Dexter—who was in need of some help for a little while. His long-time human helper had family business to take care of in the Lower 48.

There's not a lot I have to do. Chaldis doesn't feed on live humans very often, which is a damned good thing, because there aren't a lot of humans per capita in this part of Alaska from which to choose.

He also orders a lot of bagged blood. For hunting, he mostly feeds on cattle and wildlife. He runs a cattle ranch, so he's never lacking in choices. If he happens upon fishermen or hunters or tourists who are out and about at night, he sometimes chats them up and grabs a nip from them. There's a higher-than-usual number of tourists around here because they film some homesteader "unscripted documentary" TV show nearby.

The people who work at the ranch think Chaldis is an elderly recluse in poor health. Normally, everything is handled through Corbin, his human helper. But Corbin's older brother is battling cancer, and it's looking grim. The timing worked out perfectly that Chaldis had just contacted Neimus the day before, looking for possible references.

This is where I come in. I'm Chaldis' "niece." Or so everyone has been told. I don't have to deal with the day-to-day ranch operations. I'm simply a go-between and errand-runner.

Meaning I keep an eye on the time and, on the nights Chaldis wants to hunt, I prepare a special four-wheel-drive RV kept parked in the enclosed garage, so it's ready to go at safe twilight. I drive him out to his favorite hunting area and then literally wait with the motor running to drive him home again. There's a portable, light-proof crypt inside the RV, just in case we get stuck or don't make it home before dawn. I also run to the store for him when he needs anything, and I help with chores around the house.

It is a rather nice house, large, even though on the outside it doesn't look like much, doesn't draw any attention to itself. Inside, it has every modern amenity. All the bedrooms are made securely light-proof with roll-down shades inside, and louvered shutters on the outside to keep sunlight from directly entering. The rest of the house has louvered shutters on the outside, and roll-down shades on the inside that are triggered by light sensors. The front and back door entry rooms are set up not to allow light into the main house, so there's no danger to Chaldis. In addition to all this, he has heavy-duty storm shutters that can be rolled down, and can withstand hurricane-force winds.

He's 1,727 years old. While the morning hits him hard and drops him into the daily stupor, he rarely sleeps more than four hours. Sometimes, not even that long. Apparently, the wild fluctuations in Alaska's days and nights have altered his vampiric circadian rhythm over the years.

Once he wakes up, he'll talk with me while he helps me take care of chores around the house.

I was a little creeped out by that, at first, worried he might try to feed on me. But then I realized it's just that he's...

Well, he's *lonely*. Fortunately, he's not creeped out by his inability to thrall me, so I guess we're even there.

He had a vampire mate, but she was killed in World War II while they were trying to escape from Europe. After losing his mate, Chaldis made his way east across Russia to Alaska, where he lived feral in the wilderness for several years before pulling himself out of his depression and building a life here. Like Dexter, he's very ethical in that he doesn't wish to harm innocent humans, and he hasn't killed any humans in over a decade.

It won't be much longer before he'll have to move on. The locals think he's in his seventies, and through his thrall he hasn't let anyone recognize him in over thirty years. He looks like he's in his late thirties or maybe in his forties, barely. Handsome guy, with dark brown eyes and brown hair, six-two and slender in build. Bet he looks good in a suit, even though I've never seen him in one.

Nothing like my not-Ianto, though.

Chaldis is giving serious thought to moving to Tucson, and that's one of our frequent topics of conversation, even though it makes me miss Dexter like freaking crazy.

I told Chaldis I'd contact Lucius for him, if he wants, and make the introduction. Hell, I'd even vouch for him.

Look at me, vouching for another vampire.

I'm sure Garrett would be shaking his head at me right now.

Meanwhile, Corbin's brother will likely pass away soon, but Chaldis has offered to let me stay on, if I want, even after Corbin returns.

As much as I'd hate the winters...I'm thinking about it. I'm secure here. The pay's decent, especially since he provides room and board. The guy's loaded, and he's not at all a criminal. He's slipped his fingers into a lot of very legal and lucrative pies over the years, since he's been in Alaska for so long.

The problem is, when you get into winter in Alaska, besides the fact that it's fricking cold as hell, you get *days* that are barely six hours long.

To a vampire who isn't susceptible to cold?

That's fucking *awesome*. It's a goddamned Garden of Eden.

To a human like me? Who has *legit* reasons to not want to face nights that long?

Not so much.

Especially when I'm alone.

Yes, I tearfully confessed to Chaldis what drove me from Tucson. I wanted him to know about the stupid whatever the dog-thing is, the gwiggle, or weewee, or whatever the fuck Lucius and Dex called it. I showed him the pictures I took of the security camera video screen. Since we don't get cellphone reception at the house, unless I tap into our Wi-Fi and activate that setting on my phone, I was able to turn on my old phone and download the pictures to my computer without worrying about it pinging and giving away my location.

I'm pretty sure Dex was right about one thing—I'm now convinced the ring is some sort of key. When I look back, several times when I've put it on my finger, within a couple of days—usually sooner—is when I've had a problem and needed to move.

Dex puts it on his finger, and the creature shows up only a few hours later?

And the night Mom died, it was on *her* finger.

Well, *that's* pretty damned conclusive. So, if I can keep ahead of the damned thing and just never, ever wear the ring again, or let anyone else wear it...

Maybe that'll keep me safe, and keep those around me safe.

One day, maybe, I'll work up the courage to destroy the ring.

Right now, I'm sitting on the deck outside the house and staring at the damn ring, where it's threaded through its chain.

Maybe I should toss it into Kachemak Bay. The currents would carry it away, never to be seen again.

But something deep inside me rebels at that. Despite the trouble it's possibly brought to my life...it's literally the *only* thing I have of my father.

I don't even know his real *name*.

No pictures of him.

Again, I think what if Dex *is* right? If maybe the things that have hunted me all my life are being sent by him through the ring? What if Amber's right that he's alive, but she's wrong that he misses and loves me?

Maybe Mom wanted to spare me the truth. Maybe I wasn't wanted.

Maybe my presence is a threat to some family fortune or something.

But would Mom have cried over him as much as she did? I know all the nights I awakened to find her sobbing and trying not to wake me up gouged deep ravines into my soul. I think that's why I reacted to Dexter's story so hard. I can believe he still mourns.

Dad was the love of Mom's life. She never so much as had coffee with anyone else, unless it was a group of friends. But as far as I know, she never put on the ring, until that night she was killed.

And every time we had to move when I was a kid...

I groan. It was after I had usually stuck a finger in the ring, where it hung from the chain, while she was in the shower, or asleep, and I was fascinated by it and played with it because I missed Dad so much.

Dammit.

From sitting on the bluff where the property is located, I stare out at the bay. Today it's breezy and choppy, and the waters look dark, nearly black.

Unlike my stupid hair, which turned golden blonde my third day on the run and hasn't changed since.

Amber's words come to mind—that my father's not dead. That Mom thought he was dead since he didn't return, but she didn't actually see him...*die.*

What if it really is *a kind of homing beacon?* It'd make sense Dad would give it to Mom if that was the case, right?

But then what are the phantoms?

I hold the ring in my fist and close my eyes. There are

murky memories in my brain, no doubt stirred up by Amber's words. I remember Mom's beaming smile whenever Dad returned from being away, how I'd run to him and he'd sweep me into his arms.

Mazbushka. My little Mazbushka.

How worried Mom would act whenever he'd have to leave for days or even for weeks at a time for "work."

Maybe he was a criminal?

Most of my life's been spent in fear, on the run. It's difficult to remember there were large swaths of my childhood where it was the three of us happily spending evenings together, or mornings, depending on Mom's schedule. Or the four of us, if Dad's friend, Zuzu, was there.

Or me and Dad, when he'd take care of me while Mom was at work. How we sometimes spent time on hikes with Zuzu. And, sometimes, Zuzu stayed with me and Mom when Dad was away. Or Dad would take me to Zuzu's.

How Dad hated that Mom had to go to work at all, but there were reasons we couldn't go stay with him when he had to leave for work.

Their shared looks that, even at that age, I viscerally understood meant a secret I was too young to know. The way one of them would always distract me whenever I asked, to the point I forgot I even asked.

Not like there aren't crazier things in the world. Vampires. Shifters. Fae.

Maybe this ring *is* an artifact of some kind.

The colors of the labradorite stone flash in the sun. I stare at the markings on the side and wish I knew what they meant. No matter how much I've searched, I cannot find anything else like it. No known runes, or cuneiform, or any kind of markings match them.

I had some hope when Dexter thought it looked familiar, but even Lucius scratched his head over it.

If two two-thousand-plus-year-old vampires who each speak a bunch of languages can't recognize it, then...

Yeah.

Down in town, a small plane circles on final approach to Homer Airport. It's not one of the normally scheduled planes, meaning it's probably some rich person who chartered a plane for a special trip out here. The place is laid-back and beautiful. Not a bad place to end up, I suppose. The end of the world, in a way.

I wish Dexter was here to enjoy this with me.

Yeah, and whose fault is that, girlie?

Mine. It's mine, because I got my hopes up, and look what happened? Worse, it's not just my heart I broke, but probably Dexter's, too.

I hate myself for that.

When I hear Chaldis call for me, I stand and make my way back inside the house, where I find him puzzling over a cookbook he just received yesterday. "What's up, boss?" He's barefoot and wearing soft, faded jeans and a black Henley that already has flour on it because he forgets to wear the *Kiss the Cook* apron Corbin got for him.

Chaldis smiles. "Still won't call me Chaldis, hmm?" He has a slight, sexy Italian accent.

"No offense, but it's a *me* thing, not a *you* thing, boss." I sit on the other side of the kitchen island and nod toward the cookbook.

He turns it around and points to the section giving him trouble. "What does *that* mean?"

Cooking is his new hobby, I guess. Corbin warned me about it, that I'd better figure out how to slip in daily workouts, or Chaldis' cooking would fatten me up in no time. He frequently makes more than enough food to feed the ranch hands, and I take it down to them, or package it in containers for them to take home to their families. The vampire's toying with the idea of opening a restaurant one day, because it's something he's never done before. A new challenge.

It's fricking adorable, and who'd a thunk I'd ever say *that* about a vampire?

Other than Dexter, that is.

"You have to separate the egg yolks from the whites," I tell him. "I've never done that." I reach for the tablet that lives on the kitchen bar and call up YouTube. I find a cooking tutorial, and we watch it several times before he attempts it and gets it perfect on the first try, grinning like a kid at his success.

He's annoying like that. I think it's a vampire thing.

"Was that a plane I heard earlier?" he asks with his eyebrows arched in a way I've already come to know means hopeful eagerness. He's adorable. He really is. If my heart wasn't totally shattered—#selfinflicted—I'd be tempted to ask if he was interested.

Seriously tempted.

But, no, he's my boss, and quickly becoming a friend.

#vampzoned

Besides, he might not be exactly...single.

"Yeah. Small private passenger, not a cargo delivery."

"Ah. Darn."

I swipe through to the FedEx app to track his package. "Your *cocotte* isn't scheduled to land here until tomorrow, boss. It's still on its way to Anchorage." He placed an order for a Le Creuset Dutch oven and he's dying to get it, even though he already has *three* fricking Dutch ovens.

They're expensive as hell, but apparently the recipe he

wants to try uses *that* particular one, and he's an old, rich, stubborn, and borderline anal-retentive vampire. Even though he can use one of the others, he wants to use *that* one, because fates forbid he deviates from the recipe in the slightest, even though it says you don't *have* to use that particular one.

#shrug

What are you gonna do?

Plus, he's got a special edition Star Wars one coming with it. Which, I mean, *seriously*, I've spent less money for a full set of cheap new tires on the 4Runner in the past than he did on two damn pieces of cookware.

We should also receive his next order of human blood in tomorrow's delivery. It's a regular shipment, designed to keep ahead of his need so there's no worry about him running low should there be any supply line issues. It is fricking Alaska, after all.

"Any news from Corbin today?" he asks a little too casually.

"Not yet." I glance at the time. "He'll probably check in soon." He checks in every day. I suspect there is way more than an employer-employee dynamic between the two. Maybe I'm reading too much into it, but the way Corbin sends me reminders about things to do for Chaldis, and the slightly too-casual way Chaldis asks about Corbin, pings my instincts.

Meaning I'm reasonably sure there's something *there*. Corbin's single and has worked for and lived with Chaldis for over fifteen years, even though Corbin barely looks like he's older than his mid-twenties. I suspect there's been at least a few blood exchanges between the two. Probably quite a few receiving on Corbin's end, if I take Corbin's youthful appearance into account. Maybe Corbin's a sweetblood. Who knows?

But it's not my business.

At allll.

I mean, the fact that I'm in the second-biggest bedroom, which is a guest room, and Corbin apparently sleeps in the same bed as Chaldis, is another *huge* honking clue.

But the men didn't mention it, so I won't be so gauche as to bring it up. They're both consenting adults, right?

"I hope he's all right," he quietly says. "I worry so about him when he leaves."

"Why don't you travel with him?"

He snorts. "The logistics are insane." He glances my way. "I am rich by human standards, but I am not Lucius Frangelico or Dexter Van Sussex rich. I also don't wish to place an extra emotional burden on my b—I mean, on him."

"Burden on your...?"

Okay, so I am a little nosy. Sue me.

He sighs and plants his hands on the counter before meeting my gaze. "You are an intelligent woman. You tell me."

"He's *yours*." I close the tablet's cover and set it aside. "He's your boy, right?"

He nods. "Does that bother you?"

"No. Should it? I mean, did you compel him to be that to you?"

He smiles as he shakes his head. "No. He arrived in Homer, and we met at a hotel bar. I did not have to compel him. Not that first night, or any other since. He loves me, and I love him."

"Well, there you go, then. Sounds copacetic to me. Consenting adults."

"I hate that I cannot be there with him to help him through this, but I know I cannot, for many reasons." He focuses on me. "But what about you? Seems like you've referred to your Dexter in a way that's more than friends or lovers."

"We talking as equals now and have a trust box?"

"Of course."

I blink away the unexpected tears. "I thought Dexter and I were going to have...*that*. Him be my Sir. He's definitely an in-charge kind of guy, and he's the first man I've ever trusted enough to let go to like that. First vampire I was ever with, too."

"I am sorry, my dear. I suspected there was more to your tale, but I wished to respect your privacy."

Next thing I know, I'm crying the whole damn story out to him, and he's passing me paper towels.

"You know what's so stupid?" I blow my nose. "He said I was his, and that when he woke up we were going to have a conversation about our future." I dab at my eyes. "I finally, *finally* let my guard down, and then *bam*, I see the phantom dog. I mean, how ironic is *that*, right? I find the perfect guy for me, and I have to leave."

"You didn't have to leave. I'm sure he would have helped you with it."

"I don't even know what it is! Tucson isn't Homer. If I'd stayed there and that thing stayed there, too, it wouldn't be long before someone noticed it. That's not something containable. That would draw a lot of the bad kind of attention to vampires and shifters, and I'm not going to be that reason."

He sadly sighs. "I promise I will not interfere, but I would bet your Dexter is likely very upset over your departure. Are you ever going to contact him and at least let him know you're safe?"

I sniffle. "I don't know. I need to figure out a way to do it where he can't trace me."

"Please take this advice in the way it is intended, but it is intensely painful to know someone you love needs help, you can offer that help, but are not allowed to due to circumstances. Please, consider contacting him, *hmm*?"

"Don't you fricking dare, boss."

"What about your friend, Neimus? Could he not pass word for you?"

"And have Dexter hound him? Yeah, no." I've been playing with the ring while we talk. "Maybe if I could finally figure this part out, see if the ring really is connected, that'd be different. But I don't have any answers."

"May I see your ring?"

"Yeah, just don't put it on. I'm convinced there's a connection between it being worn and the thing appearing. Dexter was the last to put it on. That's the other reason I don't want him here, because I don't want the thing focused on him, if that's the case."

He nods.

I hand it over and he studies it, finally shaking his head as he returns it. "I am sorry, but it doesn't look familiar to me. Although I spent relatively little time in that region throughout the years. Most of that time was in the last couple of centuries."

"Thanks anyway." I tuck it back under my shirt.

"Listen. Tonight, I'll grill us some steaks on the deck. We'll drink, and toast our missing loves, and stare at the stars, and share stories."

"You're a big softy."

"Yes, well, you never met me in my youth. You would not say that about me if you had. Frankly, I prefer myself this way. I feel it suits me better." He sadly smiles. "I thought I would miss the thrill of the hunt and kill. In my youth, I never imagined a sedate, peaceful life such as this would appeal to me so much. Somewhere along the way, Corbin snuck into my shattered heart and gently started putting the pieces back together before I even realized it." He cocks his head at me. "Well? What about dinner?"

"As long as you make me those crispy potatoes with the truffle oil." I smile. "I love those."

He happily rubs his hands together. "*Perfetto!*"

Who'd a thunk a vampire's love language was cooking? It reminds me so much of someone, but I can't quite grab the memory. It feels like it's painful, so I dodge it and focus on what I'm doing.

I'm washing dishes for him a few minutes later while he's still working on whatever this latest dish is when the gate intercom down at the road chimes.

We both look at each other, because normally packages come to the other entrance, where the main barn and office for the cattle ranch are located. But a few times a week, tourists who get lost looking for the famous homestead will end up at the house gate.

I walk over to the wall and hit the intercom button. "Hello?"

It's a man. "Hi, I'm trying to find the Olsson Homestead?"

I simultaneously relax and feel something ping at the outer reaches of my mind, like maybe it's a familiar voice. Before I can reply, however, Chaldis has blurred over and mashed the button.

"You are still a mile from their driveway," he says. "Continue northeast approximately one mile. On your right, you will see two reflective orange triangles by their gate."

"Oh, okay. Thank you."

"You're welcome." He turns off the intercom and stares at me.

"What?" I ask.

"You. Why did you react like that? Your pulse shot up."

"I...I don't know. It just..."

"Yes?"

I blow out a breath. "It's stupid. His voice sounded a little familiar."

He smirks. "Well, we know it cannot be your Dexter, because it's still sunny out."

I laugh. "I know. It wasn't him, definitely. It probably reminds me of someone I heard at the nightclub once."

"Are you certain? I can call the ranch hands to go investigate. Tell them we're worried about an intruder."

"No. I'm fine. I'm sure it's nothing. We were overdue a lost tourist, anyway."

"*That* is something else we will do tonight." He guides me back to the kitchen. "You are overdue for another target practice session."

Yeah, the vampire wants me able to shoot. Apparently, because the risk here is more four-legged predators, not two-legged ones. "As long as I get crispy truffle potatoes out of the deal."

He smiles. "Deal."

But now that my mind's thought about the club again, Dexter's there, too, front and center.

Chaldis is probably right. Dexter's probably missing me, worried about me, and that fills me with guilt.

I need to contact him, somehow. Maybe I can send a letter to Corbin while he's gone and he can mail it for me, to hide my location.

But what do I even say to Dexter at this point? *Sorry I broke your heart? Sorry I ran? Sorry I'm a chickenshit who doesn't know how to stand and fight for myself when it comes to this?*

Sorry that we had a taste of perfection and I ran?

I didn't exactly burn that bridge, but I damn sure didn't adult very well.

Dexter can find someone better than me.

Unfortunately, I suspect I'll never find someone as good as Dexter.

30

E _ilidh_

"*Dude. How* did you use up *all* the fricking salt?" I ask Chaldis as I emerge from the root cellar about an hour later. "I *just* bought ten pounds two weeks ago." I realized we were almost out when I went to prep the steaks and let them sit out with salt on them, just to realize—

"For the salt-encrusted salmon I prepared last week. You said yourself it was divine."

Word. That salmon *was* heavenly. Melted in my mouth like *butter.* "How'd it not end up on the shopping list, *hmm*?" I arch an eyebrow at him the way I saw Corbin do.

He looks playfully abashed. "Perhaps...because I forgot to write it there?"

I roll my eyes at him. "That means a trip into town. I'll check your PO Box while I'm there."

"I'm sorry, Eilidh." Yes, I told the guys my real name.

Neimus said I can trust Chaldis and Corbin not to tell anyone. I'm "Hayley" to everyone in town and at the ranch.

Close enough.

I'm tired of running. I'm heartsick and missing Dexter. I miss Garrett and Amber and Selene and even Lucius and his men.

I miss the club's slutty household humans, and I miss the horny Fight Club shifters who always tried to get me to go out with them when I had to run errands for someone and met there to discuss the deets.

I miss Tucson.

I miss the desert.

I miss my life.

And yet, this comfortable, safe landing pad, this welcomed retreat, hasn't been all bad. I hate Alaska the *idea*, and the reason *why* I'm here, not Chaldis, or his home, or our long talks, or the quiet introspection I've had here, or even the land itself.

I do, however, hate the mosquitoes the size of fricking fruit bats this place has.

I'm about to leave—I always drive his Land Rover, because my Toyota is safely parked inside the enclosed attached garage to keep it hidden—when the house phone rings.

I answer. "Bianchi residence."

The caller sniffles. "Hey, Eilidh. Is Master awake?"

My heart sinks at Corbin's quiet, tearful tone. I know exactly what it signals, especially since he slipped and called Chaldis that. Usually, he asks for him by first name. "Oh, sweetie. I'm so sorry. Hold on." If I didn't know their dynamic already, that would've clenched it.

But when I turn, Chaldis is already standing there, reaching for the phone, a blank expression on his face.

I step out to the deck to give them privacy, even though I can still hear nearly every word both of them say. Curse my super hearing and the lack of city noises to cover their conversation.

If I hadn't been certain about their love before, I am now, from the tender words Chaldis uses to try to console his broken-hearted lover. Corbin can barely speak and spends most of the call crying.

Once they end their conversation, I return inside to find Chaldis standing there, hands in his pockets and staring at the phone.

"I'm sorry."

He nods, finally running a hand through his brown hair. It's a little shaggier than he usually wears it, because Corbin always cuts it for him. I offered to try, but he wanted to wait.

I guess that was another clue—there are things Corbin does for him that Chaldis gently refuses my offers to do. It's *their* things.

I can't blame him.

This is why I can never agree with Garrett when he calls them leeches. Sure, some of them...well, *suck*, but then there are vampires like Neimus, Dex, and Chaldis, and even Lucius at his good times. And Selene. They're not all murdering assholes without consciences. This is exactly one of the reasons why Lucius has instituted among his sired a ban on siring without his permission.

I should head to the store, but I wait, sensing Chaldis needs to talk.

Finally, he tips his head back, staring at the ceiling, and I spot the tears he's trying to blink away. "I *hate* this," he whispers. "I *hate* that I cannot *be* there for him when he needs me so much right now." He sighs. "This is why I know your Dexter must be missing you."

I ignore his last comment. "We can overnight you via charter or overnight freight cargo. We can use the crate from the RV. I can fly out with you and have a cargo van ready, prep a hotel room, all of that. It's a little spendy, but I've arranged flights like that before, and I'd fly with you because it's accompanied cargo. Probably an uncomfortable jump seat, but still, it's doable."

He shakes his head. "I haven't traveled like that in years. There is too much risk to consider. Besides, if I am traveling there like that, he will be worried about me instead of focusing on his family. I have kept him away from them already for too long." He sadly smiles and finally looks at me. "But thank you, dear. You are very sweet to offer."

"When is the funeral?" I mean, I know, but I'm trying to be polite.

"In three days. Wednesday evening." He smiles. "As if you didn't hear."

"Well, you know..." I don't know where to go with that.

"I don't know when he will return. I will try to get him to spend time there, with his family." *There* is Georgia, where Corbin's originally from. "The other reason it's probably best not to go is that his family...does not know." He sighs. "About...*us*."

"That he's gay?"

He nods. "I do not wish to drive a deeper wedge between them and him than already exists. Corbin suspects if he came out to them that they would ostracize him. He left there right after high school and made his way out here, where we met. They think he is a wilderness guide. We send them money and pay his parents' property taxes every year. We sent them money to help with medical expenses. We are, in fact, paying for the whole funeral. His brother wished to be cremated, so no graveside service." He plays with the ornate gold band on his right ring finger.

Now that I'm thinking about it, I realize Corbin wears a ring on his right ring finger, too. I remember seeing it when we met.

Ahhh.

#Imadumbass

All the clues have been there the whole time.

"But if you go, you can charm people to think you're nothing more than friends. Or—now, hear me out—you could charm them to accept that he's gay, and then you two could openly be together."

He seems to consider it, then resignation washes in again. "Yes, but it will still stress him out." I walk over and offer him a hug, which he accepts. "Thank you for all your help, Eilidh. I meant it when I offered you a permanent position here. Please, consider it. I know winters are harsh, but we will make sure you want for nothing. It is good for him to have another human here to speak with, whom he doesn't have to hide anything from. And you are very pleasant company."

I know he means that in a friendly way, not a romantic one. "I'm thinking about it, boss. Let's table that, for now."

"He wants me to turn him, but I'd rather wait. His aging has slowed somewhat, but if I turn him, it will make him visiting his family impossible. I'm hoping to wait until at least his parents have passed. By then, he will look a little older, close to my appearance. I would welcome you as our human helper, should you wish to stay on."

"I can't make you any promises, boss. I told you that."

Look what happened the last time I got my hopes up.

"I know. I just want the offer to be extended."

We end the hug and I grab the shopping list. "Anything else we need?" I ask.

He starts to say something when the gate intercom goes off again.

I'm closer and answer it. "Hello?"

It's a different man, and I don't recognize his voice. "Sorry, but is this the Olsson Homestead? I think I'm lost."

"Sorry..." I give him directions and turn to see Chaldis standing there and frowning.

And he's holding the nine-millimeter handgun he's been teaching me target shooting with. I'm not bad with it. He must have blurred to get it.

He's also holding the concealed carry waistband holster. "Take this with you to town," he says.

"Really?"

He arches an eyebrow at me—Dom eyebrow if I ever saw it—and shakes it at me. I don't like to carry and he knows it.

"Fine." I strap it on, making sure my T-shirt and light jacket cover it. "Happy?"

"And take a sat phone."

"Overkill much?" But I grab one of the three he keeps on the kitchen counter. Like a cell phone, but they get reception everywhere.

"Perhaps, but I take no risks with your safety."

"I'm sure it's fine." I grab the list, the PO Box keys, and the Land Rover's keys, and head to the garage. I always make sure the door to the inside is securely shut before rolling up the overhead door. Once I back out, I wait until the door has rolled all the way down before I leave.

The gate opens automatically for me when I leave, and I pause to make sure it closes securely behind me before continuing on to town. The PO Box first, then the store.

There were a couple of other things on the list we needed, but they could've waited until I made the trip tomorrow. Down at the airport, I see the small plane that arrived earlier is being unloaded, a cargo crate about the size of a large chest freezer being moved from the rear of the plane into a windowless panel van while three guys stand by closely supervising.

At the grocery store, I make sure to smile and say hi to everyone. Because while I'm new, I'm now considered a "local," in a way, since I'm a "relative" of a long-time local.

Besides, if I do end up staying on, I don't want to alienate everyone.

I've walked away from enough people in my life. It gets harder every time, and this time, I ripped my heart out in the process.

As I'm digging money out of my wallet to pay, Sandy, the clerk, lets out a sigh. "Wow, *he's* cute. Never seen him in town before. Must be a tourist."

I look up but see nothing more than the back of a jean-clad guy disappearing around the end of another aisle.

As I load my purchases in the Land Rover, I freeze when the hint of a scent drifts to my nose.

Shifter.

Wolf. Not one that I know, but *definitely* a wolf.

Fuck!

With my pulse pounding, I slam the back hatch closed and jump behind the wheel, peeling out of the parking lot before I even put on my seatbelt.

Instead of heading toward the homestead, I race in the opposite direction. I have all the roads and tracks and trails in the immediate vicinity that can take the four-by memorized, just in case I ever needed to know them. I've learned a lot about the local terrain from driving Chaldis around at night, too.

I keep glancing in the rearview mirror, but no one's following me.

My pulse finally slows, and I pull off and wait a couple of minutes not far from a turnoff I can take to make my way home, just to make sure.

The gun's in my hand and ready.

No one follows me.

Chaldis has been careful not to make enemies while in Alaska. There's no wolf pack here in Homer, no other vampires. No resident shifters. He doesn't draw attention to himself, meaning there's no reason why anyone should be hunting him.

Hopefully.

Feeling stupid, because of *course* there are shifters in Alaska, I finally head home, not relaxing until the garage roll-down door's safely shut behind me.

The door to the house opens and Chaldis is standing there. He immediately frowns and blurs over to the driver's door. "What's wrong? Are you all right? You smell stressed."

"That's freaky. I'm fine." I tell him about scenting the wolf.

"Homer does have an airstrip. It's not unusual for shifters to pass through, on occasion."

"Dude, you sound about as convinced as I do, and it's not making me feel any better." The house line rings, and I walk over to the garage wall phone to answer. "Bianchi residence."

"Miss Hayley? This is Jarred down at the barn. Mr. B's regular food shipment just arrived down here. Want me to send the delivery driver up to the house?"

That means his blood shipment. They think Chaldis

receives regular shipments of special perishable nutritional supplements. I turn to find Chaldis standing right next to me, scowling as he listens.

He shakes his head.

"No, I'll come get it," I tell him. "Down at the barn?"

"Yeah."

"I'll be right there." I hang up.

"Give me the gun," Chaldis says.

I do, and he blurs into the house. He returns a moment later with it. "I replaced the rounds with silver-tipped ones." And he's holding a different holster, the hip one. "Wear it visible."

"You're freaking me out." I swap the holsters out.

"I'm simply taking precautions, dear. And take this." He hands me a knife. "Silver."

"Now you're *really* freaking me out." I clip the knife's holster inside the back of my belt, hidden under my shirt and jacket.

"I am concerned and cautious. Give me the groceries and take the Land Rover. Stay in the vehicle. Fire through the vehicle's door, if you have to." He points to his head. "Aim for the head. A body shot, unless it pierces their heart, might not stop them. A silver bullet to the brain will kill."

"I've *got* this. You're overly nervous because of Corbin being gone."

"Yes, but I am also nervous because there are too many coincidences this afternoon."

Once he's safely inside with the groceries, and the inside door is closed, I open the overhead door again, back out, wait for the door to close, and head down the groomed track that leads to the barn.

There's a muddy blue Jeep I don't recognize parked in the yard in front of the barn, next to where the ranch hands park their vehicles and ATVs. I pull up close to the office door and roll down my window.

Jarred walks out, followed by—

Fuuuuuuuck.

The dude's definitely the same wolf I scented in town. He's carrying a clipboard and the large, sealed cardboard box holding the Styrofoam shipper with the cold packs and blood in it. The thing weighs about thirty pounds, but he's carrying it like it's empty.

I keep the gun in my lap, safety off, my finger along the trigger.

"I need a signature, ma'am," he says, his gaze heavy on me.

Oh, shit. It's the voice of the second tourist today, the one on the intercom.

I'm not stupid enough to look him in the eyes and risk trying to jumble his mind, in case he's an alpha and can resist me, but I keep my focus on his nose. "Jarred can sign for it. Just set it in the back hatch."

The wolf's gaze remains on me as he walks past the driver's door. From the way his nose wrinkles, I can tell he's just scented the gun.

Or he's picked up Chaldis' scent from me.

Keep walking, dude.

My heart's pounding, racing in a way it hasn't any of the times I saw that...*thing.*

This is a strange shifter, where one has no business being, and I smell like a vampire.

It's daytime.

I have to protect Chaldis.

But Jarred signs the clipboard after the wolf sets the large box in the back hatch and closes it. The wolf walks past my door again, pausing, nose barely upturned, but I know he's sniffing.

Barely parting my lips, I whisper low, in a way I know the wolf can clearly hear and Jarred can't. "I know you're a wolf. Stay off this land, and there will be no trouble. We want no trouble with you or your kind, but you are *not* welcomed here. Do *not* test me."

And I cock the hammer on the nine.

I *know* he heard that, because he freezes. He tips his chin up to show me his throat, signifying he's capitulating and won't fight me, then dips his head to me in a respectful nod. He briefly holds his hands up in front of him to signal he's withdrawing and takes a slow, deliberate step back before turning and quickly leaving.

Jarred walks over as I flick the safety on and ease the gun's hammer down. "You all right, Miss Hayley?" he asks.

I watch as the wolf gets in his Jeep and leaves. "Yes. If that man ever tries to set foot on this property again, do not let him, even if you have to shoot him." This is fucking *Alaska*. All the hands openly wear sidearms, because of bears, for starters.

He laughs, until he realizes I'm serious. "Um, yes, ma'am."

"Anyone else show up today you haven't seen before?"

"Just a couple of tourists. Same as always. Got 'em pointed the right way."

"Okay. Thanks." I get the Land Rover turned around and speed back to the house as fast as I dare, bouncing over ruts in the track. Once the overhead door is shut, the inside door opens and Chaldis blurs over.

He's armed, another nine on his hip. "Well?"

"Same fucking wolf. He was definitely the second tourist who buzzed at the gate. Get all the heavy storm shutters closed. *Now*. I don't know what's going on, but we might need to move you down into the crypt." The storm shutter system can handle bears and hurricanes.

I just hope it can handle werewolves.

"I'm *not* leaving you upstairs alone," he says.

"Yeah, well, you don't pay me to let someone set a trap for you, either, and it's daylight." There's an emergency exit, a small tunnel leading from the deep, rock-lined basement where his original crypt is, to a spider hole about a hundred yards down-slope from the house, just at the edge of thick, hilly woods with plenty of small, dark rocky nooks and crannies he could safely hole up in during sunlight, if forced to.

The escape tunnel has three branches off it, leading to sealed but easily opened exits, just in case the main exit is ever discovered and blocked. There's an old windowless ammunition storage bunker from World War II farther out on the property. They keep the roof and walls maintained, a secure door, and an emergency crypt with some supplies there in case he ever needs to use it.

He takes the container of blood into the kitchen, where we open the box to examine it. It doesn't look like it's been tampered with. The inner foam cooler's seals are also intact, as are the inner wrappers for the blood bags, which are, obviously, disguised as liquid nutritional supplements.

Chaldis leans in, his nose almost touching it as he sniffs. "You're right—I can smell the wolf on the outer box, but I believe the contents are all right. I smell nothing on or inside the cooler or on the blood bags, except the usual techs who pack the shipment. You didn't recognize him?"

"No. If I did, I wouldn't be so damned freaked out right now. I'd just be irritated that they'd managed to track me. If it was a Tucson wolf I knew, I could call Garrett and ask him to pull him off me. This is too much coincidence, though. I know you don't travel much anymore, but there are a *lot* of shifters out there who hate vampires. We'll need to get you down below."

"I'm *not* leaving you up here alone to face a potential threat."

Stubborn vamp! "You might not have a *choice*, boss. It's still *daylight*."

"Perhaps you should call your friend in Tucson and see if they sent him?"

"No. If Garrett did, then this wolf's not a threat, and he won't attack. If he didn't send him, that'll just reveal my location to him, and he'll tell Dexter."

Although I really want to call Tucson, for a *lot* of reasons.

The main one being that, right now, I'm scared, but I have a job to do.

I always could fight hard for others.

For myself? Not so much.

We get the house's storm shutters closed tight and I nervously pace inside, checking windows. As soon as twilight gets dark enough around 10:30, I go upstairs and use a pair of night-vision binoculars to scan the surrounding property.

I've just completed one lap around the upstairs, to sweep the grounds around the house, when I spot a blur of movement too fast to be a bio-bear or a werewolf, coming from the direction of the front gate. Before I can yell a warning to Chaldis, the doorbell rings.

I race downstairs, taking them two at a time. Bullets will usually *not* stop a fucking vampire, but a bow or crossbow can. I grab the crossbow Corbin gave me to use—complete with silver-tipped wooden bolts in case of werewolves—that

I'd readied earlier and left leaning against the wall in the foyer.

"*Go*," I whisper to Chaldis as I shove past him, where he's standing near the kitchen doorway. I point toward the door to the cellar.

"No. I won't—"

I turn on him. "Dammit! *Go!*"

He glares at me. "A shifter would've already tried to burst through the shutters. It would've jumped on the roof and tried to rip a hole in it, not give warning by ringing the doorbell like a civilized person. You grabbed the crossbow, meaning you saw a blur. A vampire *cannot* enter without permission." He takes the crossbow from me and aims it at the door. "Go ahead and see who it is."

The heavy storm shutter is rolled down over the outer storm door, but the button for the doorbell is located on the wall just outside it. That means looking out the viewfinder won't do me any good. The intercom is inside the storm shutter, though, protected from the weather, and not accessible by someone outside the shutter.

I draw my gun and, standing to the side, I unlock the heavy front door and ease it open a hair. "What do you want?" I yell. "You're trespassing. This is private property. You are *not* welcomed here."

The man's growly response nearly makes me drop my gun. "Then how the bloody *hell* am I supposed to give you a well-deserved spanking for disappearing the way you did, love?"

31

D exter

MAKE NO MISTAKE—THERE *absolutely* will be a spanking in her immediate future.

Earlier, when Mark returned and confirmed he thought it was Eilidh, it took everything I had not to race out into the sun.

Fucking *Alaska*. My girl just *had* to end up someplace where summer days are longer than anywhere else, and the nights are barely five hours long right now.

That's hardly long enough to fit in one of the spankings my girl's earned herself.

Then, when Noah, one of Garrett's cousins from Seattle, reported back that he'd nearly gotten himself shot by a woman who obviously knew he was a wolf, and who definitely smelled like the scent he'd been given to look for from

Eilidh's wig I had, I *knew* we'd found her. Although he reported her hair is blonde, not black.

What other human would be brave—or feckless—enough to *knowingly* and so brazenly face down a potential werewolf threat the way she did?

Only my Eilidh.

Holy fates, am I proud of her, too. She's all mine.

If I can catch and keep her long enough to get her to stop running and allow me to help her solve the problem of her mysterious spectral canine stalker.

And now here I stand, with nothing but a storm shutter and a glass storm door separating me from my love. I can smell the strange vampire and my Eilidh.

I'll kill him if he's so much as laid a finger on her, much less if he's blooded her.

The wooden door slowly swings open, and Eilidh's scent fills my lungs. *There's* my girl, and for the first time in over seven weeks, relief and peace fill me.

"*Dexter*? Wh-what the *hell* are you doing here?"

I stand in the doorway, in front of the storm shutter, and peer through the cracks at her. I brace my hands on either side of the doorway, much as I did in her apartment doorway that first night she took me there. "What do you *think* I'm doing here, love? I'm here to claim what's *mine*, dammit." I see the vampire standing behind her and force myself to remain still. "*Let* me in, Eilidh."

"That is *my* decision, I do believe," the vampire replies. "Since she works for me, and this is *my* house." He's got a slight accent I can't quite place. I want to stake him, revive him, and stake him again for being so goddamned good-looking and continental European-ish as he stands next to *my* girl.

"Back up, Dexter," she warns.

Reluctantly, I do. I hear her flick a switch and the storm shutter slowly rolls up.

Now I can see my girl. Yes, her hair's changed color to golden blonde, like in the picture I saw of her and her mother. I believe I like it better than I did the black. My gaze doesn't leave her as the vampire steps forward, a crossbow leveled at me from the other side of the storm door.

"Dexter Van Sussex, I presume?" He sounds amused, so that's something, I guess.

"You presume correctly, and that's *my* girl in there."

He studies me for a moment and then tips his head toward Eilidh. "You're right. He does look like Ianto Jones."

She nods. "I know, *right*?"

He smirks. "Funny, I somehow pictured you older."

"I'm over two thousand years old. How much older do you think I should look?"

He snorts. "Okay, Boomer."

"Let. Me. In."

"Dexter!" she scolds. "Quit being an asshole. He loves his boy, whose brother—FYI—just fucking *died*. You want in, Fangster Hunkadoofalus? Then show some respect. He hasn't blooded or touched me. He's my *boss*—I *work* for him. And he's a friend. Chillax."

My girl knows exactly what to say to calm me down, I'll give her all credit for that. "My apologies." I take a deep breath. "I am truly sorry for your loss. May I *please* come in and talk to Eilidh?"

"*Hmm*." He looks down at her. Now the asshole's just fucking with me because he's smiling. "Do you wish for him to come in, Eilidh?"

"As long as he promises to behave himself and not act like a dick."

She is soooo getting spanked. "I swear, I will respect this home and all within it."

The vampire reminds me a little of Lucius in his mannerisms, the way he taps a finger against his lips, dragging this out before nodding. "Then yes, I suppose you may enter. I invite you in." He reaches over and opens the storm door for me.

Eilidh lets out a squeal as I blur through the doorway, grab her, pin her against the wall with my body, and kiss the hell out of her.

Fuck.

I've.

Missed.

Her.

"You are getting one *hell* of a spanking, girl," I mumble against her lips as her fingers twine in my hair, and she hooks a leg around the back of mine.

"But—"

"*Shh.* I'm not done kissing you yet. First the kissing, *then* the spanking." With my lips slanted over hers, I take full ownership of her and her mouth. My erection strains the front of my jeans, and I press it along the notch in her thighs and start grinding. She moans into my mouth as her body molds against mine.

This. I've had nightmares about never holding her in my arms again, so this is blissful relief, to have her wrapped around my body once more. I grab her ass and hike her up so she can drape her legs around my waist.

Yessss. This is *much* better. The scent of her arousal fills my senses, and I'm already reaching down to unfasten her jeans when behind us, the vampire chuckles.

"Oh, no. Please, don't mind me, Dexter. Make yourself right at home. Ravish my helper in my foyer. Go right ahead. It's not like we have beds or anything for that purpose."

I can't quit kissing her, so she mumbles it against my lips. "Dexter, Chaldis Bianchi. Chaldis, Dexter Van Sussex."

I blindly extend a hand behind me, and Chaldis shakes with me.

"I'll give you two a moment," he says, chuckling again as he steps out of the foyer.

She's the most beautiful sight in the world. "Don't you *ever* scare me like that again. You are *forbidden* to ever leave me again."

Her beautiful violet eyes stare up at me, all humor draining from her. "It showed up at the club," she quietly says. "I *had* to lead it away from you all."

"Lucius and I watched the security camera footage. You are *never* allowed to do that again. We face it *together*. Besides, I think we have a lead." I lean in for another kiss, but she pushes on my chest and unwraps her legs from my waist.

"Wait, *what*? What lead?"

I steal another kiss and then tell her what we've discovered about the stone rings. "So, we need to return to Wales with your ring. I think maybe—"

"Wearing it might trigger the appearance of the thing?" she asks.

"Yes. Perhaps even during full moons. How did you know?"

"Lucky guess. You put it on that morning when we took our shower. And I think in the past that's triggered it."

I run her hair through my fingers. "We can leave tonight. Full moon in five days. We can try again right there."

"No, we can't."

"Why not?"

"Because I have a job, Fangster Hunkadoofalus. I can't leave until Corbin comes back. Although…" She looks thoughtful.

"Although what?"

"Chaldis!" she calls out. He almost immediately reappears, still holding the crossbow.

"Yes?"

She rolls her eyes at him. "Dude, put that down. Dexter's fine. Listen. Where in Georgia is Corbin?"

Chaldis frowns. "Not far outside Atlanta. Why?"

My girl smiles up at me and wraps her arms around my neck. "If I agree to the spanking, can I ask a favor? *Sir*?"

"You'll get the spanking regardless, *girl*."

"I'm serious, Dexter."

"So am I." I deliver a playful swat to the seat of her jeans. "You aren't going to sit easily for a few weeks, once I'm finished with you."

"How'd you find me, anyway?"

"In a moment. What's the favor?" Like I could honestly tell her no about anything within my power to give or do.

But she's *absolutely* still getting the spanking.

"We need to transport Chaldis to the funeral in Georgia, so he can be with Corbin, and put him up in the appropriate housing, *and* get him safely back to Alaska."

"Done. When do we need to leave?"

"Wait, what?" Chaldis asks. "Can we back up a little?"

When my girl smiles, the world feels like it's righted itself—finally. "We're going to fly you to Atlanta on Dexter's private plane, so you can be with Corbin for his brother's funeral. And we'll put you up." She looks like she just got another idea. "Oh! That was Mark at the gate earlier, wasn't it? I thought I recognized the voice."

"Yes. And Noah." I lean in and playfully nibble the side

of her neck. "And that was very naughty of you, threatening to shoot Noah after he was nice enough to agree to come with me to help track you. He's Garrett's cousin from Seattle." I pull out my phone, so I can call Mark and John, but find I have no cell signal, dammit.

She takes the phone from me, quickly swipes into settings, and plugs me into the house's Wi-Fi. "There. No cell service out here, sorry."

I reach down and swat her ass again, enough to make her playfully yelp. "Thank you, love."

Chaldis points to her. "You owe her dinner, by the way. I'd promised to grill us steaks on the deck tonight, but we thought you were coming to attack us, so she got homemade chicken pot pie instead."

Yeah, I do feel a little bad about that. "Sorry."

She sticks her tongue out at me, but the way her eyes crease at the outer edges tells me she's trying not to laugh. "Be *really* sorry about the crispy truffle potatoes. That *really* torqued me."

"Can we let Mark, John, and Noah in?" I ask. "They're down at the gate."

I notice Chaldis looks to Eilidh, who gives him a thumbs up before he nods in response. She walks over to a control panel and hits the intercom button. "Mark, John, it's Eilidh. Come on down to the house. Everything's fine. We didn't shoot Fangster Hunkadoofalus. And you can bring your wolf friend, Noah, if he's not still pissing himself after I scared him. I promise I won't shoot him, either."

"Thanks," Mark replies, when he gets done laughing. "We'll be right there."

Chaldis wears an annoying smirk. "You let your girl call you *Fangster Hunkadoofalus, hmm*? Interesting pet name. My boy just calls me *Master*. Perhaps I should renegotiate that."

"It's not so much a matter of 'let' as it is we're still in the early stages of defining our dynamic." I reach out and swat her ass again. "It's growing on me. Although I think I prefer *Sir*."

"Hold up," she says, looking at me. "That was *you* in the crate I saw getting off-loaded from the plane earlier today, wasn't it?"

"Guilty."

"You mean you've been hanging out in the back of a fricking panel van until it got dark?"

"Well, yes. You nearly shot poor Noah."

"'Poor Noah' could've nutted up and said he was *with* you, you know. They could've backed the van into the garage and we could've unloaded you there. It's light-proof. The whole house is vampire-safe during daylight."

"I told him not to reveal who he was, unless you tried to kill him. I didn't want you to run again before I could speak with you in person. I'm considering handcuffing you to me, by the way."

Chaldis looks far too amused by this turn of events. "I'll loan you a pair of ours if you promise to return them cleaned of bodily fluids."

Outside, I hear the men arrive. I let them in and make the introductions to Chaldis, and formally introduce Noah to Eilidh.

Noah chuffs. "Lady, all due credit, you gotta set of balls on you," he says as he shakes with her. "Garrett warned me you can handle yourself, but that's the first time a human's ever got the jump on me. Especially a human female."

"I recognized your voice from the gate intercom. Also, I smelled you in town, at the grocery store."

He scowls. "How?"

I lean in. "I did warn you she's not your average human."

The wolf carefully eyes her. "I'm gettin' that."

"Let me call Lucius and Garrett and tell them you've been found," I add.

She sticks her tongue out at me again and I pull her in for another long, deep kiss, followed by another hard smack on her ass. "You, baby, are in sooo much trouble."

"How did you find me, anyway?"

"Jackson King's mate, Kylie. She's a hacker. She finally discovered you'd taken the ferry to Alaska. Spotted your license plate and then was able to trace that you were a passenger, and where you disembarked. From there, we tracked down blood shipments coming to this area and narrowed the options."

"Goddammit," she mutters. "I *knew* I should've stolen a license plate somewhere."

John laughs. "Good job, by the way. You should give classes in hiding out. I have never seen this man so frustrated as he has been searching for you."

"Frustrated, hmm?"

"Very," I growl as I give her another long kiss.

"I take it this means my blood shipment wasn't tampered with?" Chaldis asks.

"No, it wasn't," I tell him. "Sorry about intercepting it. I charmed and bribed a guy at the freight company in Anchorage to let us take it. Please, don't be upset with him."

"Couldn't have hijacked my *cocotte*, I suppose?" He sighs. "I would have thrown you a *literal* hero's welcome had you done that."

"What?"

Eilidh groans and rubs her forehead like she's trying to hold on to her patience. "*Dude.* You have *three* other *fricking* Dutch ovens you could use. *Pick* one!"

"But I wish to use *that* one!"

I leave them to their friendly bickering, which apparently also has something to do with Star Wars, and step into the living room to make my calls to Lucius and Garrett, so they can call off the search.

By the time I return, Eilidh's detailing to John and Mark the logistics she wants arranged for Chaldis and Corbin—who I assume is the vampire's human partner—and my men are already making notes.

"Needless to say," Chaldis says, "you are all welcome to stay here. The night is rather short, and we have plenty of room."

Noah clears his throat. "If it's all the same to you, no offense, I'd prefer to stay back in town at the hotel. Garret vouches for you, Dexter, but in all honesty, I won't get a bit of sleep here. Sorry. Nothing personal."

"No worries," I tell him. "Meet us here around four in the afternoon."

"Will do." He bids us all good-night and departs.

Eilidh looks at Chaldis. "Remind me to tell Jarred in the morning that Noah's okay after all. I might have given him shoot-to-kill orders. I'll tell them he's an old friend of Corbin's."

Chaldis laughs. "I shall remember that."

After Eilidh shows John and Mark to their guest rooms, I pull her into her room and close the door. "About that spanking, love."

"Can we do it later? I want to get these arrangements nailed down while you're still awake."

I kiss her again. I *cannot* stop kissing her. "Do you have *any* idea how worried I've been?"

⁓

Eilidh

"Yeah, well, I do feel a little guilty about that."

I really do. But hey, this works out all right, if we have a chance of solving my phantom dog problem.

And if we can get Chaldis to Corbin's side.

"*Never* run from me again, Eilidh," he growls. "I will *always* chase you, love." Dexter sits on the side of my bed. Before I can even process it, he's unfastened my jeans, yanked them and my panties down, and pulls me face down over his lap. "For starters, I love you." *SMACK!*

"*Ow!* Motherfucker!" That was no playful swat. I try to sit up, but it's like pushing against a damned glacier. "That hurt!"

"It was supposed to, love." *SMACK!* That one hurts nearly as much. "Either take it, or safeword. You scared the hell out of me. I love you, and apparently I need to do a better job of showing you." *SMACK!* At least he rubs that one in.

I twist around enough so I can stare up into his eyes. "You...love me?"

"Yes. I thought I'd made that clear to you, but apparently, I didn't." He meets my gaze with a steady one of his own. "So, either safeword and tell me I completely misread you, or settle in, *girl*, and take your spanking."

Epic.

Stare-down.

I break first. "I love you, too," I whisper.

He flips me over and sits me upright, so he can kiss me again. "I don't know what part of 'I am sinfully rich and will figure this out for you' didn't clearly come through in my actions before, but I am, and I will. Do you *want* to be mine?"

I nod. "I don't want anything to happen to you, though."

"That is *not* your worry. It's mine. Step one is you stop running and *let* me take care of you."

"What's step two?"

His gaze narrows as his lips curve in a very predatory smile. "We're going to finish this spanking. Which, to be clear, is only the first of many. This is a 'fuck I'm glad I found you and you're safe' spanking. And you *will* take it."

"So, I just, what, let go and let Dex be Dex?"

"Exactly, sweetheart." His gaze softens and I realize he's listening to my pulse.

To my fear.

"Are you scared of me?" he softly asks.

I shake my head.

One left eyebrow—arched.

"No, Sir," I whisper.

"Good. But you should be." He immediately flips me face down over his lap again. "You belong to *me*, Eilidh. You're never to run away like that again. We face threats *together*, understand?" He resumes spanking me.

I try kicking my feet, but that's not doing anything except earning me harder smacks. "Yes, Sir!"

"I love you, Eilidh, and you *will* let me take care of you and protect you." *SMACK SMACK SMACK!* "I promise you, I will figure out what this is, and keep you safe."

Kicking and squirming is difficult when my jeans are still bunched up around my feet and shoes, but then he slides two fingers between my legs and straight into my pussy.

Which is wet for him.

The cooter can't lie. At least, mine can't. Damn sure can't lie to him.

All the squirmy fight goes right out of me, making him chuckle. "That's right, sweetheart. This belongs to me, too. The pain and the pleasure."

He fingers me and gets me nearly to the point of coming when he yanks his hand out and starts spanking me again.

Holy fates!

Time folds and compresses as he repeats this, spanking and fingering me but not letting me come. By the time he finishes the spanking, my ass feels hot and stinging, making the contrast of his cool hand rubbing and massaging my ass cheeks much more dramatic.

"Are we in agreement, girl? No more running?"

I sniffle back tears. "Yes, Sir."

"Repeat after me, 'Sir will take care of and protect me.'"

Saying that terrifies me. How stupid is that? "Sir will take care of and protect me."

"Good girl. Now say, 'I will not run from Sir.'"

"I will not run from Sir."

"Excellent." When he sits me up, I wobble a little, and he's smiling as he steadies me. "That's just a starter. You *will* be getting a much harder one later."

I'm not even mad. "Okay."

"Okay?" He arches an eyebrow at me.

"Yes...Sir?"

That earns me another kiss. "Sooo much better, baby." He nuzzles his nose against mine. "I'll let you come later, when we go to bed. For now, let's rejoin the others."

I nod. "Yes, Sir."

He stares into my eyes. "You have me, and Garrett, and Lucius ready to fight for you. I know you've been alone a long time. So have I. But I swear to you, I would not give you hope if I didn't think we can figure this out and beat it. I will never lie to you. Ever. I just need you to trust me."

I throw my arms around him, burying my face against his neck. "I missed you so much. I'm sorry I scared you."

He wraps his arms around me, holding me. "I hope you're still happy to see me after your next spanking, love."

He helps me put myself back together. By the time we return to the living room, John's already notified the pilot about our plans to fly to Atlanta, and has reserved several suites for us not far from where we need to be. With that handled, Chaldis retreats to his bedroom to call Corbin and tell him.

When he returns a few minutes later, I can tell he's been crying. He walks over and hugs me, then Dexter. "Thank you so much. My boy and I are forever in your debt for this kindness."

What little alpha male-Dom-vamp-whatever posturing Dex might have still been feeling evaporates, because I see the way he relaxes and genuinely hugs Chaldis back. "It is I who am in your debt for keeping my girl safe."

They end their embrace and both of them look at me. "I'm not sure how much assistance she needs in that department, Dexter. She's amazing. Truly. It's been wonderful having her here helping me. I can see why Neimus spoke so very highly of her."

Dexter looks shocked as he returns to my side. "You know Neimus?"

"Um, yeeeah? He was my first vampire boss. The one who taught me the pencil trick. He hooked me up with Chaldis. Why?"

Dexter looks shook. "I just..." He takes a deep breath, his gaze unfocusing for a moment. "I told you about my grandson." I'm guessing he means the one he turned, so I nod.

"They were friends. Neimus is the one who told me of his death."

"Oh."

Dexter runs a hand through his hair. "Once life settles down, love, please remind me that I wish to reconnect with him."

"Yeah, will do."

Dawn quickly catches up with the vampires. Chaldis locks himself in his bedroom, and Dexter and I retreat to mine after Mark and John bring him his things.

"I must admit, love, you found a perfect hideaway. Except for the hellishly unreasonable hours." We strip, and I let him pull me into his arms, where he kisses me. "You're still getting another thorough spanking."

He sits, and I let out a yelp as he effortlessly flips me off my feet and face down over his lap again, pins me down by the back of my neck this time and starts to spank me with his other hand.

To his credit, I know he's not spanking me a fraction as hard as he could be, but it still fucking hurts.

Which I realize is the point.

Not that I mind. Not really.

Because, as he did before, he's mixing the spanking with sexy fingering, playing with my clit and nearly driving me crazy with need. "Will you ever run away from me again, girl?"

"No, Sir!"

"Who do you belong to?"

"You, Sir!"

"That's right." He spanks not just my ass but the backs of my thighs, too. "And first thing I'm going to do is fix this for you. Because the second thing we're going to do is spend the rest of our lives together."

He sits me up facing him, straddling him and impaling me on his dick, so he can fuck and kiss me.

He feels soooo perfect, every stroke perfectly dragging against my clit and driving me closer to the edge. Like we were made for each other.

Why'd I run again?

Oh, right. Scary demon dog ghost.

His hands settle on my hip even as a gorgeous, peaceful smile fills his face. "Ready to let me take care of you, baby?"

I guess in the grand scheme of things, the fact that he's a vampire should be the last thing I care about. He's a good man, sweet, hunky—rich.

Really rich.

He spent the last seven weeks searching for me when he barely knew me and could've easily given up. And haven't I cried gallons of tears and called myself every name in the book for walking away from him?

Guilty.

A sudden and intense wave of visceral, possessive need sweeps through me. No, I don't ever want to leave him again. I don't want him leaving me, either. I pull my hair to the side and tip my head, exposing my neck. "Do it," I whisper, wanting it.

Needing it.

I don't have to repeat myself. As his fangs sink into my neck, it's like my world explodes in colors and sounds never imagined by humans before. Like I've been living in black and white, and now, I get full visual palettes previously unheard of.

My mouth prickles, my teeth suddenly feeling too large, too big, and my clit's throbbing because I'm coming harder than I ever imagined possible.

Everything's just...too damned *much*! Like my nervous

system has literally just been plugged into an electric socket. I bite down, hard, on his shoulder to stifle the primal, rolling scream bubbling up unbidden from deep inside me.

He gasps and releases his bite on me, and I'm still chewing on him. His cock throbs inside me, his fingers digging into my ass, and I realize he's coming, too.

There's a taste in my mouth. Not only his blood, but something else, like a warm, slick, syrupy tang I've tasted hints of before but never like this.

"Eilidh!" he gasps.

I growl.

Oops.

I mean, I *literally* cannot help it.

He falls back onto the bed with me still biting him, his fingers spasming against my ass as my teeth remain locked in his flesh. Like there's two parts of me, one with my hands planted on either side of his head and refusing to give up her yummy chew toy, and the other, who's horrified and trying to convince me to let the fuck go.

Dexter releases my ass, and his right hand flails, grabs, finally locks his fingers around my left wrist and forcibly drags it to his mouth, so he can bite down hard on my lower arm.

"Ow! Fucker!" But it breaks the spell—I've let go. He releases his bite on my arm and limply lies there staring at me. At first, I think it's sunrise starting to pull him under, but it's not quite time yet.

This is...

Like he's drunk.

He's breathing heavily and tries to lift his head but can't. Instead, it sort of just lolls back and forth.

Panic flows through me. "Dex? Are you all right?"

A chuffing sort of laugh escapes him, and he nods. Kind of.

I grab his hand and press it against my cheek. "I'm sorry! I don't know why I did that!" The place where I bit's already healing, thanks to his vampire metabolism. My teeth don't feel weird anymore, either, although when I run my tongue over them, I can still taste something strange.

After several tries, he flips over and drags himself up the bed, where he motions for me to snuggle with him.

"Dex? Are you okay?"

He nods again, makes a really drunken attempt to kiss me, and then passes out with his face securely pressed against the crook of my neck.

Shit! Did my blood do that to him?

Wait...it couldn't have. He would've had that reaction to drinking it bagged, and he didn't. Lucius and Selene didn't, either.

That weird taste is *still* in my mouth. Not his blood. This is different and separate from that. I run the tip of my tongue over my canines, but they feel like they always do.

Don't they?

Did him biting me trigger something weird in me?

Oh, what fresh hell is this?

Dexter

What.
 The.
 Fuck?

I lie there, struggling to make my body work. This isn't a dawn-induced stupor.

This is...

Different.

My mind feels like when I was a human and drank way too much mead or ale.

I haven't felt like this in...

Well, *ever*, because it's definitely something far different than intoxication. Like a pleasant, wet heat has quickly spread from where Eilidh sank her teeth into my shoulder and bit me.

I feel like a sweetblood deep in subspace looks after a hard scene, an even harder orgasm, and being fed on.

Shit.

My mind swirls and grows fuzzy, even as my cock throbs and tries to grow hard again.

Except...

I float.

Just before I drop into a dark, welcoming chasm of sleep, a picture floats into mind. Of Eilidh and her mother.

Of the marks on her shoulder.

And I wonder...

32

D*exter*

LESS THAN FORTY-EIGHT hours after I touched down in Alaska, my airplane is being rolled into a hangar at a small private airport outside Atlanta just at dusk. When the cabin attendant opens the hatch, he waves a human man aboard.

Chaldis immediately stands, and the two fly into each other's arms, the human softly sobbing as Chaldis comforts him.

I ease Eilidh out of the way and motion Chaldis back to the private cabin. "Please, take a few minutes."

"Thank you."

On their way past, Corbin hugs Eilidh, and I suppose it's progress on my part that I don't feel the slightest bit of jealousy over it. I can tell the two men are devoted to each other. Had Corbin been present in Alaska when I arrived, I likely would not have felt any jealousy toward Chaldis then.

Or, maybe I would have. I am rather possessive of my girl.

Eilidh and I load into the awaiting SUV, and she snuggles into my arms. "Thank you, Sir." She kisses me. "I love you so much for doing this."

"Yes, well, he seems like a nice enough guy. You know, for a vampire," I playfully add.

But her gaze remains on me and she doesn't smile. "Are you okay, Sir?"

She's been incredibly attentive and worried since I awakened hours after our encounter still somewhat fuzzy-headed and borderline high but feeling much better. It took several more hours for the effects of whatever happened to wear off.

I'm ashamed to say I didn't tell her my suspicion, because I honestly don't *know* what it means.

Only that I know damn well wolf mates who get marked feel a euphoric "high" from the wolf's venom. Humans especially so.

Except Eilidh's not a wolf, and even wolves are in agreement with that. She isn't a shifter.

She's *not*.

And yet...

At one point during our flight from Alaska, while she was in the forward cabin with the others, and Chaldis and I were awake and alone in the private cabin in back, I opened my shirt collar and asked him to look at the mark on my shoulder.

He agreed it looks like a mating mark.

What does it *mean*?

I don't know, but next to Lucius, Chaldis is the only other vampire I'd trust to ask this, because he's spent time with Eilidh—far more than I have, ironically—and he obviously cares about her as a friend. I'm not even sure I'd trust Lucius to ask this, quite honestly.

It's on my list of things to puzzle out once we've solved the question of her *gwyllgi*.

One conundrum at a time, if you please.

"Aww, I'm not Fangster Hunkadoofalus any longer?" I ask her. "I was growing rather fond of that."

That finally wins me a smile and she snuggles even closer to me. "Only when you're a jerk, Not-Ianto, Sir."

I nuzzle my face in her hair. "You, my dear, are biased."

"Damn right I am."

If it wasn't for my promise to her to get to the bottom of her *gwyllgi*, I would have simply asked Chaldis if Eilidh and I could lock ourselves in her bedroom and not come out for a couple of weeks. I wouldn't mind spending some uninterrupted time with my girl in Alaska.

I spent nearly two months desperately searching for her. In that time, I imagined nearly every conceivable horror that could have befallen her, hardly daring to hope I would ever again be here with her right now.

The only reason we aren't doing that is that I swore never to lie to her. Meaning I have to uphold my promise to her to *fix* this for her.

Once we solve this, however?

My girl is taking a well-deserved vacation, whether she wants to or not. Because we're going to relax and focus on each other, finally get to know each other in all the ways we need to. I want to know how she likes her coffee—if she even likes coffee. I want to cook brunch with her, and hear her childhood stories. I want to make her laugh as we dance in a midnight rain, and help dry her tears when something makes her sad.

I want to be the brightest moon in the galaxies in her

gorgeous violet eyes. I want to earn every bit of trust she places in me and never let her down.

And that has to start here, by upholding this promise I made to her. My instincts tell me those answers will be found in Wales.

The men join us shortly, and soon we're off to the hotel. I have two trusted men meeting us there who've prepared our rooms, and who will stay behind with Chaldis and Corbin, along with John and Mark, while we continue on to the UK. I want to be at the standing stones well before the full moon. Depending on how long this takes, either we'll detour back through Atlanta to pick up Chaldis and Corbin, or my men will arrange for another private plane to fly them back to Alaska and help them safely return.

Chaldis stares out the window with Corbin contentedly snuggled against him as we speed through the streets. "The world has changed so much. Seeing it on television doesn't do it justice. I feel guilty I am keeping you from this, boy."

"I don't want to be where you aren't, Master," Corbin softly replies with his face buried against Chaldis' shoulder.

"Perhaps we should investigate Tucson," Chaldis says. "Maybe start spending winters there."

"I will attest that the winters in Tucson are *not* sucky," Eilidh jokes. "Not in the slightest."

"We would be happy to host you as our guests," I add. "If you'd rather come for a visit first before committing to purchase a home there."

Chaldis nuzzles Corbin's head. "Would you like that, boy? A few months in the sun instead of the cold darkness of Alaska?"

"But you would be stuck indoors all the time, Master."

"I would not mind if you are there, boy."

They are adorable together, and while my heart is full

with Eilidh at my side, watching the men reminds me so much of my Robert.

It also reminds me how fleeting humans' lives are compared to ours. As my gaze briefly connects with Chaldis' before his focus returns to Corbin, I'm certain he's thinking the same thing. How fragile are our sweet humans, and how blessed we are to love them.

To be loved *by* them.

We don't have a very long layover here, but I'm not about to waste a chance to make love to Eilidh right now. Especially since the sun will catch up with us during our flight to Wales. I coax her into the shower with me, where I pin her against the wall and kiss her.

"You'll need to decide where we're going on vacation after we finish this task. Anywhere in the world, love. Your choice."

"Scotland," she softly says. "I want to see your estate there."

I didn't think I could love this woman any more than I already do. "And after that?"

She smiles. "Where do you want to go?"

"Anywhere you are. I've seen the world. Literally."

She wraps her arms around me. "Maybe we can talk to Amber and see if she can give us an idea where my father is, and we can work on that mystery next?"

Ah. There is that matter. "Of course we can, love. We *will*."

She smiles, and all is right with my world, for now. I slant my lips over hers again. There's the urge to slide inside her and slowly stroke, but once I do that, I know I'll spill too quickly, and I want this to last.

I want to give my girl every reason to want to stay with me.

Dropping to my knees in front of her, I nudge her thighs apart, draping one of her legs over my shoulder for better access. Licking her sweet pussy fills my mouth with her taste and hardens me even more.

The things this woman does to me. I haven't felt like this in...

Too long.

Gently pushing aside old memories, I anchor myself here, now, to her. To my sweet girl, my beautiful enigma. I understand why Lucius fell for Selene, even knowing she was trying to kill him, even understanding there was a trap.

I understand.

I don't care why my radiant little sun was brought into my life and placed in my path. Now that she's here, I will not let her escape me.

The sweet, needy sounds she makes as I swirl my tongue around her swollen nub help drive away my inner darkness, leaving nothing but clarity and intense purpose in its wake. Please my girl, keep her happy, keep her safe, solve all her problems.

She joked that Chaldis' love language is cooking. I suppose mine is fixing her world and making it perfect so she has no worries.

Only then am I happy, seeing *her* happy.

I lick from her clit to her ass and back again, every deep, eager moan rolling from her fueling my own desire. I get her over the first time and, when she tries to push my mouth away, I capture her wrists in one hand and slide two fingers inside her with the other, forcing her over the edge again and again.

Maybe my cunning, evil plan is to keep her so well-fucked and satisfied that she can barely walk.

#relationshipgoals

I lose track of time, and of how many times she's come, and only relent once her knees are trembling and I know she's nearly at the limit of her endurance. Then I stand, rinse and dry us both, and carry her into the bedroom.

No spanking right now. Plenty of time for more of those.

For now, I want to stare down into her beautiful violet eyes, smile over her sweetly glazed expression as I pin her wrists over her head and slowly fuck her.

"Think I can coax one more out of you, love?"

It's adorable when she bites down on her lower lip, and I dip my mouth and lick it, too. "I don't know, Sir."

"That's not a no, girl." I smile. "I'm an overachiever."

Slowly thrusting, I watch her, listen to her pulse and breathing, as I adjust my angle and strokes until she is once again rocking in time with me, chasing one last orgasm for me.

My precious, good girl.

My miracle.

My radiant sun.

I lose track of time, mesmerized by her climb, until I feel her body clamping down on my dick and her back arches under me. Soft cries I muffle with my mouth as I chase and catch up, joining her, my climax making me see stars and need to catch my breath in a way I cannot remember feeling before.

Falling still inside her, I brush my lips over hers and ease my grip on her wrists. I see her wits slowly drift back into her mind as her gaze clears and focuses on me. "Why didn't you bite me?" she softly asks.

I smile. "Because I fed from you in Alaska, love. I honestly don't know how much I took then, because *someone* distracted me." I nuzzle her nose with mine. "There might be times I literally feed from you, if you feel up to it, and times, I playfully bite you and sip just a little, for fun. But while I truly love you for trusting me enough to give that to me, the next time we do it, I'd rather be more controlled and make sure I never take too much from you, love."

She wraps her arms around me and plays with my hair, which I love. Who knew such a sweet, innocent gesture would be such a balm to my soul? "I trust you, Sir."

I rest my forehead against hers. "I never dreamed I'd ever again find someone I trust as much as I trust you."

I wish we didn't have to move from that room, but less than six hours later, before dawn, Eilidh and I are in the air once more and winging toward the UK. We'll head to Wales immediately. She hasn't been able to pinpoint exactly when all her other sightings happened, but we were able to discover her mother died on a full-moon night. A call to Neimus reveals that he clearly remembers it was a full moon when Eilidh left after seeing the thing in Toronto years ago.

It's not conclusive by itself, but it is certainly a coincidence we'd be stupid to ignore.

"Tell me what you remember of Wales, love." We're lying in the bunk in my private cabin in the back of the plane. It's set up to prevent any intrusions of sunlight and includes a secure foyer.

She sighs as she snuggles against my side. "I remember I liked living there. We used to go for walks on the beach. Sometimes, when Mom had to be away for a few days at a time because of work, me and Dad would go on hikes in the country with Zuzu and go visit him. Or he'd come visit us and take care of me."

"With who?" I study her expression, because there was a hesitation in her voice as she mentioned the name.

"Zuzu." A ragged laugh escapes her. "*Damn*, I've hardly

thought about him in...years." I hear a painful tightness in her tone and pay closer attention despite the late hour.

"Who was he?"

When her eyes drop closed, I give her a moment. "He was Dad's best friend. I remember he was a lot shorter than Dad. Kind of slender. And he had beautiful lavender eyes."

"Lavender?" Again, a color not really seen in humans.

"Yeah." Her eyes open and she looks up at me. "Is it possible I'm misremembering that?"

"Perhaps. What else do you remember?"

"Earrings." Her brow furrows. "He and Dad wore matching earrings. In their right ears." She reaches up to her ear lobe. "Little gold balls. I once asked Dad if I could get one." She pauses, her brow furrowing. "Holy crap, I haven't thought about *that* in years, either."

"Anything you remember could be very important. Can you remember Zuzu's last name? How long you knew him? Anything that might help us identify who he is or where he lived?"

"He was always there. In my life, I mean. I remember that much. He lived in a strange house."

"Strange?"

"Yeah. Different. Like it wasn't...*normal*. And he always made me these cookies that were some sort of fruit, but for the life of me, I can't remember what they were called. They weren't anything we could get at home."

"Do you think you could find his house?"

"I..." She blows out a breath. "I don't even know if I could tell you where *we* used to live. We moved around, even before Dad died. And..." Her scowl returns. "Dad used to play a game with me all the time. From as long as I could remember. He'd blindfold me when we'd go into the woods, and before I knew it, we'd be at Zuzu's. I remember we had this green checked scarf that I think Zuzu gave him. It was like we walked through a..."

"A what?"

She sits up. "The trees and plants would be different."

"Different *how*?"

"*Different*. Like...*different*." She stares at me. "You know how you can watch TV, and they're trying to say the show is happening in one place, but you *know* it was filmed somewhere different because you *know* the plants don't look like that there, because you've *been* there? I mean, does that make sense?"

I nod.

"*That's* what it felt like." Her gaze goes unfocused. "That's something else I haven't thought about in years."

"You were homeschooled, weren't you?"

"Yeah. When Mom had to leave for work, when I was really little, I remember if Dad had to go to work, he'd take me with him to Zuzu's. Or, sometimes, Zuzu would come stay with me." She frowns. "But that can't be right. Dad said he worked where Mom did, but we'd sometimes go to Zuzu's when Dad was working." Confusion fills her expression, and I realize this literally is something she hasn't thought about in years.

I can imagine there are many reasons why that would be, and most of them are not pleasant.

I'm trying not to get a bad feeling about someone I've never met before, but I'd be remiss if I didn't ask. "Did Zuzu ever molest you?" Maybe that's why she doesn't remember him.

"*No!*" She hesitates. "I mean, I don't think so." Another long pause, then she firmly shakes her head. "*No*. Zuzu never hurt me. I loved him, and he loved me like I was his daughter." She blinks back tears. "Why didn't I think about him before now? I remember when we had to leave his house after visits, I would cry because I didn't want to leave. Sometimes, I'd try to run off and hide in the woods so they couldn't find me and I could stay, but they always found me. Or if Zuzu visited us, I never wanted him to leave. When me and Mom left Cardiff, after Dad died, I cried because we couldn't see Zuzu again or talk to him. I could never call him on the phone. Dad said our phones wouldn't call him, even though I remember he had something like a phone at his house. It looked weird, too."

"Weird, how?"

"I...' She sniffles. "*Weird*. It was a phone, but it looked different. Sounded different, too. The tone was different. Not like an American phone, either, it was just different. I would sometimes pick up our phone and pretend like I was talking to Zuzu because we couldn't just call him."

She wipes away tears. "I guess I must have blanked all that out. Mom was so scared when we left Cardiff when Dad died. I asked if we were running from Zuzu, and Mom said no, but we had to leave. I asked why we couldn't go to Zuzu's, but she said we needed Dad for that. And that Zuzu couldn't follow us because Dad was gone."

"Are you certain Zuzu was real and not an imaginary playmate?"

"He was real." She stares into space again for a moment. "I *know* he was real."

"Do you have any pictures of him?"

She sadly shakes her head. "I don't even have any of my dad," she whispers.

I grab my cell phone and text both Kylie and John with what little I just learned, to see if they can locate anyone who might have gone by "Zuzu." Kylie and my people have been trying to retrace Sorcha Connover's history in Wales with patchy luck thus far, outside her tenure working for the BBC as a stuntwoman. They've confirmed Eilidh's birth certificate is real, but have yet to track down any trace of her father's existence beyond that slip of paper. Parxon Smith must be a pseudonym, but we've yet to track him down, either. His birth, or his supposed death.

All this traveling is playing hell with my body, too. Exhaustion not quite as strong as my daily stupor is creeping in, so I cuddle Eilidh in my arms. "Rest, love," I murmur. "We can talk later."

"I love you, Sir."

I kiss her one last time. "Love you, too, girl."

Eilidh

Long after Dexter falls asleep, I lie there wide awake and feeling like a shitty human being.

Zuzu.

How on *earth* could I ever have forgotten *him*?

You were eight, *dipshit.*

I mean, I didn't *forget*-forget him, but I haven't *actively* thought about him in years. Now, I silently cry and remember the man I loved like a second father for a good chunk of my childhood. He was never *not* in my life, just like Dad and Mom. I remember how I loved exploring his home, how he had pictures of him and of Dad all over the place.

Pictures of my...

Grandsire?

Grandfather, right?

No...

Grand*sire.*

That's...*weird*, but that's something now sticking in my head.

How they sometimes spoke to each other in a foreign language I didn't understand a lot of, even though I knew some of it.

They were friends, like brothers, but...not.

How we had the hiding game. If there were ever any visitors when I was at Zuzu's, it was *very* important for me to hide in a closet or somewhere and remain perfectly still and silent until either Dad or Zuzu called for me to come out. Because they worried someone might take me away from them if I was ever discovered there.

And Zuzu always gave me *rhozhen* candy after I hid, and told me what a good girl I was...

My eyes pop open.

What the hell is rhozhen *candy?*

Except now I can *taste* them in my mouth, sort of like a cross between chocolate and fruit taffy, sweetly tart and lightly fluffy, like a truffle candy. My mouth even waters as I think about them.

Candy I've never been able to find anywhere else despite now realizing I've spent fruitless years trying to find something to replicate them.

Mazbushka. It's what Dad called me.

It's also what Zuzu called me.

The man who helped Dad with my schoolwork, but like he was learning along with me. Laughing as we played hide-and-seek in the woods and around a bunch of rocks and...

The blindfold game.

How many of my childhood memories are...*gone*?

One of my earliest memories... A cold winter's day, and we'd gone to visit Zuzu, which was odd, because usually we saw him at night. After the blindfold game, we'd met Zuzu in the woods.

But then we heard voices, and Dad hustled us back the way we came and made me close my eyes as he passed me to Zuzu. Dad said something, the same phrase he always said when we played the blindfold game. And then...

The sounds changed. We were back in the Cardiff woods, just me and Zuzu, without Dad, but Dad promised to return soon. We were near the rocks that were so familiar to me.

I remember how Zuzu looked full of wonder as I named trees and animals for him, and he carried me, almost like he clung to me in his amazement. He usually didn't get to see Cardiff's woods in the daytime.

His absolute terror, followed by child-like delight, as he stared up at an airplane flying overhead and I told him about planes. Like he'd never seen one before.

Zuzu.

Dad bought Cat and Dog for me, but it was Zuzu who picked them out for me in the shop.

My heart races as I remember that afternoon, when Dad played the blindfold game with me. But instead of going to Zuzu's, when I opened my eyes, Zuzu was *there,* and he came with us back to town. I remember showing Zuzu my favorite places, going shopping, stopping at a chip shop for lunch. Like he was seeing things he'd never seen before.

Zuzu picked out Cat and Dog at one of the shops we visited. Cat and Dog are currently safely packed in my luggage, along with all my other clothes. Everything else is safely stored in my 4Runner back in Chaldis' garage. We'll retrieve all of that later.

I remember taking Zuzu back to our apartment, his wonder at watching TV, Dad saying things to him in a sweetly teasing tone in that strange language they spoke, me chiming in, too. How we all cooked dinner together, and it was like Zuzu had never tasted those foods before.

Is he even alive? Does he miss me? Does he remember me?

How the *hell* would I even go about *finding* him again?

I'd planned to sleep during the flight over, while Dexter was asleep, but now that Zuzu is fully in my mind and heart again, I sit up, thinking about him, unable to sleep.

What if I can't remember him again?

How could I have *ever* stopped thinking about *him*? He was such a huge part of my life before...

Before Dad died.

But what if Dad's *not* dead?

Mom liked Zuzu, too. I remember that. Except Mom never went with us to visit Zuzu, although Zuzu frequently came to the apartment when Mom was there. He'd stay with me if Mom and Dad were both gone. Sometimes, he'd come back with Dad after Dad had gone away for a while for work. Once, Zuzu stayed with us for a whole month, sleeping in my room while I stayed on the sofa. But I didn't mind being out of my bedroom, because every day, Zuzu was there, and he was part of our family.

I was his daughter, too.

No, Zuzu *never* hurt me, even though I understand why Dexter asked me that.

I've had no sleep by the time Dexter awakens not long before we're supposed to land. It's not quite safe dark yet, but the plane is wheeled into a hangar and the doors rolled shut.

Dexter pulls me aside. "Are you all right, love?"

"No." I slowly shake my head. "What else have I forgotten if I forgot Zuzu?"

He sadly sighs and cups my face. "Let's tackle one thing at a time. After we deal with this stone ring, and dispatch your *gwyllgi*, you and I will sit down and see if I can possibly find any other lost memories that might help us find your father."

"But you can't thrall me."

"I know. Maybe we can find a way I can access your mind. Perhaps hypnosis. Once we're both able to relax and focus."

I'm willing to try.

His people have already purchased everything we'll need to prepare the hotel room and stowed it in a rental car, which is also ready for us in the hangar. While we wait for it to get dark enough we can leave, I eat dinner on the plane, and our luggage is loaded into the car. Once it's safely dark, we set off with Dexter driving, because like hell am I going to try driving a right-hand car for the first time tonight, especially when I'm this brain-fried and exhausted and jet-lagged.

And heartsick.

The hotel is over an hour away from the airport. I wish I could look at the landscape and see if anything is familiar, but it's dark, and I'm too...overwhelmed. Too exhausted and wired to even sleep now.

We get checked into the hotel, and Dexter won't let me help him unload the car. While it's a new hotel, the room is smaller than the one he had in Tucson and the one we had in Atlanta. As I help him tape the tarps to the inside of the windows, he chuckles.

"My people here are good, but they don't know I'm a vampire, just that I have a severe sun allergy. It's easier to do this ourselves." He told the clerk at the front desk that we'd be blocking the windows because of his "sun allergy" and used his thrall to make it sound like the most natural thing in the world.

I step back and check our handiwork. "How do we know we didn't screw up?"

"I don't die." I know he's joking, but I'm so exhausted, mentally and physically and emotionally, and overwhelmed, that I burst into tears.

"Oh, love." He pulls me into his arms. "I'm sorry, sweetheart. I was joking."

"B-but what if you *do* explode?"

"*Shh.*" He gently rocks me back and forth. "I have survived this long. I think I have it well in hand." He kisses my forehead. "Let's take a shower to freshen up and then head to the stone ring for a look around, *hmm*? Full moon is in three days."

Just under an hour later, we're on our way again. As he drives, I keep one hand on his thigh and hold the ring in my other. This...

Feels right?

Which is weird and fucked up. But it's like even the air *smells* right.

Maybe not perfect, but it seems less *wrong* than the rest of my life has.

He navigates with the car's GPS and, eventually, we're parking off a quiet country lane, next to an iron gate. It's almost two a.m. local time. We have three hours before we need to return him to the hotel before local sunrise.

"It's down this way." He picks me up and literally jumps over the gate as if it's not even there.

"That's handy," I snark as he blurs through the woods. We're at the stones seconds later.

You ever have déjà vu so strong that it nearly knocks you over?

Yeah, *that*. I *literally* have to cling to Dexter's arm as I stare at the stones, because...

I've been here before.

How could I *not* have remembered this?

"Love, what is it?"

I swallow hard. "You're...you won't believe this."

"Believe what?"

I look around. It even *smells* familiar here, and I don't mean faint whiffs I'm getting from Dexter's previous visits. The trees are different, obviously—some taller, some small saplings that weren't here before, some missing that used to be here. But there are several rock piles scattered around the outside of the stone ring, and I *know* I've seen them before.

When I was a child, this ring sat within the middle of dense, thick woods. Some of these rock piles weren't even visible then, where they lay just outside the standing stone ring. Dad always parked on a little dirt track on the other side of the woods from where we're parked now, because we came in from the other side of the ring, but *this* is the place.

I close my eyes and softly clap my hands a couple of times as Dexter keeps a steadying grip on my left shoulder, letting me walk as I listen.

The acoustics.

Unbidden, I remember a Welsh nursery rhyme Mom and Dad and Zuzu used to sing to me, and I start singing it.

"Heno, heno, hen blant bach..."

I freeze, listening. Then I turn, close my eyes, and sing the first verse again, my bearings now solid. Opening my eyes, I zero in on one of the rock piles just outside the ring, where I drop to my knees and wrestle one of the larger stones out of its place. Reaching into the void behind it, I feel around...

Sobbing, I pull out the tattered remains of the green checked scarf Dad always used to blindfold me.

"I've been here," I sob as Dexter drops to his knees next to me, his eyes wide with shock. "I've *been* here. *This* is where we used to play the blindfold game. *This* is where we used to come so we could go see Zuzu!"

33

D *exter*

STUNNED, I stare at the scrap of fabric in Eilidh's hands as she literally crumples to the ground sobbing.

This is the first shred of hard proof we've had tying her to her past with her father besides the ring.

I gather her into my arms, her ragged crying ripping my soul to shreds. I instinctively know we are about to reach the heart of whatever that thing is pursuing her, and perhaps it will intersect with the mystery about her father.

"How could I have stopped thinking about Zuzu?" She gently fingers the ragged scrap of fabric that time and moisture have done a number on. "How could I *not* have thought about him in so long? They called me *Mazbushka*. Zuzu said it meant 'sweet little angel.' He said I was his little angel, like a daughter to him. How could I have forgotten the stones?

Dad always said it was special magick. That when I was older, he'd teach me."

"The mind has ways of protecting us, sweetheart. Maybe it was so painful to you, to lose your father so suddenly and then lose his friend, that it shut things out that hurt too much because you missed them so keenly. Your mother was scared, you had to move, you ended up in the States. It's not surprising. Survival mode took over."

She stumbles to her feet, the fabric clutched in her hands and a wild look in her eyes. Then she closes her eyes and starts whispering to herself in a language I don't recognize. She turns, changing directions, until she stops and stares at me. "I need you to hold me."

I stand and rush to embrace her, but she steps back. "No, I mean like I'm a kid. Carry me on your hip."

"Why?"

"Just...do it! *Please*?"

"All right." I dip my knees and scoop her up, settling her on my hip. She clings to me like a child would as I straighten, then she closes her eyes again and repeats the phrase. I recognized the lullaby she sang earlier as Welsh, but this...

It sends chills ricocheting along my spine. It feels like very old, very powerful words, but I do not recognize them.

Her eyes open and she looks around, has me turn, and closes her eyes again, repeating the phrase, a little louder this time. She opens her eyes again, looks around, and is obviously getting frustrated.

"The trees were different. There was a certain way Dad always stood, facing certain stones." She has me turn a little, and once again chants the phrase. "Why isn't this *working*? It should *work*!"

Nothing around us but a still, clear night under a nearly full moon, with the barest hint of a breeze.

"Wait!" She pulls the ring off the chain, puts the chain around her neck again, and then, with a deep breath, she slides the ring onto her left ring finger. "*Lazgo mandem tanneh cahl. Fozun rostray sephiahl.*" She chants it, like a spell, and...

I am not ashamed to admit that while her jubilant screams are of success and celebration, mine are of shock and, yes, fear. My entire body tingles as, around us, the Welsh night shimmers and dissolves, replaced by a thickly wooded clearing that's just larger than the rock piles outside the stone ring.

"Yes! *Yes*, motherfucking *yes!*" she screams, climbing out of my arms because, frankly, I'm too stunned to do anything but stand there, staring, turning around in a circle.

She darts around the stone ring, cackling in glee, whooping with her success, until a thought finally hits me. I blur to her side, grab her, and clap a hand over her mouth.

"*Shh!*"

"What?" she mumbles behind my hand.

"*Quiet!*" I hiss, listening.

A gentle breeze stirs the leaves of the trees in the woods around us. The creaking and chirping of some insects softly overlay that sound, but there are no cars or planes, nothing like that. I see no distant light pollution.

It even...*smells* different here.

When I look up, the moon is the same phase, and the stars all look like the constellations I'd expect to see, but every hair on my body is standing nearly on end as I realize we've...

Crossed.

Through the stone ring.

This is the stuff of cable TV shows and romance books, not reality.

Right?

Then again, I'm a vampire who's about to sign a lucrative business deal with a werewolf, whose mate is apparently part psychic fae.

Sooo...yeah.

After a minute, I realize I'm hearing something that fills me with dread—the sound of something large, an animal or a person, moving through the trees some distance away, but heading toward us. I realize she hears it, too, because her eyes widen.

I grab her and blur, moving into the trees on the far side of the ring from where the sounds are coming, and I hold her in my arms, so she doesn't accidentally shuffle her feet and make a noise. Also, so I can leap to safety, if necessary, and carry her with me. I have the ability to cloak my presence from the average human, but I've never tried it before while holding someone.

I try it now and hope it works with my girl in my arms.

"Stay silent," I whisper, and she nods.

The footsteps approach, closer, until the person making them finally breaks through into the clearing on the other side.

The man stops at the edge of the woods, his nose to the air, hesitating. If I didn't know any better, I'd say he was scenting us.

Before I can stop her, Eilidh gasps and throws herself out of my arms like a wild little demon badger. "*Zuzu!*" she screams, running through the trees and toward the stones.

Dammit! I'm already starting after her and attribute my delay in reacting to my shock over the fact that we're apparently in another *fucking* dimension.

Except the man's equally startled cry in reply pulls me up short. "*Eilidh*?" He screams in joy and drops the canvas satchel he carries slung over his shoulder, engulfing her in his embrace as she slams into him, crying now as hard as she is. "*Mazbushka!*"

He looks exactly as she'd described him, except this man can't be older than Eilidh. In fact, he looks like he's barely in his late twenties, if that.

And it takes my breath away to see how much he also resembles my Robert. That guts me, rendering me unable to do anything except stand there and witness their tearful reunion.

They both collapse to the ground, crying as he rocks her in his embrace and speaks to her in a language that...*yeah*.

I have *no* fucking idea what he's saying, but if I had to guess, it's the same language she chanted in the stone ring. I mean, there are plenty of languages in the world I do not know, but in this part of the world, there are none that I can't at least hear a few words of and recognize the language, even if I don't understand everything being said.

This?

It sounds like *nothing* I've ever heard before.

But even I am not stupid enough to try to make him release my girl right now. So, I stand watch, listening for anyone else approaching, trying to stay alert to potential threats despite emotionally reeling over this latest development.

"I'm *not* crazy," she whispers. "I'm not crazy. I forgot you, but I'm *not* crazy. I *didn't* imagine you. You're *real*."

"Of course, I am real," he tearfully says in accented English. "My sweet, darling Eilidh. There has not been a single day I have not missed you and thought about you and longed to hold you in my arms again. My sweet, sweet *Mazbushka*."

I let this continue for a good twenty minutes, trying to compartmentalize that a) we are no longer in Wales, and b) this man apparently knows her, and c) we *ARE NOT IN FUCKING WALES at this moment in time.*

But the night is also thinning, and either we need to move someplace safe for me, or we need to return to the hotel.

To the hotel in *fucking*.

Wales.

Because I *will* be turning into a flaming pumpkin if we do not. Life just got extremely interesting in incredibly incomprehensible ways, and I'd like to stick around for a while longer and see what happens next.

Especially with Eilidh.

"Beg pardon," I say, my old Scottish accent returning somewhat in my shock, "but who the bloody hell are ye, man?"

He smiles up at me, apparently completely unconcerned by my presence. "Zeuzehn. *Oh!*" He grabs his satchel and pulls out a small package of what looks like waxed paper and opens it. "I suppose it's been forever since you had these, my little one."

He pops one into her mouth and her eyes widen, then drop closed as she slowly chews and happily moans, tears rolling down her cheeks.

"*Rhozhen* candy!" she mumbles, laugh-crying as she leans against him, her head on his shoulder. He protectively drapes an arm around her again, holding her, his face pressed against her hair.

Part of me wants to feel jealous and part of me is terrified because we're *not* in fucking *Wales*.

The rational mind that's kept me alive for longer than one of the world's major religions has existed says I need to wait this out, as long as I'm keeping an eye on the time.

The rest of my mind is freaking the absolute *fuck* out right now.

There are literally dozens of questions I want to ask this man, the first and foremost one being where the bloody *hell* are we, but...

Eilidh.

I'm terrified if I'm this shaken how upset she must be feeling right now.

Okay, correction, there *is* a question that takes precedent above all others. "Are we safe here?" I whisper.

"**Yes**," the man says, smiling as he feeds her another candy. "We are perfectly safe here."

"All right, then." I drop to the ground and sit next to Eilidh, my hand on her thigh, willing to wait this out for a little longer.

She removes the ring from her finger, pulls the necklace off, uses a lark's head to loop the chain through the ring, and puts it on again.

Then she tips her head against the man's shoulder and contentedly chews another candy he pops into her mouth before he kisses her forehead and smiles.

I should be jealous.

I should be ripping his throat out.

But this is Eilidh raw and real and emotionally bleeding. Yet she also looks more contented in this moment than I've ever seen her.

Although, technically, once again *here* is someone who has apparently known my girl longer, and, in some ways, knows her better than I do.

I'm not conceited enough to deny this simple fact.

It's *right* here before me. I might be desperately in love with her, but we've spent barely a week together.

He strokes her hair, sniffs her, holds her close, still rocking her like a father would a child.

Yeah, that's the other reason I haven't killed him—because the vibe I'm getting is definitely father-child, not lover.

"I am so glad my call finally worked, my little one," he softly says. "I was hoping it would. Parxon told me I was tearing my heart out to keep trying, but I would never give up. I came before, during, and after every full and dark moon, and even the quarters, and kept trying. Next to the day you were born, *this* is the happiest day of my life."

"Wait." Okay, so I will interrupt. "You're so glad *what* worked?"

He holds up his left hand, where I see he wears a near exact mate to the ring Eilidh has, except for a small crack in the labradorite stone. "It will rarely work to allow a crossing unless you do it perfectly on the strongest nights. But it could still signal, or so I hoped. I would try to send a *fahnihr* to her, to find her, in hopes we could talk to her, or to let her know we were here. We never knew if it was working, but I hoped one day it would. A few times, I saw her through the stones."

"Wait, *we*?"

He nods. "Me, and Parxon." He smiles at her, so full of love and parental adoration it makes my own heart ache. "Her father."

34

E *ilidh*

"WAIT...*WHAT*?" I stare at him. "My dad?"

I mean, yeah, I know Amber said he was alive. Yet, somehow, I hadn't managed to convince myself of that.

Zuzu nods. "Yes."

"Where is he?"

"He is away doing research but will return later today." He smiles. "Wait until he sees you, love. This will bring such joy to him."

I look at Dexter to confirm I heard what I think I heard. "He *said* that, right? He *really* said that? My dad's *alive*?"

Dexter smiles and tucks a strand of my hair behind my ear. "Yes, love. He said that."

Zuzu literally doesn't look a day older than I remember him. He smiles and touches my cheek, runs his fingers through my hair. I remember him braiding my hair when I was little, singing to me as he did.

"And who is this man, little one?" he asks, nodding toward Dexter. "Is he someone important to my angel?"

"Oh. Um, yeah. This is Dexter. He's...mine."

My *what* is still up for debate, I suppose. Gawd, are we *ever* going to get an uninterrupted stretch of time together where we can sort of, ya know, sort *our* shit out?

"It is very nice to meet you, Dexter," Zuzu says, reaching out to shake hands with him. "I am Zeuzehn."

"Why does she call you Zuzu?"

"Because when she was a baby, she couldn't say my name and started calling me that." The loving smile on his face—the paternal smile—nearly shatters my heart, and I throw myself at him for another long, desperate hug.

I'm afraid to move, afraid to leave the ring of stones for fear Zuzu will disappear and I'll never see him again. I'm terrified this is some sort of dream I'll awaken from, and none of this will be real.

That I'll lose Zuzu again.

That I'll lose any chance of reuniting with my father.

Dexter takes over the questions and I'm honestly okay with that. Zuzu's familiar, comforting scent fills my lungs, and I really would rather just sit here, for now, and process the flood of memories spilling back into my soul.

Honestly? I don't think I can even walk right now.

"So, it was *you* who sent the phantom dog after her?"

He nods. "Yes. That was the easiest form for me to conjure with the ring. To track you and hopefully lead you to me. The rings can summon each other. Act like beacons, when they're worn. It was the only form I knew I could conjure with any accuracy."

Dexter slowly nods while Zuzu pops another candy into

my mouth like I'm five, and he's just retrieved me from hiding because—

"Sers," I gasp. "Uncle Sers." A flood of fear washes into me. He was like a bogeyman. I always had to worry he might discover me.

"*Oh*," Zuzu says, his voice suddenly filled with venom I've never heard him speak before. "You *never* have to worry about him again, little one." He hugs me tighter. "He is dead, long in his grave." He kisses my forehead again. "I am so sorry about your mother. We tried so hard to find you and come to you. It nearly destroyed your father's sanity."

I cling to him. "Did...my uncle kill Mom?"

I feel Dexter's hand gently settle on my back as Zuzu answers. "Yes. I'm so sorry. We didn't know Serxon had a crossing ring until he attacked your father that day. We tried to find where he hid it, but he would never reveal it. Your father left your mother with his, thinking he would take Serxon's."

"Can we start over?" Dexter softly asks. "Her mother told her that her father died." I'm so stunned over all of this that I can't even appreciate how sexy Dex sounds with a Scottish burr.

Zuzu sniffles. "Sorcha likely believed that. Understandably so. There was a weekend camp you wanted to attend. Arts and crafts." As Zuzu tells the story, he plays with my hair. "So they enrolled you. Your father had to come here, and he brought your mother over for a visit, since you were to be gone overnight at the camp. But we didn't know Serxon had arrived on the estate. He followed your father and mother when Parxon was going to take her back, and Serxon confronted them. Attacked them. Your father took her through the crossing, but then Serxon followed.

"That's when your father realized Serxon had a ring no

one knew about. Parxon left his ring with your mother and fought with Serxon, forcibly dragged him back through the crossing. Unfortunately, Serxon got away from your father and hid his ring." He sadly shakes his head. "No amount of bribery would make him give up the location. He was so angry at your father for mating and marking Sorcha."

"Why?" Dexter asks.

Zuzu sighs. "I am afraid I am not doing this story much justice," Zuzu says. "It is very complicated. There are so many things you do not know about us, or how we do things here."

"Where *is* here?" Dexter asks.

"It is still your Earth. It is a different...dimension, I think is the word? We call it *Jotnunlm*. This is the old world, the *original* world. Where you come from is the land where the old families sent the sorted ones after the ruling class decided to separate our kind, the *jotnun*, from the rest. During *rangnork*. The sorting. The ones who'd had the virus, and the shifters, and females. The hybrids who could mate with the females, but who weren't Alphas or omegas, and who couldn't give birth. What are now called humans, I guess you could say? And others who wished to go with them. There was very old magick here in this dimension, and none that they were aware of in the other."

I find my voice. "Wait, *what*?"

"There is so much to tell you, *Mazbushka*. Oh, your father will be so joyful when he returns and sees you."

Something pings my brain. "Wait, when is sunrise?"

He lifts the sleeve of his tunic, exposing what appears to be a digital watch on his wrist. "Less than two hours. Why?"

I look at Dexter. "You have to go back."

"Like bloody hell I will."

"We *have* to send you back."

"I'm *not* leavin' without ye, girl."

"And *I'm* not leaving until I see my father." I focus on Zuzu again. "How far away is the house?"

"Not far, but I have a crew coming this morning to finish repairs on the roof. They will be there for most of the morning. And the estate crews will arrive soon, too, for morning tasks. I should not take you across the open fields while they are there. There is nowhere to hide." He smiles. "Do you remember our hiding game?"

I nod. "Sort of, yeah."

"You were always so good. No one ever saw you during your visits."

"Why can't anyone know about her?" Dexter asks.

"Because they will immediately know she is not of here."

"But how? Can't we disguise her?"

"The problem is that she is female."

"So?" Dexter and I both ask.

Zuzu sighs. "It has been so long, little one. Here, in our world, there are no females. There haven't been since the rangnork sent all the others to your world, long, long ago. When the ruling class decided. That's when the stone rings were created by the old families who controlled the magick. They were used to move the sorted, and anyone else who wished to go, to the other world. The old magick was centered here, but those who were sorted didn't care because they were then free of the ruling class and could do as they wished."

I'm glad Dexter looks as confused as I feel right now. His Scottish accent keeps bleeding through. "Then how do ye have babies if ye don't have women?"

"Omegas, mostly. Like me. Some zetas and gammas, although most cannot, anymore. Some betas can father children with omegas, but most cannot with zetas and gammas."

"So, does that mean ye're her...mother?"

Zuzu laughs. "*No!* Parxon marked Sorcha and mated with her. He was secretly visiting that world to compile research when they met. He fell in love with her instantly and mated and marked her. I helped them keep their secret."

Zuzu smiles at me. "And then our miracle happened. I'm not sure who was more shocked—Parxon or myself—when Sorcha caught with child. We had no idea she could catch so quickly, or even at all. Some couples here try for decades before catching, if ever. I will never forget the day of your birth. I am so glad I was there for it."

"An' who are ye, then? Yer relationship to Parxon an' Eilidh?"

Zuzu strokes my hair, smiling at me. "Technically, I am Parxon's mate, although we never consummated it and he never marked me. In your world, I suppose I would be called his husband."

I reach up and touch Zuzu's ear, where the gold earring still sits in his lobe. "You always matched."

He smiles. "Yes. One for mates, and an additional one each for offspring." His smile fades. "We could not, of course, add one for you without revealing our secret." He sighs. "You are my heart's child, little one, and always have been. I love you so much and have missed you terribly."

"Then we'll stay here," Dexter says. "I'm feckin' rich. We'll make it work somehow, even if I have to bribe people."

Zuzu's eyes widen. "*No!* You do *not* understand—this magick is old and forbidden. We would all be killed if her presence is revealed." He wrinkles his nose at Dexter. "You, perhaps, could stay. We could pass you as a distant cousin from far away. You don't smell too different. But she is *female*. Females only exist here in myths. It would mean our deaths."

"Did ye love her mum?" Dexter asks.

Zuzu nods. "I loved Sorcha as I do Parxon—as a sibling. That is why Parxon and I never consummated our mating and he never marked me. We both knew we did not have those feelings for each other."

Dexter looks as confused as I feel. "Then why are ye together?"

"Because it was arranged by our families when we were children. Parxon and I practically grew up together as siblings. We were both from old families, with ruling class Alpha sires. I am an omega, and he is an Alpha. The hope was that we would produce an Alpha heir to carry on the family lines."

I sort of...tune out as they talk and Dex asks questions. I can't stop staring into Zuzu's eyes—lavender eyes. A clear, light color that reminds me so much of my own. All while a bad feeling grows and swells inside me until it smacks me in the head, and I jump to my feet.

"Dex, what time is it?"

He and Zuzu both stand. "How long until dawn?" Dex asks.

Zuzu checks his watch. "Fifty-nine minutes."

"We have to get you out of here!" Panic threatens, tightening my chest and making my pulse gallop.

Dex grabs my arm, his Scottish accent gone again. "Listen to me, *girl*, I am *not* leaving you. You *promised* no more running. That we'd face everything *together*."

"Yeah, but that can't happen if you explode into a pile of ash!"

Zuzu's eyes widen. "Wait...he has the virus?"

We both look at him. "What do you know of that?" Dexter asks.

"No one has had that in... Well, since rangnork. The sorting. But people rarely got it so bad that the sun burned them like that. Especially if they mated with an Alpha or beta. That usually neutralized the worst of it."

I try to process that. "Wait, *what*?"

He's getting distracted. "We can talk about this later. You need to leave. *Now!* Come back at night, when it is safe, and I can bring you to the house."

Dexter runs a hand through his hair. "Isn't there someplace dark, without sunlight, where I can hide for the day?"

Zuzu looks as panicked as I'm starting to feel. "Not close enough to make it. She's right—you *must* return for your safety."

"You're going back." I take Dexter's hand and lead him into the center of the stone ring. "Because I can't lose you, and I need to see my dad."

He stands there like the stubborn fucking vampire Dom he is. "You come *with* me, *girl*, or I stay. Those are the *only* two options. I will *not* be separated from you again."

Noooo...actually, there's a third option.

And I'm reasonably certain Dexter's *not* going to like it.

35

D^{exter}

I LOVE THIS WOMAN, but she is about to drive me insane because she will *not* quit arguing with me. I don't understand what she doesn't understand about this situation. Leaving her side is not an option.

I guess I need to spank her more. Maybe she enjoys the spankings too much, and I need to use my belt or a cane on her to drive the message home.

"You can't stay, Dex. It'll be dawn in less than an hour!"

"Then let's leave. *Now*. We can return tonight once it's dark." I don't want to force her to go, but I will, if I must.

"And what if we *can't* return? I'm *not* leaving here until I see my father. Maybe you've been alone so long you don't remember what it feels like to *not* want to be alone, but I spent most of my life thinking he's dead. I'm *damn* sure not going to lose him, or Zuzu, before I even get them back!"

Before I can process what she's doing, she pulls the ring off the chain, sticks it on my left ring finger, and grabs my hand. "March, mister. Go to the hotel and come back tomorrow night. We'll be waiting here." She spins me around to face the stones and utters that rhyming phrase. Then, she shoves me, hard, toward the outside of the stone ring.

Normally, she wouldn't have been able to budge me an inch, much less push me off-balance. Except I'd started to turn back to her. In the process, I stumble over a rock and find myself falling backward, into air, landing hard outside the stone circle on the cold, dewy grass in what I instinctively know from the smell is my own world.

I jump up and whirl around, seeing nothing but the looming dark shapes of the stones.

I am alone.

"*Eilidh! Zeuzehn!*"

No answer, just the sound of the breeze swirling around me. I let out a roar and fling myself back inside the ring of stones.

Just to find myself still *here*.

Without her.

"Dammit! *Eilidh!*"

If I still had a pulse, I know my heart would be hammering in my chest, my breath coming in ragged gasps.

Wait. Actually, my pulse *is* hammering. *Weird.* Come to think of it, it's been doing that a lot since Alaska. And I'm breathing, too.

Double weird.

Closing my eyes, I take a few deep, cleansing breaths and think about the phrase she chanted. I say it, chant it, spin around inside the stones and try to replicate how she said it earlier when we came through. No matter what I do, even though I feel a few strange tingles, it's not working.

Except, problem. *Massive* problem.

She was right. It's close to dawn, and I should've been sealed up in our hotel room by now. As much as I want her safely back in my arms, I can't do anything for her if I explode into a pile of ash.

Cursing myself and my body, I experience a brief moment of panic when I can't find the rental car key fob in my jacket, just to remember it's in my jeans. I could blur to the hotel, but I don't remember the exact way and need the car's GPS. I blur back to the car, climb in, and spin the tires as I race toward town.

I've had close calls before in my life. The last and worst was in World War II. I found myself trapped in London during the start of the German bombings. I had been in the city on business and opted to stay there instead of risking a drive back to my estate to the north.

That was an unfortunate decision.

I was lucky I wasn't killed when a bomb fell five houses from mine. It'd been strong enough to rattle me—literally and metaphorically—where I had just settled myself into my basement crypt to await the next evening.

When I emerged to assess the damage, I discovered the blast had destroyed my car. Meaning I had no way of easily leaving London by vehicle and putting me on foot. I realized escaping the city wouldn't be a simple matter. Not if I wished to survive the rapidly approaching daylight. It's one thing to run fast, but I still needed a safe place to hunker down for the night, so I ended up deep inside an air raid shelter.

I wasn't sure if my cloaking ability would work while I was asleep, but there wasn't any alternative. It was too far for me to blur to my nearest estate to the north of the city. Thus, I wedged myself as far back in a corner of the air raid shelter as I could, moved some boxes of supplies so they blocked me from the view of others, and pulled a blanket around me.

My presence, up until that point, had not even been acknowledged, so I knew my cloaking ability was working. Fortunately, my spot remained undisturbed when I awakened at dusk and promptly exited the shelter before it was sealed for the night. I found a soldier and compelled him to drive his jeep, headlamps off, to the northern outskirts of London, where he ran out of petrol, and I once again ran out of luck.

From there, I blurred as the bombings resumed, sought refuge in an abandoned cottage the next morning, and that night barely made it to my estate before the following dawn. The Blitz had begun in earnest, and I was now trapped in the UK. Leaving for America via ship was foolhardy, due to the presence of U-boats in the Atlantic. All I could hope was the bombings didn't reach my small corner of the world.

Although I did venture out a few times and drink from bomb victims. They were dying already, and I eased their suffering. I never took from someone I thought might have a chance to make it, only those who were in agony.

Why let their deaths be a waste, or prolong their pain?

I am once again on the run in the British—all right, Welsh—countryside.

All these thoughts assail me as I speed to the hotel, unable to touch my Eilidh.

Make no mistake about it—she is *mine*.

How I shall get her back is a puzzle I pray I can solve. If this takes too long, I shall find myself purchasing an abode locally, so I have a secure base of operations from which to work.

As I race through the waning night, my left thumb strokes the ring. Why did she do that? How will I make it back through to her?

Less than thirty minutes before dawn, I pull up in front of the hotel and don't even speak to the attendant when I snatch the valet slip from the man's hand. Stalking across the lobby to the stairwell, I opt to blur all the way up, stopping in front of my own room seconds later.

Certainly faster than the elevator.

Excuse me—*lift*. I am back in the UK. Perhaps I should remember the lingo.

The lock clicks green as I wave the keycard in front of it. Putting out the *Do Not Disturb* card, I lock myself in, secure the deadbolt and safety bar, stick the wedged doorstop under it, lock myself into the bedroom and stick the wedge under that door, too, and start checking the bedroom windows.

The tarps and curtains look intact, best I can tell. Let's hope I haven't missed something. In my agitated state, that's totally possible and would be a fatal mistake.

Unfortunately, I realize too late I left the body bag in the car's trunk. I'd tucked it in there in case we were delayed returning to the hotel. I could have curled up inside it in the trunk and been safe while Eilidh remained in the car.

After putting my phone on the charger, I snatch the blanket and duvet cover from off the bed closest to the windows and retreat to the bathroom, with the door cracked just enough I can see the mirrored closet door if I move a little. Any light should reflect off the mirror without exposing me to the deadly sunrise. If I have to, I can spend the day in the bathroom with the door closed, since it doesn't have a window.

The daily stupor isn't working its way through my body as it usually does, but I am exhausted and jet-lagged, so I suppose that's the issue. As stressed and worried as I am over Eilidh, I imagine I won't stay awake very long this morning.

I'm beginning to despise my existence. The trade-offs for immortality and power increasingly look like they're not worth it.

Except for Eilidh.

She is worth it.

If I can't get her back—*again*—I don't know what I'll do.

That girl is definitely getting handcuffed to my side, though, once I reunite with her.

Again.

After I redden her pretty ass.

Once I know it's several minutes past dawn, I realize the room isn't any lighter, so I risk peeking at the mirrored closet door and find the room is still dark and safe.

Thus satisfied, I drag myself out of the bathroom, wrap myself in the covers, settle on the bed farthest from the window, and close my eyes to await my daily oblivion.

It takes me far longer to fall asleep than I expected, but my last thoughts before doing so are terror for Eilidh's safety, fear over possibly never reuniting with her, and anger at myself for not reacting faster, for not grabbing her arm and dragging her through with me.

If I can't cross through the stones, and she needs the ring to cross...

Will I ever see her again?

That is a future I do not wish to contemplate. I'd rather embrace the dawn.

It's BEEN countless ages since I last dreamed.

I missed dreams, at first.

Over the centuries, as my strength grew, I learned I could drop into a state of mind more like meditation and still think about things while safely sequestered.

But these tortured imaginings my mind now conjures—of losing Eilidh, of her being attacked and me unable to protect her—are worse than anything I have ever dreamed.

Unfortunately, I'm powerless to stop the visions, much less help her.

I finally snap awake with a gasp and realize it must be sundown, or close to it.

My phone, however, says it's only one o'clock in the afternoon. Obviously, I'm still alive, meaning this remains a relatively safe space. Still, I'd prefer something less vulnerable and far more under my control.

Eilidh.

I need to plan. I didn't survive this many years by racing into battle unprepared.

That means thinking this through.

If Amber truly can see the future—and the jury is still out, as far as I'm concerned—maybe she can tell me what my next step should be.

I'm not sure Garrett will be happy his mate is helping a "leech" again, but perhaps if I frame it as helping Eilidh, he'll let her try.

I call Garrett first as a matter of courtesy.

"What do you want now, Dexter?" he gruffly answers. Wolves have their own hierarchy and dominance bullshit. We might be business partners, but I'm still "the enemy," to him. Especially since Eilidh fled Tucson, and he blames me for not keeping her there and safe, which upset his mate.

But I must talk to the man's mate, so I adopt an appropriately respectful tone. "I have to speak with Amber, please. It's urgent. It's about Eilidh."

Worry fills his tone. "Why? Where is she? I thought you two were back together, and she's safe?"

"That's exactly what I need Amber's help with, and why I wish to speak with her." I quickly detail what happened and feel a modicum of relief when the shifter's tone changes from gruff to sympathetic.

"Oh, shit. Hold on, Dex. I'll get her for you."

Seconds later, Amber's voice fills my ear. "Hey, Dexter. This is serious."

I close my eyes. "It is. What do I do?"

The sound of her breathing is the only thing I hear for a moment, and I find myself breathing in time with her. "She's alive and safe, for now."

"That's reassuring, but not very helpful."

"I feel like I'm trying to look at her through a fluffy, crocheted blanket. Like I can sense her, sort of, but I can't really *see* her. *Oh!* It's *exactly* like when I see her father. It *has* to be due to where she is. Through the stone ring, I mean. Wherever that is. That must mean her father's there, too."

Fear fills me. "Is she in danger? Apparently, it's a very precarious situation."

"Not necessarily. I don't feel fear for her safety. Not right now." She pauses for a moment, and I sense her thinking, so I don't interrupt. "She'll be safe for a few days, at least. She's really worried about you, though."

Dare I feel any measure of relief? "Can you see any way for me to get through the stones?"

Another long pause. "Not right this minute, but I see you

in the future through that same...fuzziness. You cross again, somehow. Hold on." I hear the muffled sound of her speaking to someone, assumedly Garrett, then she's back. "I'm going to put you on with Garrett. We'll fly over to join you."

Relief so powerful it's nearly painful sweeps through me. "Thank you. I am in your debt. *Again*." I don't say that lightly. "I can send a private jet for you."

"Nah, we got it. Should take us a day to get there."

I speak with Garrett again. They'll keep in touch with me and let me know when they arrive on UK soil, and he agrees it's better not to tell Lucius anything about what's going on right now.

Ten minutes later, we've ended the call and I'm staring at my phone.

At a picture I took of Eilidh before we left Alaska. Of her natural hair—honey gold with reddish lowlights.

I love her.

I love her so painfully, I'd rather embrace the dawn than lose her again.

Except...

I will lose her, won't I? Humans have ridiculously short lives compared to vampires. In fifty or sixty years, I will likely be alone again. Even the extra decades we might gain with blood exchanges are still not enough.

Because turning her isn't an option for me right now. Because I don't wish to lose her like that—it would destroy me, I'm sure of it. I lost Robert, but he was already sick and dying. She is young and healthy, and we should have plenty of time.

If I can just keep my feckin' hands on the lass.

Dragging myself to my feet, I take a shower, change clothes, down three of the bags of blood I'd brought with me, and talk to John, my office, and deal with some business issues.

Because I still have a business to run if I wish to support my runaway girl's lifestyle, don't I?

Once it's dark enough, with Eilidh's ring on my left ring finger, I head downstairs to retrieve the rental. I need to find a way back through the stones.

I need to find a way back to *her*.

36

E *ilidh*

WHEN DEXTER DISAPPEARS, I'm relieved to realize I'm still there, with Zuzu. Dexter has been sent back through to what I hope is safety.

Except Zuzu lets out a horrified cry, startling me.

I wheel around. "What?"

"You...sent him back!" I don't understand why he sounds so...distraught.

"I had to! He's a vampire. He'll *explode* in sunlight. He *needs* to get back to our hotel."

"But you sent your ring *with* him!"

"Well, yeah. But he can come back tonight. You have one."

Wide-eyed, he walks over to me and places his hands on my shoulders. "*Mazbushka*," he whispers, "he's of *that* world.

He cannot cross alone, and I don't know if we can make the damaged ring work to allow you to cross to him."

My heart pounds. "*What*?"

"I am sorry. If I knew you were going to do that, I would have warned you to take him and cross back yourself *with* the ring. Perhaps if you had mated with him and claimed him. But your mother could never cross alone with the ring, not without you or your father wearing it, because she was human."

"You mean...I just sent the guy I love back...and might *never* see him again?"

His agonized expression mirrors the way my soul feels. "I do not know." He pulls me in for a long hug. "If we can make the damaged ring work properly during full moon, there might be hope. But we have not been able to manage a crossing in so long. Because of the damage to the ring, it has to be on a perfect full moon when the chance is best. Your father almost didn't make it back the last time."

"Full moon," I mutter.

He nods. "*Your* ring is undamaged. It will work in daytime or at night during full and dark moon cycles. At night only on the perfect quarters. But the damaged ring, we've only been able to make it work for crossings at night during perfect full moons, and even then, rarely."

I'm...stunned and processing, and I hate that he looks worried for me.

"We must get you back to the estate and hide you, some-how. I *must* keep you safe."

Taking my hand, he leads the way, and it feels so familiar and yet so strange that I can barely process it. We move quickly through the dark woods, but I sense dawn's twilight closing in on us. It's hard to fight the edge of panic gripping my system, to remember that *I* am not in danger from the sun.

I've lived my life for so long respecting the cycles of the sun because of who I worked for and because of my personal issues that I didn't realize exactly how much I had internalized that fear.

When we reach the edge of the woods, we drop down behind a large boulder at the outer perimeter of the fields. "No, this will not work," he mutters. "I cannot risk taking you across the fields. It is too bright already."

As the sky lightens to the east, I spot the large house from my distant memories perched in the middle of the group of fields and surrounded by shade trees.

"Come." He takes my hand again and, once more, we're moving through the trees at the edge of the fields, angling away from the fields until they are no longer visible through the forest. Eventually, he pulls up short and leaves me in a thick copse of trees. He walks ahead, returning in a few minutes.

"You *stay* here. You will be safe here."

"Where are you going?"

"I will return to the estate and get a vehicle from the garage. I will say I need to fetch something from the market. Parxon doesn't like me driving and prefers I take a driver, but the driver is not at the estate this early. I will travel to town to buy something from the shops to set my story. On my return, I will pull over and call for you when it is safe. You will stay hidden in the vehicle until we are in the garage and I confirm the house is empty."

Terror fills me. I'm honestly not sure if I could find my way back to the stone ring by myself now. If I can't get there, I can't reach Dexter. "How long?"

He hugs me. "Not long, little one. Maybe an hour. Here."

He removes his watch and fastens it to my wrist. I realize now the numbers don't look like numbers I'm used to, but I can still read them.

A memory pops into mind, of Dad and Zuzu teaching me their alphabet and numbers.

How did I not remember *that*?

Then he kisses my forehead again and is off like a flash before I can stop him.

The woods begin to fill with a purply kind of light as dawn crests and breaks beyond the large, gentle valley the estate sits in. I pull my cell phone out of my back pocket and look at the time. 5:48.

Of course, I have no signal.

Obviously.

A hysterical burp of laughter bubbles free before I can stop it.

When I compare the time on the watch to the phone, it matches nearly identically, only a few seconds off from each other when the minutes change.

Okay. I can do this.

Maybe.

God, I hope Dexter made it to the hotel okay. I turn off my cell phone to save the battery. It'll go dead quickly at this rate, as it tries to find a signal.

That's when the shakes hit me, along with a renewed bout of tears.

I remember nights spent sleeping over at Zuzu's, the two of us curled under a blanket on the couch in the living room in front of the fireplace, with him reading adventures to me from books that were ornately illustrated in a way I never saw in books at home. Pictures that almost seemed to shimmer and move, as if alive. I remember standing on a chair in his kitchen and learning how to chop *orhtan* for soup, a root vegetable like carrots. Baking cookies with him.

Maybe that's why I suppressed so many memories. Maybe Dex is right, that it was too painful to lose both of them. I remember feeling a flash of anger that Zuzu couldn't be with us when Dad was gone, wondering why he wouldn't come to us.

Wondering why he'd leave us alone if he loved us so much.

I can look back on what I remember now and clearly see the duality of existence that wasn't visible to me as a child. I see the lengths the three of them went to keep this secret.

To protect me.

I curl up against a tree, my arms wrapped around my knees, and rock back and forth as I try to process...everything.

This is why I was always able to accept the secrecy Mom imposed on me. Why I never asked about our nomadic lifestyle.

The unquestioning acceptance of non-humans, like vampires and shifters.

Because it was always a part of my life, even when my brain locked the knowledge away because the memories were too painful to bear.

When we lost Dad, I spent days crying for him and Zuzu. Mom had to hold me at night, because I threatened to run away, to take the ring and find the stones, even though I didn't know where to begin because Dad always drove us out to the woods.

I'm not cold but I'm shivering, my teeth chattering, when I eventually hear my name softly being called. I struggle to stand and can't.

Sobbing, I start crawling when I hear someone rushing through the brush.

It's Zuzu, looking worried. "Oh, my little angel." He picks me up and bundles me in his arms even though he doesn't look like he'd be strong enough to carry me, and he hurries with me back to the edge of the trees.

The vehicle parked along the unpaved road is some sort of car, greyish silver, two large doors, and the trunk lid is open. I know it's running, but it barely makes any sound. He rushes over with me, gently setting me in the trunk.

"Be very quiet, love. Do not move and make no sounds. Once we are inside the garage, and I know it is safe, I will open the trunk and let you out, right?"

I nod. "I love you, Zuzu. I missed you so much."

He sadly smiles and kisses my forehead again. "I missed you like my heart had been torn from my body, love. Now, be my good girl and stay still. It won't be long." He carefully covers me with a blanket and then gently shuts the trunk.

We're underway again seconds later. I feel the vehicle swerve from side to side, plenty of bumps in the road, and I think it's because it's a dirt road.

Until I remember something Dad once said in a teasing tone when we were going somewhere in our car.

"Zuzu, I love you, but there is no way I will allow you to drive here. You are many wonderful things, but a good driver is not one of them."

That's why Dad has a driver for him.

He drives for several minutes. I stay quiet and still and listen as we slow, then stop. I hear voices, including Zuzu's, and laughter. Finally, we start moving again, although much more slowly. Another pause, and then we ease forward, bumping over something, and then the car stops, the engine shutting off.

One of the vehicle doors opens and the car slightly rocks as Zuzu gets out and shuts the door. I hear the creak of a door being rolled shut, another door being opened and closed, and then silence.

Panic soaks into my soul. *What about me?*

It feels like forever, but is probably only a few minutes, until I hear the other door open and close, and footsteps across a concrete floor.

I slap a hand over my mouth when the trunk opens, but it's Zuzu pulling the blanket off me. Flinging myself into his arms, I cling to him and refuse to let him go.

This place...it smells familiar.

It smells like *home*.

"*Shh shh shh,*" he whispers. Scooping me into his arms, he carries me into the house.

Into a house that looks virtually unchanged from when I was a little girl.

He carries me upstairs to a room I remember because it was *my* room, and there are paintings on the wall Zuzu and Dad bought for me, and some of my old toys still sit on a shelf. He's closed the shutters on all the windows and put on music somewhere downstairs. But as he sits on the bed with me in his arms and rocks me, I softly cry, clinging to him, refusing to let go.

When I wake up, we're still in my old bed. Zuzu sits up, his back against the headboard. In sleep, I'd clung to him, my head in his lap. I look up to find him smiling down at me.

"Good morning, little one," he whispers.

Above us, I hear muffled bangs and footsteps, the workers on the roof.

"How long was I asleep?"

"Not long. Perhaps an hour." As upended as my soul feels right now, he looks equally contented and happy. "We have missed you so much, *Mazbushka*. I never gave up hope."

I don't want to move. So many good childhood memories were made with him. "When's Dad coming home?"

"He is scheduled to arrive before evening."

"Can we call him?"

"We do not have portable phones like you do. Even if I could call, this is news best revealed in person. He will be so excited."

There's something in his tone, though. "Why don't you sound happy about this?"

He sighs, playing with my hair for a moment before answering. "Because now we must find out how to send you back."

"I don't want to leave you!"

"You must, sweetheart. You can't live in this world. It is too dangerous. Your father will come with you." He *tsks*. "He will be very cross with me for continuing to try after he gave up, but he will not be upset for long."

"What do you mean?"

"He travels a lot for work. I think it hurts his heart too much staying home. Missing you and your mother. He stays busy to keep his mind occupied. He feels guilty about Sorcha dying."

"Why?"

"We will never know all the details. Apparently, Serxon figured out how to signal with his ring. To home in on your mother's ring. We tried to guard the stones to keep Serxon from crossing, but he slipped through and somehow made it to her. Killed her." His tone turns bitter. "All because he wanted to ascend to the ruling class."

"I...I don't understand."

"He wanted power. Your father caught him upon his return, and Serxon bragged about what he did. Once an Alpha marks a mate, that is their mate until one of them dies. An Alpha cannot have a child unless they mark their mate. Serxon killed Sorcha to try to force Parxon to mark me to produce an heir. Your father raged and killed him, but in the fight, Serxon's ring was damaged."

He curls locks of my hair around his fingers as he talks, stroking them. "We hoped your mother had told you about all of this, but when full moon after full moon passed, and you never appeared, we suspected you didn't know. Parxon had trouble crossing with the damaged ring, to the point where the last time he attempted it, he almost did not make it back.

"As the years passed, I kept trying to contact you. I never abandoned hope. Grieving, your father threw himself into his work."

"But...what about you?"

"What about me, angel?"

"You're...alone."

He sadly smiles. "Your father is a kind, loving man. He is my friend. We have leaned on each other through these years. The plan was to reunite him with you, move him to your world, and we'd fake his death here so I inherit everything, and then I could start a search for my own true mate."

"We'd never see you again."

"You will come visit with your ring."

"Why don't you look any older?"

"Because we live so long, sweetheart. Your father is a

little older than I am, but we are very, very young in our time. I am 162 and he is 169."

I sit up. "*What?*"

"*Shh!*"

I drop my voice. "You're *162* years old?"

He nods. "We can live thousands of years. I was thoroughly scandalized when Parxon told me Sorcha was only twenty-five when they met." He softly giggles. "I was imagining her as a child. Then I met her, and he revealed humans age so much faster. That she was, comparatively, a little older than us, possibly a quarter of her life already."

Stunned, I'm trying to process that. "I'm half...whatever."

"Half jotnun Alpha, yes. And half human."

The implications are sinking in. "That means..."

"You should far outlive the average human, yes."

That's why I look so young.

Good genes, indeed. "Why didn't Dad...mark you?"

"Where you come from, it is, relatively speaking, easy for babies to be born. Here, it is difficult for a pregnancy to be achieved, and there must be a soul-deep connection between the couple for it to happen. While the ruling class tries to deny this is true, I've seen the secret studies your father and others have done. He knew that my greatest desire has always been to become a parent."

He strokes my hair again. "Not that I don't love you, because I do, Mazbushka. But your father and I knew we had no choice but to mate, thanks to our families. So, we agreed to pretend he marked me. That way, we would not be permanently tethered to each other."

"That's...sad."

He shrugs. "But he was right."

"I have..." I finally look around the room and remember

things I haven't thought about in years. Memories I thought happened in Cardiff.

Not...*here*.

"I have so many questions," I whisper.

"I know, love." He untangles himself from me. "You will feel better after a bath and breakfast." He playfully smiles. "*Matshush-keks*. You have not had them in years, right? Your old favorite?"

I remember those, like a cross between pancakes and blintzes. "I love you."

His eyes go bright as tears fill them again, and he cradles my face in his hands. "I love you *so* much, my sweet little angel." He kisses my forehead, lingering, then hugs me. "Come." He stands and holds out a hand to me. "I will set up the large bath for you, and then you will come downstairs, so I may cook for you."

Wiping my tears away, I nod and take his hand. I'm worried about Dexter, but for the first time since I thought Dad died...

I finally feel like I've come *home*.

Except if I can't figure out how to get back to Dexter, to Earth...

This might really end up being my permanent home.

Alone.

The thought of never seeing Dexter again *literally* hurts, like a dagger rammed straight through my heart.

Did I just exchange soothing my inner child's aching, lonely soul for an even worse pain?

37

E *ilidh*

THE ONLY WAY I'm going to survive this without losing my mind is to do what I've always done and focus on placing one foot in front of the other, taking things one day at a time.

Right now, that means a bath.

Oh, my *god*. This bathtub, an ornate copper thing large enough for three people.

Holy cow, it's *huge*.

I remember Zuzu bathing me in it when I was little, the floating toys I had. It's in the master bathroom because I just have a shower in the bathroom attached to my bedroom. But I loved playing in this tub when I was a kid.

He sets it up with scented soaps and his own fluffy robe and soft towels, then leaves me to my privacy.

I remember bubble baths and singing. I remember Zuzu

brushing out my hair for me, and the soft, dark blue robe I had.

Zuzu practically raised me.

The more I think about my childhood, the more I remember. How, sometimes, we'd drive out to the woods, me and Mom and Dad. Dad would leave for "work," which meant walking into the woods. We'd wait there and, pretty soon, Zuzu would walk out of the woods in his place. Mom would drive us back to town and Zuzu would stay and take care of me at the apartment. We'd spend the days exploring Cardiff on foot.

Going to the beach.

Working on my lessons. He'd cook for us and do the shopping, and while Dad was gone, Mom would rely on him to help care for me.

How she said he was like a brother to her.

I'm trying to rationalize that I shouldn't be here, that this is dangerous, that being caught in this house could literally get all of us killed.

But I'm also clinging to my memories, and I want my truncated childhood back.

I want someone to take *care* of me, and cuddle me, and feed me candy and tell me everything's going to be okay. Since I was eight years old, I felt like I had to grow up fast and live in fear. Always looking over my shoulder. Never able to trust, because I didn't know who I could trust, especially after Mom died.

I want Dexter.

That pain lances through my heart again.

Is that why I fell so hard for him? Because I feel safe with him and he has the ability to take care of me, to protect me? Because I've spent so many years living and working literally among the world's most dangerous beings, and Dexter makes me feel...*safe*?

Because I'm half...jotnun, or whatever the hell I'm half of, and Dexter is stronger than me?

I sink below the water and get my hair wet. Dexter has a deeply nurturing streak, infinite compassion. If he was here right now, I know he'd be bathing me, tending to me.

Trying to make things better for me.

Look how long and hard Dexter searched for me after knowing me less than a *week*. He didn't give up when any other guy likely would have said *FTS, adios, chica*.

In some ways, Dexter reminds me of a mix of Zuzu and Dad both.

I reach up to my neck, where he bit me in Alaska. Sometimes, it feels like it's still throbbing, but in that good, sexy kind of way.

Will I ever see him again? Did I just condemn myself to a life of loneliness, hiding, and darkness? Never setting foot outside in the sunlight for fear of it meaning my death should I be seen?

Never again having a partner, or knowing romantic love?

#irony

Upstairs on the roof above me, I hear the workers doing their thing, and it reminds me I really need to finish my bath. I wrap my hair in a towel and put on the robe and let the water drain from the tub.

Even the soaps and shampoo smell the same as I remember, something else I've subconsciously sought all my life and never matched. How many hours have I spent in stores, sniffing different concoctions and never quite replicating what I didn't realize I needed and desperately missed?

All of this brings a belated clarity to my life. A peace I always chased and never found.

For the first time since losing my dad, I feel like I'm not emotionally treading water. Like I can actually reach out and accept what Dexter's offering me, fully embrace it and the life he wants to give me.

Again, the irony does *not* escape me.

I have to find a way back to him.

I grab the hairbrush and head downstairs, carrying my dirty clothes with me so I can put them in the small washer there in the kitchen. When I step into the kitchen, it hits me that I didn't even hesitate while winding my way down the stairs and through the back hallway.

I knew the way by heart.

Zuzu's pulled the curtains and shutters on the windows in the kitchen, casting it in shadows but giving us privacy. No one will be able to see inside. He's standing at the huge copper and enamel stove, and already I smell the tasty scents of my youth.

"There you are, angel." He turns and smiles at me and…

Yeah.

The wounded child within me *howls*. I don't want to leave. Not at all.

"What's wrong?" He moves the pan off the burner and hurries over to me, embracing me.

"Why can't I stay?"

I feel like a kid again, hating it every time either he or Dad hustled me out of the house under the cover of darkness so we could return to Cardiff. Daytimes were full of love and light and laughter.

Nighttime frequently meant—

Oh.

Leaving.

Loss.

Well, shit.

Nail, meet hammer.

"Sweetheart, you belong in your world, with your father, and your...guy."

"But what about *you*?"

He sighs. "This was always the plan, angel. Even before your father met Sorcha. Your father *wants* to live in your world. He *loves* it there. He wanted a chance to escape from the ruling class, and all I wanted was true love and a child of my own." He smiles. "Then you came along and everything changed. Our lives changed."

His smile fades. "Then *Serxon*." He spits the words. "He ruined everything. He ruined everything he touched and always did. Selfish man. All he had to do was wait. He had every comfort, every need met. He would have ascended once Parxon faked his death and I found another mate. But he couldn't wait, even though he would have been far better off. And now, he's dead."

He bundles me over to the table. "Come, sit. I haven't cooked for you in so long."

And...that's what we do. He asks me about my life, and it feels so weirdly normal to sit here talking to Zuzu in the kitchen and telling him about vampires and werewolves and...

Yeah. My crazy life.

A life I'm desperately missing, even as I yearn to stay here.

He sets out the food on the pretty cobalt blue plates I remember so well, and then I'm crying again as I eat the most delicious home-cooked meal in...

Well, no offense to Chaldis, but he's no Zuzu. Zuzu's love

language has always been cooking and caretaking. Nurturing his loved ones.

After we finish eating, I help him with the dishes, and then we move to the living room. There, I perch on the same old hassock while he sits on the sofa and brushes through my damp hair as he sings to me.

Maybe this would be creepy in any other context, but this is *home*.

"Why does my hair change color?"

He laughs. "Because you are a jotnun Alpha, little one. Well, half-Alpha. You are most definitely your father's child, but you are as beautiful as your mother. When Alphas are upset, or happy, or in love, they can change their hair color."

"My hair used to change all the time."

"Especially before and after visits." He chuckles. "You hated to leave here, or for me to leave you if I visited there. That was one thing that used to fluster your mother. She didn't know how to explain that to people, so it's a good thing we educated you ourselves."

"I still have Cat and Dog," I admit.

"You do? Oh, sweetheart. I remember that day. We had so much fun. That was the first day Parxon brought me into Cardiff."

"Remember that day in the .woods when you saw an airplane for the first time?"

He chuckles. "I do. He'd told me about them, but I didn't believe him until I saw them for myself. Your father was always so adventurous."

"That day, we heard voices. Who was that?"

"Serxon." He gently brushes out a knot. "I think perhaps even then Serxon had the ring and was hoping to catch your father crossing, so he could learn the secrets. He'd followed us. Then he asked where I was, I guess, and your father told him that I'd returned home because of him. It was no secret that I did not like Serxon."

Zuzu tells me the story of how my father's brother stole the ring from their sire's uncle and then killed him and made it look like he'd taken his boat out and drowned, the body never recovered.

"Once again, had Serxon waited, he would've eventually been passed that ring, in time. No patience." As I sit there, I look around and see photos of Dad and Zuzu together, from very young, to even more recent ones.

Except in the most recent ones, my father's grief weighs heavy on him. Deep lines furrow his brow, and sadness darkens his eyes, even though he still looks very young, as young as the last time I saw him.

"I need a picture of you, Zuzu. I can't leave without pictures of you and Dad."

"Of course, love." He finishes brushing my hair and I curl up on the couch with him, my head in his lap, the way I used to do.

"Why don't you take a nap?" he suggests.

I close my eyes, a wave of exhaustion washing through me. "Why were you in the woods this morning?"

He strokes my hair. "When your father is gone, I always go out to the stones. He has his ways of coping, and I have mine." He sniffles. "And here is our angel."

All those years I spent running. Had I known the truth, I would have gladly embraced and followed it.

I just hope my running hasn't permanently run me out of Dex's arms.

∽

I DREAM.

I dream that I'm back behind the bar at Club Toxic, and hunky not-Ianto walks in. But instead of seeing me, he ignores me and dances with some pretty young twenty-one-year-old who's out celebrating her birthday with her friends. He dances with her, sliding her already short dress up around her hips and his hand down the front of the strip of fabric masquerading as a thong.

I try to call out to him, to beg him to look at me, not to be with her, and then he bites her. She undulates in his arms and he dances her off the floor and down into the dungeon while I stand there being ignored by every vampire in the place.

My voice is silent. I can't scream, I can't—

"Eilidh."

My eyes pop open, and I'm staring into the red-rimmed violet eyes of my father. He's crying.

"*Shh!*" he reminds me in time for me to clap a hand over my mouth to muffle my happy scream.

"*Daddy!*"

I throw myself at him, and we both tumble onto the floor with Zuzu laughing from where he still sits on the couch. "I'll be right back," he says. "I need to use the toilet. She slept for nearly six hours, and I couldn't bear to disturb her."

Dad and I are both crying—god, I've literally cried more in the past day than I have in years—and if this is my new reality, then I'll figure out a way to be okay with it.

I would miss Dexter like hell, but maybe I'm proof he can love again and move on from Robert. Maybe that was my brief purpose in his life.

It'll take me a while to figure out what his was in mine when my heart hurts so bad from missing him.

Living the rest of my life confined to this house would still be a blessing.

"I love you, Daddy. I've missed you so much."

"I've missed you, too, *Mazbushka*." He sits up with me, helping me onto the couch where I cuddle in his arms like I'm eight again.

No, this isn't a nightmare. This is a dream come true, and one I never thought possible.

"Zeu said there's a story."

I nod, and he hands me a tissue. "It's a looong story."

"But...where is the ring?"

"That's part of the story."

I end up using the bathroom next and then, sitting on the couch between them, I tell him the story with Zuzu's help.

Dad looks pensive when we finish. "We will need to go out tonight then and try." He reaches over and ruffles Zuzu's hair. "You wish me to say it now?"

He smiles. "I do."

"You were right, and I was wrong."

Zuzu throws back his head. "*Yes!*"

"It isn't full moon tonight, though," Dad says. "We will keep trying, even if it doesn't work tonight. First, I have a question." He turns those violet eyes on me, and I nod.

"Is this man good enough for you?"

I snort. "Yeah, Dad. He's good enough for me."

"How do you know?"

"He spent almost two months hunting for me after only knowing me a couple of days. And I've never met anyone like him before. He's different, in a good way. I can see myself spending the rest of my life with him. And he makes me feel safe."

"How do you know it's love and not obsession?"

"The two are not mutually exclusive, Parxon," Zuzu

teases. "I remember a certain man obsessively in love with a human woman."

He grumbles at Zuzu but focuses on me. "Do you love him?"

"I really do."

"Then we'll see what we can do to get you back to him."

I reach up and rub my chest at the thought of never seeing Dexter again. "It physically hurts, missing him," I admit.

They both scowl. "Have you marked him, then?" Dad asks.

"What?"

"Bit him."

"I..." I stare at him. "Wait. I did bite him." I tell them about it.

He smiles and opens his mouth, indicating his canines and pointing to my mouth. I open so he and Zuzu can both look. "Yes, look here," Dad says, pointing. "They've come in fully. That only happens when you have left a mating mark."

Zuzu nods. "Our little girl has a mate."

"Does that mean... Wait, what *does* that mean?"

Dad's stomach grumbles. "It means I need dinner, and we'll talk while we eat, little one."

I don't even mind him calling me that.

Frankly, it's the best sound in the world.

BY THE TIME we finish eating dinner, I've been dressed in some of Zuzu's old clothes that fit me—sort of. They're a little big. But Dad now knows about Dexter being a vampire.

And...I *marked* him?

"This is good, though," he says. "Having him marked and being so powerful, it improves his chances to use the ring. And possibly to help neutralize the virus."

"Wait...what?"

He looks at Zuzu. "Did you explain the rangnork to her?"

He nods. "Briefly."

Dad focuses on me again. "So, before that, before the sorting, there were humans, and the hybrids. There were the ones susceptible to the virus, and they were also of the same lines as the ones who carried sifting genes. The rangnork was to send all of them away to Earth, to keep the jotnun lines 'protected.'" He scoffs. "Narrow-minded foolishness. Before that, it's reported in the old histories that when a jotnun Alpha mated and marked someone with the virus, the venom usually helped neutralize some of the impacts. I mean, these are very old reports, passed down in the secret records of the old families who still controlled the rings, but it is worth exploring."

"You mean it'll cure him being a vampire?"

"Probably not cure. Perhaps help some of the symptoms. Especially if you mark him more than once. For example, instead of burning to ash at dawn, he might merely be sensitive to sunlight. Or, it might remove his need for blood. But, it could also change some of his other powers—being able to move fast, his extraordinary strength. It is difficult to know. You will need to test that out."

I think about the hairs that day in my apartment. How they *poofed* into ash. "That would be...amazing."

It'd also mean one massive logistical hurdle...*gone*.

"First of all, sweetheart, we'll need to get you back. That might take some time. Probably more than one moon phase. Let us hope he is a patient and persistent man. Then again, you crossed without my assistance from just your memory. You may be stronger. I was..." He chokes up. "I was grieving your mother, and it might have impacted my ability to cross."

It feels good-weird to eat as a family again. To *have* a family again. I grab my phone and power it on, putting it in airplane mode, so it doesn't use as much juice. I take a shit-load of pictures and some video of the three of us before turning it off again.

At least I'll have that when I go back.

Proof that I have a family.

I mean...*if* I go back.

Once it's dark, Zuzu packs us snacks and two water canteens, and we set out. Now that my brain has somewhat re-engaged, I recognize things here and there. Rocks, dips in the path, and my childhood feels like I can reach out and touch it.

I could only go outside at night here, because then we were alone, with no one to see me.

Those nights were magick and beauty and fun and full of laughter, except on the nights when I had to return to Cardiff and leave Zuzu's.

When we approach the stone circle, I pause, staring at it. I have to ask it. "There's no way for me to stay here?"

Dad hugs me. "One step at a time, angel."

"What do I do?"

"We'll stand inside the stones," he says. "I'll let Zeuzehn try to contact him first, since he knows how to do it already. Once you see how he tries it, then you try it, because you have the stronger connection to Dexter."

We've been at it for hours when I finally feel a slight tingle, like what I felt when I brought us through. Before us,

I see a faint shimmer, and there's Dex, faintly, standing in the middle of the stones.

But before I can call out to him, everything fades, and that knifing pain in my soul returns.

Zuzu lets out a cry. "That was it! You did it!"

"But how do I know he saw anything?"

"It's full moon tomorrow night," Dad says. "We will try again then. You need to rest."

I start to argue with him, but I suddenly feel really freaking dizzy. Next thing I know, I'm cradled in his arms and Zuzu's dabbing at my face with a damp cloth.

Oh, and I'm on their sofa.

"How'd we get back here?"

"You fainted, angel," Dad says. "Meaning you *need* rest. It was bound to happen. It can be very draining, at first."

I don't want to rest. I want to sit here and *talk* to them.

This is like being given access to Heaven for a limited time, and I don't want to waste a second.

Except, I'm overruled. Dad carries me up to my old bedroom, where they crowd in on either side of me, and I quickly fall asleep, happier than I've felt in decades.

The only thing that could make this better is if Dexter were here with me.

Somehow, I've *got* to make that happen. Because like hell do I want to give up on him.

38

D*exter*

BOLLOCKS.

For a moment, standing there in the stone circle and chanting, it feels like I am connecting with...something. Then I see the *gwyllgi* and know I am on the right damned path.

Followed by what I'm positive is a glimpse of Eilidh, Zuzu, and another man...

And then nothing.

A wave of fatigue slams into me, staggering me to the point I have to take a step back to maintain my balance.

Damn.

I don't want to give up, but I'm exhausted and afraid if I give in to the nearly overwhelming urge to sit down and nap right here, I might wake up dead and charbroiled.

Not a great look in any dimension.

I am spanking that girl's ass sooo fucking hard when I get her back.

I refuse to quantify that with an "if."

It's "when."

When I get her back.

I will accept no defeat on this.

Returning to the hotel, I reserve a room for Garrett and Amber and leave word to call me on the room phone when they get in. They're in the air already, Garrett having connections of his own to obtain rapid transportation. They'll arrive sometime late this afternoon, and as soon as it's dark, we'll head over to the ring and try again.

I thought solving the *gwyllgi* problem might be tricky, never dreaming that was the *easy* part of this whole equation.

All I want is a few uninterrupted weeks alone with her, so I can collar her, spank her, fuck her, and *prove* to her that I want only her in my heart, bed, and personal dungeon. And if she continues letting me feed off her, all the better.

I think of Chaldis and his boy, and that's what I want for me and Eilidh. Peace.

That's not too much to ask, I don't think.

Before I collapse into bed, I call John and update him with the latest developments in our story. Including Zuzu, and that her father is alive, and what the stone ring is and does.

Which I'm sure he'd find difficult to believe if he didn't know I was a vampire and...

Well, yadda-yadda.

But I need him to know what's going on, in case I disappear for a few days. Or longer. So he doesn't assume something horrible happened to me.

I thought I would sleep late, but I'm awake by nine a.m., which is completely unheard of for me. Jetlag must have really screwed up my body's clock, which is now at war with the sun's schedule, I suppose.

But since I am wide awake, I feed and start answering e-mails, returning phone calls, and dealing with business-related items.

None of which completely take my mind off Eilidh.

Please let her be okay.

I take a shower and rummage through her things, finding Cat and Dog.

I set them on her pillow on her side of the bed. That looks better. Like they're simply awaiting her return.

Her imminent return.

When my room phone rings late that afternoon, I practically jump on it. "Yeah?"

"Dex? It's Garrett. Thanks for the room."

"Come on over. I'm awake." I pull on a T-shirt and move the doorstop to let them in.

"You're up early," he says by way of greeting.

"Tell me about it."

Once they're inside, Amber smiles. "Told you her father's alive."

"Yay. How do I get her and him and Zuzu back here?"

She closes her eyes and is silent for a moment. "We've got plenty of time for Zuzu later." She opens her eyes. "I know this is scary for you, but this has helped her heal so much past trauma, it's unbelievable."

"She's getting a spanking when I get my hands on her."

"She needs a leash and collar locked on her, is what she needs," Garrett jokes.

I mean, I think he's joking.

Sort of.

Although it's not a half bad idea.

As soon as it's dark enough, we head back to the ring, where I let Amber walk around first. She touches the stones and cocks her head, like she's listening.

"It's full moon," she says, nodding. "This'll happen."

"What do I have to do?"

"You know what you have to do." She waves Garrett into the center of the ring with her and holds his hand. Then she holds her other hand out to me. "With our help."

"Are you sure?"

"Yes," she says.

"No," Garrett grumbles at the same time.

I can't blame him. I wouldn't be happy holding my hand, either, if I were him.

I join them and hold hands with them. "Now what?"

"Say whatever you're supposed to say. Are we standing in the right place?"

I glance around and try to remember exactly how I was standing when Eilidh sent us through. Then again, she sent me back and shoved me, hard, so maybe how I'm standing isn't so important.

"*Lazgo mandem tanneh cahl. Fozun rostray sephiahl.*"

Nothing.

I try again, and again.

And again.

We stand there trying for over an hour when I'm ready to take a break. I'm more exhausted than I thought I would be. I release their hands. "Maybe I need to listen for her. Maybe they'll send a message."

"No. Don't stop," Amber says. "We'll chant with you."

"You sure, babe?" Garrett asks.

"Yes. You won't catch vampire cooties, Garrett. Hold his hand again."

He snorts but doesn't argue with his mate. He extends his hand to me and I take it, then we shift our little circle around and try again.

EILIDH

I STAND INSIDE THE STONES, holding hands with Dad and Zuzu as we chant. They have me wear the ring. If we can send the three of us across, we'll have the good ring to use. If we can't get this to work, we'll try signaling, but I suspect Dexter is standing right here, somewhere.

I *feel* it. Along with the increasingly sharp pain in my chest that I know is from missing him.

He wouldn't *not* be here, not unless something stopped him. I know he survived the first night because we saw him last night.

When the tingling sensation starts, I fight the urge to scream in triumph because I don't want to interrupt the process. "*Lazgo mandem tanneh cahl. Fozun rostray sephiahl!*"

Except I jump back, releasing both Dad and Zuzu's hands, when a very solid and wolf-scented man appears directly in front of me, his back to me.

And we're still...*here*. We didn't cross.

He wheels around, biting off a growl rumbling from him. "Eilidh?"

"*Garrett!*" I throw my arms around him, just to hear a very vampiric growl from behind him.

"You, my lovely girl, have just added an infinite number of strokes to your spanking."

I peek around him to see Dexter standing there, and now I scream again.

A good scream.

I also throw myself at him. He catches me as I wrap arms and legs around him and hug him tightly.

"I love you so much," I tell him, over and over again. The pain in my chest is blissfully gone.

"I love you, too, sweetheart."

It's the sound of the woman clearing her throat that brings me back. Amber's standing there, smiling. "Hiya."

"Amber!" I release Dexter and hug her. "Why are you guys here?"

"When my business partner calls asking for help," Garrett drawls, "especially when I know a very lucrative real estate deal is being held up because his girl disappeared, *again*, I'm going to help." He smiles. "I'm getting you a locking collar, leash, and trackable GPS ear tag for him to put on you for your wedding present."

I laugh. "Thanks. Sorry about this. This one was..." A wave of dizziness sweeps over me, and I stagger. Zuzu and Dexter catch me.

"Love?" Dexter asks.

"I-I'm okay, I..."

∾

DEXTER

WHEN EILIDH'S eyes roll back in her head, I scoop her into my arms before she can hit the ground. She goes completely limp in my arms and I've never felt so helpless in my very long life.

Except one other time.

Fates, *please* don't let this be like that. It would utterly destroy me.

The strange man I assume is her father, Parxon, gently pats her cheeks. "She's all right. She's not used to doing this, and it takes a lot out of her. Especially bringing through three people with a damaged ring. Let's get her back to the house."

"First of all," Zuzu says, and he works the ring off my left hand and hands it to Parxon. "*You* hold on to *that*."

He slips it onto his finger. "Good idea."

Then Zuzu removes the ring from Eilidh's finger and puts it on his own.

We race through the night, Garrett carrying Amber on his back, and quickly make it back to...

Well, a house that looks...*different*. Just as Eilidh said. It reminds me of a fusion of the Spanish-influenced adobe-style buildings I've seen in Tucson, and concrete-block ranch-style houses very common in Florida. Except it's two-story.

It's also large and rambling, and the grounds and house look neat and well-maintained, so I suppose that indicates wealth.

We're hustled inside, where Zuzu securely bolts the door behind us.

"Take her upstairs to her room," Parxon says to Zuzu, who leads the way. "I'll be right there." He indicates for Garrett and Amber to follow him, and I assume they're adult enough to handle their own introductions.

This is a child's bedroom, but with a very large bed. I gently lay her in it, terrified because she's still so deeply unconscious.

"Are you sure she's all right?"

Zuzu smiles. "Yes. She fainted last night after trying to contact you. She's fine. Parxon used to faint all the time when he was young, before he learned how to master it. So did I."

"You can use the rings?"

"Mostly. Better with his ring than this one, obviously."

Parxon appears in the doorway. "I settled them in the living room, for now. How is she?" He steps inside, his gaze on her.

"She's fine," Zuzu says. "Exhausted and sleeping."

Then Parxon's attention turns to me. "You must be her man, Dexter."

We can hammer out the finer points of that later. "I must." I have to force my attention away from not just Eilidh, but also Zuzu. I cannot get over how much he reminds me of Robert. Now that I've been safely reunited with Eilidh, my mind can process that fact.

The larger man holds out a hand. "Parxon. Eilidh's father." He has her violet eyes but barely looks older than Zuzu, maybe thirty, if that.

I shake with him. "Sorry our first meeting is under such chaotic circumstances."

"Me, too." He's as tall as I am, and broad-shouldered, with dark brown hair just to his shoulders and tied back. If I didn't know he wasn't a shifter, I'd assume he was, just from the very air swirling around him. His scent is nearly identical to Eilidh's, too. "She was distraught when she thought she might never see you again."

"Yes, well, that makes two of us." I look down at my beautiful girl. "Is there any way to chain her to the bed?" I smile, hoping he realizes that's a joke.

He chuckles. "I heard the story." He pats me on the shoulder. "You sound very dedicated to her."

"I love her. She's mine."

"But are you hers?"

I take a deep breath, an easy breath with her scent once again on me and in my lungs. My pulse finally levels out and calms. "Forever."

"Good. Come. We shall talk."

"But—"

"She'll be all right." He nods toward Zuzu. "Please, let him attend to her. He needs this time with her. You and I will have a lifetime at her side."

It hits me what he means—Zuzu won't leave this world and we will. After leaning in and kissing Eilidh, I follow Parxon back downstairs. We stop by the living room, collect Garrett and Amber, and then end up in a kitchen that...

Well the whole house, actually, reminds me of some sort of fusion between rustic Art Deco and old French country, with a healthy dose of the Craftsman movement.

Parxon motions for us to sit at the table and then pulls dishes of food from what I assume is the fridge and passes out plates, cups, and a pitcher of what I think is some kind of tea.

"For starters, thank you very much for whatever you did that helped bring him back here," he says. "Secondly, I hope you were not planning to return tonight. It will be tomorrow night at the earliest before I can return you. I am too exhausted, as is Zeuzehn, and Eilidh is obviously in no condition to go. But you will be safe here with us until then. We will keep the doors locked and the shutters drawn and wait until nightfall to take you back. We are still within the phase where my ring can transport you. But we must return you tomorrow night, or you will be stuck here until the next phase."

Relief fills me. "Excellent."

He leans back in his chair and studies me as he eats pieces of fruit that look like grapes. Then he focuses on Garrett. "You know this man, correct?"

Garrett looks reluctant to answer. "It's complicated."

Amber elbows him. "Yes, we know him. Dexter's a good man."

"You are the one who can see things?"

She nods. "That's me."

"Meaning he is a wolf, correct?" He points to Garrett.

Garrett darkly scowls, but nods.

"Do not worry. I have lived my life keeping secrets. I cannot wait to finally be able to join my daughter in her world. I have dreamed of this for so long and honestly had lost hope. Thank the fates and old ones for Zeuzehn's faith and efforts. I truly do not deserve that man's friendship."

I lean forward. "So...yeah. About that. Our talk got interrupted the other night. What's the deal with you two?"

"He is my husband, but we are not mates—we are friends." He points to my shoulder. "Let me see where she marked you."

"*What*?" me and Garrett both ask.

Amber smirks.

"She is half jotnun Alpha, and she said she bit you. She didn't know what it meant." He points at Garrett. "We all share common ancestry, from before the old families. People who could shift were among the sorted. People with the virus." He points at me. "Alphas still mark their mates in our world. We have a kind of venom that bonds our mate to us, and us to them. She instinctively marked you because you are her true mate."

Garrett stares at me in shock. I finally unbutton my shirt and show them the mark.

Parxon nods after he examines it. "That is good. She

should mark you several more times. Because that will only improve your chances of her venom overcoming aspects of the virus." He pops another grape into his mouth.

"*Aspects*?" Garrett and I ask.

We could take this duet on the road.

Parxon nods. "We will need to test. It's possible her venom might neutralize it in some ways. According to the old stories accumulated throughout the ages. But she is half human. And your version of the virus is far older and different in many ways. Mutated over the eons."

"You're kidding, right?" Garrett asks.

"No." Parxon eats another grape. "As I told her, it might not mean you can tolerate direct sunlight, but, for example, perhaps you no longer explode. It might only mean a bad sunburn."

Stunned, I stare at him. "*Seriously*?" Amber smiles and sips her drink, so I focus on her. "What did you see?"

She shrugs, the playful smile still curling her lips. "Just you and her walking in sunlight. Carrying a baby."

Garrett must be thinking along the same wavelength I am. "Holy shit!" we gasp in unison.

"Or maybe not," Parxon said. "It could possibly manifest in a number of ways. As I said, we must test. Most importantly is for her to rest so we can return you all to your world tonight."

"What about you?" I ask. "Come with us—I can support you and Zeuzehn both. You can walk away, right now, and I can set you up, anywhere in the world. Eilidh needs you."

"I can't disappear yet," he says. "I have too many loose ends to tie up first. I'm the last heir of one of the last old families. If anyone figures out the old myths are true, and I can still cross, it could be devastating for both worlds. There's a reason this was kept a closely guarded secret by the old families, and why it was forbidden and punishable by death to engage in the old magicks after the sorting was completed. They will destroy Zeuzehn and bury the evidence if we do not properly prepare. I cannot let that happen to him."

"Then how do you set it up?" I ask. "This *is* kind of my specialty. I've built and rebuilt hundreds of lives. Maybe I can be of some help."

"I need to move some things across to your world from this realm first. Knowledge that should not be destroyed, but I cannot risk leaving it here, because if we ever need it again..." I understand what he means.

"If we need the ability to stop anyone who figures out how to cross?"

He nods. "Exactly. Once I've taken care of that, then I can place Serxon's body and make it look like mine. No one knows we never cremated him." He grimly smiles. "We disinterred old bones and placed them, along with cattle meat, in the coffin on the pyre. As my mate, Zeuzehn helped me perpetuate the ruse. We were the only two allowed to bathe and tend and prepare Serxon's body, per our old customs. We sealed Serxon's body in a freezer in my lab in hopes of one day using it to stand in for my body, when I was finally able to cross. I'll stage it on our land, and there will be no investigation because there will be no birthright claims."

"I'll buy you a house in our world," I tell him. "Near the stones, so you can move things there, for now. I'm beyond wealthy in our world. I will completely support you. Whatever you need." In my head, I'm already calculating how much I'll need to spend to buy all the properties surrounding the stone ring.

It's pocket change, really.

Especially when it means Eilidh's happiness.

Finally, it looks like we will get our chance to settle down and enjoy our new life together, without dark mysteries lingering over our heads.

Parxon nods. "Thank you. I am very grateful."

"Is there anything we can take with us now?" I ask.

"Yes. I have several boxes of notes, journals, and old books and scrolls that need to be moved off-world."

Garrett scratches the back of his head. "And nobody else can cross, except you?"

"Other than Zeuzehn and Eilidh, and now possibly Dexter? Not that I'm aware of. To my knowledge, there are only two other intact stone rings in this world. I'm not sure if they are still viable here, or in your world, or if there are even crossing rings left which correspond to them. Stone rings only work with the particular crossing rings created at the same time to be used with them. The runes on the crossing rings are particular to that stone ring. Now that I have my crossing ring back, I hold the last two crossing rings for this stone ring. And Serxon's is damaged and unreliable."

"The crossing rings are like an airport code," Amber says, sounding awed. "They were tuned."

Parxon nods. "Exactly." He smiles. "Of all the things our world has created and accomplished, our fear of high-altitude flying and the refusal to fully embrace it has baffled me the greatest."

"Can a crossing ring be re-tuned to a different stone ring?" Garrett asks.

"Definitely not by anyone alive. That was knowledge and old magick that died with the creators. Knowledge perhaps best lost to time, now that I see the dark side of their deeds.

Our population truly deserves to die out. Who knew the sorted were the lucky ones?"

"Can we trust Zeuzehn?" Garrett asks.

Parxon nods. "He is beyond reproach and will protect our secret. He is a brother of my heart and my closest friend. He is Eilidh's spirit sire. I could not have made it through these long, lonely years, especially through my grief, without Zeuzehn's support."

Maybe he can answer another question. "Vampires, in our world, usually have the power to compel humans. Make them comply, wipe their minds. But Eilidh is immune to that. Not just with me, but with any vampire she's ever encountered. In fact, she can sort of do it a little with some vampires and humans."

"That is a jotnun Alpha trait," he says. "Try it on me."

I look into his eyes...

Nothing.

"Alphas are immune to it from other Alphas," he says. "Ironically, a claimed mate who is marked is also immune to that."

"But humans are turned into vampires by the virus that gives us our powers."

"The virus appeared in far distant history," he says. "But it never did the things that Eilidh told us it can. Daytime lethargy. A need for blood. The virus also removed some abilities, especially from Alphas, like reduced our speed and strength. It did not impact omegas or others as strongly. It did not impact the ability to sire or have children. In fact, children born of those with the virus were most often immune to it. I suspect that, somewhere in history, after the sorting, as hybrids and those with the virus mated, there were more mutations, more hybrids, until it changed into vampirism. Just as those who eventually became shifters evolved."

"Wow," Garrett softly says. "That's...holy cow."

"This is why I have dedicated my life to research. It will not be long before Jotnunlm is empty, and the last laugh will be had by those on Earth, without any knowledge of their true history."

39

D *exter*

Zuzu joins us shortly. "She is still asleep, but she will be fine. Dexter can, obviously, sleep in her bed. But do you wish to share a room?" he asks Garrett and Amber.

"They are mates, Zeu," Parxon says, smiling. "I believe they will wish that, yes."

Zuzu playfully smacks the back of Parxon's head. "Just asking. Not assuming." Then he looks at me. "The curtains and shutters in her room will keep out direct sunlight, but there still might be light visible. The windows face south, not east. Is that safe, or do I need to tack quilts over them for you?"

"As long as it's not direct light from dawn, or a direct sunbeam, I will be fine." I remember how my Robert worried any time we changed residences, how he panicked if I emerged before dusk in a new place, despite me assuring him I knew what was safe for me and what wasn't.

Those thoughts get shoved to the side. I'll unpack that later, once Eilidh and I are safely home.

The GPS ear tag is looking like a better idea by the minute. Maybe I could use one of those radio collars, like Yellowstone bears are fitted with.

We retire for what's left of the night. In the bathroom, I use the toilet and wash my face and hands. Standing at the sink, I stare into the mirror, where the ornately tiled shower wall behind me is visible.

Because I am not. Not my body, at least.

I am used to this. Used to shaving by touch, to brushing my teeth and hair by feel, seeing the items in my hand floating in mid-air, or my clothes mysteriously standing by themselves. A century or more ago, I unconsciously started thralling people in public bathrooms, once I realized they all have mirrors in them. A quick glance at someone to tell them there's nothing amiss, nothing to see.

It is amazing how anonymous one can be in larger cities with very little effort.

Eilidh, however, *sees* me, and has from the moment I walked through the doors of Club Toxic.

She was attracted to me without me needing to use any powers on her.

No need to smile and look her in the eyes.

She loves me for *me*.

I strip and snuggle in bed with her, relieved to have her in my arms once more.

Perhaps it is time I nurture myself a close circle of friends and put down permanent roots, with Eilidh as my hearth and home. It's time for me to stop living in the past and move forward to build a life with her. Robert wanted me to live and be happy. Since losing him, I've only half succeeded at that.

Eilidh's arrival in my life finally means I can fulfill my promise to him to be happy.

She makes me happy.

For the rest of our life together—what looks like might be a very long life together—I will spend every moment doing whatever it takes to make her happy and show my love.

I know dawn must be coming, but I lie awake with her warmth snuggled against me.

Of *course* my cock hardens when she shifts position against me in her sleep.

Dammit.

I softly sigh, but like hell am I going to reach down and take care of myself and risk disturbing her. She needs her rest.

Except she shifts again, and then her hand brushes me, and I realize she is more awake than I thought. Only then do I hear her breath and pulse quicken as she wakes up and finds herself draped over me.

Her violet eyes gaze down into mine. "I love you, Sir," she whispers.

Yesss. This is worth *everything*. I stroke her hair. "I love you, too, girl."

Her lips slant over mine and she starts trying to squirm out of her clothes.

Being the helpful chap I am, I hook my fingers in the waistband of her borrowed trousers, and she's soon naked from the waist down. The heady scent of her arousal immediately hits me, even before she wiggles into position and impales herself on my cock. She's wet and ready for me, her body warm and welcoming and her sweet moan as she fully seats herself on me makes me twitch inside her.

Instead of controlling this, I'd rather savor the feel of my girl using my body. My emotions have been whipsawed from jubilation to despair over the past couple of weeks, and I just want to *be* and *enjoy* this.

She stops kissing me only long enough to sit up and whip the shirt off over her head before she leans in to kiss me again. I could spend forever just doing this, tasting and teasing her. It feels like I've never kissed anyone before, and she makes me welcome the wonder exploring her body brings me. My hands settle on her hips, and while it's tempting to work in some of her overdue spankings right now, I'd rather her father and Zuzu not hear that.

Slowly, she rises and falls, her gaze meeting mine and growing darker with every languid stroke. I knead her flesh as she rides me, skimming my hands up her sides, to her breasts, where I run the pads of my thumbs over the tips of her nipples. They pebble under my touch and she bites down on her lower lip, softly gasping, her wet heat fluttering around me.

Cupping her breasts, I squeeze, playfully at first, then digging my fingers in to gauge her tolerance. More than the average human woman, that's for sure. Except now I know she is anything *but* average. Squeezing harder, I feel her clenching around me, her breath quickening.

"More, love?" I ask.

She nods.

I pull her down so I can suck her nipples, graze my teeth over them without piercing her flesh yet. I want to feed off her sweet blood. I want to leave bites all over her breasts, along her inner thighs, mark every sweet spot on her body so her every memory is of me and my love for her.

Yet, I hold myself back. I don't want to weaken her before the crossing home. We'll have ample time to experiment after our return. But I do suck hard, leaving love bites all over them, pinching her nipples with my fingers and enjoying every soft, mewling sound I can draw from her.

Eventually, I flip her over and kiss my way down her body so I can spread her thighs and bury my face there. Her fingers twine in my hair and I don't even mind the sharp tugs as she grips me and grinds her pussy against my mouth. I lap up every bit of her I can, my tongue teasing her clit, sliding it inside her and drawing breathless, sweet gasps from her.

Wrapping my fingers around the tops of her thighs to hold her in place, I graze my teeth over her clit, forcing myself not to bite, to feed, just playfully nip and suck. That kicks her over the edge and makes her come.

But I'm not finished with her yet.

I ease up, lightly licking, flicking with my tongue, not letting her push me away, until she's once again squirming and eagerly grinding on me.

This time, I don't let her come. I sit up and let her push me back onto the bed, so she can go down on me.

Holy fates, the woman's mouth is *perfection*. I lace my hands behind my head and watch her, her gaze on me even as my cock disappears between her lips. She swirls her tongue around the head, tracing every line and ridge, flicking the tip along the slit and playing with my pre-cum. I want to grab her head and fuck her mouth, which is exactly why I keep my hands right where they are.

I refuse to rush.

There's no desperation in our passion now, other than building desire and chasing pleasure. She feels like she's all here, with me, in every way, without her mind trying to pull her in other directions and dividing her focus.

Eilidh's all mine, and I won't have to say good-bye to her any time soon.

My persistent fears of losing her to time versus turning her can finally be put away, so I can do nothing but love her.

I know she would eagerly suck a climax out of me, but before I get too far along I pull her up and let her ride me again. She does so with purpose, like she's quickly closing in on her pleasure, so I watch and wait and enjoy the ride. Because, believe me, I *am* enjoying it ever so much, the simple pleasure of making love to the woman I love because it's perfection, and not with purpose.

Her eyes grow darker, intense, and faster than I realize she's doing it, she leans in, tips my head to the side, and her teeth sink deep into my shoulder.

Liquid fire flows from the bite and quickly makes its way through my body. My cock grows rigid as my balls empty, the white-hot pleasure searing me and making my back arch. Still, she rides me, her own orgasm hitting her and her body clenching around my dick, milking more cum from me, until she finally releases the bite and licks the spot.

Around me, the room spins, swirls, as my girl happily sighs and snuggles tightly against me, draped over me.

I crash into oblivion.

∼

DREAMS.

The things this woman does to me, the *dreams* I have.

This time, it's of the two of us walking in woods I recognize as being at my estate in Scotland. It's an overcast day, and we're further shaded by the thick canopy of trees. Eilidh looks radiant in a blue sundress, her breasts round and full over a tummy already swelling again, and in my arms...

I carry a sleeping baby not quite a year old.

I instinctively know if he was to open his eyes, they would be violet, like hers, like Parxon's—

grandsire

—and her laughter as she races ahead of me fills my soul with warmth I never dreamed possible to experience again.

We come to a clearing, where three men are setting up a picnic for all of us. I recognize Parxon and Zuzu, but while I think I should know the third, like he is familiar to me, his back is turned and I cannot see his face or hear his voice.

But in my arms...

I can smell the baby's sweet scent, a mix of Eilidh and my own. We've named him Robert, and while I know this is a dream I can understand now why Eilidh doesn't want to leave her father's house and return with me to our world.

This joy, it is addictive, a new obsession for me to chase.

Unbounded happiness, my soul full and at peace and healing in a way I never thought possible.

So many impossibilities within my grasp.

And then it all fades to thick, inky blackness, leaving me to crash into oblivion.

I AWAKEN that afternoon to the glow of sunlight around the curtains covering the bedroom shutters and, for the first time in what feels like forever, I'm not choked with panic. Fear and dread no longer fill me.

Neither does the usual stupor that arrives with the sun. That was simple exhaustion—and maybe an effect of her bite—that sent me to slumber, not the sun's dawning.

Not this time.

Eilidh lies snuggled next to me, sound asleep, exhaustion carving lines deep in her face that are nearly painful to my soul. She doesn't deserve to worry—she's suffered enough of it in her life. I want to take care of her, make her smile, ease every burden.

Moving slowly, I extricate myself from beside her and climb out of bed...

And with the dream still in my mind, I pray.

Carefully, I tug one of the curtains open, and a lone sunbeam spills through a tiny gap at the top of the shutters. I stand there watching it, where it's picking up dancing dust motes and flowing over a shelf on the far wall.

Reaching up, I wince as I yank a couple of hairs from the back of my head. Then I lay them on the shelf and nudge them just to the edge of the sun's path.

And I step back into safety and wait.

The minutes creep past. Not believing it, at first, I watch as the hairs are fully enveloped by the light.

They do not dissolve into ash.

My breath—my *breath*—escapes from me in a whoosh. I realize that, unlike before, I haven't been automatically starting to breathe before I wanted to speak.

I've...been *breathing*.

Reflexively.

Possibly for days, now that I think of it.

When I hold my fingers to my neck...I have a pulse. It's not me consciously willing my heart to beat, either.

It's...*beating*. I no longer can start or stop it at will.

Time to experiment. When I hold my breath deliberately, I find my lungs soon aching, until I suck in gulps of fresh air.

Doing the stupidest thing probably in the history of ever, as my girl might say, I reach out and let the sunlight spill over my hand and arm.

I gasp. My vision blurs, triples, as I stare at the golden light cascading over my body. I turn my hand over and back again, marveling at the sight and the warmth of it on my flesh.

"Dex?"

I can't speak, can't move, except to breathe and turn my hand back and forth.

"Dex!" I hear her throw the covers off her and climb out of bed, her hands suddenly on my back.

Her breath against my shoulder.

"Dex," she whispers.

I can't take my gaze from my arm. "Look!" I whisper, terrified this is a mirage, an impossible dream.

"I see."

"Am I awake?"

"You are."

We stare at it for long, silent minutes with her arms wrapped around me. "What does this mean?" I finally manage.

"Well, I think it means Dad and Zuzu were right, and me marking you worked. My venom was able to neutralize the virus. At least, partially."

My tongue seeks out my fangs. I feel them slide into place as my stomach grumbles and I realize I haven't had any blood in over twenty-four hours. "I'm still a vampire. I still need blood."

"But...this is *huge*."

"I know." I can't stop...*looking* at it.

The way the light picks up the hairs on my arms.

Her canines lightly rake across the back of my shoulder, instantly giving me a throbbing erection.

Before I even realize I'm doing it, I spin around, grab her, and we land on the bed with me on top and her wrists pinned over her head.

Her violet gaze burns up at me. She hooks a foot around my leg and nearly manages to flip us over, until I lean in and bite down on the side of her throat, piercing her flesh so I can feed. Her fingers flex and curl as she wraps her legs around me and grinds against my thigh.

The thick, sweet scent of her arousal fills the room, my dick aches to be inside her, all while the warm, honeyed taste of her blood fills my mouth. I fill her pussy, shoving in deep and hard until I bottom out.

"Yes!" she gasps.

I chuckle against her flesh and slowly thrust. My sweet, radiant sun.

Who's also far more than she appears.

Digging in deeper with my fangs makes her come, and her body clamps down on my cock, nearly milking my climax from me. So I ease up and lick her sweet flesh after I withdraw my fangs. Every thrust I take inside her prolongs her pleasure, keeps pulling those sexy gasps from her, makes her clench around me.

My stomach is happy, my cock is about to be happy...

And my sweet girl is *very* happy.

I kiss my way up to her ear and nip, my hips still rocking against her. "We can fuck our way through sunrises and sunsets, my love." I thrust hard and deep, digging in and actually coaxing one more orgasm of her before I finally let go and my own climax hits. Pleasure the likes of which I've never felt before builds and explodes, snapping free and setting off fireworks behind my eyelids. Wave after wave sweeps through me as I fill her with my cum before eventually falling still inside her.

Kissing her tastes like heaven and perfection. I lace my fingers through hers and gently squeeze.

"I love you so damn much, Eilidh."

She smiles. "That the orgasm or the mating mark talking?"

"Both. And more. Sooo much more."

We stare at each other for a long moment. "I want forever with you," she whispers. "Master. *Husband.*"

It feels like the breath just got sucked out of me.

No one's called me either of those since Robert.

I release her hands and sit up, pulling her with me, cupping her head in my hands as I kiss her again. "I love you, baby. I want forever with you, too. Never letting you go." I rest my forehead against hers. "No more running."

She smiles. "No more running. Looks like I'll have a really long lifespan." She wiggles against me. "Hope you're ready to put up with me."

I grin. "I am. And I'm looking forward to having inlaws."

She giggles. "I think you won them over."

Every breath I take brings her sweet scent and the aroma of our shared passion into my lungs, filling me, giving me life. "We should get up and eat before we go back."

She pouts. "Do we have to? Go back, I mean. To our world."

"You know we do, sweetheart. They said it's dangerous."

"We could send Garrett and Amber back and stay here."

"No, sweetheart, we can't, and you know why. But we'll prepare for your father to move to live with us permanently, and we'll visit with Zuzu as often as you like."

Her tone tells me she's not totally happy about that, but she understands it's the way things have to be. "Okay."

We end up snuggling until the call of nature strikes me. I kiss her, extract myself from her sweet embrace, and head to the bathroom without turning on the light in there.

It's the flash of movement in the looking glass that startles me. I'm not too proud to admit I scream, which brings her running.

"What? What is it?" She flips on the light.

"I..." I'm staring into a pair of blue eyes and at a man—a naked man—who looks startlingly like Ianto from *Torchwood*.

A man whose movements mirror mine.

When I hold up my right hand, the man holds up his. When my jaw drops open in shock, so does his.

Eilidh lets out a cackling laugh as I struggle to process this. "That's *you*, Fangster Hunkadoofalus!"

"Me?" The man's got tousled light brown hair, looks kind of brooding.

Bet he looks good in a suit. Any suit.

Other than a birthday suit.

Although, I have to say, he's rocking that, too. I turn, so I can get a better look at the guy's ass. Definitely not bad. I'd fuck him. "That's...*me*?"

She wraps her arms around me. "That's *you*, Not-Ianto."

I pull her into my arms as I stare at us in the mirror. I've spent my life never truly seeing myself. Never in a modern mirror. The last time was the day before I was turned, in the surface of a calm pond.

"Get your phone, baby," I whisper.

She darts out of the bathroom. Now that I know the full truth, I see that those flashes of spookily fast movement are part of who she is.

Of *what* she is.

Vampire 2.0.

Or, maybe it's more accurate to say I'm Vampire 2.0 and she's half Vampire 1.0.

She returns with her phone and unlocks it for me, handing it over.

I call up the camera app and take a picture of the mirror.

"Oh, naked pics," she snarks. "Thanks."

I gasp as I stare at the image.

The two of us.

Both of us clearly rendered in the image.

I remember when the first cameras came out, my bitter disappointment to realize that the blur marring the image plates wasn't just a glitch, but all I'd ever see of my own face for the rest of forever.

Forever.

I had a vague idea of what I looked like from IR and FLIR imaging experiments, but they don't give an accurate representation. Ditto body doubles. They resembled me enough to pass with people who didn't know me very well, but they weren't...

Me.

Eilidh nuzzles her head against my shoulder and takes the phone from me. She deletes the picture before repositioning the phone to take a selfie of the two of us.

Necks up.

No boobies, unfortunately.

Hey, look at that—I have a decent smile.

Hers is gorgeously perfect, as always.

"*That's* the guy I fell in love with," she softly says. "That handsome, toothy fucker, Mr. Fangster Hunkadoofalus. The guy who turned my life upside down in good ways. *All* the good ways."

I pull her into my arms and stare down into her eyes.

Violet eyes.

Perfect eyes.

"All the good ways?"

She drapes her arms around my neck. "Yeah. *All* of them."

40

D*exter*

WE SHOWER AND DRESS, and I don't fail to note the looks of shock on Garrett's and Amber's faces when we walk into the kitchen.

"Holy...*dude!*" He stands and slowly paces over to me, circling me. "You *do* realize it's daytime, right?"

Amber giggles and throws herself at me for a hug, then Eilidh. "It worked!"

"Yeah, it did," Eilidh says. "My dad and Zeuzehn were right. Where are they?"

"They'll be back soon," Amber says. "Your dad is down in his lab, and Zeuzehn ran to the market."

Garrett's still staring at me in shock and reaches out, poking my shoulder.

Normally, that might offend me, but not today.

Nothing can shake my good mood today.

I grin. "You think *that's* cool? Check *this* out." I walk over to the kitchen door, open the shutter covering the window, and, after testing it against my arm first, I stand in the sunlight spilling through, closing my eyes against the glare as I tip my head back and greet the warmth of the sun.

"*Shhhiiiit!*" he gasps.

"This *has* to stay a secret in our world," Eilidh says.

I turn and step back inside, closing the shutter behind me. "Why?"

"Because if it doesn't, I become a target of Data-X and others," she says. "So would you, most likely. If you think they'd lock me in a lab to make me a breeder, they'd do the same to you, if they thought your sperm would father hybrid children, or that they can use your blood to cure or trigger vampirism. If they find that they can't use you, they'd kill you."

Garrett runs a hand through his hair. "She's right." He looks to Amber. "Thoughts?"

She closes her eyes for a moment, her arms crossed over her chest. When she finally opens her eyes, she grimly nods. "There are still secret programs out there. Our work's not done closing down the labs. Not just Data-X, but others. I can see more now. A lot more. Stuff that didn't make sense before, but does with this new context."

Garrett throws his head back, hands on his hips. "Aw, *shit*," he mutters. "I was afraid you were going to say that."

Parxon walks into the kitchen and pulls up short at the sight of me standing there. He slowly approaches, smiling as he looks me up and down. "It worked, I take it?"

"Yes!" Eilidh says, smiling up at me. "It did."

He briskly nods. "Excellent. But you can't let anyone know."

I chuckle. "Already covered that."

"They're right," Garrett says. "You *especially* can't let Lucius and them know. None of the other vampires can ever know about this. About you and the sunlight. You absolutely *cannot* tell them. And if you ever turn her, and she retains the ability to handle sunlight, you have to hide that from them, too."

"Yeah, I *get* it." I turn to Garrett. "I need your permission to do something."

"To do what?"

"I need to see if there's something I can still do. I need to find out now, before we return, so I don't screw up and do something that we can't fix. And there's only one human here."

We both look at Amber.

She nods and says, "Okay," as Garrett says, "*Fuck* no!" and moves to stand between us.

Amber puts her hand on his arm. "It's okay."

"*No*, it's *not* okay! I'm *not* letting a leech put you under his powers!"

"*Garrett!*" she snaps. "You *know* he's not like that!"

"No." He shakes his head, glaring at me. "Absolutely not."

"We need to find out," Amber says. "We *need* to know. This is *huge*."

"First, Selene is turned into a vampire," Garret growls. "A shifter with even more powers than she had. Who *knows* what happens if she turns on *us*? And now Dexter is a day-walking vampire? This is *not* good, babe."

"Then it's good we've got three new secret weapons on *our* side now, huh?" She indicates me, Parxon, and Eilidh. "They're *pack*. Everything I've seen about them makes total sense now. I've seen them as pack from the start. I understood that with her, but not with Dexter, and of course, I didn't know who Parxon was until I met him. It didn't make sense to me, which is why I didn't tell anyone about that part of my visions. I just thought I was wrong.

"But I wasn't wrong—I wasn't listening clearly to the visions. Parxon, Dexter, and Eilidh are *pack*. Their first allegiance is to us, *not* Lucius and his nest. And literally the survival of *all* shifters and vampires depends on us treating them as pack. And Zeuzehn, obviously. Ditto Chaldis and Corbin. We can trust them. But he's right—we have to know if he can still thrall a human."

"*Shit.*" He paces in a circle, hands still on his hips. Then he turns and jabs a finger in my face. "You hurt her, and I'll hurt *her*." He points at Eilidh.

"I won't hurt her. I swear. I won't touch her memories at all. Just a harmless test."

He curls back a lip and growls, but finally moves to the side.

Amber steps forward and offers me a nervous smile. "Go ahead."

I'm still not looking her in the eyes. "I just want to see if I still have the ability."

"I know. I trust you."

Garrett growls a little louder, deeper. "Get it *over* with!" he roars.

I look into her eyes and feel the connection take hold. "*Hi*," I whisper into her mind.

She smiles and lifts her hand in a wave. I immediately disengage and turn away while Amber blows out a breath and Garrett rushes in to check her.

"I'm okay," she quickly says. "I'm okay, Garrett. He didn't hurt me. All he did was say *hi*, and ask me to smile and wave."

Eilidh touches my arm. "Well?"

I nod. "I can still do it. At least that much. It felt the same, like I still had the strength." I stare at my hands, which are illuminated by a sliver of sunbeam flowing through a gap in the shutter over the kitchen window.

It's still hard to believe I'm not dreaming. This is a day I never thought would ever come.

Not without it bringing my immediate death.

"Now what?" Garrett asks.

"Tonight, we take you to the stones and send you home," Parxon says. "Before anyone discovers you're here. I will meet you there at the quarters, dark, and full moons to move things to your world."

"But what about you coming with us?" Eilidh asks. The pain in her voice rips at me.

If she stays, I stay. I will never be separated from her again.

I keep saying that, and this time, I fucking *mean* it, even if I have to handcuff her to me.

"I must prepare first," Parxon tells her.

"How long will that take?" I hate how *lost* Eilidh sounds.

"Not long, *Mazbushka*." He smiles. "No longer than a few months. The story must be perfect, to protect Zeuzehn. I cannot leave unless I am certain he is protected."

Eilidh throws her arms around him. "Please do it fast, Daddy," she says. "Don't let your ring get damaged. I'd never see you again."

Okay, so, yeah, Daddy play is going to be a hard *no*, for sure.

Parxon sadly sighs as he holds her. "*Mazbushka*, nothing will ever keep me from you again, now that I've found you. And you will have the other ring."

"Why can't we bring Zuzu, too?" Eilidh asks. "We can take care of him. Please help me talk him into it."

"I doubt he would leave." Parxon clasps his hands together. "Unlike me, he still has a chance of finding true love here in this world, because I never marked him."

"He could probably find love in ours, too," Garrett says. "It's a big world. Lots of people. Dating apps."

"Yes, but it's doubtful he could birth a child of his own, and *that* is his heart's desire and always has been. Ever since we were children. He needs an Alpha of our kind to do that. I have never marked him, so he can still find another Alpha. With me declared legally dead here, Zeuzehn will ascend to the ruling class and have the ability to find a suitable mate of his choosing. Or, at the very least, he can live comfortably and independently.

"My leaving must not cast shadows on his reputation and possibly have people thinking he killed me. Especially since Serxon supposedly died in an 'accident.' I will send Zeu traveling, and make sure he is away from the estate, with plenty of witnesses to attest that he is gone, and I am alive, and then I will stage a fiery accident."

Parxon's got a good heart, thank fates. I was honestly worried we'd find out he was a shitty asshole. Like his brother. And that I'd have to kill him to protect Eilidh.

"Should we destroy the stone circle once you're in our world for good?" Garrett asks.

"*No!*" Eilidh yells, silencing us all with her vehemence. "How will I see Zuzu if we can't get to him?"

Amber closes her eyes and we wait until she opens them. "No. Definitely can't destroy it. We'll need it again. For more than just visits."

"Why?" Parxon asks.

"I can't see exactly who yet, but we'll need to send someone over here for their safety. Not one of us," she adds. "It's vitally important they be able to cross and get to

Zeuzehn. And Eilidh needs to be able to visit with Zeuzehn."

If we can't convince Zuzu to move across with us, scratch my plan to send in bulldozers once I own all the land around here, and then say *oopsies*, and pay whatever considerable fine would be levied against me by some government antiquities agency. Or, at the very least, to shift the stones off their moorings enough to permanently deactivate the ring.

There's a knock at the front door, silencing all of us. Garrett herds the rest of us upstairs, and he and I listen at the top of the stairwell while Parxon answers the door.

A moment later, Parxon appears at the base of the stairs. "It's safe," he calls up. "It's only Zeuzehn back from the market."

We all return to the kitchen. The omega smiles when he sees me. "It worked. How have you enjoyed your first view of sunlight since forever, my son?"

My heart does an uncomfortable summersault at his expression. "It was incredible, thank you. I will never take it for granted again."

His smile turns bashful. In another life, another universe, before meeting my Eilidh, I would be sorely tempted to make him mine. He reminds me so much of my Robert, it takes my breath away.

You would think after such a life long-lived that I wouldn't be able to remember individual faces, but you'd be wrong.

That face is imprinted on my soul forever, the way my children's faces are imprinted there.

The love never dies.

Ever.

Parxon rests his hands on the omega's shoulders. "We

will send them back tonight, but this means it is finally time for us to put our plans in place."

Zeuzehn sadly smiles. "I understand. I will miss you, dear friend." He looks at Eilidh. "But at least my *Mazbushka* has returned. Promise to come visit."

"I will."

Parxon gently squeezes the omega's shoulders. "We can bring you with us. You can live with us. We'll care for you for the rest of your life, and you will have no worries."

"While I would love to see more of that world, you know my heart. Perhaps you can bring me to visit. I will leave notes for you, friend, the way we used to." He covers Parxon's hands with his. "You have a chance to go on and find new love in that world. You have much time to make up with Eilidh. You have been more than kind to me throughout the years, but we both know where my future happiness lays, and it must be *here*, if it is to be at all. Perhaps if I grow too lonely and have no success and miss all of you, I will change my mind. For now, I do wish to try."

"I can't believe *I* of all people am saying this," Garrett grumbles, "but there's more to life than having pups. *Babies*, I mean."

Amber snickers and hugs him.

"I know this," Zeuzehn says. "I have a full life, a well-rounded life that few can match. For some, it is plenty. Our objection to our sires' plans for us were never the plans themselves. It was that we didn't have the freedom to find true mates. I have always wished for more children besides Eilidh."

He looks up at Parxon. "We knew at our first meeting as children, long before we were joined, that we didn't feel a mate bond. We most likely wouldn't have produced viable heirs, even had we consummated our mating. There is a reason the jotnun birth rate is dropping so dramatically, and it is because too many people are mating for money or convenience or family estates, instead of love and instinctive attraction.

"Instinctive attraction means the best chance of having children. We've settled into a...lazy way of pairing off. It is evident in our race's decline, yet our rulers have decided to ignore all the evidence to the contrary and fall back on old and ineffective ways. By enforcing a class system, it's reduced the ability to freely choose mates, since genetic diversity has also decreased.

"The elders who decided on isolating what became humans, vampires, and shifters from the rest of us didn't anticipate what the loss of natural diversity would do to our kind eons later. They worried about the hybrids' abilities to reproduce faster than us and were concerned that females were 'weaker' than males. They thought they were 'purifying' the jotnun race by isolating us, but instead, they merely doomed it to inevitable extinction. Mixing what we are would only have made us all stronger, eventually.

"And, of course, they found sympathetic ears within the representatives for those races, who were being given an entire new world they could shape however they wished, without our restrictive ruling class in charge. At our population's current rates of birth and attrition, we will likely quit producing offspring within a thousand years, and effectively die out completely in less than ten thousand. Which might sound like a long time, but considering our life spans can easily be two thousand or more years, that is not long at all. Just a few generations. Parxon and I are still very young by our race's standards. Barely adults."

"Well, *that* sounds familiar," Amber snarks. "Trying for

species 'purity.'" She shoots a glare at Garrett. "Your dad and uncle would fuckin' *love* it here."

He blushes a little, like she hit a nerve, but he doesn't reply.

Interesting.

"Serxon was younger than I am," Parxon says. "He was incredibly selfish and immature, and he never cared if I was happy. All he ever cared about was the prestige of finally ascending to the ruling class, and that I sire a legitimate Alpha heir to make it happen."

"Why couldn't he just mate and sire one of his own?" Garrett asks.

"Because I'm the eldest, an Alpha, and have a registered mating without an Alpha heir. Even had he mated and sired, it would still be ruled common class. Only if he was elevated to ruling class through *me* would *any* heir he sired be a ruling class member. That was put into place to prevent younger siblings from trying to kill off elder ones to improve their status."

"*That's* fucked up," Eilidh says.

Zeuzehn smiles. "Yes, it is. But with our declining birth rate, people are loathe to challenge the system. They feel a more strict dedication to it will turn things around, and that's simply not the case. The ruling class tightly holds their power, and the common class blithely believes no change can be had."

"I'm surprised Serxon didn't try to kill you off from the start," I comment.

"Because of our laws," Parxon says, "at that time, every-thing would have then gone to Zeuzehn's family by default, since he is my mate, because of my will and our sire's will and his birthright statement. I also had many protections around Zeuzehn to keep him safe from Serxon, in case he tried to harm him. My plan had been to rewrite my will and birthright statement so that if something happened to me, only once Zeuzehn mated again would Serxon ascend. I was obviously not going to tell Serxon that, however."

He looks down at the smaller man. "But then Zeuzehn was the last of his family, and Serxon murdered Sorcha. Once I killed Serxon, then our full focus became locating Eilidh."

"As the last of my family," Zeuzehn says, "if Parxon is recognized as dead, because of his will, everything reverts to me. Including the bulk of my family's estate, which, as my legally recognized mate, Parxon's been controlling since my sire's death. Without an heir, my status will be converted to full ruling class member, as if I am an Alpha. Once I have ascended to ruling class, I can freely choose any mate I wish, regardless of their class, and they will also ascend to ruling class, if they are not already."

Parxon drapes a protective arm around the other man's shoulders and nuzzles his chin against the top of Zeuzehn's head. It makes my heart ache for both of them, especially since the omega reminds me so strongly of my Robert.

"Zeuzehn told me to keep hope alive," Parxon says. "He was correct."

"I'm surprised you didn't kill Serxon sooner," Garrett says. "He sounds like an asshole."

"I was not aware he knew anything about the crossing rings. My sire passed on the knowledge to me before his death, and he was the last to know from his generation, with his brother dead. Told me to keep tabs on the other world so the knowledge wasn't lost. To pass it down to my eldest heir. He was part of an old, secret organization that monitored events in that world, and he conferred those responsibilities to me, even though he was the last of the members, as far as he knew. Had Serxon not killed our uncle, he would have passed his ring and the knowledge to Serxon because our uncle had no mate or heir.

"The night Serxon attacked me and Sorcha, I needed to be at our estate to oversee the annual assessment. Zeuzehn had covered for me as long as possible, until I could cross back here. Every crossing period, he would leave messages for me at the stone ring for me to retrieve, so I would know when I needed to be present. We told people I travelled a lot for my work as a researcher and historian. Technically, not untrue. I gave Serxon a generous stipend we thought would keep him living a life of leisure far from the estate. Bought him a large, beautiful home in the city, paid for him to go to school and travel.

"That worked, for a while. Zeuzehn was happy and contented running the estates, which my brother never showed any interest in. My brother's ways were, I was certain, destined to get him killed. We knew if we waited long enough, his fate would take over. He was always picking fights, drinking, gambling, getting arrested, angering people. He was like that from childhood.

"I brought Sorcha through to me for an evening visit, because I wasn't sure if I'd be able to return until the next crossing phase. The stone ring is on our land. I didn't know Serxon had returned and spotted me sneaking Sorcha from the residence, or that he followed us.

"He caught up to us at the stone ring, where he attacked us. He saw her mating mark and realized what had happened. He also wasn't expecting Sorcha to be as tough as she was. We got free and ran from him, crossed back, and I was shocked when he crossed through behind us moments later. I gave your mother my ring and told her to run. That I would drag him back, take his ring, and find her."

"Plus, you thought I'd be able to bring us back through at some point," Eilidh quietly says.

"Yes. She knew she couldn't use the ring on her own, but we already knew you could."

"Because you sometimes had me sing the song during the blindfold game," she softly says.

He nods. "Exactly. Anyway, that night, I fought with Serxon and dragged him back through to our world. Demanded to know where he'd obtained a crossing ring.

"He admitted he plundered his ring from our sire's younger brother when Serxon killed him several years earlier. Serxon apparently got him drunk one night, and he confessed we were one of the old families, that the rings were for crossing, the secret society—everything. Everyone thought my uncle had drowned at sea in an accident, the body never recovered.

"Obviously, Serxon couldn't reveal to anyone he had the ring, or how he'd obtained it, or the knowledge he held. Fortunately, he didn't know *how* to cross. He didn't realize when he killed our uncle that there were only certain times the ring worked, or what the proper chant was. Since our sire was dead, Serxon knew he couldn't kill me if he ever wished to fully understand its secrets. But he couldn't let on to me that he knew because that would have implicated him in my uncle's death.

"Your mother likely thought I was dead because I swore to get Serxon's ring and return to her. She knew crossings were only possible during certain moon phases and times. Unfortunately, my brother escaped me and hid his ring. Refused to tell me where it was. Taunted me. Said if I changed my will and faked my death to give him the estate and Zeuzehn, he'd give me the ring. Otherwise, he expected me to keep funding his lifestyle. I had no recourse. I could not kill Serxon without first obtaining the ring, and he couldn't kill me because he knew he'd lose the secrets to crossing, as well as any chance of ascending, or having a birthright, or milking me for support. Stalemate.

"If I retaliated, he threatened to reveal what he knew about me, which could have threatened Zeuzehn, too. Serxon and I both knew if either of us revealed what we could do with the rings, we would *both* be killed. It's ancient, forbidden magick. Serxon also knew that, as long as your mother was alive, I would never take another mate and produce an heir, meaning he would never ascend to ruling class.

"What Serxon didn't know is that, long ago, I'd told Sorcha if anything ever happened to me, when you were eighteen, Sorcha was to give you my ring and tell you the full truth and the secrets of how to cross. To disguise yourself as men and cross and look for Zeuzehn immediately upon your arrival."

"And that's why you never reported Serxon to the authorities here," Garrett says. "Because it was mutually assured destruction."

"Exactly. Zeuzehn and I tried to keep vigilant watch on the stones during the crossing times. As you can imagine, we had to keep our actions a secret. My brother must have been watching us and finally puzzled out the pattern, that only certain times were crossing nights. The rings can home in on each other during crossing times. I guess he heard us discussing that while we tried to find Sorcha. At some point, Serxon slipped through when we weren't guarding the stones and killed Sorcha..."

When his voice chokes, Zeuzehn consoles him. "I was delayed getting there that night for my watch. I knew something had happened because I felt such a sharp, deep pain, like my very soul was being rent. But I was there when Serxon returned the next night. He sounded...smug. Triumphant. Told me I could now mark Zeuzehn and get busy siring an heir, since Sorcha was dead. In my grief and rage, I attacked Serxon and killed him, but his ring was damaged during the fight. Zeuzehn helped me stage the accident and provided an alibi."

"Wrecked a perfectly good vehicle on such a waste of a soul as that man," Zeuzehn darkly mutters. "Better he'd not been born at all for all the grief he caused, the beast."

EILIDH

I DRAG my feet as we cook dinner together and eat. Dexter lovingly hovers without getting between me and Dad and Zuzu. And when we sit to eat, I sit between them, and nobody comments about me crying.

I take lots of pictures of pictures on the walls, and of them, and me with them. I'll be printing these out when we get home.

"Oh, wait." Zuzu darts off and returns moments later with a small photo album. "I keep this in the safe. It's too risky to leave it lying around. I cannot believe I almost forgot about it. Sorcha gave it to me for my birthday one year."

I burst into tears when I realize it's filled with pictures of when I was born, when I was a small child.

Pictures of the four of us together. A family.

My hands are shaking too hard to take pictures of everything. Dexter gently takes the phone from me and does it for me while Zuzu and Dad hold me.

Amber walks over, smiling as she hugs me. "I know this hurts right now, sweetie, but please be strong. Good things —great things—are coming. I'd tell you more, but I don't want to jinx them."

"Well, you were right about Dad being alive. You've got a great track record, in my book."

Once it's dark, we head out to the woods, with all the men carrying boxes of notes and journals and other items we're moving now. I want to dart off the path and run away, a familiar feeling from when I was a kid, but I know Dexter and Garrett would quickly catch up with me if I tried.

The way Dad and Zuzu used to catch up with me and hold me, trying to calm me down when I cried and begged not to leave.

I just wanted my family together all the time. That's all I ever wanted.

I now understand why I hated the night for so long.

I also understand why I suppressed all those memories.

Because it hurt.

Saying good-bye hurt and always did.

I haven't had the heart to tell them about the cage fighting Mom resorted to in her attempts to keep us afloat. Dad and Zuzu both feel horrible enough as it is about what happened.

It wasn't their fault. I just wish my fucking asshole uncle were still alive so I could have the satisfaction of killing him myself. I'd stab him with so many pencils, he'd look like a fricking porcupine when I finished.

Once we reach the stone ring, I stand outside it, hesitating. Zuzu smiles and walks over to me, slipping the ring on my finger. "You can signal to me. You know how now. You can leave me notes in the rocks, where the scarf was. And your father will bring you notes, and we'll visit."

The scarf. I have it in my pocket. "What if you don't find love, Zuzu? You'll be alone here."

"I have friends, angel. They will comfort me. And you will come visit with me, and I will visit with you."

"But what if you don't find love?"

He sighs. "If I make a promise to join you if I give up, will that help?"

Parxon shakes his head. "Zeu—"

"No, it is all right. She is our daughter." He envelops me in his arms. "I promise, my little one, if I feel I would be happier with you, in your world, absolutely, I will come." He laughs. "And then I will move in with you, and your man will never spank you again because he will fear me overhearing."

I tearfully laugh with him.

"Well, he's not wrong," Dexter jokes. "And we'll come back for the dark moon to visit. That's only two weeks away."

Without fanfare, Parxon takes Garrett and Amber and all the boxes of stuff through the ring, returning seconds later.

I feel like my heart is breaking all over again. "Please come with me. Please don't leave me again."

"*Shh, shh*, angel," Dad says, holding me, rocking me. "It will not be long before I will be there with you all the time."

"Zuzu, *please*, come with him."

"*Mazbushka*, I made you a promise, and I will keep it." He kisses my forehead and pulls me in for a hug. "We will see each other. This is not good-bye. And if things do not work out to my liking, then we will talk about me moving there. Besides, you have a man to love and let spank you. He will take care of you for us. He seems like an agreeable fellow."

I sense Dexter step in behind me. "It'll be all right, love."

"Both of you come over. Please?"

Dad nods and, seconds later, we're back in Cardiff.

John and Mark are standing there, talking with Garrett and Amber.

"You have your ring, angel," Zuzu says. "Your father has his. Please, do not cry. Be happy that soon he will be here all the time. This is not an end, but a beginning."

I nod, but it doesn't comfort me.

"Love you." He kisses my forehead, my cheeks. "See you soon, my little angel. Be good until I return." It's what he always said to me.

"Love you, too. Both of you."

Dad hugs me tightly. "Love you so much. This will be all right. I will see you soon."

I nod, but I'm crying too hard to talk.

After one last round of hugs with everyone, they step back into the stones and...

Gone.

I'm not too proud to admit I plop down right there, on the ground, clutching the ring on my finger against my chest while sobbing my agony to the stars.

41

Five Weeks Later...

Dexter

THIS IS the second most beautiful sight I've ever seen in my life—watching the sun set over the mountains west of Tucson on our first night back from the UK. I sit in front of the living room sliding glass doors that lead out to our balcony as I sip a chilled Moscato Eilidh picked for tonight.

We've moved two comfortable chairs here so we can watch the show.

Eilidh is my most beautiful sight—waking up to her curled at my side, with the late afternoon sunlight picking up the golden honey highlights in her hair.

And then spending the better part of an hour spanking

her ass. She gets spankings every day when we wake up, to remind her who she belongs to.

A nice side effect of that is that it makes her wet and makes me hard, so she doesn't mind very much.

Right now, the fingers of my right hand are laced through the fingers of Eilidh's left, and we're sitting here, just inside the living room, watching this...

Amazing view. Except it blurs slightly...

"Are you crying, Sir?"

"I guess I am." I blink them away. "Something else I haven't done in what feels like forever." The last time I cried before meeting Eilidh was for Robert. I thought losing him burned out what little soul was left inside me.

Then I met my beautiful, radiant sun. She not only led me back to the light—literally—but she lit my soul, as well.

She turns in her chair, tucking her legs under her so she can face me. "We get all the sunsets we want now. And sunrises."

I gently squeeze her hand. It comforts me that her life-span will be far longer than a human's. All I want to do is focus on making her happy, and on helping Parxon complete his move to Earth from Jotnunlm.

For now, I want to enjoy *this* simple pleasure, just sitting here with her. It's almost enough to make me want to retire permanently, except I like a challenge. Building a new empire in a new location.

Besides, I don't want Lucius to get suspicious. The last thing I need is other vampires trying to figure out how to eliminate the sun's danger to them. It would put Eilidh and I both at risk. A world can only handle so many apex predators, and I don't want Lucius getting any grandiose ideas and thinking he can expand his power base or tip the balance of power.

I also don't want anyone looking too hard at Eilidh and her abilities. Especially not my fellow vampires, who want a way to up their game against shifters. And I don't want shifters thinking they can out-vamp vampires.

Meaning I'll tread very carefully and only indulge these rare moments when I know there's no chance of being observed by my fellow vampires or their human companions. Eilidh and I can retreat to my estate in Scotland and be free to roam there under daytime skies. There, Parxon and Zuzu can join us in our walks.

Meanwhile, Garrett and the Tucson pack are valuable allies outside of any agreement they hold with Lucius. The real estate deal is done, and I trust them far more than I do nearly all of the vampires.

Including Lucius.

Although Chaldis and Corbin are becoming close friends. The couple will move to Tucson before next winter. When my new resort opens, Chaldis and Corbin will run the restaurant. I've already connected him with an expert on running a restaurant to help him manage it. The two men will be able to get a start on their new life together, Corbin will more easily be able to visit his family, and Eilidh will be able to see her friends. She's looking forward to helping the men with their restaurant.

I think she's found the thing she wants to do.

Part of me is hoping we can coax Zuzu to our world permanently and get him involved with the restaurant, too. According to Eilidh and Parxon, he is a remarkable cook.

Anyway, I couldn't be happier, because she is happy.

We still don't know if we'll be able to have children. If Eilidh "marking" me also changed my body in those ways, or if my dream and Amber's vision were correct. I haven't told Eilidh about the dream I had that day at Parxon's house, about the baby.

I don't want to get my hopes up.

I guess we'll see. I'd long ago shed the melancholy thoughts about additional children, much as I learned to stop mourning the sun.

But now?

The world is alive and surrounds me and my senses with unspoken potential in a way I never dreamt possible. That means I'll wait before I take any actions. If she does get pregnant, we'll say we went through a fertility clinic. That is not unheard of among couples in our situation involving a vampire and a human. If I feel we are at risk, I'll simply move us to Scotland, to my estate. Anywhere away from other vampires who might ask too many questions.

For now, I will enjoy my love and our life together.

Meanwhile...we'll build.

EILIDH

ONCE THE SUN'S DOWN, we close the sliders and the blinds and take a shower together. I'm tempted to tackle Dexter now, but he has his heart set on going to Club Toxic tonight and scening there with me.

To put on a show.

To publicly stake his claim on me in front of all the vampires, and to make sure we throw off any and all suspicions about him and me, both.

"I thought you weren't sure you could ever scene with me in public?" I tease.

He pins me to the shower wall by my throat and my pulse spikes even as a flood of moisture pools between my thighs.

His other hand slides in there, two fingers easily gliding inside me while he leans in close. "*What* was that, love?"

I'm too horny, too eager for him, my body craving him and his domination over me. "You heard me, Sir."

Oooh, there's the evil smile. *That's* what I wanted.

He hooks his fingers perfectly inside me, thumb on my clit and slowly massaging exactly where he knows I need it. "Tonight, I'm cuffing your hands to a cross and letting you feel my singletail all over your back. I'm going to lick every welt I leave and not let you come. Then, I'm going to fuck you and make you beg for me to bite you and make you come." He licks my cheek. "Everyone's going to see the needy, horny girl willingly asking for my marks."

Yes, please!

His hand withdraws from between my legs, and I'm already whimpering and pleading for more, making him chuckle. "Not right now. You can't come until we're at the club."

I feel like pouting. I guess I actually give him pouty lip, because next thing I know, I've been spun around and his bare hand is spanking my ass, every impact pressing me against the shower wall and firing my need.

Dammit! When'd I become a masochist?

Apparently, he turned me into a *slutty* masochist.

Well, slutty only for *him*, obvs.

I totally understand sweetbloods now, why some of them are addicted to the process. I guess I am, too.

Only for this particular vamp.

Anyone else tried it, I'd rip their dick off and feed it to them before I stabbed them with a pencil.

I guess it also makes sense now why I never wanted to be with another vampire besides Dexter—because I'm basically an Alpha, too. It took someone like Dexter, a very old, strong vampire with more than enough of his own Alpha in him, to break through my natural defenses. Someone not only strong enough, but someone comfortable enough in his own skin, without something to prove, someone worthy.

I miss Zuzu and hope he can find someone like that for him. I told him we could help him adopt a houseful of children needing his huge heart full of love.

I know Dad and Dexter are right that I have to let Zuzu live his life, but I feel like I already lived one, and now I want him back in it.

After our shower, Dexter dresses me the way he wants me dressed—a tight, short black dress with spaghetti straps. No panties, no bra. The Jimmy Choos.

A leather collar he buckles around my neck. A collar that is huge and leaves absolutely no doubt it's a collar.

Show-off.

The ring, for tonight, is locked in the safe here in the apartment. That way there's no risk of losing it. I've mastered the signaling and homing abilities with it and can even cross with it during full moon.

Knowing I can do that helped ease my separation anxiety with Dad and Zuzu. Dexter bought them a home close to the stones, and that's a base of operations, for now.

Dexter's hand sharply connects with my ass. "Mind on me tonight, girl," he says. You belong totally to me, and everyone's going to see that."

"Yes, Sir."

I'm not about to press my luck there. Last time I tried to, he introduced me to tease and denial.

Anyone says that's not torture is a damned dirty liar.

Dexter wears jeans, a black button-up shirt, a midnight blue vest I love, the black boots, and the belt.

Ahhh, the belt. Next to his hand, that's been used on my ass almost as frequently.

I loooove it.

We head out to Club Toxic in my new Audi SUV. I wouldn't let him get rid of my 4Runner, and it's parked in one of our spots in the parking garage. I don't know where we're going to build or buy our Tucson house yet.

I don't care. Dexter now owns this building, and we'll be safe here.

It's Saturday, and the line is down the block. But when we roll up, Theophilus is at the door. He smiles as he pulls the velvet rope back for us. "Look at you, Blondie. Good evening, Dexter."

"Good evening, Theophilus," Dexter says, shouldering the strap of the duffel bag over his shoulder. "She is ravishing, isn't she?"

"Yes, sir. I take it the collar means she is your private property?"

"You take it right, and I will take the hand off anyone who tries to lay their hand on her."

"Yes, sir. I do *not* blame you there."

We head down to the dungeon, where Lucius immediately descends from his throne—jesusfuck that pretentious dude, anyway—to greet us.

"There's the runaway. Looking ravishing, my dear."

"Thank you, Mr. F."

"Ah! You are his now. I *insist*."

I glance up at Dexter, who finally nods.

"Thank you, *Lucius*," I say.

His smile beams. "Now was *that* so difficult? May I?" He motions to my hand, and Dexter nods again.

I feel a trill of panic until I realize Lucius is just kissing my hand. "Lucky bastard," he says to Dexter, shaking with him. Lucius motions to the dungeon. "Anywhere is yours, nephew."

Of course, Dexter points to a St. Andrew's cross that's practically in the center of the room and right where Lucius can easily watch from his perch.

There are several sweetbloods and household humans down here, and several vampires. They all watch as Dexter takes my hand and leads me to the cross.

I was hoping for a little warm-up, a toe in the water, but we're doing this.

Sure, I could safeword. He reminded me of that just before we arrived.

Except...I don't want to.

I want this, and I want Dexter.

We don't know if what I've done to him can wear off, so we've developed a ritual. I mark him, and he feeds off me, which makes us both come, and then we both collapse in a gooey, sticky heap, and happily sleep for hours.

I did ask if I could take my shoes off when we scene, though. I don't want to break a fricking ankle.

Or a heel.

He moves an implement stand over and quickly takes items from his duffel bag and hangs them on it—crops, canes, floggers, a singletail whip, and a variety of other implements.

They've all tasted my flesh, except for the singletail.

He's been saving that for tonight.

He also removes a set of leather cuffs and quickly buckles them on my wrists and ankles.

Then he smiles and kisses me, dipping his knees and

catching the hem of my dress with his fingers, easing it up and over my head, leaving me standing there naked.

I keep my focus on him, on his blue eyes. I also asked for no blindfold. If something happens, I want to see what's going on. He also agreed to use panic snaps on the wrist cuffs, so if I needed to free myself, I could. My ankle cuffs will remain unattached.

I mean, I trust Lucius and the club staff, but it *is* a Saturday night. Shit can happen quickly.

He hooks the panic snaps to my wrist cuffs, turns me face-forward against the cross, and hooks them to the chains on the cross. The smooth lacquered wood and vinyl padding feels cool against my naked flesh as he turns back to his bag.

Dexter steps behind me, the length of his body pressed along mine. "And for your peace of mind, love." He presses the fingers of both my hands around items, and when I look, I realize they're two sharpened pencils.

Yeah, I fricking *snort*, okay? I'm...

Well, I can't say I'm only human, can I? Not anymore.

His fingers slip between my legs, where I'm wet for him still. I moan as he teases me, pressing two fingers deep inside me, and he nips my earlobe. "Is this where I make a joke about it being bigger on the inside?"

I laugh so hard my knees nearly give out. "Asshole."

Never should have got him started on *Doctor Who*. He's still salty that I didn't warn him they fridged Ianto in *Torchwood*.

Got one hell of a spanking when that episode made him cry.

But everyone was a winner, because I got spanked, and then fucked. Only losers that night were Ianto and Captain Jack.

He smacks my ass, hard, with his other hand. "*What* was that, love?"

"Master Asshole."

And then we're laughing, when I'm not yelping, as he fingers and spanks me and uses nearly every toy he brought on me.

Because we laugh.

A *lot*.

All the fricking time.

I don't even know how long we've been there because time sort of dissolves when he gets me in the zone.

Yeah, yeah, I get it now. No more looking down my nose at the slutty little club Dobbys. I *get* it.

He moves in close. At some point, he lost the vest and unbuttoned his shirt because I feel his bare chest pressing against my back. "Almost done, girl."

The singletail cuts a stripe of fire across the back of my right shoulder, and now funtime's over. I let out a shriek before I clamp down on it. I'm certain every eye in the place is probably on us now, but I'm keeping my eyes closed.

I just want it to be us.

Me and my Master.

The second hit is to the back of my left shoulder, another deep one that I'm certain drew blood.

He leans in and licks the first one, then the second, slowly, every touch of his tongue making my lady bits clench and ache to be filled.

I hear him smack his lips as he sucks the popper on the end of the whip, too, kinky bastard.

Another two flicks, to my already tenderized ass this time, and yeah, those hurt like a motherfucker.

Except he licks the pain and blood away, and I know what he's doing.

He doesn't want me to have open wounds that will attract too much attention and make him have to wave in a DM to back off another vamp.

Because what he's doing is biting the inside of his cheek, so he's licking his own blood across my flesh and healing the marks.

He pauses to finger me, and I'm just on the verge of coming before he pulls his hand away and lays two more whip strokes against my flesh. When I think I can't take any more denial, I start begging.

"Please make me come, Master!"

"*Hmm*. Someone sounds very needy."

"I am!"

He chuckles in my ear. "What will you give me?"

"Everything!"

"Forever?"

"Yes, forever. *Please*! Master, I need you forever!"

He uncurls the fingers of my left hand from around the pencil—How the *hell* did I manage not to drop that?—and I feel something small and cool slide over my ring finger.

My eyes pop open, and I'm staring at a *huge* amethyst and diamond ring. "*Forever*, girl."

He tips my head back and kisses me. That's distracting me, so I don't realize he's unfastened his jeans and pulled them down until his cock's already sliding inside me.

And then his teeth sink into the top of my left shoulder.

Fuuuuuck! I come unglued, and it's a damned good thing he has me hooked to the cross because I want to turn around and mark him.

Oooh, that's why he kept his shirt on—to hide the mating marks.

That's literally the last coherent thought I have before the world unhinges around me, and the hardest orgasms

I've ever had in my life go off like a nuclear chain reaction and pull one from him, too.

And then he's licking my shoulder, his arm around me and holding me up as he unfastens my cuffs and cradles me against him. A fleece blanket appears from somewhere, and he wraps me up in it, and we go cuddle on a couch.

I'm still holding the pencil in my right hand. I finally tuck it behind his left ear and close my eyes as I rest my head on his shoulder.

This amuses him greatly, because he chuckles. "Love you, Eilidh," he whispers.

Life is perfect. "Love you, too, Master Fangster."

He snorts. "Brat."

"Your brat."

He sighs. "Thank goodness."

∾

http://www.LesliRichardson.com

WANT MORE MIDNIGHT DOMS?

Click here to sign up for news!

Read the whole series for more of your favorite vampire BDSM club:

Alpha's Blood by Renee Rose & Lee Savino

Her Vampire Master by Maren Smith

Her Vampire Prince by Ines Johnson

Her Vampire Hero by Nicolina Martin

Her Vampire Bad Boy by Brenda Trim

Her Vampire Rebel by Zara Zenia

Her Vampire Obsession by Tymber Dalton, writing as Lesli Richardson.

ALSO BY THE AUTHOR

Please sign up for my author newsletter, where I post info about both my Lesli Richardson and Tymber Dalton pen names, and never miss a new release or update: https://tymberdalton.com/newsletter/

Determination Trilogy:

(A stand-alone trilogy set in the same world as the Governor Trilogy.)

1) *Dignity*

2) *Diligence*

3) *Desire*

Devastation Trilogy:

(A stand-alone trilogy set in the same world as the Governor Trilogy.)

1) *Dirge*

2) *Solace*

3) *Release*

Inequitable Trilogy:

(A stand-alone trilogy set in the same world as the Governor Trilogy.)

1) *Indiscretion*

2) *Innocent*

3) *Incisive*

Maxim Colonies:

1) *Jailmates*

2) *Farborn*

3) *Saudade*

Of Boardwalks and Bison

Cross Country Chaos

Poly

Her Vampire Obsession (Midnight Doms Series)

Coming Soon:

Deviant Trilogy

Devout Trilogy

How Many Times Do I Have to Say I'm Sorry? (Maudlin Falls 1)

Lesli Richardson is better known by her more prolific Tymber Dalton pen name. Please check out her website for more info on all her titles under both her pen names, including full book and series listings, trivia, character information, and more.

http://www.tymberdalton.com

ABOUT THE AUTHOR

Author Lesli Richardson, who is better-known by her more prolific wild-child Tymber Dalton pen name, lives in the Tampa Bay region of Florida with her husband (aka "The World's Best Husband™") and too many pets. She writes a wide variety of heat levels and genres, from mainstream sci-fi all the way to scorching ménage.

The USA Today Bestselling Author (as Tymber) and two-time EPIC award winner is a part-time Viking shield-maiden in training who loves to shoot skeet and play D&D with her friends. She's also the author of over one hundred and sixty books and counting, including *The Reluctant Dom*, *Cross Country Chaos*, the Bleacke Shifters series, the Governor Trilogy, the Determination Trilogy, The Great Turning Trilogy, the Suncoast Society series, the Love Slave for Two series, the Triple Trouble series, the Coffeeshop Coven series, the Good Will Ghost Hunting series, the Drunk Monkeys series, and many others.

She lives in her own little world, but it's okay—they all know her there.

She loves to hear from readers! Please feel free to drop by her website and sign up for her newsletter to keep abreast of the latest news, snarkage, and releases.

Honest reviews are always welcomed. They help with a book's visibility and can boost its placement on book retailer sites. Even a few lines about what you felt reading the book will help. Thank you so much, it's greatly appreciated!

Newsletter: https://tymberdalton.com/newsletter/
http://www.tymberdalton.com
http://www.facebook.com/AuthorLesliRichardson
http://www.facebook.com/tymberdalton
http://www.facebook.com/groups/TymbersTrybe/
http://www.twitter.com/TymberDalton
http://www.instagram.com/tymberdalton